MOONLIT SEDUCTION

T.J. grinned at Carrie Sue, a grin that said he had more in mind than a late night swim. "I'll meet you in the water," he said.

Carrie Sue knew what she wanted tonight — him — and she was quivering with anticipation. She headed for the river's edge and undressed near a tree, then stepped into the cool water, enjoying the feeling of the water against her bare flesh.

T.J. dove in, then surfaced within inches of her. Just a glance from him seemed to awaken every sleeping emotion within her. Despite the cooling water around them, she felt aflame with desire. She trembled as his lips nibbled at her ear. She had promised herself never to trust another man, but how could she not trust this man she loved and craved? Merciful heavens, could she even trust herself?

ZEBRA'S REGENCY ROMANCES
DAZZLE AND DELIGHT

A BEGUILING INTRIGUE   (4441, $3.99)
by Olivia Sumner

Pretty as a picture Justine Riggs cared nothing for propriety. She dressed as a boy, sat on her horse like a jockey, and pondered the stars like a scientist. But when she tried to best the handsome Quenton Fletcher, Marquess of Devon, by proving that she was the better equestrian, he would try to prove Justine's antics were pure folly. The game he had in mind was seduction—never imagining that he might lose his heart in the process!

AN INCONVENIENT ENGAGEMENT   (4442, $3.99)
by Joy Reed

Rebecca Wentworth was furious when she saw her betrothed waltzing with another. So she decides to make him jealous by flirting with the handsomest man at the ball, John Collinwood, Earl of Stanford. The "wicked" nobleman knew exactly what the enticing miss was up to—and he was only too happy to play along. But as Rebecca gazed into his magnificent eyes, her errant fiancé was soon utterly forgotten!

SCANDAL'S LADY   (4472, $3.99)
by Mary Kingsley

Cassandra was shocked to learn that the new Earl of Lynton was her childhood friend, Nicholas St. John. After years at sea and mixed feelings Nicholas had come home to take the family title. And although Cassandra knew her place as a governess, she could not help the thrill that went through her each time he was near. Nicholas was pleased to find that his old friend Cassandra was his new next door neighbor, but after being near her, he wondered if mere friendship would be enough . . .

HIS LORDSHIP'S REWARD   (4473, $3.99)
by Carola Dunn

As the daughter of a seasoned soldier, Fanny Ingram was accustomed to the vagaries of military life and cared not a whit about matters of rank and social standing. So she certainly never foresaw her *tendre* for handsome Viscount Roworth of Kent with whom she was forced to share lodgings, while he carried out his clandestine activities on behalf of the British Army. And though good sense told Roworth to keep his distance, he couldn't stop from taking Fanny in his arms for a kiss that made all hearts equal!

Available wherever paperbacks are sold, or order direct from the Publisher. Send cover price plus 50¢ per copy for mailing and handling to Penguin USA, P.O. Box 999, c/o Dept. 17109, Bergenfield, NJ 07621. Residents of New York and Tennessee must include sales tax. DO NOT SEND CASH.

JANELLE TAYLOR

Kiss of the Night Wind

ZEBRA BOOKS
KENSINGTON PUBLISHING CORP.

ZEBRA BOOKS are published by

Kensington Publishing Corp.
850 Third Avenue
New York, NY 10022

Thirteenth printing: February 1996

Printed in the United States of America

For:
Linda Morgan and Mary Coker,
two very special sisters.

And:
Marianne and Kenny Rogers,
two very special friends.

Come with me, my fiery vixen,

"And I would love you all the day,
Every night would kiss and play,
If with me you'd fondly stray
Over the hills and far away."

John Gay

"And o'er the hills and far away
Beyond their utmost purple rim,
Beyond the night, across the day,
Through all the world she followed him."

Alfred Tennyson

Until for Rogue Vixen's heart did burn,
Until for Rogue Vixen's soul did yearn,
Until for Rogue all else did fade,
Until Vixen Rogue had betrayed . . .

Chapter One

If this doesn't work out and you get caught, Carrie Sue Stover, as surely as the summer's hot, you'll either swing from a rope or waste away in some awful prison! Ever alert and wary, Carrie Sue scanned her surroundings and strained to hear each sound, her senses sharpened from years on the run. Being with strangers always made her nervous, as she constantly feared being recognized and arrested even this far from Texas and her infamous reputation.

The redhead continued dressing in a small room which she had shared last night with another female passenger at the "home station." She had traveled from Fort Worth on this stage line, a coach which halted every night, unlike the Butterfield stage which halted once every twenty-four hours for passengers to get sorely needed sleep. Between these rustic inns which were owned and operated by the Garrett Overland Company, the coach stopped for fresh horses at relay stations where the passengers could eat and freshen up.

Her roommate, a soldier's wife from back East, had completed her grooming quickly and left the cramped room, almost as if she were afraid of Carrie Sue. The redhead frowned, knowing that her thoughts were groundless and it only proved that she was too mistrustful of

9

most people. She had given the timid woman no reason to be afraid of her. The soldier's wife, who had joined them yesterday at Fort Bowie to complete her journey to Fort Verde, had jumped at every twist and turn, at every sudden voice or stranger's glance. Without a doubt, she concluded, the Eastern female was petrified of her own shadow. How, the redhead wondered, would the pitiful creature ever survive the wild west?

Carrie Sue shook her head in sympathy. She vigorously brushed her long hair to remove as much trail dust as possible. Whether it be in a rented tub of hot suds or in a cold stream, she hated not having daily baths. She was eager to reach her destination where a good scrubbing from head to toe would be her first priority.

Carrie Sue glanced at the brush she was holding whose handle was marked with a painted "C.S.S." Suppressing guilt, she repacked the confiscated belongings of Miss Carolyn Sarah Starns. She wanted to believe that fate had decreed that the Butterfield Stage would overturn between St. Louis and Fort Worth during a robbery attempt by her brother's gang. All the passengers had been killed, including a Texas Ranger and the young woman whose identity and possessions she had stolen in a moment of desperation.

If the driver had reined up that day near Sherman, Texas as ordered by Darby Stover instead of recklessly charging her brother's gang and trying to outrun them, the fatal crash would not have occurred. Carrie Sue wished it could have been avoided, but no one could bring the innocent victims back to life. Upon learning the female passenger was dead, Carrie Sue had been compelled by some inexplicable force to search her belongings to learn something about the unfortunate woman. From the woman's letters and detailed diary, Carrie Sue had made a startling discovery and found the answer to her problems.

Carolyn Starns had been a twenty-one-year-old orphan

who was heading to Tucson to become the town's new schoolmarm. The lovely brunette would be a stranger there. By the time the gang had completed their task, Carrie Sue knew what she wanted to do, what she had to do. The chance at a new life had been too tempting to ignore. Carolyn looked enough like Carrie Sue . . . but their initials and sizes were eerily the same. It had to work!

So, after her brother helped her bury the teacher's body miles from the scene of their crime, on April twenty-eighth of '76, Carrie Sue Stover became Miss Carolyn Sarah Starns. Today, May tenth, she was on her way to blissful freedom in a Tucson schoolhouse as long as no one recognized her. That was a strong possibility since her wanted poster was done so poorly, by Quade Harding's nefarious design!

The redhead was tired of running and hiding, tired of being scared, tired of being shot at, and tired of being pursued until she was exhausted or provoked into lethal self-defense. She was tired of innocent people getting hurt, and of being accused of crimes which she and the gang hadn't committed. She'd been forced into a life of crime at the tender age of seventeen—she'd never wanted to live this way! Several times she had tried to "go straight" and once she had risked turning herself in to the law and ending this awful existence. All of those desperate actions had failed. Too, she had heard of how horrible prison was for women, and that three female outlaws had been hanged in the last few years by crazed mobs!

Carrie Sue wanted a normal life. She longed for peace and safety. She wanted to fall in love, to have a husband, a home, a family. She wanted this soul-wrenching loneliness and misery to end. She wanted to ranch again, to work alongside her family. She wanted to be the Carrie Sue Stover she had been at seventeen before her life was torn asunder by a greedy man named Quade Harding.

The lovely outlaw sighed wearily as she braided her hair. She secured the long plait near her nape and fluffed her thick, wavy bangs over her forehead in an attempt to avoid calling attention to the fiery locks that had caused the law to brand her the "Texas Flame." How she yearned to gaze toward a bright future rather than looking over her shoulder for trouble. This opportunity had fallen into her lap like a miracle, and she had taken advantage of it. In a way, she was giving God a helping hand with her survival. If no one recognized her, her dreams could be realized. She had to make this work. She had to!

So far, Quade Harding had still not released an accurate sketch of her that could insure her capture or possibly cause her death. No, Quade Harding wanted her alive, wanted her as his private prisoner. In May of '74, Quade had furnished the law with her name and a poor drawing of Darby Stover's sister, but only to frighten her and to remind her of her precarious existence which he could destroy at any moment.

Unlike posters for the other members of the Stover Gang, her wanted poster demanded that she be turned in *alive* to Quade Harding for a payment of five thousand dollars in gold. The law, on the other hand, was offering two thousand paper dollars for her capture, *preferably* alive. She knew the reason for Quade's stipulation; he wanted to use his power and money to obtain control of her. As long as no one learned she was the "Texas Flame," Carrie Sue was safe; she could make a fresh start in Tucson. But what, she mused frantically, if Quade decided he would see her dead if he couldn't have her alive? All he had to do was release a better description.

"Breakfast!" the station keeper shouted and interrupted her worrying.

With increased haste Carrie Sue finished her task. As she buttoned the front of her dress, she was relieved that Carolyn's clothes, although rather plain and inexpensive, were comfortable and appropriate for her new status. Judging from the way she had packed her belongings, Carolyn had been a precise and careful person.

"It's on the table and going fast!" the second announcement came.

Carrie Sue entered the adjoining room. The mouth-watering smells of cat's-head biscuits, fried bacon, perked coffee, and flour gravy reached her nose. She inhaled, realizing how hungry she was. *No more trail food,* her mind sang happily, and no more choking down food on the run or on the impatient Butterfield stageline which she had used earlier. Thank goodness the frugal Carolyn had wanted to save money by purchasing a ticket between Fort Worth and Tucson from Garrett lines which traveled more cheaply but much more slowly. Knowing the routine by now, she walked toward a wooden table to join the driver, guard, woman, and the men who had caught the stage two days ago.

Instantly she sighted a handsome stranger sitting there and eating calmly. At her approach, he glanced her way for a moment, his rapid and probing gaze sliding over her before it returned to his meal. Everything and everyone in the room except him vanished briefly. Her heart pounded in trepidation. Numerous questions about him filled her mind. She trembled, but struggled to regain her poise.

The only vacant seat was across from the black-haired male whose presence seemed to fill the room, and Carrie Sue took it. She eased her chair to the table and placed the red-checked napkin in her lap as her mother had taught her long ago. *Relax,* she ordered. *He's only a customer. If not, you can bluff your way out with Carolyn's identity.*

When he looked up from his plate, she was astonished to feel weakened and warmed by his smokey gray gaze. Why was she feeling this way? She had lived among men for years!

13

In what seemed to be only a second, the darkly tanned stranger scrutinized her thoroughly. She could tell his mind was quick and keen, so she tried to keep her expression blank. His stubbled jawline and upper lip said he hadn't shaved in a day or two, but his face and hands were freshly scrubbed and his collar-length hair was combed. He was dressed in a faded gray shirt and jeans, both snug enough to evince a muscular body and worn enough to imply his funds were limited. Sleeves rolled to his elbows revealed a lean hardness in his forearms. He looked up again and nodded a polite greeting which caused a midnight lock to fall across his forehead, and he left it there as he returned to his meal.

A drifter? she wondered. *Can't be,* she reasoned. *His body is too well-honed and his movements are too controlled for an easy-going cowpoke. Who is he and what's he doing here? That sketch hardly favors me, but what if he guesses the truth and challenges me?*

Carrie Sue tried to keep her hands from shaking and rattling the dishes as she served herself. For a reason which she couldn't grasp and a reaction which she couldn't halt, she had difficulty eating, and more difficulty keeping her disobedient eyes off of him. She had been around countless men, but none had affected her this way. She found herself wanting to stare at him, to talk with him, to share passion with him. That was crazy! He was a stranger, perhaps even a threat to her.

Beneath lowered lashes as she nibbled at a large biscuit, she eyed the enticing span of hairy chest which was showing above the three buttons which he had left unfastened. His features were strong and appealing.

She observed the way he sat in his chair, leaving room between his chest and the table and between his back and the chair to allow for rapid movement if it was required. The other men chatted amiably, but the stranger kept quiet. Even so, she realized that he caught every word spoken and each move made, that he was in full control of himself and any situation. The others might think he was totally relaxed or distracted, but she knew better. Yes, he was alert and guarded; those were traits which she recognized too well. She knew he could spring into action swifter than she could blink if danger approached. She wondered on which side of the law this man stood. And was he here to eat or was he biding time for an unknown purpose?

The stranger finished his breakfast and laid his fork on the empty plate. After his coffee cup was refilled, he propped his left elbow on the table and placed his thumb along his sturdy jawline with his first two fingers entrapping a cleft chin between them. As if in deep thought, he absently rubbed his jawbone with his thumb, causing the dark stubble growing there to make a noise which he did not seem to hear. Those smokey gray eyes boldly studied her in a manner which warned her that he knew she had been furtively doing the same with him, studied her as if he were trying to figure out a crucial puzzle. Maybe, as Kale Rushton had told her long ago, fear had an odor, and this man had detected it in the air. Certainly that would cause a gunslinger, if that's what he was, to become intrigued.

Carrie Sue struggled to ignore him, but his pull was too strong. Her gaze fused with his, and she felt as if he was probing the depths of her soul. Her cheeks flushed slightly. The handsome stranger glanced at her dark blue cotton dress with small white cuffs and collar and at her neat hairstyle. She heard a deep inhalation and exhalation of air through his shapely nose as his eyes narrowed, but not in a menacing way. For an instant she read doubt in those smokey depths. His gaze shifted to her left hand. One brow lifted inquisitively. He studied her again and confusion—an obviously unusual emotion for him—briefly filled his eyes.

15

"Can I give you anything, Miss?" he asked, his voice teasing over Carrie Sue's flesh like blazing sunshine on a frigid day. When her expression said she was astonished at him speaking to her, he half-grinned—only the left corner of his sensual mouth lifting—as if to imply she should have expected his response to her behavior. He lifted his cup and sipped coffee as he brazenly observed her over its rim.

While she collected her wits, Carrie Sue watched the steamy curls from the hot coffee tickle his nose and dampen it. She noticed the enticing humor in his potent gaze which implied that his real query had nothing to do with food. She was baffled, as he did not seem to be the kind of male who flirted with a strange woman, or one who had to make any effort to get a female's undivided attention. There was something about the way he was eyeing her that made her tension increase. This was something more than a man admiring a pretty face; there was an array of emotions battling within him.

What if he's a bounty hunter? What if he's playing games with me? Or trying to decide what to do about me? How she wished she had her Remington revolvers nearby for comfort, but they were concealed in Carolyn Starns's baggage. Besides, she doubted she could defend herself against this particular man. The way he moved, looked, even breathed told her of his enormous prowess. The flaming haired female shifted in her chair, unnerved by his overt attention. Maybe he was only intrigued by her scent of fear, or responsive to her unintentionally enticing behavior. She reminded herself to behave as the respectable and studious schoolmarm. "No, thank you," she replied in a ladylike manner and dismissive tone. She focused her eyes on her food, but was intensely aware of him.

Suddenly he stood, pushing back his chair with his legs, and walked to the front wall. Recovering his gunbelt from a peg, he strapped it around his firm waist, the way he buckled it exposing that he favored his . . . *right* hand. Strange, she would have sworn he was left-handed. The holsters held two Frontier Colts, the '73 model, six-shot, forty-five caliber, single action. As he bent forward to secure the dangling thongs about his thighs, Carrie Sue observed his lithe movements. Before putting a dark hat on his ebony head and settling it into place, he pulled on a brown leather vest which was as worn as his shirt and jeans. He retrieved a Winchester '73 lever-action rifle from where he had leaned it against the door jamb.

"A fine meal, Sam," he told the station keeper and smiled broadly, a smile which captivated Carrie Sue and sent tingles over her body.

The burly man in a stained white apron smiled and responded, "Most folks say I got the best vittles on any line. Stop in again to fill yore belly. I cook a kill-for stew on Tuesdays and Thursdays."

The appealing stranger tossed Sam an extra coin, glanced back at the beautiful redhead, shrugged as if she puzzled him, then departed.

Carrie Sue heard a horse gallop away, but only half-prayed she had seen him for the last time. She waited patiently while the other passengers, the two men and the soldier's wife, completed their meals. The driver and guard loaded their baggage and summoned them.

For a moment, the fleeing desperado wondered if she should buy or steal a horse and escape this area as swiftly as possible, just in case that virile stranger was after her. No, she bravely decided. This chance for a new life was too good to pass up without proof he was on her trail. If he had delayed her capture with the hope of her leading him to Darby and his gang, he would have a long wait!

"All's away!" the driver shouted to let the passengers know he was leaving so they wouldn't be thrown backwards roughly when the horses jerked against the harnesses and the stage's weight.

17

Tomorrow night, she would be in Tucson. There were only a few more stops for fresh horses, meals, and one night's sleep between her and her destination. Suspense, eagerness, and hope filled Carrie Sue Stover and diverted her from thoughts of the stranger.

The stage had passed the Dragoon Springs station where an Apache massacre had occurred in '58. The road was flanked by impressive mountains. They had made it through the Chiricahua range which had been Cochise's stronghold until four years ago when the infamous Apache chief had agreed to settle on a reservation. Carrie Sue looked out the window, as did the other three passengers. No one chatted, which suited her just fine.

The arid countryside possessed a wild beauty with its abundance of blooming yuccas, entangling catclaw, bean laden mesquite, paloverde, snakeweed, and countless other sturdy plants and small trees which could survive this harsh area and climate. A variety of cacti, some crouching low to the ground and some standing tall and green against the blue skyline, was scattered before her line of vision. The coach had passed through many mountain ranges, but the landscape in this flash flood region was relatively flat.

She watched the scenery alternate between scrub-covered areas with an occasional hill, to sparsely vegetated areas, and sites with countless boulders and brown mountains on all sides. In some places, grass was a yellowy tan, or pale green, or nonexistent. At times thousands of yuccas grew on both sides of the road; at other times, only scrubs and small trees were visible. She noticed that the mountains had an almost purply brown color—unlike the vivid reds, grays, and blacks of Texas mountains or the heavily forested green ones of Georgia.

Carrie Sue's eyes had rested enough to return to her task, which was a difficult one in the jouncing coach. She wanted to read Carolyn Starns's letters and diary as many times as possible before she reached Tucson so she would know the woman's life by heart. She could not afford any slip-ups when she met her contact tomorrow and began her new job. She had practiced signing Carolyn's name until she could do it perfectly. She had learned why Carolyn had purchased a ticket for this cheaper stageline, to save money. The brunette was intent upon saving enough to buy a dress shop with a small home attached.

Carrie Sue hated sewing. But when she claimed the money which Carolyn had transferred to the Tucson bank, she would not squander those hard-earned dollars; she would use them wisely. Carolyn had no need for them and she had no family to claim the shattered-dream fund. Carrie Sue would use the money for a promising future, just as Carolyn had meant to do.

She also studied the school books in Carolyn's baggage to refresh herself on "reading, writing, and arithmetic," along with history and geography. She was glad her mother had insisted on educating her and that she'd always loved learning. She went over sample lesson plans to familiarize herself with presenting information to various ages, as the Tucson school included first through eighth grades. Carrie Sue smiled, for she felt confident she would make a good schoolmarm. If she didn't like teaching, she could change jobs later, after she was certain her new identity cloaked her securely.

Following the midday meal, the other three passengers dozed in the warm stage which was traveling at an almost rocking pace in the heat of the day. Carrie Sue leaned her head against the coach and closed her eyes to think about her brother and their stormy past. While there was not an accurate picture of herself on her wanted poster, Darby and his gang were not as fortunate. She worried about her brother. Darby had been such a cheerful, easy-going, likable person before Quinn Harding and his lecherous son Quade had ruined his life. She fretted over how Darby was changing, especially during the last two years since Quade had released her brother's picture and name and had tagged his band the Stover Gang: a vicious trick to flush her into the open again. The longer Darby was an outlaw and the more he was forced to do to survive, the harder he would become.

She and Darby had been born and raised in Georgia, until a greedy Carpetbagger wanted their farm following the War Between the States. The northern controlled law had refused to protect them when they were forced to sell out for less than half of the land's value or risk imprisonment for allegedly unpaid taxes. After her father secretly took revenge on the villain, they had left Georgia to make a new life elsewhere, finally settling in Texas. Her parents, Martha and John Henry Stover, had come upon another Southerner in dire straits and purchased his ranch near Brownwood. But Quinn Harding and his son had wanted to add it to their large spread, the QH Ranch, a fact the seller—who despised the Hardings—had not told them. Her father had refused to sell out to the Hardings, refused to be forced from his land and home again. Within a year, her parents had been killed and the Hardings had taken control of the small ranch with a coveted water supply and lush grasslands. This time, their unpaid bank loan had been used as the so-called legal means to steal all the Stover's possessions. Lacking evidence against the Hardings, there had been nothing she and Darby could do, or so the Hardings had believed.

In '69, at the age of seventeen, she had gone to work in the Harding home as the housekeeper's helper to spy on them for her brother. The elder Harding, a hateful man, had treated her as a slave—someone to dominate and cruelly tease. She had despised waiting upon Quinn Harding, who had been crippled three months earlier from a fall. It was that accident which had placed Quade in control of the QH Ranch, their evil plans, and all of their

20

hirelings. She had learned about payroll shipments, cattle drives, auctions, and more—information she had passed on to Darby and the gang he had formed to destroy the Hardings. The unknown band of outlaws had cut fences, rustled cattle, burned barns and fields, and stolen payrolls—anything to punish the Hardings.

In the beginning, she and Darby had been concerned only with justice and revenge. But her furtive activities had been discovered by the lustful Quade who had watched her too closely. After seven months on the ever-increasing QH Ranch, she had been compelled to flee Quade's wicked demands and his threats about unmasking her brother.

From his wheelchair, "Old Man Harding" had ordered his devious son to hire gunslingers to guard his spread and bounty hunters to destroy his persistent enemies. Quade had agreed to a certain point but, despite his family's losses, he had not told his father or the law about Carrie's involvement or about the gang's identity. She had been surprised and confused by Quade's silence, until she guessed his motive: he wanted to capture her, not have the law do it.

After several run-ins with detectives Quade had hired, Darby had ceased his harassment of the Hardings, and they had fled into the Oklahoma Territory. They had lain low there all winter, until a lack of supplies had forced them to pull off raids in Oklahoma and Kansas. For a year, dressed as a boy and masked, she had ridden occasionally with Darby's gang as they eluded Quade's relentless detectives and struggled to survive. But unless it was too perilous to leave her behind, she remained in hidden camps because Darby didn't want her—a fiery-haired female—to be sighted and remembered. The same was true when the boys visited towns in small groups, which was possible since their faces and names were unknown. Still, no matter where they journeyed, they had to be on con-

21

stant guard. And she, at eighteen, could do nothing except tag along for safety.

With no place to live and on the run from Quade's cohorts and the law, Darby's gang had begun to commit other crimes, mainly robberies and rustlings. Carrie Sue had realized her brother's gang was becoming too much like other outlaws or the men she wanted to punish, but she was caught up in the band's crimes and too fearful of capture to leave.

When the men had grown restless in camp and supplies had run out, the gang had made their raids. Yet, Darby Stover was careful not to kill, and he never attacked poor folks. Sometimes, he gave money to people in dire straits whom they met along the way. For those reasons, his reputation became the colorful one of a hero more than that of a ruthless outlaw. Darby's rule had been "Never kill anybody unless you have to save your hide 'cause it only gives lily-livered men the guts to join posses and chase our tails to kingdom's come. Folks will allow robbing but not killing. They know we'll treat them fair, so they yield without trouble. Some of them even enjoy being held up by the Stover Gang."

In late '71, she was desperate to break free from her offensive life and Quade's obsessive pursuit. She tried to make a fresh start by working in a mercantile store in Sante Fe. To go unnoticed, she dressed plainly, kept her eyes lowered timidly to hide their color, and covered her fiery hair with a dark brown net. Her freedom lasted only ten months before one of Quade's detectives tracked her down and delivered his intimidating threat: "Marry me and I'll get the charges against you dropped. If not, I'll see to it you and your brother are imprisoned and hanged."

Carrie Sue had heard tales about the treatment of female captives. The law could kill her as punishment, but never send her to prison! She would do just about anything to avoid that degrading existence. She had used her wits and skills to overcome the clever detective. She had fled to one of Darby's hideouts and nervously waited for three wintry months until her brother arrived to lay low and found her there.

At twenty, she was thrown into the gang again, and rode with them from March of '72 until April of '73. To protect her identity, she continued to dress as a boy, to conceal her hair, and to wear a mask.

Things had changed over the years, mainly because they were charged with crimes which they hadn't committed. Clearly the gang's reputation was suffering from the false accusations and wild newspaper stories, and sometimes from the bitter truth. During her absences, Darby had begun hiring other outlaws to help pull certain jobs. Her brother was a strong leader who tried to choose his men carefully, but a "rotten seed" sometimes slipped past his keen wits. It was those rare mistakes who were hard to control at all times, mistakes who got them into trouble with unwanted violence. Still, Darby Stover was responsible for his gang's actions.

Carrie Sue admitted to herself that she wished she had never gotten involved in such a wicked existence, even to punish the Hardings. Perhaps the grief and anger she'd felt after her parent's deaths had made her too susceptible to Darby's scheme.

In April of '73, Darby and his men had grown tired of roaming and of being chased. They had realized their luck could not last forever. One truth could not be denied or halted: every fast gun and strong body eventually slowed, every keen eye and mind dulled with age.

The men who had ridden with Darby from the start put their money together and purchased a ranch near Laredo from a widow who could no longer manage alone. On April nineteenth, for a pleasant change, she had celebrated her twenty-first birthday in happiness and peace.

As they had always been masked during their crimes and Quade had continued to hold silent, their identities had remained unknown. Still, they had taken the precaution of changing their names. For eight wonderful months all went well, even if Darby wouldn't allow her to leave the new seclusion of their new home. Then, Quade's detectives had located them again, forcing them to leave the ranch and new life behind. They had fled to Mexico for the next few months.

That time, Quade became desperate, impatient, and dangerous. He released the descriptions and names of Darby and his men in hopes of flushing the gang—no, her—into the open. He hired an artist to provide the law with accurate sketches of the men. Yet, Carrie Sue's wanted poster still lacked her sketch and identity, containing only a vague description of a fiery-haired female. He had labeled her the "Texas Flame," a nickname which had stuck to her.

She had been lucky to remain a secret over the years. Her family had not lived near Brownwood very long when they were slain, so few people had met her there. She had been over seven years younger and her looks had changed greatly since '69. Her short, dark auburn hair was now—due to hours beneath the sun and years of growing—a long "flaming red mane with a golden soul" as Darby put it. Nor was she a "skinny kid" any longer. Anyone who might have met her as the sixteen or seventeen year old Carrie Sue Stover was either employed by the Hardings or had been run out of Texas by them. No doubt, Quade had ordered everyone on the ranch to keep silent about her looks and, considering her scanty poster, his father must have agreed to let Quade have his way in this matter, if the old man even knew about it.

Maybe Quade's relentless pressure was partly her fault. At times, she had led him on, boldly and vindictively tantalizing him with what he could never have. She had made him crave her to the point of taking any risk or paying any cost to have her. Yet, as an innocent seventeen-year-old, she had not fully understood the hazardous trail she was taking with that unpredictable villain. But marry her? She didn't believe him. Probably Quade wanted to force her to become his defenseless and slavish whore, to punish her for duping and eluding him! Without a doubt, both Harding men were evil and cold-blooded.

For the past two years, she had stayed with the gang, becoming widely known as the mysterious "Texas Flame." She had given up trying to tuck her thick hair beneath a hat and banding her breasts tightly to conceal the shapely feminine figure which her cotton skirts and snug jeans insisted on revealing. But she still wore a mask to hide her identity and made certain to keep her distance from their victims to prevent anyone from noticing her unusual periwinkle eyes.

She knew what most men thought and said about her, "a wildcat to be tamed" or a "sly vixen to be captured and punished." Yet, Carrie Sue only shot in self-defense if she was cornered. Even then, she gave her pursuer many chances to retreat or yield before firing.

But things had worsened over the years. With the men's faces and names known, they could no longer travel at will. And they all feared that Quade would panic and expose her at any time. Carrie Sue was sickened by the accidental deaths like Carolyn's and the Ranger's two weeks ago, and a mother's and her child's in March near San Angelo.

Her worst experience had been in August of '75 when a Texas Ranger snared her. She had the drop on him, but couldn't shoot him, so she surrendered. The vile lawman had physically and mentally abused her, and had tried to ravish her. With skills taught to her by Kale Rushton — a half-Apache member of Darby's gang — she had thwarted the wicked Ranger and escaped. That experience had taught her that the law couldn't be trusted. She also had learned that the authorities were no longer lenient with female criminals, especially those without children.

She had been given no choice except to stay with the gang. Anger and resentment gnawed at her. Being a woman, she couldn't take off to faraway places without plenty of money, a job, or a partner. Often women were trapped in terrible situations because good and safe choices were so few. To have raced off with the blind hope of finding a lucky opportunity would have been reckless. Every time she had been on her own, numerous men had tried to take advantage of her. She was a good shot and fighter, but she could not call attention to herself by going around killing or beating wicked men all the time! And once Quade raised the amounts of his rewards, listing "Dead or Alive" in all cases but hers, bounty hunters and vicious gunslingers became a threat to them. Everyone knew that bounty hunters were like badgers; they never let go of their prey. At least she had her brother and his gang to protect her from beasts like the Hardings, their detectives, bounty hunters, posses, lawmen, and gunslingers.

Off and on for seven years she was a daring desperado in Texas, Oklahoma, New Mexico, and Kansas. But she had faced the truth long ago. Her deeds were no longer a matter of honor and vengeful justice. The harsh demands of a criminal's life—the cold, the rain, the dust, the hunger, the desperation—were wearing. She couldn't pretend to be cold, hard, and tough any longer. She was tired of having no home, no meaning to her life, and no friends except other bandits. And, she admitted, she hated what people thought about her.

Too, real life was passing her by swiftly. She was twenty-four, a spinster by custom. She had never been married, never had a child, never even had a lover! To keep galloping down the wrong road was like recklessly racing toward a box canyon with a crazed posse hot on your tail. Surely Fate had forced this life-saving decision upon her.

After concealing Carolyn's body and fleeing the soldiers who were approaching the overturned stage, Darby and his men had headed for a hideout in the Oklahoma Territory, hoping to stay unnoticed for a few months while "heads cooled a mite in these parts."

The soldiers had taken "Carolyn Starns" to the next Butterfield station to continue her journey following a "lucky rescue just in the nick of time." Since that tragic day, she had switched to this Garrett stage in Fort Worth for the remainder of her trip to Tucson.

The redhead knew her brother was worried about her daring plan, but he had agreed with it because he was more concerned about himself and his gang endangering her on the trail. If anything went wrong, she knew where and how to contact Darby.

Gunshots filled the air and ceased her musings. Carrie Sue glanced out the window and sighted the trouble. As the driver urged the horses to outrun the bandits who were attacking it, the stage lurched wildly, hurling the two passengers on the other seat toward her and the man beside her. Obviously the driver had seen the six masked men galloping from behind a hill toward them and had decided to make a desperate race for the next relay station, which baffled and alarmed her because it was twenty miles down the road. It was a policy of stagelines to yield to robbers to safeguard passengers' lives, but the rash driver must have felt that he and the guard could successfully discourage the bandits, as he surely could not race the horses at breakneck speed for hours.

Carrie Sue and the other man helped the two fallen passengers back into their places. The holdup made no sense to her, as it was common knowledge that the Garrett line carried no mail or strongboxes; the Butterfield line performed those perilous tasks. The Garrett line was known for its passenger comfort because of its slower pace and fewer robberies. Averaging five miles an hour for nine to ten hours a day in comparison to Butterfield's rapid nine miles per hour and fewer stops, this line only covered forty to fifty miles a day and halted every night instead of every twenty-four hours for sleep. They had been on the road for five hours today, and Tucson was about sixty miles ahead of them. So close for trouble to defeat her!

The stage bounced up and down roughly, shaking them about like cotton bolls in a flour sack. Many sounds assailed her ears: the driver's whip slapping against horse-flesh; the metal and wood creaking in protest; the pounding of many hooves and the labored breathing of the frantic animals; the exchange of gunfire. The soldier's wife began screaming hysterically and the two men cursed in fear.

Carrie Sue saw the guard's body fall from the stage and tumble several times upon the hard ground. Hills, trees, yuccas, and brown mountains flashed by swiftly. The man on the seat beside her slumped into her lap as a bullet caught him in the head, staining her dress with blood. She did not shove his body aside because it would probably only fall her way again. The other man drew a small pistol and began firing at the outlaws. She shouted a warning but he sneered at her. He, too, was shot and killed.

As Carrie Sue peered out the window to see how close the gang was, the soldier's wife—in a panic over the horrible tales she had been told about the Wild West—screamed, "They'll rape us and murder us!" The woman seized the dead man's gun and shot herself in the head before Carrie Sue could grab the weapon from her. The redhead gasped at the shocking sight. She looked at the three bloody bodies which surrounded her and heard the peril closing in on her. These bandits were merciless, and she did not want to imagine what they would do to her.

28

Now she knew what it was like to be a helpless victim. As Kale vowed, she had actually smelled fear and death in the air, and its odor was foul in her nostrils. Carrie Sue knew she wasn't anything like these heartless outlaws; yet, she wanted to gun them down! Dare she reveal who she was? Would it matter to them that she was Darby Stover's sister, that she was the "Texas Flame?" If she exposed herself, probably they would take her with them and there was no telling what would happen to her in their camp!

Outlaws were galloping on both sides of the coach. The driver reined in and yielded only to be shot by the bandit leader. Carrie Sue wished fervently she had her revolvers or rifle inside the coach. She was an excellent shot and her aid might have swung the odds in their favor. She knew better than to hide her money—no, Carolyn Starns's money—even in her bodice. She knew better than to give the cutthroats any trouble. She knew from experience.

Suddenly she wondered if the handsome stranger at the relay station was in this gang, if he had been scouting the stage while pretending to eat. Would his presence help her?

During her brief distraction, the door was jerked open and Carrie Sue was yanked outside. She lost her balance and fell, skinning her hands and dirtying her already ruined dress. Quickly she flipped to her seat and glared at the despicable ruffian, preparing to defend herself. She watched the man's expression change upon viewing her face.

A lecherous grin revealed his perilous interest in her. "Whatda we have here? Seems this stage was carrying two prizes, boys. Get that strongbox while I have a look-see at this pretty thing."

As the lawless bully bent forward to seize her, he was shot in the throat near his collarbone. His body fell past Carrie Sue, hitting the ground with a thud. The other bandits whirled to check out their danger, but not in time to prevent two more from taking lethal rifle bullets.

The rescuer, who was galloping toward them without fear or hesitation, nearly concealed behind his horse's head, shoved his rifle into its saddle holster and drew two pistols. The remaining two outlaws fired at the lone gunman who rode to the side of his horse Indian-style and fired guns from either side of the animal's neck. One bandit yelled in pain as his chest accepted two deadly shots.

The last man grabbed Carrie Sue's wrist and yanked her to him to use as a shield and hostage. Wanting to protect herself and to aid her defender, she fought the cowardly villain like an unleashed wildcat as he struggled to control her while defending himself. Their actions caused her braid to fall. He cursed her and threatened her, but she did not let up on her attack of nails, fists, and kicks. As his hand tried to band her chest to imprison her, his rough fingers snagged the edge of her bodice and, as she attempted to escape his grasp, popped off several buttons and scratched her tender flesh. Provoked further, she whirled on him and landed a fisted blow to his mouth. "The Devil take you, you bastard!" she screamed.

Carrie Sue broke free and scrambled beneath the stage to give her rescuer a clear shot at him. She knew the bandit didn't have many more bullets in his two revolvers and he was winded from his fight with her. As he damned her to hell and scurried behind the coach for cover, she saw him shove an emptied weapon into one holster.

She kept her gaze on the nearby bandit and shifted her position as he did. Hurriedly her mind plotted how to help defeat this killer. She risked a quick glance at her rescuer, but he had dismounted and rushed behind a tree which was too small to offer much protection. Yet, the faded gray shirt and ebony head were familiar. Excitement traveled through her. She saw him duck a bullet, and knew she could not allow the bandit time to reload his weapons.

She looked about for a rock or stick; none were available. If she tried to climb on the driver's box or into the coach to get a weapon, the outlaw would hear and feel her movements. Then, she spotted a dead outlaw's pistol not far away.

Carrie Sue checked the bandit's stance which said he was peering around the back of the stage. Rapidly she scooted toward it. Her rescuer fired several times. Obviously he had seen her action and was giving her time and cover by distracting the ruffian. Seizing the weapon, she turned and fired beneath the coach at the man's legs.

He yelped in pain and staggered into the handsome stranger's view. The raven-haired man jumped into the open. His right hand cocked the hammer and his left hand pulled the trigger in one fluid motion which required no more than a split-second. The last bandit was slain.

The smokey-eyed gunslinger with whom she had eaten breakfast shoved his revolvers into their holsters and stalked forward in a purposeful stride, a black stallion trailing him out of love and protection. He glared at her and shouted, "That was a stupid thing to do! You could have gotten killed! Why didn't you stay under the stage?"

Distressed by the mayhem of the day, and angered by his ridiculous attitude, she shouted back, "If you had gotten yourself shot playing the hero, I would have been in deep trouble by now! I couldn't take a chance on your being killed for helping me! I wasn't about to let that ba . . . beast get his hands on me again!"

The man glared at her as if no female had ever dared to argue with him, and she glared back. His left thumb tipped up his hat and that obstinate ebony lock fell over his forehead once more. He sighed loudly in annoyance and shook his head. "What about the others?" he finally asked.

Carrie Sue knew he meant the people inside the coach. "All dead."

He rubbed his jawline as if saving her life had cost him precious time and energy which he resented spending. This vexed the redhead even more than his previous behavior. She suggested coldly, "If you'll help me load the bodies, I'll drive the stage to the next relay station and you can be on your way."

His eyes widened as he looked her up and down in astonishment. She was the most beautiful and desirable woman he had ever seen, even more so in her highly agitated state. Her tawny red hair seemed aflame beneath the brilliant sun. Strands had pulled themselves free of her plait and now danced about her dirty face like a fiery glow. A defiant expression filled her violet-blue eyes and tightened her enticing lips. She faced him squarely able to meet his gaze without craning her neck though he was over six feet tall. What an armful she would be!

When she wiped at the perspiration on her face, it mingled with the dust and created playful smudges on her forehead, nose, and above her upper-lip. Her dress was dirty, torn, and blood-stained. He noticed the scratches on her chest where the bodice gaped and revealed a white chemise. Observing his line of vision, her free hand lifted to clutch the severed garment together. The revolver was still dangling from the loosened grip in her right hand. He recalled how she had fought the bandit, even shot him. And hadn't he heard her curse the man? Where had that prim and proper lady from breakfast gone? What a surprising spitfire she was!

All that shyness and gentleness which he had observed this morning was now masked by a strength, confidence, and boldness which he found unexpected, befuddling, and appealing. Yet, he still sensed that same wary nature he had detected earlier. This intriguing vixen could definitely take care of herself, if the odds weren't too uneven.

Long ago he had built a strong wall around himself to prevent ever being hurt again, and had honed his skills to make certain no one ever took advantage of him. In a few minutes this morning, this wild filly had nearly kicked a hole in that sturdy wall, and he had been willing—eager— to let her! That was crazy! He was a loner and she was a stranger, a ravishing and troublesome type. At the station this morning, he had lost his wits for a while. No, this beautiful thief had stolen them! He had tried to dismiss her from mind after leaving, but found that task impossible. He had caught himself riding slower and slower and sticking close to the road just to be near her once more when the stage halted for the night at the last home station. While he halted to get control of himself, the stage had passed his hiding place. Now he was glad he had hung back.

What was so different and alluring about this particular creature? Was it her entrancing eyes which exposed such vulnerable innocence and such defiant fire? Her beautiful face with its rosy gold hue? Her shapely body in that simple cotton dress? Her fiery mane which enticed his fingers to enter it? Or some elusive and irresistible aura which he couldn't name just yet? Whatever her magic, he didn't have time to test it, enjoy it, or become ensnared by it! He had to get to Tucson to kill a man. Afterwards, there were other men to track and slay.

As the man stared at her, Carrie Sue felt that strange heat and tension crawl over her body once more like a dangerous viper seeking a vulnerable spot to strike. She had not expected him or wanted him to be so . . . whatever! Being alone with him was intimidating. Never had she been more aware that she was a woman. "Why do you keep gaping at me so rudely, just like you did at breakfast? Your mother should be whipped for failing to teach you any manners!"

The stranger's eyes chilled and narrowed. He forcefully jabbed his thumbs into his gunbelt as if controlling the urge to strike her. "Why is it people always blame a mother's failure for their bad traits and weaknesses? Obviously your mother failed in the same task or you'd be thanking me for saving your pretty hide instead of being so smartmouthed," he scolded. "When a man sees such a beautiful woman, naturally he's gonna stare a minute or two. At your age, I would think you'd be used to it by now," he added, but made it sound more like an insult than a compliment. He watched her violet-blue eyes blaze with fury. He lowered his head and inhaled deeply several times, chiding himself for his callousness. Obviously she had endured a bad scare and wasn't herself just now. When he looked back at her, he asked, "Have you ever driven a stage or wagon before?"

His mood, expression, and tone had changed. Maybe it was the heat or lethal battle which had put him on edge. They both had to settle down because there was a grim chore to perform. "A wagon, yes; a stage, no," she replied, mastering her own unleashed temper.

He was visibly impressed by her self-control. In a teasing tone, he said, "No insult intended, Ma'am, but you don't look strong enough to handle six half-broken horses and a heavy stage. If you have no objection, I'll drive it to the next station."

"You seemed in such a hurry that I didn't want to put you out any further," she responded in like manner.

"Won't delay me much. I'm heading for Tucson just like you."

"Why?" the question jumped uncontrollably from her lips.

His expression waxed to one of curiosity. "Does it matter?"

Carrie Sue dared her cheeks to turn that unnatural red again. Her body must have feared her threat, because it obeyed. "Not to me. I was just wondering why you didn't travel with us. If you'd been . . ."

Knowing her words, he interrupted, "I travel alone,

34

unless it suits me otherwise. Your stomach strong enough for this task, or you want me to load the bodies alone?" he inquired, his voice softening.

The lovely fugitive liked the change in his tone and expression. "I've seen and touched plenty of dead people before. I'm just angry because this attack was stupid, a waste of lives. The Garrett line never carries anything of value. I'm glad you came along when you did. I've never witnessed more courage or prowess than you displayed," she said without thinking. Unnerved by her slip, she rushed on, "Let's get busy. It's four hours to the next station. What about those bandits?"

His smokey gray eyes glanced over them. "I would leave 'em here for the vultures, but there might be a reward or two on their heads. I see no reason not to collect it for my trouble. I might even be persuaded to split it with you. Let me check your hand," he said and reached for the one which had struck the last bandit.

Carrie Sue jerked it from his light grasp and stepped away from him. She hoped her face didn't pale and her trembling didn't show. "Are you a bounty hunter?" she asked, her tone laced with revulsion.

Chapter Two

He was surprised by her reaction. "A bounty hunter?" he echoed in a matching tone of aversion. "Not me, but it's foolish to pass up a possible reward when you've earned it. Why do you feel so strongly about them?"

She looked relieved by his reply, but ignored his question. "You're awfully good with a gun," she hinted for information.

He responded to her evocative tone and expression, "I manage to stay alive and healthy. What riles you about bounty hunters?" he persisted.

"I've heard many times that they hunt men down like wild animals, that they get their shooting and questioning out of order. They're nothing but glorified killers using the law to carry out the evil within them. What do you do for a living?"

"Rescue beautiful women in trouble," he quipped. The stubble on his face and his dark tan made his teeth appear snowy white when he smiled.

She frowned. "Hold the jests, please. What are you? A gunslinger? A drifter? A lawman?" she inquired.

He chuckled to prevent her from realizing that he was aware of her excessive anxiety. He knew she was afraid of something or someone because her lips remained parted, her respiration was shallow and swift, and she seemed to hang on every word he spoke as if seeking life-sustaining clues in them. In a casual tone and manner he said, "I'm

36

intrigued by your choices. I've had lots of jobs in the past. When I get bored with one or the place I'm in, I move on to the next challenge. I guess that makes me a drifter of sorts, doesn't it?"

"Not necessarily. A real drifter roams aimlessly, but you sound as if you plan your moves before taking them. You left the station before the stage and a horse travels faster, so how did you fall behind?"

He eyed her up and down and grinned. "Very observant and sharp-witted. Was I suppose to be in a hurry to reach Tucson?"

"What's in Tucson to lure you there?" she kept firing questions at him since he seemed willing to answer them, which surprised her.

"Mighty nosey about strangers, aren't we?" he teased.

"Since we're trapped out here alone, I'd like to make certain I can trust you. For all I know, that could be your gang you double-crossed and gunned down so you could steal that alleged strongbox for yourself. You could have been checking us over this morning at the station. Do you mind answering my questions to calm my worries?"

"I certainly don't need or want an hysterical female on my hands. I'm heading for the mines near Tucson. You've heard of the Specie Resumption Act of '75. The government needs lots of gold to trade for those worthless greenbacks. Arizona has plenty of gold and silver."

"You don't look like a miner to me."

He laughed. It sounded rich and mellow, and his smokey gray eyes filled with amusement. "I'm not. Freight lines need drivers and guards, and those jobs pay plenty. Might be interesting for a while."

Carrie Sue tugged on her lower lip with her upper teeth, a habit which revealed her suspicion of him and his words. "You don't look like a wagon driver or guard either."

He was impressed by her cunning, wits, and courage.

She was direct without being forward. From now on, he needed to pay close attention to what he said and did around her. "I take it you've seen enough miners, drivers, and guards to recognize them at forty paces."

She frowned again at his new jest. "What I meant was, you don't strike me as a man who takes or follows orders from others. Isn't that right?" she probed.

"Maybe that's why I can't stay put for long in one place. But a man has to eat, so he needs money. If he gets it the wrong way, his lazy days are over. Frankly, Ma'am, I don't hanker to have the law on my tail day and night, so I watch my steps and guns."

Once more Carrie Sue's teeth toyed with her lower lip, exposing her mistrust. This man was not behaving as he should! She knew that loners were not talkers, so why was he doing so much of it?

The gunslinger wondered the same thing. Everywhere he went, people accused him of being silent and moody, of being cold and hard and tough. Yet, this clever female had a strange way of pulling words from his mouth, of warming and disarming him. He was actually enjoying their controlled banter. But he wanted to know a few things about her. He wanted to ask why she hid her exceptional looks beneath plain dresses and simple hairstyles; why she had no ring on her finger; why she was so curious about him; why her hand had gone to her waist at the home station like a reflex of a gunslinger; why her hands were so rough and her nails so jagged; why she was scared of him; and why she had watched his presence and departure so intensely. Those queries would certainly frighten her into silence. Perhaps she was fleeing a brutal father or a cruel marriage and was wary of strangers. All he asked was, "Why are you heading for Tucson, Miss Starns?"

"How do you know my name?" she demanded, looking and sounding angry and distressed.

He wondered if he had read a brief gleam of terror in her lovely eyes. He also noticed how her hand tightened on the gun butt in her hand. "I asked the guard before I rode off this morning."

"Why?" she asked in a strained voice.

He shrugged and replied, "You caught my eye."

Carrie Sue could not suppress a smile. "What's your name?"

"T.J. Rogue."

Her violet-blue gaze widened and she looked him over again. She recognized his name. He was a famous gunslinger. Gossip said he was one of the fastest, if not the fastest, guns in the West. Rumor also said he hired out to settle dangerous problems for other people. He was supposed to be tough, cold, hard, and relentless, but she did not find him that way. If anybody knew how gossip could be exaggerated or fabricated, she did! At times she had observed a resentful, almost bitter, air about him and wondered what had birthed those emotions. One thing, he was careful and highly intelligent because he wasn't wanted by the law, as far as she knew.

T.J. realized she had heard his name before, but if he had met her in the past, he would certainly recall it. "You've heard of me," he said, a statement instead of a question. "Where? When? What were you told?"

"Are you really as good as your reputation claims? One of the best guns in Texas? A man who settles problems others can't? Or should I say the fastest gun in the entire West?"

"No man is the fastest and best for very long. Another gunman always comes along who is swifter and better. Does it frighten you to be alone with the notorious T.J. Rogue, Miss Starns?"

"Actually, Mr. Rogue, having heard of your enormous reputation and having witnessed your skills, it makes me feel safer. If rumor can be trusted, you're more legendary than notorious. Tell me, does it make you feel odd to be the subject of countless campfire tales?"

"A man can't help what others say or think about him. Let's get moving. I want to reach the next station before dark." He tugged his hat down on his forehead and wiggled it into place, indicating their conversation was closed for now.

The redhead inquired, "Don't you think you should check those bandits. Someone could be alive."

"Not unless I'm losing my touch, Miss Starns. When I pull my gun, I shoot to kill. That's something you should always remember: never draw a weapon unless you intend to use it or you'll get hurt. You know any of these passengers?"

"No. They've only been on the stage a day or two, and I caught it at Fort Worth. None of us were talkers."

They gathered the outlaw's bodies and loaded them inside the stage with the slain passengers and driver. Carrie Sue glanced at the soldier's wife and unwillingly recalled another woman's murder in March near San Angelo. But that time, a small girl had been slain, too. She had to forget those incidents; she had to look to a bright future.

While her ebon-haired partner retrieved the guard's body down the road and fetched the horses, Carrie Sue recovered her purse and buttons and hurriedly changed clothes, a fact T.J. noticed when he returned. He liked the multi-colored dress she was wearing; its brighter colors suited her better. He secured the horses' reins to the back of the stage, but allowed his black stallion to remain free.

"You forgot your horse," she told him.

"Nighthawk stays with me unless I order him otherwise. He'll run alongside of us." As he replaced her smaller bag atop the coach, he pointed to the large chest hidden beneath the driver's box and commented, "Gold makes men go crazy with greed; it gets 'em into trouble. Obviously those bandits knew this stage was loaded."

"I wonder how," she mused. "I thought Garrett lines didn't haul mail or strongboxes to insure passengers' safety and comfort. That's why I chose them over Butterfield in Fort Worth. They're responsible for this slaughter. I'll register a complaint when I reach the next station."

He concurred, "I would too; it nearly got you killed. Let's tend those scratches and get moving."

The daring desperado allowed T.J. to doctor her scrapes with soothing ointment from his saddlebag. His touch was surprisingly gentle and warm. She wondered if he was tempted by the gold. All he had to do was get rid of her — the solitary witness — and take it. No one would guess the truth and he'd be rich.

When she trembled, his eyes left her injuries to look at her. She hurriedly averted her gaze and stood silently before him. When she began to fidget, he knew he was affecting her in the same way she was affecting him. He released her hand. "What's in Tucson for you?"

Carrie Sue kept her telltale gaze on her hands. "I'm heading there to become the town's new schoolmarm."

His gaze narrowed, but remained pleasant. He inhaled and exhaled deeply through his nose, a clue the redhead already guessed revealed his doubts about something. "A teacher. That explains why you're so inquisitive and ask so many questions."

"It's the best way to learn anything and to stay out of trouble."

"Only if people tell you the truth," he nonchalantly refuted.

"If you're smart enough to know they're lying or being evasive, that tells you a great deal about them and the situation."

He chuckled and his smokey eyes glowed. "You're right on that point, Miss Starns. You're very smart and brave."

"For a woman?" she teased.

"For anybody," he replied, then grinned.

T.J. helped her onto the driver's box and lifted the reins and whip. "Ready?" he asked.

Carrie Sue placed the pistol in her lap and nodded.

The gunslinger glanced at it, then looked into her periwinkle eyes.

"Just in case there's more trouble, I want to be prepared."

"Like I said, smart and brave."

As they traveled along the dusty road, Carrie Sue contemplated the man beside her. He didn't seem tempted by the large amount of gold beneath his feet if it meant killing her and breaking the law to obtain it. Perhaps if they'd all been dead when he attacked the bandits, he might have taken it just as she had stolen Carolyn Starns's identity and possessions. He was basically a decent and honest man, but private. He had not tried to capture her. Surely that also meant he hadn't guessed her dark secret, as that much gold should be more tempting to a gunslinger than the rewards posted on her and her brother's gang. Normally she was not this open and talkative, nor was he. Obviously there was an attraction between them which relaxed them. She wondered how long he would stay in Tucson. Yet, it couldn't matter to her. It was too risky starting a romance with any man, particularly a man like Rogue. It would make her too vulnerable to discovery and defeat. She had to resist him.

T.J. was thinking much the same. She didn't look like a school teacher, and she possessed a trail instinct which most men would envy. Her lips were full, her nose was wide, and her eyes were large. Separately none of those features were beautiful, but put them together beneath a flaming head of hair and the result was exquisite. At this moment, she looked so soft and vulnerable. But he knew better. Lordy, what a fetching and intriguing vixen she was. And frankly, he was aching to make her *his* vixen.

That was impossible. He would never be able to love her as she deserved to be loved. He was always on the move and doubted he could settle down in one place. He had tried, but had failed in every attempt. To date, the women he had known fell into two sacks: spoiled daughters of rich and powerful men, who pretended to be angels outside but were black devils inside, and whores in saloons who were filled with bitterness, most too weak to break away from a life they despised. But this woman was different, and different could mean trouble for him!

For the first time he asked himself if he was as cold and hard as people claimed, or he led them to believe. He had been forced to become that way to survive. His parents had been killed by Apaches when he was seven and he had been raised by the Indians until he was thirteen. After being rescued by the cavalry, he had been placed in Father Rafael Ortega's mission in San Antonio, Texas. He had become a street kid—"a half-savage rogue"—until running off to the war in '62 to see how the white tribes battled. Upon returning to Texas in '65, he had wandered aimlessly, facing new challenges every day, always into trouble, never fitting in anywhere.

Yes, he admitted, he had been tough, unrelenting, embittered. He had been separated from his brother after their capture and had never seen Tim again. Then, last winter he'd learned that his brother was a major at Fort Davis near the Mexican border. But fate had played him cruel again, allowing Tim to be slain by Mexican renegades before they could be reunited.

Then, the beautiful Arabella and precious little Marie had been murdered two months ago during a holdup near San Angelo. He had planned to give up his perilous existence and settle down with them, but that ill-fated dark cloud over his head had prevented it. As soon as he hunted down and killed the piece of scum who had barbwired him to a tree, he would stalk the gang responsible for Arabella's and Marie's deaths. The law wouldn't interfere if he killed them on the spot!

Despite his earlier troubles and "sorry attitude," he had always managed to stay an inch on the right side of the law by finding a way to provoke an enemy into a legal showdown. Hopefully he could do the same with those cold-blooded killers of his loved ones. Nearly everyone and everything he had loved had been taken from him, so it was a big risk to lean toward the woman beside him. Maybe his destiny was to remain a loner who cleared the earth of vermin, so why keep fighting it?

He glanced at the gold chest below his feet. That much treasure would tempt any man, including him. He couldn't steal it. But, Lordy, he could dream about taking it and the fiery treasure beside him! What a fine life that would be. . . .

Carrie Sue furtively observed T.J. She wondered what was more important to this man than easy riches. When he glanced her way, she read such resentment and anguish in his smokey eyes before he swiftly looked ahead again. Her heart twinged in empathy. She wanted to ease his suffering. Terrible things must have compelled him into his miserable existence. She wondered if he even realized how unhappy he was, how much he wanted and needed love. Yes, underneath that hard exterior was a gentle man aching for peace. She was certain of it because she felt the same. Was he the kind of man, the only man, who could understand what she had done and been, could forgive it and forget it?

Back off, Carrie Sue. You're dancing too close to the fire, she warned herself. She didn't know much about love and commitment, but she knew a tormented man like T.J. Rogue could burn her badly.

"Where are you from, Miss Starns?" he interrupted her musings.

Carrie Sue called Carolyn Starns's life to mind. "Originally from back East, but I've been teaching in St. Louis for the past two years. I lost my job to the mayor's daughter. She wanted it, so papa got it for her. I read about the position in Tucson in the paper. Fortunately I was the only teacher to answer their advertisement. I don't know why because the pay is excellent. Lots of successful ranchers and miners in that area. I've been traveling for weeks, so I'm more than ready to get there and take on those little hellions."

"Little hellions?" he echoed.

"If you've been to school, Mr. Rogue, surely you remember how boys behave when cooped up like feisty roosters all day."

They shared laughter before he remarked playfully, "You don't look like a schoolmarm to me."

"And you would recognize one at forty paces?" she teased.

They laughed again. "Nope, but I've never seen one who looks like you. Those boys will be lucky to face you every day."

"Only if they do their lessons the night before. I can be very tough."

"I know you can, but I wouldn't have believed you if I hadn't seen how skillfully you handled yourself back there. You surely know a lot about a lot of things."

Carrie Sue smiled. "I read and study all the time, an occupational necessity and curse. Too, if I weren't strong and hard, those children would run all over me. Fear, Mr. Rogue, is the only way to control boys twice your size and nearly your age."

He eyed her with a sensual grin. "I'd imagine you have other ways to control rowdy males. Just give 'em a smile and they'll do anything you ask." She smiled radiantly and he laughed. "I didn't mean for you to use that power on me. You forgetting we're out here alone? If you want me to remain a gentleman, better holster that weapon and

45

don't draw it again unless you intend to use it."

As if trying to obey his mischievous warning, Carrie Sue placed her left hand over her mouth as merry laughter spilled forth. "You're quite a charming man, Mr. Rogue."

"That's one word which hasn't been used before to describe me. Why don't you call me T.J.?" he suggested.

"If you'll call me Ca-rolyn and tell me more about you."

"Why not? My folks were killed by Apaches when I was a boy. Then, I was raised in a mission orphanage. I ran away at fifteen to see what all the ruckus was about in the East. I fought a few battles and returned to Texas when the war ended. I've had just about every kind of job there is, but none of them kept my interest, and certainly didn't pay me enough to become my own boss. The last job I had was herding cattle to market. Months on a dusty trail in all kinds of weather. I plan to rest up a spell in Tucson, then hire out as a mine guard. When I get bored, I'll move on. One thing, you learn a lot while drifting around and trying out different jobs. You a widow?" he asked suddenly, returning the conversation to her.

"No, I've never been married. Have you?"

"Was that your choice or was every man you've met dumb and blind?"

He guided the stage off the public road to the Garrett station. Although it couldn't be seen through the dense growth of billowy mesquite, thick paloverde, and numerous branches of cacti, T.J. knew something was wrong: it was too quiet, and he smelled recent smoke. Just as those perceptions settled in, the winding road reached the clearing.

Before she could respond to his question, he shouted, "Hold on tight, Carolyn! Trouble ahead! Whoa, boys!" The moment she braced herself, he stomped on the brake lever and pulled back hard on the reins, halting the stage with skill and strength. He scolded himself for his lack of attention, a result of his intriguing companion.

Carrie Sue's eyes went from his scowling face to the scene before them. The home station had been destroyed by a fire and bodies were sighted here and there, with arrows protruding from them.

"Renegade Apaches," he commented knowingly from their colors and patterns. "Must have broken from the reservation. No buzzards circling yet. Stay here while I take a look around."

He climbed down slowly, adjusting his gunbelt when his boots touched the ground. He retrieved his rifle from Nighthawk's saddle and cocked it. He closed the distance between the stage and the station. He scanned all directions with keen eyes, then dropped to the ground and listened for any sound of hoofbeats as the Apaches had taught him. He examined the bodies, the charred remains of the house and barn, the empty corral, and tracks on the earth. He returned to the coach and said, "Happened late yesterday. She was dry and burned quickly, but the odor's still fresh. They won't be back this way. We'll camp here for the night, then leave at dawn."

Her wide eyes checked their surroundings and her ears strained to pick up any unnatural sound. Mountains were visible in all directions over the tops of the thick growth which encircled the clearing. Her lips were parted and her breathing was shallow and swift. She knew what Indians on the warpath could do, and was wisely afraid. If Indians came galloping down the narrow road, they would be trapped. "I don't like being boxed in like this. You're sure it's safe?" she pressed.

"No reason for them to return. They stole the horses and supplies and destroyed everything else. Besides, our horses have to rest and graze before they can take us on to Tucson. We'll load those bodies in the stage to keep the vultures off them and leave the stage here. We can make better time on horseback. I'll let you ride Nighthawk and I'll use one of these horses. Can you ride?"

"Yes, but what about the gold and my baggage? Other bandits might come along and steal everything before the company can send someone to recover them. Can't we just take the stage on into town?"

T.J. gave her reminder some thought. The gold was too heavy for them to lift out and bury. If anything happened to it, someone might point an accusatory finger at them and mess up his schedule. "You're right, Carolyn. We can't risk losing that gold and falling under suspicion for its theft. We'll take the stage on to Tucson at dawn."

Although he hadn't mentioned her possessions, she thanked him for agreeing with her. She certainly didn't need to fall under suspicion for a robbery! She climbed over the edge of the driver's box and made her way down, with T.J.'s hands securely about her waist. "What's first?" she asked.

"Let's put these bodies inside the coach. Too many to bury, and families might want to claim them for burial at home."

Carrie Sue and T.J. carried two more bodies to the stage and added them to the eleven already there. To foil vultures, they had no choice except to pile them on the seats and floor. She wished there were blankets in which to wrap the bodies, but none were available in the warm month of May. She watched her partner lower the leather window shades and secure them tightly to keep insects away.

Afterwards, he unhitched the team and placed the horses in the corral where unsinged hay and a water trough were located. Nighthawk was placed with them so he could drink and feed. T.J. motioned to a spot on the western side of the clearing where a few trees didn't have limbs teasing the dry ground. "We'll camp there in the shade. Your nose is already pink. You need a hat, Miss Starns."

She touched the sensitive area and said, "I didn't even

think about it in all the excitement. I'll unpack one for tomorrow's ride."

Carrie Sue followed T.J. beneath the trees, both having to duck to avoid low branches. He spread out a blanket and told her to have a seat while he gathered firewood and prepared them some "grub."

"I can help, T.J.," she offered. "My rear can use some relief. That shotgun seat is harder than the benches inside the coach."

He chuckled when she rubbed her sore behind. He was accustomed to doing chores alone, but he welcomed her company and assistance.

Being careful around the bristly cacti, sharp-tipped yuccas, and thorny catclaw, they scouted amongst the scrubs for dead branches and dry weeds to use for a fire. When they finished, T.J. raised his left pant leg and withdrew a large knife from a sheath which was strapped to his calf. He dug a shallow pit and built a fire within it.

On the lip of the hole, he placed a circle of rocks to contain the flames and heat. Around it, he jabbed a three-prong metal holder into the ground from which to suspend a small cooking pot. He opened his pouch and dropped strips of dried meat into the pot, then cleaned and used the sharp blade to open a can of beans to add to it. Next, he put some coffee on to perk near one edge of the fire. "It'll take a while. Which one of your bags do you need for the night?"

"Why don't I go with you? There's no need to lift a heavy bag down and up when I can climb up there and pull what I need from it."

"Good idea. Come along, partner."

They went to the coach and mounted the driver's box. T.J. pulled her largest bag forward so she could reach it easily.

Carrie Sue opened Carolyn's bag and withdrew a washcloth, dress, hat, and undergarments for the next morning. She was glad she had hidden her rifle and six-guns on the bottom of the case where he couldn't see them. She closed the bag and fastened the straps, leaving a tiny gap which would tell her if the bag was tampered with during the night. If he was anything more than the gunslinger T.J. Rogue, she would know by morning. And if he was, she would deal with that problem then. She inhaled deeply to distract him and said, "That coffee smells wonderful."

"Let's see if it's ready." He helped her down and they walked back to their small camp. "Not yet," he said while stirring the beans.

Carrie Sue excused herself to use the outhouse, the only unburned structure. Borrowing his canteen upon her return, she washed her dirty face and hands. T.J. handed her the ointment from his saddlebag and suggested she rub more on her scratches, which she did.

"I only have one set of dishes and utensils. You can use the plate and fork, and I'll eat from the pot with a spoon. I'm afraid we'll have to share the cup," he told her. "Sorry, but I don't have any sugar."

"It doesn't matter; I drink mine black," Carrie Sue replied, having been forced by years on the trail to adjust to unsweetened coffee. "You're handy to have around, T.J., and you're most generous. I'm sorry I accused you of not having manners; clearly you have plenty."

He glanced at her and teased, "Don't swell my head, woman. I guess we were both a little edgy back there. Sorry." He pulled two biscuits from a cloth and put them on a hot rock to warm. "Sam gave 'em to me this morning. Been craving 'em all day."

After dining on coffee, beans, biscuits, and dried beef, darkness surrounded their cozy campfire. T.J. suggested, "We'd better turn in so we can get an early start at dawn. We only have one bedroll, so we'll have to share it too. You mind?"

"Not if you remember you're a gentleman," she teased

pointedly.

"I promise not to forget that fact, Miss Starns. I wouldn't want the Tucson town council tracking me down for molesting their teacher."

Carrie Sue stayed in her clothes as she settled down to spend the night beside the handsome man. She turned on her side away from him, and he did the same. Yet, as time passed, she remained aware of his close proximity and her body burned to feel his touch again.

T.J. couldn't sleep; the woman near him was too desirable. He wanted to turn to her and pull her into his arms, to smother her lips with kisses, to caress her shapely body, to run his fingers through her fiery mane. He knew that would be a mistake, for both of them.

Carrie Sue struggled to locate dreamland where she could unite her torrid flesh with his, but her search was in vain. He was too real; this moment was too real. She attempted to concentrate on their surroundings. Not far away was a coach filled with bodies. She was heading for a new life, one free of complications. He was T.J. Rogue, a famous—or infamous—gunslinger who could destroy her without meaning to do so. He would call attention to her presence. Their match was perilous; their attraction was dangerous.

"Carolyn?" he whispered, "are you awake?"

"Yes," she replied.

"I'm going to bed down near the corral, else neither of us will get any sleep. Don't be afraid; I'll be nearby."

"T.J. . . ."

"Yes?"

"Thank you."

"I know," he murmured hoarsely.

He left the area and his body was engulfed by darkness. She listened as he crossed the open space and flopped down on hay near the corral. How she yearned to call him back to her side, but she dared not. How long, she wondered, before she would feel safe to yield to her desires? How long before another man like this appeared?

Carrie Sue thought about Quade Harding's lust for her. It had been seven years since they'd met. Why couldn't he forget about her and settle down with another woman? How could he sustain his obsession for so long? He must have spent a fortune on detectives. Anyone would think he'd weary of the chase and setbacks. But time seemed to increase his hunger for her. Merciful heavens, what would he do next to locate her?

The lovely fugitive's mind drifted to her brother. Had Darby and his men made it to their hideout? What if peril forced him northward and she needed him to rescue her? Would he head to El Paso in early July as planned? If she ran into trouble, would that old Mexican deliver her message to Darby as promised? Would Darby keep his gang out of Arizona as promised so her new life wouldn't be threatened? And, how long would Quade hold silent? Or that Ranger she had shot and thwarted last year? If the vile lawman had reported her deed, news of it had not been released. After all, it would be her word against his that she had surrendered, then been forced to shoot and flee.

Carrie Sue recalled the Stover farm in Georgia before the War Between the States had destroyed their lives the first time. Her family had raised cotton and done very well at it. She remembered how to plant it, pick it, and gin it. After the war, greedy northerners had forced them off their prized land and out of business. Finally her father had yielded reluctantly, bitterly, and sold out to a persistent Carpetbagger in '67. The moment the evil man moved into their home, her father had robbed him and had burned the barns, house, and fields so he couldn't profit from his wickedness. Afterwards, they had made their way to distant Texas and purchased a ranch in early '68 with the villain's stolen money. Perhaps that was where Darby had learned the motives and means of just revenge which he had used against the Hardings in '69.

Men, could any of them be trusted? Carrie Sue wondered sadly. First, the northern soldiers had terrorized her family in Georgia. Next, northern Carpetbaggers had ruined their life and driven them from their home and land. Then, the Hardings had destroyed their new chance for happiness in Texas. Now, countless lawmen, bounty hunters, and others wanted nothing more than to see her and her brother's gang dead.

If only they could be left alone for a while, allowed to cease their criminal life and settle down. Both she and Darby should be wed by now with homes and families. But fate had dealt them heavy blows. Everywhere they went, trouble followed. Everyone they loved, fate destroyed. T.J. Rogue had enough trouble without taking on hers!

Carrie Sue grimaced as if in physical pain. Never had she known a man whom she wanted to know intimately. It was too late. When she reached Tucson and he departed, she must forget him.

T.J. glanced toward the cluster of trees. It was too dark to see the woman camped beneath them; yet, he knew she was still awake, awake and miserable like he was. He felt the heavy tension in the air, sensed the odd mingling of powerful attraction and necessary rejection in both of them. Why had he allowed her to get under his tough hide? How could he simply scratch her out like a troublesome chigger? He had to ignore her, resist her pull, forget her. But could he?

At last, the distraught redhead and agitated smokey-eyed male were fast asleep and the remainder of the night passed swiftly.

Chapter Three

Carrie Sue stirred and awakened on T.J.'s bedroll. She nestled her cheek against the material which held manly scents along with those of leather and horseflesh. Accustomed to such smells, she did not find them offensive. In fact, the gunslinger's scent was quite arousing.

To break its hold over her, she sat up and looked around, but didn't see the charming Rogue anywhere. The sun was just peeking over the distant mountains to the east, so her shade would be stolen soon. Except for the neighing and movements of the corralled horses, few sounds were heard in the "Southwest Corner of Hell," as early travelers had described this dry and sunny area. At first glance one might think this landscape was desolate and dreary, but on closer inspection, it was filled with life and wild beauty.

The creaking of metal and splashing of water caught her attention and she turned to find the black-haired man near a water pump at the corral. She stood, straightened her dress, removed the washcloth from an overhead branch, and headed his way. Used to being around males who were half-dressed, she thought nothing of joining him. "Good morning, Mr. Rogue. We did pass the night safely as you promised."

He met her smiling gaze and grinned. "I was hoping I wouldn't have to awaken you to start breakfast, but I was getting mighty hungry." His mellow gaze roamed her sleepy face and rumpled clothes. "I found a bucket in the yard and filled it with fresh water. I put it behind the coach. Why don't you get washed up and changed behind the stage while I prepare some coffee and vittles?"

"Sounds marvelous to me," she replied, stretching and yawning. She watched T.J. fingercomb his wet hair and use his dirty shirt to dry off his muscled torso and darkly stubbled face. That willful lock fell forward to tease at his temple and she had the urge to twirl it around her finger. She eyed the two rows of curious scars which ran across his furry chest, arms, and over his flat stomach. Then, she noticed matching ones across the backs of his wrists. It appeared as if he had been bound tightly by a metal rope with jagged edges.

T.J.'s smokey gray eyes went from her inquisitive expression to his chest and arms, then returned to her face. He reached for the bib-shirt which he had thrown over the fence and began pulling it on. "Barbwire," he murmured as he fastened the buttons.

"What?" she said in confusion.

He left the top part of his shirt unbuttoned and flapped to one side. As he tied a brown bandanna around his neck, he revealed, "I ran afoul of a man in Texas so he had his hirelings ambush me and tie me to a tree with barbwire."

"Merciful Heavens, T.J.! How did you get loose without tearing yourself to pieces?" she asked, imagining those sharp points biting viciously into his handsome body.

His eyes narrowed and chilled, but he joked lightly, "I stayed real still until somebody came along and cut me free. Didn't take but two days. I was so hungry and thirsty and mad by then, damage or naught, I would have broken myself free in another hour or two. Worst part was all those blood-sucking insects wanting a drink from me."

"How could anyone do such a despicable thing? Did you kill him?"

T.J. withdrew a comb from his saddlebag and ran it through his ebony hair. "I caught two of them later and let them enjoy the same experience for a while. Their friend will cross my path one day and I'll make certain he recalls who I am. As for their boss, I couldn't prove he was involved, as if anyone would believe a notorious gunslinger over a respectable rancher. He even had a different kind of wire used on me so the evidence wouldn't point a finger at him. But he'll make another mistake some day, and I'll be there to repay him. I know right where to find him and he isn't going anywhere."

"Was he trying to kill you for some reason, or just torture you?"

"Yep, I made a fool of him in front of others. A man doesn't forget or forgive humiliation. He planned for me to rot at that tree, real slow and painful, but I fooled him." T.J. chuckled coldly.

"Why didn't you sneak to his ranch one night and get revenge?"

"I'm letting him simmer and sweat. Fear is a perfect first course to a fine meal of vengeance. About the time he stops looking over his shoulder, I'll be standing there. Guess that sounds pretty cold-blooded to a genteel lady like you, Miss Starns."

"No, it sounds like justice to me. Sometimes men have to take the law into their own hands to obtain it. Evil men don't deserve to live."

"Lordy, woman, you think like me."

"Is that why your reputation says you take on villains the law is afraid to touch or can't touch?"

"It's a job like any other, but one I seem to enjoy a lot," he admitted. His gaze wandered over her lovely face and tousled hair. Her eyes were wide and alert, but enticingly soft. When she looked away, fell silent, and shifted her weight nervously, he knew he was making her uncomfortable with his stare. "We'd better get busy."

T.J. headed for the campsite beneath the fragrant mesquites and squatted by the fire ring. Carrie Sue's gaze followed his retreat and lingered on his back for a time as he pulled items from his saddlebag. She sighed heavily and made a trip to the outhouse before going behind the stage to bathe and change clothes. She wanted to look her best when she entered Tucson later today, as the impression she made on the people there would be vital. With their grim baggage and tale to be exposed, their arrivals certainly wouldn't go unnoticed; that worried her.

At least she would look fairly well-rested. Actually, she was amazed at herself for sleeping so deeply; she hadn't even noticed T.J.'s stirrings at dawn. Obviously she felt at ease with him. But, she wondered, should that please her or make her nervous? Merciful Heavens, it was scary to trust a stranger!

She slipped off the dress, glad Carolyn was accustomed to dressing alone and had all of her garments made with buttons up the front. The only exception was an elegant gown and it wasn't appropriate for her mission today. But at least she had a proper dress if a special occasion arose.

Carrie Sue discarded the cotton petticoat, chemise, and bloomers. Using the bucket of water and washcloth, she bathed as quickly and thoroughly as possible. She dried herself and pulled on the clean undergarments and dark green dress. She wondered if Miss Carolyn Starns favored darker garments because of her position as a schoolmarm. She knew the dress was plain and sturdy, yet it did nothing to flatter her coloring and figure. But she shouldn't want to appear beautiful to T.J., or showy to the town council in Tucson. She must present the image of a virtuous and respectable school teacher.

Delectable odors assailed her nose and her stomach rumbled in hunger. She climbed upon the driver's box to stuff her things inside her baggage. She smiled when she noticed the case had not been tampered with during the night. If the gunslinger mistrusted her or was playing games with her, he would have searched her baggage while she was asleep. Relief and joy swept over her. She placed her hat on the shotgun seat, ready for use later this morning when the sun's heat and glare increased.

Taking her brush, she joined T.J. beneath the trees. He looked her way as she unbraided her hair and brushed it. The fiery mane was long, thick, and wavy, and golden highlights shone in the sunny light. T.J. felt his groin tighten at the ravishing sight before his eyes.

Carrie Sue rebraided her hair neatly and secured the looped plait to the back of her head as she had done yesterday. When she put aside her brush and looked his way, T.J. was still staring at her. "Is something wrong?" she inquired apprehensively.

T.J. shook his head and murmured, "Nope." He returned his attention to his chore. Lordy, she was one tempting female! With that flaming hair unleashed, she looked like an angel imprisoned on earth.

Carrie Sue grinned as she realized what kind of expression had filled his eyes: desire. Her own body was burning with it. She noticed what he was cooking and asked, "Where did you get those?"

Without looking up again, he replied, "One of the chickens must have gotten loose during the Apache attack. She was nesting in a thicket, but a coyote got her. Wasn't a total loss; she left behind three eggs. I fried enough salt pork to stuff inside our last two biscuits so we won't have to halt at midday to make dinner. Sam gave me six, so we can have two this morning. I can't wait to reach Tucson and get some good food," he chatted on nervously.

"What could be better than fried pork, scrambled eggs, coffee, and biscuits? You're an excellent cook, Mr. Rogue. I'm going to miss all this attention when we reach Tucson."

"Attention is what you'll get plenty of, Miss Starns," he muttered, sounding resentful.

"Not like yours, T.J., not without demands attached."

T.J. glanced at her again. "I guess that is a problem for a

beautiful lady like you."

"It's nice meeting a real gentleman for a change."

T.J. eyed her up and down and shrugged. It might be nice, but it surely was damned hard where she was concerned! "It's ready." He dished up her portion of the meat and eggs and placed a warmed biscuit on the plate. He set the coffee cup near her and focused on eating his own share of the meal.

Feeling happy and relaxed, Carrie Sue devoured the food and sipped on the coffee, from a metal cup which he occasionally used. When they finished the silent meal, she gathered the dishes and carried them to the pump to wash. After rolling up his sleeping bag and collecting his supplies, he joined her there and put them away.

"I'll hitch up the team and we'll be off."

The redhead observed the smokey-eyed man as he worked efficiently with the horses and harnesses. He saddled Nighthawk but did not secure his reins to the coach. "Let's get moving," he called out.

Carrie Sue mounted the stage and took her seat beside him. She tied the sun bonnet on her head and placed the pistol nearby. When he handed her his folded blanket to sit on to soften the bench, she smiled and thanked him. She held on while he got the stage and team into motion. The black stallion galloped beside them, on his side of the coach.

T.J. was aware of the gun on the bench between them, just as he was aware that she hadn't slept with it. Since she knew who and what he was, why did she trust him so fully? Why was she at ease in his company? Not many women would strip, bathe, and change clothes within a hundred yards of a total stranger, even with a stagecoach between them. Maybe she was one of those women who was attracted to dangerous men, to adventurous rogues. No, he concluded, she wasn't like that. He was pleased that she hadn't complained one time about the heat, dust, dangers, food, or hardships of their journey. He couldn't figure her out, and that astonished him.

The wind tugged at their hats and clothes. Yet, he didn't think there was any danger of a sandstorm. He glanced at the benches on the sides of the slopes where countless cacti grew. Some places were so abundant with it that cross-country travel was impossible for man or beast. Everything around them seemed to warn people to stay out of this harsh countryside or risk a terrible death. It was rugged terrain: hot, dry, and hostile to everyone except the Indians and critters who knew how to survive in it.

They traveled in silence until midday, when they halted to rest the horses and eat the fried salt pork in biscuits, washed down with water from his canteen. For a short time, she vanished behind bushes to the right of the coach while he did the same to the left. When the journey continued, he almost hated to reach their destination, knowing she and their circumstances would alter drastically. Once she was in town, the rough edges which had surfaced briefly with him would be forced to disappear. Again, she would become the sedate lady he had met at breakfast at the way station, and his fantasy would end.

Carrie Sue hated to reach Tucson today, knowing this stimulating adventure with T.J. Rogue would be over and she probably would never see him again. She was tempted to try to prolong his visit in town, but was afraid to do so. What could come of it? Nothing. He was a drifter, and she had to settle down, settle down safely and permanently. But she longed for more time with him.

As she gazed out over the desert terrain, tears stung her eyes. She couldn't help but feel that she would be losing something special when they parted, that she would never forget him or cease wanting him. They were a good match; they could grow, change, and mature together, but she could not afford to entice him. She could cause him grave trouble, and he could do the same for her. Fate, cruel fate, was ruining her life again. Every time a glimmer of hope and beauty entered her life, vindictive fate would appear to show her the bleak reality of her destiny, her destiny to be an outcast, to have nothing and no one for very long. Bitterness chewed at Carrie Sue's soul. It wasn't fair! But she had to accept it.

Maybe, just maybe, one day they would meet again, meet when there were no threats to their relationship. If she prayed real hard and was very good, perhaps God would answer her prayers.

T.J. could almost smell the troubled air which surrounded the woman beside him. She was watching the passing landscape as if she were taking a ride to the gallows. Why were tears glistening in her lovely eyes? Why were her shoulders slumped in dejection? Why was he so afraid to ask those disturbing questions and to offer her help to solve her problems? He wasn't a coward or a weakling, but Lordy she scared him! Who was this contradiction beside him? What was in her past? Could he allow himself to get involved with her and those dark shadows?

The ground became drier, sandier, and rockier. In most spots, vegetation was sparser than it had been along their journey. Mesquite was laden heavily with green and yellow pods like cleverly decorated Christmas trees. Clusters of white flowers topped the uplifted arms of the giant Saguaro cactus. Some were over two hundred years old, over fifty feet high, and weighed more than the stage. Mountains appeared to form a distant ring around them. Dry washes occasionally crossed the road to remind travelers of the flash flood threat.

In some places, the road was narrow and winding, often causing trees and bushes to slap their limbs against the coach. Several times a white sea of blooming yuccas stretched for miles beside and beyond them. On some rolling hills, cacti stood like green soldiers at attention, ready and eager to defend their terrain against invasion.

Most of the wildflowers, trees, bushes, and plants were in full bloom; their reds, golds, blues, yellows, pinks, whites, oranges, and purples fused into a blanket of color to make Spring the desert's most beautiful season.

Tucson loomed on the horizon. Along one mountain range west of town, three peaks rose higher than others and reminded T.J. of teepees without poles out the top. It was one of the markers which had guided travelers to this area before the road had been cleared. "We'll be there soon, Carolyn. Do you need anything before we ride into town?"

"No," she replied in a hoarse tone. "I'm fine, thanks, just a little nervous. I've only spoken to these people through the mail. What if they don't like me? And refuse to hire me?"

T.J. sent her a smile of encouragement. "How could anyone not like you and want you?" he chided softly, touched by her vulnerability.

Carrie Sue bravely fused her gaze to his. "I'll miss you," she rashly confessed, then averted her eyes and scolded herself. "You saved my life and took good care of me. Thanks, T.J."

"I'll miss you too," he replied. "I'll . . . be in town for a while, if you get a hankering to spend time with a . . . real gentleman again." Carrie Sue grinned. "That's much better," he murmured, pleased with his affect on her.

It was three o'clock and the town ahead seemed quiet. Later, it would probably get rowdy when the cowboys and miners drifted into town for the evening. From reading Carolyn's notes, Carrie Sue knew that Tucson was situated on the Santa Cruz River, in a wide valley which was rimmed by mountains and surrounded by desert. In the latter seventeen hundreds, Tucson had been a presidio of the Spanish Army. Today, it was the territorial capital, and had existed under four different flags: the Spanish, Mexican, Confederate, and United States.

Carrie Sue called the brunette's diary to mind and tried to remember all Carolyn had written about this town. As a teacher, she should know such things. As a desperate fugitive, they could be vital to her.

The town had sprang up around the presidio of *San Agustin del Tucson* which had been built in 1775 by Hugo O'Connor of the Royal Spanish Army. Since that year, men and women from many countries and all walks of life had added to her history: Indians, soldiers, padres, Mexican colonials, cowboys, miners, gamblers, outlaws, merchantmen, prostitutes, wives, children, and countless others.

As they neared town, the stage passed adobe huts and houses, their sunbaked mud blocks held in place by straw-laced mortar, some with light stucco surfaces. Other homes, probably those of Anglos, were built of wood and most had lengthy porches to keep out as much sun as possible. There were barns, lean-tos, rough corrals, out-houses, and a few small stores. The ground was dry and dusty and little vegetation grew around the homes. She noticed a heavy use of dark stone which T.J. told her came from nearby Sentinel Peak, meaning "dark mountain," which gave Tucson its name.

The town was much larger and more settled than she had imagined. It seemed to spread out over a great distance in the valley. They passed two cheap cantinas which were silent this early in the day. They passed Mission Lane which led across farmlands to the *Convento of San Agustin.* She was amazed by the lovely townhome of rancher Francisco Carrillo, and asked T.J. how he knew who owned it.

"I've been in and out of this area more than a dozen times. I've watched her grow from a hole in the desert to a real town. I probably know as much about this area as I do any other. When you get settled in, you might enjoy me showing you the surrounding area. You certainly don't want to visit such secluded terrain without a gentleman guide."

T.J. described the interior of the Carrillo home with its mesquite and pine beams and its saguaro-ribbed ceilings. "Maybe you can visit it when he comes to town on business. I surely was impressed."

"How did you meet him?" she asked eagerly, not daring to make a quick acceptance of his polite offer to be her guide. She feared she couldn't allow "Miss Carolyn Starns" to be seen in his company.

"Did a little job for him years ago. Look over there." He told her about the *El Ojito,* an artesian spring which had supplied Tucson with water since the Spanish Colonial days. He pointed out *Casa del Gobernador,* a breathtaking home built by Jose Maria Soza over twenty years ago. They passed *Calle de La India Triste,* a street meaning "the sad Indian girl."

"The Garrett office is near *Calle de la Guardia* and *Calle Real.* We'll be there shortly. I guess you've noticed the attention we're getting," he hinted.

Carrie Sue had been too busy staring at the enormous adobe fort which stood before them to take note of the crowd gathering beside and behind the stage. She knew the people's curiosity and attendance had nothing to do with a slightly tardy schedule. She and the man near her were the center of attention. She discarded her study of the Presidio to focus on her task.

T.J. reined in the team before the stage office. Men hurried outside, questions spilling rapidly from their mouths at the ominous sight. The handsome man climbed down from the driver's box and helped Carrie Sue to the ground.

Sheriff Ben Myers, whose office was next door, heard the commotion and joined the crowd. T.J. related their misadventures to the gaping men. Myers introduced himself and said he'd take a look at the bandits inside the coach to see if any of them had prices on their heads.

Before doing so, he sent for the undertaker.

The thirteen bodies were unloaded and laid out on the plankway in front of Garrett's office. Ben Myers checked each man and said, "Far as I know, three of 'em have rewards posted. I'll check on the others."

"No hurry, Sheriff, I'll be in town for a while," T.J. informed him.

"I'll alert the Army about those Apaches. Until March we didn't have much trouble with 'em after Jeffords persuaded Cochise to settle down. Some of 'em riled the Mexicans and did some raiding nearby. Governor Safford got Jeffords fired last month 'cause he couldn't control 'em, and the Army's to move 'em soon to New Mexico. The Apaches are real mad. I got news a band had jumped the reservation with that Geronimo. Maybe they just needed supplies to get 'em across the border."

T.J. knew that Cochise had died two years ago and his body had been buried in a secret place in his beloved Chiricahua Mountains. T.J. remembered Geronimo and doubted that great warrior would flee to Mexico. The Indian agent Tom Jeffords was about the only white man the Apaches trusted, but Tom's hands were tied by government ropes.

A nice looking businessman joined them, and the crowd parted to let him move about as he desired. Even the noise quieted. "I heard the news, Ben. Did they get my gold shipment?"

Carrie Sue eyed the man closely, and took an instant dislike to him. He had brown eyes and brown hair; and his clothes were costly, clean, and neatly ironed though the day was hot and the hour late. She realized he was a man of power, wealth, and status . . . like the northern Carpetbagger who had stolen their Georgia farm and the Hardings who had slain her parents and stolen their Texas ranch. He noticed the bodies, but made no comments or apologies for the destruction he had caused. His only

65

interest was his gold! "Sir, you are to blame for this slaughter of good people." She bravely scolded. "The Garrett line is not suppose to carry such perilous baggage. It was your gold which lured those beasts to attack us. I shall file a complaint with the company."

The middle-aged man looked her over, then smiled. "You must be Miss Carolyn Starns, our new school teacher. We've been expecting you. I'm Martin Ferris. I own a ranch and silver mine nearby, and I'm head of the town council which summoned you."

Carrie Sue's heart lurched in panic. She could not make an enemy of this important man, important to her new beginning here. She searched for her lost poise and a safe way to disentangle herself. "Why would such a responsible man encourage the stage company to break its rules and endanger so many lives?" she inquired, her tone softened.

"My gold shipment was suppose to be a secret and it's gravely needed here for expansion. Since everyone knows Garrett doesn't haul mail or strongboxes, we thought the gold and passengers would be perfectly safe this one time. We have men who won't accept paper dollars for skills or goods, scared the government might back down on its promise to rebuy them with gold. I traded silver from my mine for that chest of gold so I can loan it to our local bank. I'll have the sheriff investigate who revealed its presence to those outlaws. He's the one to blame for this bloody attack. I hope you weren't injured."

Carrie Sue cautioned herself to behave as Miss Carolyn Starns. "I'm fine, thanks to this kind gentleman," she remarked, nodding to T.J.

Martin Ferris glanced at the gunslinger, then told the redhead, "There's no need for a lady to endure a situation like this, so I'll have someone escort you to Mrs. Thayer's boarding house. We can meet and talk in the morning after you've rested and unpacked. If we see eye-to-eye, I'll hire you after our talk." To her ebon-haired companion, he said almost coldly, "I'll have to reward you for saving Miss Starns and my gold. I'm surprised to find you're such an honest man."

"Your gold isn't worth dying for, Ferris, or rotting in jail over," T.J. replied in a casual tone, which concealed his past trouble with this man. He didn't like the way Martin Ferris was observing Carolyn or how the man had spoken to her. Too, there was something strange about the attempted theft of a "secret" shipment.

Two men gathered the bags which Carrie Sue pointed out and she followed them to the boarding house, after thanking T.J. again for saving her life. One of the men spoke privately with Mrs. Thayer—as he had done with Martin Ferris—before she showed Carrie Sue to her new home. It was a lovely set of two rooms which received neither the morning nor afternoon sun, which meant they would be cooler day and night.

The woman said there was a tub and pump in the water closet down the hall and informed Carrie Sue that supper was served promptly at six each evening, with breakfast at seven and dinner at twelve. "I'm sure after days on a hot stage you'll be wanting to get scrubbed first. The food and lodgings are good here, Miss Starns, so I know you'll enjoy living at my place."

"I'm certain I will, Mrs. Thayer. Thank you," she responded. "What do you charge for rent and when is it due?"

"I charge fifteen dollars a month for board and ten for food, due the first day of each month you plan to live here. You'll be wanting to take your meals here because the restaurants are higher and my food is better." She laughed merrily and her pale blue eyes twinkled. "Leave your key with me every Monday for changing bed linens and cleaning up your rooms. The other days are your responsibility. I don't allow no cussing or drinking or misbehaving." The fifty-year-old woman laughed again as if she'd told a joke.

"There's a laundress down the street who does a good job of washing and ironing, and her prices are cheap. It might be better to hire her rather than doing your own clothes. But if you like, you can use my washtub and iron. If you have a guest for a meal, it's fifty cents extra. You can have gentlemen callers in the downstairs parlor, but you have to leave your door open for decency if a man visits you up here. Any more questions?"

Carrie Sue returned the woman's warm smile. She liked the grandmotherly landlady. "Today's the eleventh, so how much do I owe you for May?"

"The town council is paying until the fifteenth, then you can pay for half a month's charges. If you need anything, let me know. I have to get back to my supper. We'll talk more over a hot meal."

The moment the owner left, Carrie Sue examined her surroundings. The front room, a small private parlor, was clean and decorated nicely. It contained a short couch against one wall and matching chair in a floral print on one corner. Beside each was a round table with a glass lamp. In the middle of the floor before the couch was a thick rug which looked several years old but was in excellent condition. In another corner was a desk and chair, and Carrie Sue wondered if this set of rooms had been reserved for the new schoolmarm, or had Martin Ferris requested it after meeting her earlier? She wanted to know what he and his man had said, and what the man had told the owner of this fine boarding house.

There was a window on one side of the room which overlooked a side street. The bedroom had two windows for fresh air, one which looked out over that same side street and one which overlooked a quiet back street. Situated away from the main section of Tucson, it should be a serene home. The structure, two stories high, was built of sturdy wood. The walls were covered with a pale floral wallpaper and the woodwork was painted a light yellow, giving the rooms an airy and bright effect which appealed to Carrie Sue. The floors were scrubbed and the furniture was polished. It was clear that Mrs. Thayer took good care of her property and would expect her guests to do the same.

The bedroom was furnished with a double bed, a small side table with an oil lamp, a braided rug, a squatty chest with a second oil lamp, and a washstand with a pitcher and bowl and a mirror mounted over it. Surprisingly the room had a large closet for storage, which meant no hanging of clothes behind a curtain in one corner.

Carrie Sue twirled around, eyeing everything once more. Her daring ruse was working! Everyone believed her! At last, her dreams were coming true. She had a real home.

She lifted a bag to the bed to begin unpacking. A knock on her door halted her. She froze and panicked. Then, she heard Mrs. Thayer call out to her. Carrie Sue took several deep breaths to steady her jittery nerves before she opened the door to find Martin Ferris's two men standing there with the older woman.

"They brought up the trunk which you had sent ahead. Carry it into the bedroom, boys. After you unpack it, if you don't have space for it in your closet or bedroom, you can store it in my shed out back."

"You're most kind, Mrs. Thayer. In all the excitement yesterday and today, I almost forgot about it. Thank you," she told the men as they departed.

Mrs. Thayer remarked, "They told me about the holdup and Indian attack. You've had a rough time getting here, but you're gonna like Tucson. Why don't you relax in a nice bath before supper? You can settle in tomorrow when you're rested."

"That's an excellent suggestion," Carrie Sue responded.

"You'll find towels and soap in the water closet. Don't forget to wash out the tub when you're done. There's a chamber pot under your bed. I have a Mexican girl who empties them every morning and helps me around here. You'll meet her tomorrow."

After Mrs. Thayer's second departure, Carrie Sue fetched her string-purse and retrieved the key to the lock on the trunk. First thing, she needed to make certain there were no clues inside of it to her and Carolyn's identities. If so, they must be destroyed immediately.

To Carrie Sue's surprise, the clothes inside the trunk were prettier and nicer than the ones in Carolyn's travel bags. She examined each one with pleasure and interest. There was even a riding skirt and three lovely nightgowns. Of course, there were more books, and one picture: Carolyn with her family. Carrie Sue studied it and decided it had been made several years ago. She hated to get rid of it, but she looked nothing like the parents or girl there.

Taking her knife from another bag, Carrie Sue entered the closet and knelt. She searched for a loosened board on the floor and found one. As quietly as possible, she worked it free. In the space between her floor and the ceiling of the room below, she concealed the picture and her weapons. She had the most trouble with her rifle, which barely fit because of the support beams. With great caution, she replaced the board and sat the empty bag atop the disturbed area. The clothes from it were placed inside the chest of drawers to be sorted later.

After deciding which dress to wear tonight, she put the other bags near the large trunk at the foot of the bed. Tonight, she would bathe, eat, and get a good night's sleep. Tomorrow she could unpack at her leisure, after her meeting with Martin Ferris.

Chapter Four

Friday morning, Carrie Sue dressed with great care for her meeting. She donned a lovely pale blue day dress from Carolyn's trunk and placed a matching sunbonnet on the bed, which was straightened neatly. As she brushed her hair, her mind drifted back to last night.

Her lengthy bath had been wonderful, but she hadn't washed her hair because there hadn't been enough time for it to dry before supper. She had met the other guests during a splendid meal. Mrs. Thayer had not boasted deceitfully about her cooking, and Carrie Sue had savored each bite of chicken and dumplings.

On the second floor were two more sets of rooms similar to hers and two single rooms for traveling men, who "don't need as much space as a woman or a couple," according to the genial owner. One set was occupied by a young couple who was awaiting the completion of their new home; they were too much in love and excited over their bright future to take much notice of her. Another was occupied by a couple whose home had recently burned; they were too depressed to take much notice of her. One of the single rooms was rented by a man who was having his home repaired and painted for his bride-to-be who was to arrive soon from El Paso, and he couldn't stop talking about her. The other single room was vacant.

Mrs. Thayer's private rooms, into which she invited very few people, were located on one side of the first floor. The other side of the large house contained a kitchen, dining area, large social parlor, and a small sitting room for privacy.

There was a storage shed built against a small barn for the residents' horses, to the rear of which was a small corral. At the back of the house had been attached two more single rooms, both of which were rented by men who were going to be in Tucson long enough to make staying here cheaper than renting hotel rooms. Both men—one married and one single—were taken by Carrie Sue's beauty and presence, and each did his best to obtain her full attention until the evening ended.

Mrs. Thayer had introduced her to everyone at supper and had shown her around afterwards. Carrie Sue had been impressed by the woman's property and success. She had learned of Mr. Thayer's death a few years back and of the woman's determination to keep the boarding house.

The redhead braided her hair again, twisted it into a ball near her nape, and covered it with a thick brown net from Carolyn's trunk so only her fiery bangs were exposed. Carrie Sue checked her image in the mirror and smiled; it was an excellent disguise for her flaming locks. Once her sunbonnet was in place, she concluded happily, no one would be overly aware of her hair. It would be wise to do this every day.

Last night she had gone to sleep thinking about Darby and T.J., wondering what both men were doing. To imagine never seeing either one again pained her deeply. Was freedom worth such a high price? She thought about the horror stories of women in prison and—

Someone knocked at her door and interrupted her mental study. She tensed, but not as much as she had yesterday afternoon. She was far away from Texas and her crimes. She had been accepted here as the new schoolmarm. She had fooled everyone. She had to calm her fears and worries. She was Carolyn Starns now, and forever.

But what would happen if she opened her door one day to find Quade Harding standing there, or one of his hired hunters? The lovely fugitive reprimanded herself for her cowardice. If it happened, it happened, and she must deal with it that day! She couldn't live her new life in constant terror of discovery and capture. Yet, realistically she knew she would be looking over her shoulder for a long time.

The knock came again. Carrie Sue responded to find a dark-haired girl standing there. "Señor Ferris waits downstairs for you."

"You must be Maria Corbeza, Mrs. Thayer's helper," Carrie Sue hinted. The young girl smiled shyly and nodded. "Tell him I will be down shortly. Thank you, Maria."

Carrie Sue checked her appearance once more, gathered her hat and purse, and went to join the man. She assumed he was picking her up to escort her to a council meeting.

Martin Ferris had other plans in mind. Carrie Sue found him awaiting her in the private parlor. "Sit down, Miss Starns, and we'll complete our business quickly. Then, I can show you around."

"What about the rest of the town council? Don't they wish to meet me and question me?" she inquired.

"It isn't necessary. They trust my opinion. Would you care for some coffee or hot tea?" he inquired, as if this were his home.

"No, thank you. What do you need to know about me that wasn't included in our correspondence?" she asked, getting down to business.

"Relax, Miss Starns, there's no rush, or need to be afraid." Carrie Sue didn't like his tone or his lecherous gaze. "I'm certain we'll become very good friends. If you satisfy me, the rest of the town council will go along with my wishes."

Carrie Sue recognized his kind of man. He was a cruel and greedy tyrant who took advantage of weaker people, especially defenseless females. She wanted and needed this job badly, but not badly enough to cow to a man like this! With Carolyn's money and identity and credentials, and with her determination and wits, she could find another job, even another town farther west, if this one didn't work out as expected. She couldn't allow him to get the upper hand this early in their relationship, or she would have trouble with him from now on! She had to be firm, but cautious.

In a pleasant tone and with a calm expression, she asked, "Why should I be frightened, Mr. Ferris? Either you hire me or you don't. If not, I can look elsewhere. From your recent experience, I'm sure you realize that well-trained teachers are in great demand these days and that it's difficult to lure them to a town in the desert. One point confuses me—it was my understanding that I had already been hired through the mail by Mr. Payne. Am I mistaken?"

Martin Ferris studied her intently, especially her eyes and hair. "Not exactly, Miss Starns. But I do need to interview you further before placing the children of our town in your hands."

"How many children do you have, sir?"

"None," he responded, but not a glimmer of sadness was exposed in his piercing brown eyes.

"You've never been married?"

"My wife met with a fatal accident years ago and I haven't remarried. I'm sorry to say she was unable to give me children."

Carrie Sue mentally scoffed, *Just like you to blame her for having weak seeds!* "Ask your questions because I would like to get our matter settled as quickly as possible. I've had a long journey and I'm still fatigued. Too, I have a great deal of unpacking and planning to do."

"Right to the point—I like that in a person. I've gone over your credentials and correspondence. You didn't say why you left St. Louis."

"Another woman wanted my job, and she had a powerful father who made certain she got it. I can assure you the school there will suffer greatly for hiring her; she isn't as qualified as I am." Carrie Sue wanted to demand, if you read the correspondence, why don't you know those facts? Fortunately Carolyn had kept a copy of every letter to and from this town, so the redhead knew Martin was lying.

"Confidence and courage are good traits to have, Miss Starns. I'm certain every word you've spoken and written is the truth." He watched for her reactions as he continued. "The salary is one hundred dollars a month. I know you were quoted sixty in the letter, but I convinced the council that isn't enough for a lady to live on in Tucson. It's a growing town, getting more expensive every week." Naturally Martin didn't tell her he was supplying the additional forty dollars, not yet anyway.

"I'm delighted to learn your town council is so generous and wise, Mr. Ferris. Most teachers are terribly underpaid for the difficult job they perform. The salary is most agreeable. What else?"

"The school is open Monday through Friday from eight until four. Since the children have been without a teacher for some time, we expect you to begin classes on June fifth. You can give them August off, then resume teaching in September. That allows you three weeks to get the schoolhouse in order and get settled here. I'm sure you know from experience that the care and cleaning of the schoolhouse is part of your job, unless you hire a helper from your salary. You will also receive a small budget for supplies. Is that part also agreeable?"

"Certainly."

"There will be a trial period of two months, June and

July. If all goes well, your position becomes permanent in September. I have been appointed to drop in occasionally to observe your methods and control of the children. We do expect good results, Miss Starns."

Appointed, my rump! Carrie Sue's mind refuted. She didn't need to spend time and energy on this offensive distraction when she had so much to do! "I assure you that you'll have them, Mr. Ferris. But it's my policy to hold a parent's day once every month so they can see how their children are progressing. At that time, any problem either of us has can be discussed and resolved. I'm afraid your presence in the classroom would be most distracting to the students. Most of them, especially the older ones, are shy about participation in front of strange adults. I'm certain you don't wish to disrupt the class over something you can observe one Saturday a month."

Carrie Sue sensed the man's annoyance at her quick wits and obstinance. She had been playing Carolyn Starns for weeks and her old life seemed far away, so she had the courage to battle him.

The well-dressed man stood and said, "I'll show you the schoolhouse if you'll follow me."

Carrie Sue tied the ribbons of her sunbonnet beneath her chin and trailed Martin Ferris to the door. A carriage was waiting outside with a driver, a black man who was as neatly dressed as his boss. Martin turned to assist her into the carriage. Carrie Sue did not want to sit so close to him, so she suggested, "Is it within walking distance? I can use the exercise."

"It isn't far, but you must learn to be careful in this sun. It can be a killer. Newcomers don't realize the danger because the heat dries up warning perspiration so quickly. Always remember to keep plenty of drinking water available for you and the children. We'll take the carriage today, so we can head on into town afterwards."

"I would ra—"

Martin did not let her finish her refusal. "There are plenty of people eager to meet you, and you need to learn your way around. I promised to bring you by for introductions after our talk."

The desperado did not believe him, but she couldn't call him a liar. She reasoned politely, "Couldn't we make our visits tomorrow or Sunday after I've settled in?"

"Some of the council members and important people live outside of town. It's best to catch them at their stores and offices today."

Carrie Sue felt trapped by the ride and his demands, but she had to yield. "As you wish, Mr. Ferris."

The wealthy man thought it was the bright sun which made the beauty beside him squint her eyes, tighten her lips, and flush her cheeks. He did not know that the exquisite redhead had a temper as fiery as her hair, one which Carrie Sue had learned to leash on most occasions. He felt the heat of her body, touching his from thigh to shoulder, and passion for her blazed into life.

They reached the schoolhouse soon, three blocks away, an easy walk for anyone except a man who didn't like to sweat or work. It was a stark wooden structure. The boards were weathered by harsh nature and its dull facade was unappealing. *If schools were prettier, perhaps children wouldn't be so frightened by them!* she mused as she followed Martin's lead around the outside of the building. There were windows on all sides for fresh air flow, including one near the apex of the front roof and one in the same place on the back to allow the rising hot air to escape.

The earth around it was dry, rocky and nearly barren, except for a tall saguaro cactus near the front door and a few small scrubs here and there. A bell beneath a cover was attached to the roof near the front, and two steps — over which was nailed a sign that read "Tucson School" — led inside to the one large room. Behind the school was an outhouse which looked as if it would collapse if it weren't repaired soon.

As if reading her mind, Martin remarked, "I'll have a carpenter work on it next week. We don't want parents blaming you for an accident." He pointed to a partially fenced area and informed her, "That's where the children play during recess. The boards near the ground keep out snakes and other undesirable creatures. It also keeps the children in an area you can control. Let's go inside."

There was no moisture on Carrie Sue's face, but she felt as if her clothes were getting damp. Obviously the man's warning about the climate here was accurate, something to remember. The shade of the schoolhouse felt good to her flesh and eyes. She let her gaze grow accustomed to the lack of glare before looking around. There were twenty student's desks placed in rows of fives, all facing the lengthy wooden desk upon a raised section of flooring. On the wall behind the teacher's desk was a chalkboard, flanked by shelves on each side. A long pole sat in one corner for pushing up and pulling down the two high window sashes. In the other stood an American flag with its thirty-seven stars. The bell rope was wound about a peg near the door, and she had a mischievous urge to ring it. On one side of the doorway was a bench, and on the other side was a row of pegs for winter garments.

The floors, desks, window sills, and shelves were covered in dirt. The window panes were so clouded that seeing outside was nearly impossible. It appeared as if the school hadn't been cleaned in months, and the windows had been left opened during a violent dust storm. This meant she had a lot of sweeping, mopping, scrubbing, and polishing ahead of her. Perhaps she could hire Maria to help with the first cleaning.

Carrie Sue approached the shelves behind her new desk. Small chalkboards, boxes of chalk, pencils, paper, books, and other items were stacked there. "You furnish such supplies rather than the families?"

"The parents pay a small fee which makes up that supply budget I mentioned earlier. It's easier for everyone if the teacher provides them on the first day of school. When it closed, the children were asked to leave them here so they wouldn't get lost while we sought a replacement for Helen Cooper."

"What happened to Miss Cooper? Did she move or retire?"

"I'm afraid Miss Cooper met with a terrible accident."

"What happened?" she pressed.

"Mining's a big part of our territory, so she wanted to teach the children about it. She asked to take them out to the one I own. I agreed to let her visit first to make certain she knew what she was doing. Once we got inside where it was dark and narrow, she panicked and started running for the entrance. She fell into a pit and broke her neck. Since it was my mine and she was in my care, I've taken a responsibility to help replace her. If you get the same idea, I'll have to refuse your request. But I can send one of my men here with samples to give a lesson."

"That's very kind and thoughtful, Mr. Ferris. Shall we begin our tour of your town?"

As they were leaving, he said, "I'll have notices sent out to all parents to let them know we have a new teacher and school will open again on June fifth. That is, if you've found everything agreeable today."

"Everything is fine with me, Mr. Ferris." Actually, she was getting excited about this new challenge.

"Excellent, Miss Starns. I promise you'll love it here."

As they rode past homes and businesses, Martin Ferris told her who lived there or owned them, and sometimes their history. His driver took them to where the streets *Calle de la Guardia* and *Calle Real* met near the entry to the Presidio. He helped her out of his carriage and told the driver, "We'll walk a spell."

As they did so, he pointed out the size of the old Spanish fort. The adobe wall was twelve feet high and ran for about seven hundred and fifty feet on each side. He explained how the soldiers and their families had lived inside the Presidio and how settlers had lived and farmed beyond it. He pointed out where the fiestas were still held on special occasions, and she could almost hear the music and laughter and smell the Mexican foods. She saw the home built by Edward Nye Fish and the one beside it which belonged to Hiram Stevens, his friend.

She was shown *La Casa Cordova,* one of the oldest buildings in Tucson. She saw the unusual outside of Leonardo Romero's home which was built over part of the Presidio wall. He told her that Soledad Jacome's residence had been completed only last year, that it had saguaro rib ceilings, expensive woodwork, and several corner fireplaces.

She noticed people of many races and cultures, living and working as if no one here was aware of any differences between them. Shops with Spanish and American names and goods were located here and there, and she was amazed by what this walled area contained. She studied its columns and arches, its highly decorated facade, the tile roofs, and traditional canales: drain pipes to allow water to flow off the flat roofs. Most of the private homes had been built ten to fifteen years ago, but some were much older. It was a splendid blend of cultures.

"How do you like Tucson so far?" he asked.

"It's breathtaking and amazing," she commented.

"Just as you are, Carolyn," he murmured.

As if she hadn't heard him, she glanced his way with an innocent expression and asked, "What did you say, sir?"

"I said, I promised you would love it here. We'll meet a few people, then have some dinner. It's already three o'clock. You must be famished. I didn't mean to starve you during our tour."

This man could be very charming, she concluded, but deceitfully so. She had been so engrossed by the scenery that she had forgotten about time and business, and his company. "Learning new things is always fascinating to me, so I forget everything else. Lead on, Mr. Ferris," she teased, having decided to spend more time with him to observe him. Too, she might encounter T.J. Rogue along the way. Her handsome rescuer had told her he would be in town for a while, and he did know where she was staying and working. Surely he hadn't already dismissed her from mind.

After meeting the other members of the town council, Carrie Sue sat down in a nice restaurant to eat with Martin. They were served baked chicken, rice with gravy, biscuits, jam, and canned carrots. The delicious meal was finished off with dried apple pie and coffee.

Carrie Sue shifted in her chair and sent him a rueful smile. "I must get home now, Mr. Ferris; it's late and I'm exhausted. I can see that my unpacking will have to wait another day."

"If you'll call me Martin, I'll escort you home this moment."

"As you wish," she responded with a lightness which she didn't feel.

Mrs. Thayer met her in the front parlor and asked, "Are you all right, Miss Starns? I was worried about you when you missed dinner and supper is nearly ready to go on the table."

As she removed her hat, she explained, "I'm sorry, Mrs. Thayer, but Mr. Ferris practically refused to return me home until I knew Tucson by heart and had met everyone he called 'important.' He insisted we stop to eat at four-thirty. He's a most persistent man and I didn't want to offend him so soon after my arrival."

"I thought I saw a twinkle in his eye when he arrived this morning. Be wary of him, Carolyn," she advised,

81

switching to her first name and lowering her voice to prevent being overheard. "He's a rich and powerful man, and he likes to have his way."

"Did Helen Cooper live here, too? Did he pester her like this?"

Mrs. Thayer's smile faded completely. "She moved here about a month before her death. She saw him now and again, but she seemed afraid of him. He always sent his carriage and driver after her, didn't come himself like a real gentleman should."

"He said she had an accident in his mine. Is that true?"

"She left here to visit it with him, but she didn't want to go. She'd been feeling poorly ever since she moved in. She never came back. He told everyone she got scared inside the mine and took a fall while trying to get outside."

"You sound as if you don't believe his tale."

"I've talked too much as it is. Just keep this between us, but watch him with a tight eye. And stay out of that dangerous mine," she warned like a frightened mother. "I have to get back to work."

"Thank you, Mrs. Thayer. I'll be careful."

The older woman smiled at her and tweaked her cheek. "I know you will, girl. You're smart and brave—noticed that right off. Helen weren't nothing like you. She was weak and scared. Can't blame her; she needed this job to keep her out of the whorehouse. There ain't many jobs for a woman alone, 'specially if she ain't got no money. Maybe it's best she went to her final resting place. She couldn't get enough sleep, tired all the time, tired and nervous and sick. Didn't a morning pass that girl didn't empty her stomach into her potty."

Carrie Sue noticed how the woman's speech pattern became rustic as she spoke hurriedly, apprehensively. She wondered if the woman realized what sickness she had just described: pregnancy. Was it, she asked herself, a coincidence that the single and expectant Helen Cooper was seeing a man she disliked and met with death in his mine?

"I suppose you won't be needing supper tonight since you just ate, but I'll save some pie and coffee for you later."

Carrie Sue impulsively hugged the older woman. "You're wonderful, Mrs. Thayer. I'll get my hair washed; it feels awful."

Carrie Sue sat on the floor in her bedroom with her long hair hanging out the window so it could dry before bedtime. She had unpacked a few things, taken a bath, scrubbed her head, and consumed the pie and milk which Mrs. Thayer had brought to her room.

Her lids kept closing as her mind drifted lazily. How she wished her brother was here to enjoy the sweet taste of freedom.

Another safe day had passed. Tomorrow, she would visit the school again and the laundress. And she might stroll around to see if she could sight T.J. somewhere. Of course that presented the risk of running into Martin Ferris and being unable to get rid of him.

"Who knows?" she murmured. "Perhaps he would make a powerful ally if trouble struck. If I can use him without being used!"

The following morning, Maria delivered a package to her room. When Carrie Sue unwrapped it, she found a lovely parasol and a note from Martin Ferris. She read it:

Carolyn,
To protect that beautiful head from our hot sun. Please join me for supper tonight. I'll send for your answer at noon.

83

Martin Ferris.

Carrie Sue hurriedly rewrapped the package and retied the string. She seized her hat, purse, dirty clothes, and the gift and rushed downstairs. She found Mrs. Thayer in the kitchen and explained her dilemma. She entreated, "Please put this somewhere. When Mister Ferris or his man arrives at noon, tell him I was gone when it arrived and you don't know when I'll return today to get his message."

The woman grinned with anticipation of their ruse. "It's done, Carolyn. If you see his carriage waiting outside, slip in the back and up to your room. I'll bring your meal there later. Be careful."

"I will. But don't worry about me. We'll think of some plausible excuse tonight."

Carrie Sue followed Mrs. Thayer's directions to the home of the laundress. The sturdy woman agreed to do the redhead's washing and ironing each week. Carrie Sue was to bring it to her each Monday and pick it up each Thursday, unless she had a special need of a garment.

Carrie Sue walked to the schoolhouse. She did not open the windows or leave the front door ajar, just in case Martin Ferris came by. She examined the room again and mentally made notes about its cleaning and preparation. She sat at the desk; she walked back and forth on the raised flooring; she pretended to write on the chalkboard; she imagined herself teaching a room filled with children.

Anticipation surged through her as she decided this job would be fun and challenging. She would be filling young minds, making friends, and earning respect. She wanted these people—especially the children in her class—to like her, to trust her, to want to learn from her. She recalled her school days and teachers in Georgia. Having loved school, she remembered a great deal about them, memories which would aid her now.

The room was getting hot. Carrie Sue realized she had to open the doors and windows, or she had to leave. The noises of an approaching carriage caught her attention. She grabbed her purse and hid under the lengthy desk, relieved that the front and sides were enclosed so she couldn't be seen from the door. Nor could she be sighted if Martin walked around the building, as the back window was too high.

She heard the carriage halt. She controlled her respiration so it wouldn't expose her presence. The steps creaked as Martin mounted them and opened the door. There was momentary silence as he must have glanced around the large room. She heard him swear irritably. Then, she sighted another peril. . . .

A Bark Scorpion was clinging deftly to the underside of the desk, poised there and ready to strike an unsuspecting leg or hand. She was lucky he hadn't attacked earlier when she was sitting in the chair with her legs near his hiding place. He was about two inches long, rather slender, straw colored, and had two dark bands along his back. His pinchers were moving in a threatening manner, as was his raised tail with its venomous stinger. It was said that more people died from its sting than from the bites of all poisonous snakes combined!

Carrie Sue remained motionless, keeping her full attention on the scorpion, who seemed content to hold his position for the time being. She was crouched on the other end, but her feet and legs were beneath him. If he released his hold on the wood and dropped to them . . . She knew Martin had not closed the door and left. If she scrambled from her position, her ruse would be exposed. She waited; the tiny foe waited; and Martin seemed to stall his departure for some reason.

A horrible thought entered the lovely desperado's mind: what if the scorpion had family or friends nearby, such as behind her? She dared not turn her head and look. She kept her hands in her lap with her purse. There was nothing within reach to use for a weapon. Despite her fear and peril, she knew it was best not to alert Martin to her ruse. She had been in tight spots before, so she could endure this one.

Finally she heard him close the door and descend the steps, but he walked around the schoolhouse, even called her name several times. Perhaps he thought she was in the outhouse. The scorpion took a few menacing steps forward. Carrie Sue held her ground. She kept her respiration slow and shallow to prevent as much motion as possible. She wondered if the deadly creature could sense her fear, perhaps smell it as she had smelled the passengers' terror during the holdup.

Even when she heard the carriage leave, she remained in her hiding place for a time, her gaze glued on the arachnid. Martin Ferris was sneaky, and could be standing outside to see if she suddenly appeared after his departure. The scorpion began to make his way in her direction. She had no choice but to wiggle cautiously from beneath the desk. The moment her dress cleared a spot, the venomous creature dropped to it with stinger and pinchers lifted ominously.

Carrie Sue seized a heavy book and dropped it on the scorpion. She placed her foot on it and shifted her weight. When she heard a "crunch," she leaned against the chalkboard and took a deep breath. Her shaking ceased, and she went from window to window making certain the persistent man was gone. No doubt he would return later to look for her again when she failed to appear at the boarding house.

She left the school and went to visit a seamstress which Mrs. Thayer had recommended. She didn't need any new clothes for a while, but it would take time to meet the woman and to chat for a while. Carrie Sue did not plan to alter Carolyn's image until she was assured of her unquestionable acceptance here. Then, *Carolyn* could buy and wear some prettier and nicer clothes. After subtracting her monthly expenses, she would have thirty-five to forty dollars left over to save or to spend.

One thing she needed to do was conceal money and supplies in her closet, just in case she had to flee in a hurry. And it might be a good idea to do the same outside of town, in case she couldn't get to her room following her unmasking. A horse for a quick getaway was a good idea, and it shouldn't arouse suspicion for Miss Carolyn Starns to own and ride one in this western town.

Carrie Sue made a lengthy visit with the seamstress who was close to her age, the widow of a soldier from Fort Lowell nearby. She revealed that she wanted lovelier and better quality clothes, but she had to wait a while because people had a preset idea of how a teacher should dress. The woman had laughed and understood.

Afterwards, Carrie Sue strolled down backstreets where she assumed she was safe from Martin Ferris's seeking gaze. She realized that Tucson was a rapidly growing town of very wealthy people and very poor people. Some of the poverty she observed tugged at her heart. She saw homes which were little more than adobe or wooden shacks with dirty children playing around them in near rags.

The air was hot and dry, yet she smelled a variety of odors of which Mexican food was most noticeable. The people seemed to move and work slowly in the heat of the day, aware of the demands of their harsh climate. Carrie Sue's body was warm and her clothes were damp. She knew she should get out of the unrelenting sun for a time.

She sighted a Mexican cafe which looked clean and safe for a lady to enter, as she had learned to judge places fairly well during her years on the trail. She entered it to find only a few customers present. She took a seat near a window for fresh air.

A plump Spanish woman took her order with a smile,

and returned shortly with her meal: refried beans, browned rice, a floured tortilla rolled with a chicken filling, and coffee. Carrie Sue ate slowly to enjoy the tasty meal and to waste time. She wished she could order a few sips of tequila to calm her nerves, but she dared not.

She watched Martin Ferris's carriage go down the street and wondered how long the man would search for her. Perhaps, she fretted, his patience and persistence would rival Quade's! Unable to hold another drop of coffee or food, she paid the woman and left.

She made a stop at a saddlery shop, concluding that no one would think to look for her in such a place. She told the man she was considering the purchase of a horse and a saddle, so he delighted in showing her the different kinds and making recommendations for a lady. She pretended to know little about western saddles and let him talk for over an hour. She promised, when she bought her horse, she would make her saddle purchase in his shop.

Carrie Sue was hot and tired and tense. She sneaked to the boarding house only to find Martin's carriage sitting out front as suspected. She went into the barn and climbed into the loft. She sat on loose hay which was used to feed the horses in the corral out back. She sank to her back, gazing at the beams overhead as she eased into deep thought.

She had hidden in lofts many times, sometimes while on the run during her outlaw days, and sometimes for hide-and-seek with Darby on their Texas ranch. Her location stirred many memories of those days.

Suddenly the beautiful fugitive bolted upright. She asked herself what she was doing hiding out like a terrified child. She didn't owe Martin Ferris or anyone here an explanation for her choices. This was like being on the run again! She had work to do. She was fatigued. She needed a soothing bath. She needed the tranquility of her new home. All she had to do was refuse his invitation firmly.

She couldn't hide from him every day. And she hated this feeling of being watched, followed everywhere. It hadn't left her all day or yesterday!

"What's the matter with you, Carrie Sue Stover? You're too damn edgy and suspicious. No one is trailing you, or you'd have noticed him. Get your butt in the house and get busy with something!"

Carrie Sue left the loft and entered the back door. She heard Martin Ferris's voice in the front parlor. She scowled, then headed up the back steps. She made it to her room without meeting anyone, and locked her door. After removing her hat, she fanned herself with it a few minutes. A bath would have to wait because it would alert the others to someone's presence upstairs. No matter, she had plenty of unpacking and sorting to do until Martin gave up and departed.

T.J. Rogue leaned against the building nearby. He was baffled by the redhead's behavior, yesterday and today. Something had her spooked. But what? he wondered. It couldn't be his tail because he was too good at that job to give himself away, especially to a woman. There was something weird going on with that contradictory vixen. He wanted answers to her mystery.

Chapter Five

Sunday morning, Carrie Sue dressed to attend church
with Mrs. Thayer. She knew such behavior would be
expected of her, as she was an example for the children to
follow and it would reveal her morals to the adults of this
town. She had not attended church since her parent's
deaths, and because of her past sins she found it difficult
to enter one. Yet, her ruse demanded it of her, and she
was probably in need of God's protection and guidance.

She had completed her unpacking last night and had
taken a late bath. When Mrs. Thayer had come to check
on her after Martin's departure, she had revealed her
actions of the day, and her decision to confront the man
when next he approached—no, pestered—her.

Carrie Sue pinned her hair atop her head and put on a
lovely pink and blue floral hat which she had purchased
yesterday during her wanderings. It went nicely with the
soft blue dress she had found in Carolyn's trunk. She rode
with Mrs. Thayer and one of the couples to the other end
of town to where a large white church was located. From
the number of horses and carriages and wagons, the
attendance was good.

They took seats on a pew which was halfway to the
front of the church. They had arrived just in time for the
service to begin. A woman started playing an old organ

which needed tuning; the crowd rose to its feet with hymnals in hand; and the minister took his position behind the pulpit and led the opening song.

Martin Ferris slipped into the row where they were standing. He took a place next to Carrie Sue and boldly shared the songbook which she and Mrs. Thayer were holding. His action caused him to lean close to the redhead, too close for her liking. She kept her gaze either on the page or the minister and sang softly.

After several songs were completed and they were taking their seats, he whispered, "Good morning, Carolyn. I missed you yesterday."

She glanced his way and smiled politely, then shifted toward Mrs. Thayer as she pretended to settle herself. The preacher gave them a heated lesson on the Ten Commandments from Exodus 20: 1–17. He shouted about the "wages of sin" being death. He urged them to repentance and to obedience of "God's Holy Word."

Carrie Sue felt her heart flutter when the minister expounded on God's views on theft and murder. She had not coveted the possessions of others, but she had needed some of them for survival. She had not entered her life of sin because she was evil or weak; she had done so to seek justice against the Hardings. She had not turned "the other cheek" or waited for "God to punish vile sinners." But as the preacher shouted on and on, she had to admit she had taken the law into her own hands and sought vengeance—a sin in itself.

Carrie Sue's mind wandered to the innocent victims of the Stover Gang's deeds. She had condemned herself by being a part of them, however innocent in the beginning. Guilt nibbled at her. She promised, *If you let this new life work out for me, I'll never be bad again.*

Immediately the preacher yelled that you couldn't make deals with God: live morally or pay the consequences. Carrie Sue's mind argued that she had been forced into a life of crime. But the minister yelled as he pounded his fist on the pulpit, "God don't accept no excuses for being wicked! You'll pay for your black sins in the fires of Hell, and He'll make you suffer terribly here on Earth!"

Carrie Sue's mind shouted back at him, *I have suffered terribly! I've paid for my mistakes! I've earned a right to freedom! What about those whom God hasn't punished or destroyed?*

The service finally ended, and she wanted to get away from Martin Ferris. Carrie Sue was forced to chat with him though. When he questioned her whereabouts the day before, she eyed him rather oddly, sending him a look which said he was being too forward and nosey.

Her reaction did not trouble or dissuade him. He alleged, "I was worried about you, Carolyn. You don't know this town yet and you aren't accustomed to our tricky weather. What did you do all day?"

She noticed his use of her first name. She was standing in a church, so she tried to be as honest as possible. "I visited the school to decide how much time and work was involved in getting it clean. Then, I just wandered around familiarizing myself with the town and people. I also did a little shopping," she remarked, touching her new hat.

"It's very pretty. How did you like the parasol?"

"It was kind of you to send it, Mr. Ferris, but a lady shouldn't accept gifts from strangers. I'll return it tomorrow."

He chuckled and shook his head. "It's a welcome gift from the town council, so you can't refuse it and hurt everyone's feelings." In a smug tone, he informed her, "We need to get moving, Carolyn. I planned for you to join me and some friends for Sunday dinner."

Carrie Sue was annoyed. They were standing outside now, so she lied calmly, "Thank you for the invitation, but I always rest and study my Bible on Sundays as the Scriptures insist."

"Surely you don't want to disappoint our Mayor Carlson and his wife. They're expecting us to join them at their home within the hour. I was certain you'd want to go, so I accepted their invitation for the both of us."

Carrie Sue eyed him again, then exhaled loudly to reveal her vexation. "I will dine with them today, Mr. Ferris. But in the future, please ask first before you accept invitations on my behalf."

Carrie Sue was introduced to numerous people, many of them parents of children who would be her students very soon. The adults were delighted to learn that the school would open again on June fifth, but the children seemed none too happy about attending classes in the hot summer. Carrie Sue laughed and joked with the youngsters to relax them.

Before she left the church yard, many of the children were won over by the beautiful and genial schoolmarm.

In his carriage, Martin teased, "Don't you think it's unwise to get so friendly with your students? How will they obey you?"

Carrie Sue did not smile. "It has been my experience, Mr. Ferris, that people—especially children—obey better out of friendship and respect than out of fear and dislike. A friend will go a second mile for you, but an enemy halts your journey or heads the other way."

"You're very wise for such a beautiful young woman. I stand corrected, my fetching schoolmarm."

Carrie Sue did not respond to his overture by word or expression. "Did the other council members agree to our deal, Mr. Ferris?"

"Please, you promised to call me Martin," he scolded mockingly.

"I'm afraid I find it difficult to call a man of your status by his Christian name. I am only the school teacher here, and some people might think that improper." Her remarks did not put him in his place.

"I don't care what people say or think about me," he vowed.

"I can't afford such a luxury, Mr. Ferris."

"If anyone is nasty to you, just report it to me. I'll handle him."

They reached the mayor's home and were greeted by a stocky man with heavy jowls and a prominent belly. Carrie Sue became alert.

Lester Carlson invited them inside. "We're so happy you two could join us for Sunday dinner. The wife is finishing up in the kitchen now."

"It was kind of you to invite me, sir."

"Please, call me Lester, and my wife's name is Mertle."

The man beside her jested, "If you accomplish that feat, Lester, I'll be shocked. Carolyn insists on calling me Mr. Ferris. She's worried about people's opinions of her."

"That isn't necessary, Carolyn. You're amongst friends here."

"See there. What did I tell you?" Martin teased.

"We only met recently, so it will require practice." Carrie Sue felt that Martin was responsible for this invitation and treatment.

Lester Carlson's wife and children joined them, and they took their seats at the table with Martin beside her. The petite woman served a roast of beef, rice, gravy, dried peas, cornbread, and canned peaches. The conversation was light during the early part of the meal. As everyone started on dessert—cake and coffee or milk—the talk increased, except for the three children who were trained to hold silent.

"Martin is one of our best citizens, Carolyn. I own the local bank and we can do a lot with loans on the gold he had shipped in on your stage. I know it caused you a great deal of trouble, but that was an unforeseen accident," the local banker informed her.

Probably at Martin's request, Carrie Sue concluded.

She talked with the children for a while, noting how well-mannered they were.

The mayor boasted, "I have good children, Carolyn. They're going to enjoy having you as their new teacher."

"I was told Helen Cooper was a good teacher. It's a shame about her accident." She watched the children's faces and realized they had liked the woman who had preceded her. "I promise you're going to like school and not mind spending the summer there. Learning can be fun. I'm sure I won't teach in the same way she did, but that doesn't matter."

Lester remarked uneasily, "We don't talk about that tragedy, Carolyn; it makes the children sad. I'm sure you won't mind. Martin tells us you're from St. Louis. We have family there. Their children are grown, but perhaps you know them: John and Clindice Carlson."

Carrie Sue had not considered such a problem arising, but she held her poise and wits. She smiled and replied, "Naturally I've heard of them, but we're not well-acquainted."

"Doesn't matter. You can meet them when they come to visit this fall. John wrote us about how well you were liked there."

"That was kind of him," she replied, hoping her voice didn't quaver as she obviously had given the correct response. There was no way of knowing if Carolyn Starns knew the St. Louis Carlsons, as they had not been mentioned in the woman's diary. Carrie Sue was tense. What if they came here and exposed her as a fraud?

As the two women were doing the dishes in the kitchen while the men enjoyed cigars in the parlor, Mertle Carlson asked, "How do you like Tucson, my dear?"

"It's quite lovely, like your home, Mrs. Carlson. I deeply appreciate the invitation to dinner, and I've enjoyed the meal and company."

"Martin says you're living at Mrs. Thayer's boarding

house. I hear it's the best one."

Carrie Sue smiled and nodded agreement. "Mrs. Thayer is wonderful. She's like a mother hen. I feel right at home there."

The woman's next words were alarming to the redhead. "Martin is very fond of you, my dear. I haven't seen him this interested in a woman since his wife's death, nor this happy in a long time."

Carrie Sue felt as if she'd walked into a conspiracy. "He seems very nice and respectable. What grades did your children say they were in?" she asked, trying to change the subject.

"We can talk about the children another time. I'm having a party in two weeks. You will come with Martin, won't you? It's the perfect occasion for you to meet everyone."

Carrie Sue realized she had no choice except to reply, "I'll be delighted, Mrs. Carlson. You will let me know if there's anything I can do to help."

"Certainly, my dear."

When Carrie Sue was dropped off at the boarding house, she was relieved that the man did not insist on coming inside for a short visit. She found Mrs. Thayer gone to visit friends and the other boarders were occupied. She paced her rooms, and they suddenly felt confining. She was being thrust toward Martin Ferris and she hated that disagreeable problem. Her new life was not developing as she had hoped. She had left one trap only to find herself ensnared by another! She had to face the truth: Martin Ferris was not going to let up on her and, if she made an enemy of him, things would not go well for her here.

"What to do?" she murmured anxiously. Quit this job and move on quickly? Try again to discourage Martin's interest in her? Lead him on for a while until he tired of his amorous pursuit?

"Not in a flea's jump!" she scoffed, recalling that Quade Harding hadn't given up on his chase in over seven years. "The Devil take you, Martin Ferris! Merciful Heavens, what am I going to do now?"

Carrie Sue longed to see T.J. Rogue. She yearned to have soothing and protective arms around her. She wished he would come to visit her, but she doubted he would. And she certainly couldn't go scouting for him! Besides, what could that handsome Rogue do to help her? Nothing, except perhaps to stain her new image. She was on her own now, and this new problem was hers to solve.

At supper, the two men with back rooms were exceedingly quiet, even slightly sullen. Carrie Sue wondered if Martin Ferris had warned them to stay away from her or he would damage their business in town. She knew such a threat was not beyond the offensive man, nor was carrying it out if he was challenged. He was so like the Hardings!

Instead of remaining downstairs in the parlor after supper, Carrie Sue returned to her room. She sat at the desk to go over Carolyn's class plans, and was relieved the woman had made out those for the first month. By that time, she should have learned enough to do them.

She compared the notes to the pages marked in Carolyn's books. The brunette had been very intelligent and the lessons were easy to grasp. Between now and the opening day of school, she needed to study the books daily to refresh herself on all the facts contained there.

When she grew weary of reading, she went to the couch. She leaned her head against its back and closed her eyes to rest them. She could not get over the feeling that she was being watched all the time. Yet, she never saw anyone spying on her. Perhaps she was just nervous and tired.

Perhaps it was because of too many years on the run. Or because she was too afraid of letting down her guard too soon. She was worried about Darby, and yearning for T.J. Rogue. She was irritated by Martin Ferris. She was unaccustomed to this dry heat.

And, she was afraid of what Quade Harding had in store for her. How long would his obsession for her continue? Surely there was no way he could track her to Tucson. Was there?

Monday morning, Carrie Sue put on one of Carolyn's oldest dresses for her task today. When she went downstairs, she paid her rent for the remainder of May. She borrowed cleaning rags, a broom, a mop, soap, vinegar, and two pails from Mrs. Thayer. She left her key with the woman, as this was the cleaning day for her rooms. With Maria's help, Carrie Sue carried the supplies and water to the schoolhouse.

After the Mexican girl's departure, Carrie Sue pushed up all the windows and left the door open. She tied a bandanna around her head to protect her hair from dust. To stay as cool as possible, she hadn't worn a petticoat or chemise under the cotton dress which was thick enough to be modest. She removed her shoes, and hoped no one would come by and see her in such a state.

The first thing she did was search beneath the desks, bench, and bookshelves for scorpions and spiders. She removed the webs and killed the spiders so they couldn't rebuild and endanger the children, but she found no more scorpions. She brushed down the walls and swept the floor, twice to make certain all the loose dirt was removed. Next, she washed the desks and mopped the floor.

While they dried, she sat on the front steps to eat a light snack which Mrs. Thayer had sent over with Maria. As Carrie Sue did so, the Mexican girl retrieved more water for her.

The heat absorbed the water quickly, and Carrie Sue

was eager to finish as much work as possible before she needed to head home for a bath and supper. Already her arms and back were aching for relief.

She climbed upon a chair to wash the windows, using a mixture of water, soap, and vinegar to remove the grimy dirt. She had completed the door and two of the side windows when she suddenly sensed a powerful presence behind her. Instinctively her right hand dropped the wet cloth and went to her side, but naturally she wasn't armed. She hadn't heard anyone approach, but she knew someone was there. Her flesh tingled and her respiration increased. She half-turned to find T.J. Rogue leaning against the door jamb. Her eyes widened, then she smiled as she stepped off the chair to recover the rag. "Hello, stranger. How long have you been standing there watching me slave?"

He chuckled, the sound of it mellow. "Not long. I didn't want to startle you and make you fall." He straightened and walked forward, teasing, "I see they put you right to work. How are you doing?"

Carrie Sue felt dirty, sweaty, and a mess. But she was too happy to see him to let her condition trouble her too much. She mopped at the smudges and perspiration on her face, and tossed the rag into the water pail. She flexed her sore body as she replied, "Fine I guess. The boarding house and Mrs. Thayer are wonderful. I finally got settled in Saturday night, and I even went to church yesterday."

They exchanged grins. "They treating you all right?"

She inhaled deeply and nodded. "Mr. Ferris interrogated me on Friday before hiring me and showing me around. I've met so many people in the past few days that I can't recall everyone."

"Keeping you busy, huh?"

"They did on Friday, but I sneaked off Saturday to look around and shop. Yesterday I was practically forced to eat Sunday dinner with the mayor and his family." She sighed heavily. "I almost feel like a puppet performing for these people. That Mr. Ferris . . ." She halted and glanced away from his engulfing gaze. "I'm chattering like a raucous bluejay! What have you been doing since Thursday? I haven't seen you around since we got here."

"Not much of anything," he answered nonchalantly. "Playing cards and lazing about. I've had to repeat our tale a hundred times. You'd think these people were dying for news and excitement." His smokey gray eyes slipped over her from covered head to bare feet. She was a hard worker. And, she was a beauty even in her disheveled state.

Carrie Sue warmed at his tone and at his use of "our." He looked so handsome today. His face was freshly shaven; his ebony hair was combed neatly, even if that defiant lock was hanging over his forehead. His clothes, a red shirt and new jeans in a dark blue, were clean. A blue bandanna was tied about his throat, and two Frontier Colts were strapped at his waist. "How long do you plan to stay in Tucson being lazy and entertaining?"

He shrugged his powerful shoulders. "Until Nighthawk's hoof gets well. He caught a stone under it on our way into town. He's got a nasty rock bruise which needs to heal before I ride him again. Besides, I have to wait for those rewards to arrive. With a jingle in my pocket, I can be more choosey about my next job and boss. I have four hundred dollars coming. You earned fifty of it by helping me defeat that last man; that's half of his reward."

"Shooting a man in the leg hardly makes a rewarding experience. You keep the money, T.J.; I have a good salary here. And I have savings from my last job in St. Louis. If I have too loud of a jingle in my own pocket, I'll spend it foolishly. Keep it all, please, for saving my life and getting me here."

He shook his head and grinned. "I've never known any woman to have enough money, and you don't appear a foolish spender. I can't leave Tucson before settling my debt with a partner. Ain't my way."

"Then, you'll be here an awfully long time," she playfully warned.

"Don't tell me you're one of those difficult females who loves to give any man a hard time," he jested.

"I suppose I can be bullheaded on occasion," she admitted. "Haven't you heard that redheads are stubborn, impulsive, and fiery-tempered?"

"And they like to keep you indebted to them until they need to call in a favor?" he accused with a laugh, recalling how she felt about bounty hunters who earned blood money. "Name it, woman."

"I tell you what, Mr. Rogue. Why don't you work off your debt today? And take me to supper Friday night?" she suggested in a brave attempt to keep him in town a while longer. Maybe that would give her time to make a decision about staying here, and about chasing him. The more she saw him and thought of him, the more she wanted him, the more she weakened in her resolve to avoid him.

T.J. observed her intently, surprised by her temerity. "What do you need from a gunslinger like me, Miss Starns? A bodyguard?"

She wanted to say, I want you! And didn't realize her gaze did it for her. "I don't need a bodyguard since I only have one man pursuing me, and I can handle him," she revealed in a tone which exposed her ill feelings about Martin Ferris. "What I need is a ladder from Mrs. Thayer's barn so I can reach those high windows. And I can use a strong back to fetch more water. The school doesn't have a well."

"Anything else, partner?" he inquired mirthfully.

She laughed and replied, "I'll give it some thought while you're gone, partner. I never turn down free help or a willing spirit."

"Free?" he echoed. "It'll cost you fifty dollars, Ma'am. Haven't you heard? T.J. Rogue doesn't work cheap, most of the time. Not unless he's starving and needs a quick dollar, or owes a favor."

She watched T.J. mount a strange horse, probably a rented one to use while his black stallion healed, and ride away from the secluded school. Carrie Sue hurriedly checked her appearance, doing as much as possible to improve it during his absence. She removed the scarf and rebraided her hair. She dusted her dress and put on her shoes.

The handsome Rogue returned, dragging the ladder behind the horse and balancing a water pail in each hand. She took a bucket and set it on the ground, then took the other one. T.J. dismounted and carried them inside the schoolhouse, then returned for the ladder. Together they placed it before the window over the door.

Carrie Sue added soap and vinegar to one bucket. She wet a rag in the mixture and climbed the ladder very slowly and apprehensively.

T.J. noticed her neatened appearance and wondered if she had prettied herself up for him or because she was a proud female. Even if she was mussed, she was still ravishing. He wouldn't mind sticking her in a tub and washing her all over before carrying her to— "Careful, woman," he cautioned as the ladder wiggled under her.

Without looking down, Carrie Sue began scrubbing the highest panes. As she was about to go down the ladder for rinse water and a drying cloth, T.J. mounted it, carrying both.

"I'll hold these close so you can get done quickly. You make me nervous up here. A fall like this could break your neck."

"I'm nervous, too. I'm afraid of heights," she revealed, smiling sheepishly.

"Why didn't you say so?" he softly chided her.

"This is part of my job, so I have to do it. Besides, you should know that the best way to overcome fears is to confront them."

"Even if you break your neck or kill yourself in the process?"

"I'm being careful," she avowed nervously.

"Get down and let me do these high ones."

"That's asking too much of you, partner."

"You didn't ask; I offered. Better accept my help before I get mad and leave you to do it all."

Carrie Sue glanced down at him. He was standing a few rungs below where her feet were positioned, his face near her waist. Their gazes met and searched, as if each was looking for something special to be written in the other's. She trembled. "Just hold the bucket within reach and I'll hurry," she told him, averting her gaze and going silent. His touch made her more jittery than the fearsome height!

Soon, the window over the door was sparkling clean. They shifted the ladder to the back one, and finished it within thirty minutes. When Carrie Sue's feet touched the floor, she realized she was shaking.

So did T.J. Rogue. "You always been afraid of heights?" he asked.

"For as long as I can remember. Every time I go to a loft or up high stairs, I don't look down. It makes me feel so silly. I thought if I kept doing it, the fear would finally go away, but it hasn't."

"Fear is a way of warning us to be extra careful about certain things. We usually mess up by trying too hard to overcome it, by being too reckless so we won't look like fools or cowards."

"You aren't afraid of anything or anyone, are you, T.J.?"

"Only myself," he replied too quickly.

"What do you mean?" she probed.

"A man like me is his own worst enemy, only he can

103

hurt himself."

"How?" she persisted for a clearer answer.

"Drop it, woman, or you'll make me look and feel silly."

The lovely desperado knew it was best to let the matter pass. She smiled and nodded. As she started on the lower windows again, T.J. went to fetch more clean water. Had he meant that he was self-destructive? Weren't all gun-slingers that way? Surely a man who lived by his gun expected to die by the gun. She wondered if the ebon-haired man yearned to settle down. If so, where and how and when? If she was not mistaken, she sometimes read deep anguish in him. Somewhere in his past, or more than once, he had been hurt terribly.

Carrie Sue felt sad and hungry, but not for food. She knew that T.J. was not the kind of man who opened up to many people. Yet, he seemed to be reaching out to her, even if he didn't realize that fact. If she turned her back on him, wouldn't he withdraw even more into himself? But what would happen if she didn't . . . ?

While she labored and the smokey-eyed man observed, T.J. asked, "What happened to their last teacher?"

Carrie Sue related part of what she knew about Helen Cooper. She wondered if she should reveal what Mrs. Thayer had said, and decided she shouldn't expose those suspicions at this time.

"You know more than you're saying, Carolyn. What is it?"

She glanced at him, astonished that he had read her so well. "What are you, T.J., a detective hired by Helen Cooper's family to investigate her murder?"

"Nope, but why did you say murder?" he jumped on her slip.

She halted her chore to meet his direct gaze. She cautioned herself to choose her words wisely, as such an accusation could result in an investigation that called light to her. "I don't know any facts about her tragic accident. I just think it sounds like a strange one."

"But you have a suspicion it wasn't an accident. Why?"

"Why are you so interested?"

"Because you've taken her place here and I wouldn't want the same thing to happen to you. I've seen you with Martin Ferris several times. There's something about him I don't like."

The redhead gaped at him, asking herself if his were the eyes she had felt spying on her. "You've seen us together?"

"Couldn't help it, woman; you've been with him nearly every day since our arrival," he remarked, sounding a little jealous.

Carrie Sue smiled in pleasure, assuming interest in her to be his motive for observing her secretly. T.J. had been given plenty of chances to take advantage of her, but he hadn't, so she felt she could trust him. She needed to talk openly and honestly about this problem with someone who wasn't involved. "You're a man of keen instincts, T.J., and you've earned my trust." She told him what had happened between her and Martin Ferris and revealed her ill feelings about the man, with the exception of Mrs. Thayer's revealing words and her dark suspicions. "Do you think I'm being too suspicious of him?"

"Not suspicious enough, if you ask me. I think you've sized him up right, and I think you should steer clear of him. He's dangerous."

Carrie Sue frowned. "How do you propose I do that? He is one of my bosses, probably my only boss considering everyone yields to his wishes."

"Have you ever dealt with a man like him before?"

Her expression said yes, but she replied, "What difference does that make? Aren't all men and situations different in some way?"

"Yep, but we learn from past experiences what works and what doesn't. I'd say you should make him dislike you and avoid you."

"How?" she questioned seriously. "The best way for a woman to frighten off a man is to make it obvious she's seeking marriage. Somehow I don't think that ploy would work with Mr. Ferris."

"You don't want to get married?"

"Not to him! In fact, I haven't met any man I've wanted to marry," she added, then wished she hadn't made such a deceitful reply with the truth staring her in the face.

He ignored her last statement and suggested, "Look for his weaknesses, then work on them. A man can't stand for a woman to belittle him in any way. Annoy the hell out of him and he'll scat."

"That sounds good, but it hasn't worked so far. He hears and sees only what pleases him. I've done everything but slap his face in public."

"It didn't look that way Friday afternoon while you two were looking around. You both seemed to be having a good time."

"Well, I wasn't!" she snapped angrily. Her periwinkle eyes squinted, her full lips tightened, and her cheeks flushed. "I don't like to feel like I have a noose around my neck! He's demanding, and persistent, and overbearing, and pushy! He's lower than a snake's belly! But he's a powerful man here, so I can't afford to offend him."

T.J. laughed heartily. "You do have quite a temper, Miss Starns, but don't get mad at me. I'm not the one chasing you. You think you can handle him after I'm gone?"

"I'll have to, but it'll be tough," she answered, trying to master her wild temper. Her outburst was foolish. She snatched up a wet cloth and returned to her chore. She was being too talkative with this disarming stranger!

"I don't like him or trust him, Carolyn. I'll be worried about you."

She halted and turned to face him again. There was something in his tone and expression which lassoed her heart. "I don't either, T.J., but I'll have to tolerate him. I

106

can't just pick up and leave like you do. A woman makes a bad drifter. You men can get jobs anywhere and any time, but that isn't true for women. At least not the kind of jobs we want." She began washing the window again, working the rag swiftly and roughly over the filthy panes to release her rising tension.

T.J.'s hand covered hers and halted it. He felt her tremors, from anger and resentment and from his contact. "If you need anything, any help at all, you will send for me, won't you?"

Carrie Sue leaned her forehead against the window. She wanted to fling herself into his arms and beg him to carry her away from all her troubles, away from her loneliness and pain, and further away from her dark past. "Where? You move around all the time."

T.J.'s other hand reached out to stroke her hair, but then he stopped himself and let go of her hand. Her pull was nearly overpowering, and it alarmed him to feel such weakness. It was reckless to play with this fiery torch! He could get burned badly. "I'll let you know where I can be reached in case of trouble here."

"T.J. . . . ," she began, but forced herself to cease.

He probed tenderly, "What is it, Carolyn?"

"Have you ever wanted to stay in one place, to get your life settled, to be off the trail for good? No more running just ahead of real life? No more suffering and loneliness? No more killing? Just to find a place where you can be accepted and respected? Where there wouldn't be any more cold, and dust, and rain, and hunger? A place where you can be free and happy?"

Her understanding caused him to respond, "I was going to try it once."

She faced him. "What happened to stop you?"

Lordy, she was beautiful and desirable! She made him feel hot and weak all over. Such empathy blazed within her eyes. She was so special, so precious. He could have this woman if things were different, but they weren't. He couldn't remain here, and he couldn't carry her off. Bitterly he scoffed, "Fate. I've got a bad one, haven't you heard? Men like me can't settle down." When he sighted warning moisture in her eyes, he flinched and said, "I need to go. I have a poker game set up."

Carrie Sue guessed the reason for his turn-around. She, too, was scared of the potent feelings which were passing between them, scared to surrender and scared to flee. From experience she knew it was rash to push a man or to respond to him falsely. There was no future with a gunslinger who drifted. "Thanks for the help, both times."

He inhaled deeply, then slowly released the spent air. He grabbed his hat and holster off the bench. "Anytime, Miss Starns."

As he strapped on his weapons, she teased to lighten his parting mood, "You always so formal with your past partners?"

He grinned and winked. "See you around, Carolyn."

"I hope so. You will let me know before you leave town?"

From the steps, he glanced back at her. "It's a promise."

Chapter Six

Carrie Sue worked until five o'clock. By that time, she was exhausted and soaked with perspiration. She left her supplies, except for the water pails, at the school and returned to the boarding house.

Mrs. Thayer met her at the back door with a genial smile. "I saw you coming, Carolyn, so I sent Maria to fill the tub for you. You can't clean up a mess like that in one day. I bet you're bone tired."

The redhead leaned against the door jamb for a few minutes, hating to challenge those steps with her aching legs. "I am, but I got a lot of work done. I think I can finish most of it tomorrow. That place was covered in dirt."

"Now you are," the woman teased. "Who was that handsome gent helping you today? I don't recall seeing him around town."

Carrie Sue told the woman who T.J. was and how they met.

Excitement and intrigue filled the woman's eyes and voice. "There's a man who knows how to defend himself and protect his woman."

Carrie Sue laughed. "I'm not his woman, Mrs. Thayer. This is the first time I've seen him since our adventures together."

"Do you want to be?" the graying haired woman asked.

Carrie Sue was almost too weary to think straight. "Honestly, I don't know. We're nearly strangers and it's probably best to keep it that way. He's a wild gunslinger and I'm a respectable schoolteacher."

"But you like him, don't you?"

"Yes, but T.J. Rogue has quite a colorful reputation, Mrs. Thayer. He's a most unusual and mysterious man. He could cause trouble for me. If I started seeing him socially, people might think something wicked happened between us on the trail, which it didn't. Besides, he'll be leaving soon and I probably won't ever see him again, so why take a chance of staining my reputation here?"

"Men can be changed, Carolyn."

"Not all of them. Consider Martin Ferris. He's cast in stone."

Following a long bath, hair washing, and delicious meal, Carrie Sue returned to her room for rest and quiet. It wasn't long before she was asleep, to dream of T.J. Rogue.

Tuesday she returned to the schoolhouse to work again. She polished the desks and dusted the books. She checked their condition and recorded their number, as well as the available supplies. When she heard hammering outside, she went to see what was going on out back.

A carpenter told her that Martin Ferris had paid him to repair the outhouse and the play-yard fence. The redhead thanked him and returned to her chores inside, fearing a visit from the vile man.

Surprisingly, Martin did not appear for a visit, which pleased Carrie Sue immensely. When her chores were completed, she closed the windows and door and walked home, to spend a night similar to the one before.

Wednesday, Carrie Sue remained in her rooms, relaxing

and studying for her new job. She made notes on school supplies to be purchased tomorrow, and on her own secret supplies for a quick escape in case of trouble. She had concealed Carolyn's letters and diary in her hiding place in the closet. She had decided to buy a horse and keep him in Mrs. Thayer's corral. Perhaps she could look around for one tomorrow while she was shopping.

With the door bolted, she cleaned and oiled her weapons, then replaced them in the secret compartment. Handling the guns brought back an assortment of memories, such as the day Darby had given her the pistols and the rifle, and the days she had target shot for hours with her brother. She was a good shot, nearly perfect.

Her mind drifted to her brother's gang. Off and on for years she had lived with or around the six men: Kadry Sams, Walt Vinson, Tyler Parnell, Dillon Holmes, John Griffin, and Kale Rushton. She knew the men liked her, and would do anything for her because she was Darby's sister. She was fond of them, but they had never seemed like family to her, except for Kale. She was close to the half-Apache bandit, and he viewed her as a sister. She could talk to Kale, be honest with him. He had taught her most of the skills which she possessed and he had honed them. Without a doubt, Kale would die defending her. But, she admitted, so would the others.

She wondered what Dillon—a die-hard Southerner—was doing. He had pursued her for years. She wondered if Griff—a black man—was chewing on a stick this minute as usual, and if Tyler was sipping too much whiskey, and if Walt was collecting his badges and fingering his gunbutts.

She knew Kale was watching over Darby, his best friend, and few men had his prowess. But what about the blue-eyed blond Kadry Sams? Was he pining over her? Was his Scottish burr filling another woman's ear? Would he come after her and beg her to return? Kadry loved her and wanted her fiercely, but that feeling wasn't mutual. She had tried to return his love, especially at the Laredo ranch; it hadn't worked and never would.

Carrie Sue's mind shifted to the local men in her life. She hadn't seen or heard from Martin Ferris since Sunday, and was a bit baffled by his sudden distance for days. No doubt it was some ploy of his to seize her attention. That would never work either!

As for T.J. Rogue, she was disappointed that he hadn't returned to the school Tuesday or come to visit her today. But she had expected his distance; she had seen that flicker of apprehension in his gaze, the one which said a woman was getting too close too fast.

"I bet that's the most talking you've done with a female, Mr. Skittish Rogue. Do I dare try to tame you, to really trust you?"

The flaming haired ex-outlaw called his image to mind. Her body warmed all over and the pit of her stomach tightened. "What's gotten into you, Carrie Sue Stover? You've never behaved this way before. Merciful Heavens, loving him scares the life out of me!"

Her face paled and she felt her heart drum rapidly. "Love him?" she murmured hoarsely. "You hardly know the man. Maybe it's only because he's a handsome and virile man. Not so, girl, you've seen too many of them and not been affected like this." Most women would kill to win Kale, or Dillon, or Kadry, but none of them affected her like this. "Nope, it's T.J. Rogue who's got you snared."

Carrie Sue squirmed in agitation. Now that she had admitted the truth to herself, what was she going to do about it? Could she risk messing up her new life for him? Could she risk losing this unique man forever just to remain here? "You're a fool, Carrie Sue Stover! What makes you think you can win him even if you tried? He's a loner, a drifter, a famous gunslinger. If he discovered who you are, he'd be waiting around Tucson for your reward to arrive!"

112

He wouldn't do that, her heart argued.

"I suppose you think he would understand and forgive you?" she scoffed. "He would just let those thousands of dollars slip through his hands so he could caress you with them!"

He likes you, fool, her heart reminded her.

"He likes Miss Carolyn Starns, a pretty schoolmarm, not an outlaw with a high price on her head."

No, he likes you. That's why he's hanging around Tucson. You saw how he looked and behaved with you the other day.

"He was just being nice."

A gunslinger just being nice? Never. Get off that loco horse, girl.

"I can't love him and chase him. It's too dangerous."

For whom, you coward, you liar?

"For both of us, idiot. T.J.'s already a gunslinger tottering on the line between good and bad. Think what loving you would cost him. You're a wanted fugitive. Do you want that bitter life for him too?"

Her heart remained silent, and she knew why. There was no reasonable comeback to her last words.

Thursday, Carrie Sue arose late, as she hadn't slept well after her talk with herself. Her final decision had been to leave the matter in T.J.'s hands. If he stayed around Tucson and seemed to feel the same way she did and she felt she could trust him fully, she would tell him the truth. Then, they could decide what to do about a future together. She cautioned herself to be patient with him because she didn't want to scare him off. He had to more than want her as an attractive woman; he had to love her, love her enough to discard her past as he would an unwanted poker card.

She headed for the mercantile store a few blocks away. She spoke with the owner for a time, then began shopping.

113

The man told her to pick out what she needed and he would have it delivered to the school. He said he would charge the items until she decided how to pay for them.

Carrie Sue rounded one tall counter toward the rear of the large store and nearly bumped into the man who now haunted her dreams day and night. "T.J., what are you doing here?"

"I needed some ammo and a new rope. I saw you come in, so I decided to sneak up on you and check your reflexes," he teased, warming her with a blazing smile.

"They're dull today because of fatigue," she said with a laugh. "I could have used your help again Tuesday to finish up the schoolhouse. You sure you worked off your entire debt in one afternoon?"

"Nope, I still have to take you to supper tomorrow night. What time you want me to call on you, Miss Starns?"

"I thought you might have forgotten that part of our bargain."

"Calling on a lady is new for me, but I'll try my best to do it right. Any place special you want me to take you?"

The thought of spending an evening with him thrilled her. How else was she going to test her feelings for him or his for her? How else could she discover if he was a risk worth taking? "I'm sure you know this town better than I do. You choose and surprise me."

"Some place quiet and relaxing, away from your adoring crowd?" he hinted with a twinkle in his smokey gray eyes.

"Perfect."

"What did you do yesterday?" he inquired to continue their talk and his observation of this fascinating woman.

"Worked on lessons and tried to rest up." She gave a mock sigh of distress. "School begins in two weeks, so I have to prepare myself."

"To challenge those little hellions?" he teased near a whisper.

Carrie Sue glanced around before replying softly, "Want

to help me tame them, Mr. Rogue?"

"Not on your life, woman. You couldn't pay me enough to go back to school. Always hated 'em. Father Ortega used to stand over me with a switch making me do my lessons. I wasn't lucky enough to have a teacher like you. Mine was real strict and cold."

"You went to school while you were at the mission in San Antonio?"

"Yep. The priest made all the orphans do it. But he was especially hard on me. Said I was too wild and needed settling down."

"Did it work?" she asked, suppressing laughter.

"What do you think, Miss Starns?" he answered, then grinned.

"It must have because you're very smart and well-mannered."

"For a gunslinger," he added teasingly.

Carrie Sue smiled. "For anyone."

They fused their gazes and looked at each other for what seemed a lengthy spell. Suddenly both smiled at the same time.

"I like you, T.J., you're so easy to talk to," she confessed. "It's going to be awfully dull around here after you leave."

"I know what you mean, Carolyn; you're easy to talk with, too." The moment after he made that admission, he cleared his throat and asked, "You need me to help carry your packages home?"

"Thanks, but the owner's going to deliver most of them to the school, and I can manage the rest. I'm not going straight home from here. I have some other stops to make. I'm thinking about buying a horse, so I planned to look around while I'm out today. Some places are too far for walking in the heat, and I hear it gets worse."

"Why don't I look around for you? Men sometimes take advantage of a female customer by selling her a bad horse or charging her too much. I'll pick out a couple and take

115

you to see them in a few days."

"That would be very nice of you, if you don't mind."

Of course he didn't mind, for two reasons. He didn't want her to get cheated, and he couldn't let her visit the stable where Nighthawk was staying and discover he had lied about the stallion's injury. "Be my pleasure, Ma'am," he said in a heavy Southern drawl. "I best get moving along. I'll see you tomorrow night at six."

"Thanks again, T.J. You're always there when I need help."

"What are friends for?" he murmured and left.

Carrie Sue finished her shopping and walked to the laundress's home to pick up her washing. I'll see you Monday," she told the woman.

At the boarding house, she related her encounter with T.J. to Mrs. Thayer, who seemed genuinely pleased with the news.

Friday seemed like a particularly long day as Carrie Sue planned her evening over and over while she tried to study, bathe, and dress. She had selected a lovely dress in pale yellow from Carolyn's trunk. The skirt was full and swishy, the waist snug, and the sleeves ending at her elbows. Matching lace trimmed the collar and cuffs, and Carolyn even had slippers to match the pretty dress which didn't look as if it had ever been worn. Sadly, they were too small for Carrie Sue's feet. She put them aside to drop into the school's outhouse to correct an oversight which could be dangerous if noticed by someone.

The soft shade of the dress brought out the golden highlights in her red hair and flattered her skin color. It even made her eyes appear darker and more noticeable. Carrie Sue gazed in the mirror, wondering why she wasn't covered in freckles like most redheads. She also noticed, as if for the first time, that her skin was not exceptionally pale

116

or florid, but was a rosy brown from the sun. Her brows were reddish gold to match her hair, although her long lashes were a dark brown. She knew her features were too large, her nose and lips and eyes. Yet, she decided, they blended together enhancingly.

She had washed her hair early so it could dry before this evening. It hung to her waist, thick and shiny, and curled ever so slightly to spread around her shoulders like a tawny red mane. She recklessly decided to let it hang free tonight. She gathered up the sides and pinned each behind her ears, then fluffed her bangs over her forehead.

Carrie Sue Stover stood and twisted before the mirror. She was amazed by how different she looked in a dress, compared to a cotton shirt and jeans and boots. She actually looked like a real lady, and that delighted her. She hoped T.J. liked her appearance tonight.

She paced the floor as she waited for him. He was fifteen minutes late. She worried that he had changed his mind about coming tonight. Worse, what if something had happened to him? He was a famous gunslinger, and they were often challenged by men who wanted to increase their own reputations by outdrawing legends. Who would care if T.J. Rogue died except her? She trembled. She clenched her teeth and vowed to slay any man who —

Mrs. Thayer's voice called from outside her door, "Carolyn, he's here. Are you ready?"

Carrie Sue rushed to the door and opened it. She beamed as she nodded. "Thank you, Mrs. Thayer. I was getting worried."

"So was I," the woman confessed with a sly grin.

Carrie Sue went to the front door and joined T.J. there. She smiled when he couldn't seem to take his eyes from her or speak. "I'm ready," she said to bring him back to reality before his stimulating loss affected her even more deeply and noticeably.

T.J. said he had rented a carriage. She followed him to it

117

and he helped her inside. The redhead watched him walk around the horse and take his seat next to her. She noticed his purposeful and confident stride, his alert gaze, his proud and fearless carriage, and his sensual aura. Carrie Sue had to remind herself not to snuggle up to his broad shoulder, as she was tempted to do. Happiness filled her as they rode away and she furtively studied him.

T.J. was wearing a dark gray shirt that fit his muscled chest as if molded for it. His hips were clad in ebony pants and his feet in freshly polished midnight boots. From the rich colors and excellent condition of his garments, she concluded, they were new. She wondered if he had purchased them to make a good impression on her, and she wanted to believe he had done so. A black hat rested comfortably on his dark head of neatly combed hair, and a matching bandanna was tied loosely around his neck, its edges fluttering playfully in the breeze created by the carriage's movement. His ever-present gunbelt hung below his waist, the holsters strapped securely to hard thighs. Her heart beat faster as his overpowering looks and nearness enchanted her. Courting, she decided, was delirious fun, with the right man.

T.J. asked, "You like Mexican food, Miss Starns?"

"Love it, Mr. Rogue."

T.J. wondered where an Eastern girl, even one from St. Louis, had learned to "love" Mexican food. He had seen her stop to eat at a small Mexican cafe the other day and had thought it strange. He headed for the other end of town as he, too, furtively studied the woman beside him. The gunslinger decided she looked vivacious and stunning in the yellow dress that made her appear so much the lady. He was glad she was not attired in one of those depressingly dark gowns which she seemed to favor for some odd reason. This color was sunny and warm, like she was. His hands begged to slip around her waist, which looked so small in its snug confines. His fingers itched to caress the silky skin of her arms that was exposed by her elbow length sleeves. Tonight, she seemed as delicate as the lace on her dress; yet, he knew she was a woman of strength and will, a ravishing woman of compelling traits.

T.J. halted the carriage behind a large building. He helped her down—wisely not allowing his hands to linger too long and inflamingly on her body—and escorted her inside. As he walked behind her, he watched the gentle and enticing sway of her hips beneath the flowing skirt. Although he had never been one to attend many socials, he wondered what it would feel like to have her pressed against his body while dancing dreamily to romantic music. Every time he was with the flaming redhead who got under his skin, he felt hot and itchy all over and he had to be extra careful to keep himself under tight control.

A dark-haired woman greeted them and smiled at T.J. before she led the couple to a back table. T.J. assisted her with her chair and was rewarded with a radiant smile. Lordy, he thought, how those beautiful eyes glow when she smiles. He asked himself if he was crazy to spend time with this unobtainable lady. He yearned to touch her soft hair, and to catch another whiff of her fresh and heady fragrance. He cleared his throat and asked, "How do you like my choice?"

Carrie Sue glanced around. It was decorated with Mexican tapestries, sombreros, a bull's head, colorful ponchos, braided lariats, silver spurs, and other items to give the flavor of Mexico. A mariachi trio was strolling around the front of the room, playing their native music for the customers. The serving girls were dressed in Mexican clothes. Delightful aromas filled her nostrils. She closed her eyes, inhaled, and smiled. She was out for the evening with the most appealing man alive. "It's wonderful, T.J.," she remarked, opening her eyes. It reminded her of times she had spent over the border in hiding with Darby, but those were good memories of lazy and pleasant days.

119

The woman returned to take their order. Relaxed and happy, without notice, Carrie Sue ordered her favorite dishes in Spanish.

T.J. noticed, but he quickly ordered in English. After all, she was a teacher and they often knew more than one language. He watched her listen to the musicians and sway her head in time to their beat, as if it were a natural thing to do. He realized that she was utterly relaxed with him and that was why her guard was down, because she did have a guard up on most occasions. Certain things she had said and done raced through his keen mind. Who, he mused, was this beautiful woman who had him at a loss of wits? Why did she seem like a born and bred Westerner hiding behind an Eastern face? If that was true, why the act? From whom or what was she hiding? How would it affect him?

"How old are you and how long have you been a teacher?" he asked.

"I'm twenty-one, almost twenty-two. I've been teaching for two years," she replied without looking at him. Lying to T.J. left a bad taste in her mouth, but it couldn't be helped.

"How did you get into teaching?"

"My parents were teachers back East. We lived in Charleston. But there were many problems in South Carolina after the war. Northern Carpetbaggers tried to take over everything. They even wanted to control what the children learned in school, and the new books were very biased against the South. One of the newcomers kept giving my mother a hard time. My father was forced to kill him for trying to attack her. We were lucky there were witnesses in his favor, but the law warned us it would be best for everyone if we left Carolina. We tried a few towns in neighboring states, but they didn't work out. Papa decided to move to St. Louis and open a private school there. Mama and I were going to teach in it. But there was an accident, our buggy overturned while we were looking for a place to build. They were killed and I was knocked unconscious. When I recovered, I took over the job at a local school, until a spoiled brat wanted it."

T.J. wondered why she sounded like she was reciting a lesson rather than relating her history. His intrigue gave him the chance to get other things off his mind, such as where and how this stimulating evening would end. "So you found this job and headed for Tucson."

Their conversation did the same for Carrie Sue, as she focused on her false tale. "It was in the newspaper, and I responded. Many people heading west get stranded in St. Louis, so I guess they thought it was a good place to search for a teacher. I caught the Butterfield stage to Fort Worth, then the Garrett line from there. Garrett was suppose to be cheaper and safer, and I could see more sights at a slower pace."

"What's a teacher's existence like?"

Carrie Sue hoped that her willingness to converse would inspire him to do the same. "I'll have grades one through eight. Classes run Monday through Friday from eight until four. I'm suppose to start school on June fifth and work until August. If I do a good job during that two month period, I'll be hired permanently to begin in September. I'll be paid one hundred dollars a month, which is an excellent salary."

"You don't sound too thrilled about such a good job and pay."

"Can you blame me? Martin Ferris wanted to come observe, but I hope I talked him out of it." She related what she had told the man. "He would make me and the students nervous with his little visits. This was a big move for me, T.J.; I have to do good and make it work. It could be my last ch —," she faltered at his alert gaze. "Chance to prove myself. It's important to me. Tell me more about you," she encouraged when the music halted.

"There isn't anything more to tell you than you already

121

know. I'm a simple man. I live, I breathe, I travel." Mentally he added, *And I want you like crazy, woman!* He lowered his gaze for a time to master his runaway emotions.

"And you're private and shy," she added and laughed. Carrie Sue watched him grin and listened closely to his merry chuckle, a reaction that mellowed his smokey gray gaze and softened his features. She liked the way his dark gray shirt seemed to make his arresting eyes appear the same shade and the way his sun-bronzed skin made his teeth appear white when he smiled broadly. She longed to run her fingers through his midnight mane and over his tanned face. She wanted her hands to roam his chest. He looked so splendid tonight, so clean, so healthy, so vital and alive, so downright irresistible. *Concentrate, girl, or you'll make a fool of yourself in front of everybody, especially him!* "Where are you staying?" she asked nervously.

His gaze shifted to the ceiling as he said, "Up there. That's how I know the food here is good."

"I thought that woman smiled too long at a stranger," she teased.

"Jealous?" he hinted with a mirthful laugh.

"Of course. I don't like women looking at my partner like that."

"I see," he murmured with a lopsided grin. "Possessive, huh?"

"I suppose that bad trait goes along with being stubborn, impulsive, and fiery-tempered: the ill fortunes of being a redhead."

T.J. leaned forward on the table. His left thumb rubbed his jawline as his first two fingers captured his strong chin between them. His gaze slipped over her tawny red hair, and he liked how she was wearing it tonight. The pulled back style revealed more of her lovely face and made her look more genteel and exquisite than when she tried to hide it beneath a hat or secure it in a snug bun. "Do you honestly have any bad traits, Miss Starns?"

Carrie Sue tingled at the way he was watching her. Surely his mood and gaze meant she was having the same effect on him that he was having on her, and that pleased her. She relaxed even more as she replied, "Plenty of them. Haven't you noticed?"

T.J. stared into her merry eyes and said, "Nope."

"Good, then I don't have to worry about trying to conceal them."

"Have you noticed mine?" he asked.

"Do you have any?" she parried, feigning playful innocence.

"Of course not," he answered, then licked his lips. Lordy, he mused, how his mouth hungered to close over her sweet one and to feast there. She was absolutely bewitching, and he didn't mind her magical pull at all. In fact, he found it amazing and intriguing that a near stranger—even a beautiful one—could touch him this way. As a man who liked and needed to grasp all angles of a matter, he knew this curious one would require lots of study, close and pleasant study.

The food came: enchiladas, refried beans, Spanish rice, soft tacos, and tasty burritos. *"Gracias,"* she told the woman. It was spicy, but delicious. Carrie Sue ate with eagerness.

"Well?" he hinted as he watched her with keen interest.

The smiling fugitive noticed that T.J. was using his left hand to hold his fork. Either he used both hands equally, or he wanted challengers to think he was righthanded. If so, it was a clever ruse to entice foes to watch the wrong fingers during a gunfight. She said, "The best I've had, Mr. Rogue. You were right about this place."

He grinned and asked her if she wanted to taste his tequila. She looked around, smiled, and reached for his glass. She took a small sip, rolled it on her tongue, and swallowed. "Strong," she murmured.

As he refilled the glass from the bottle left on their table, he said, "It's made from the agava, that tall yellow plant you mainly see on hillsides. It's potent, so drink it slow. If you drink too much, you get real thirsty and your head kills you the next day."

"Perhaps I shouldn't have any more."

"Perhaps, Miss Starns. I wouldn't want you getting drunk on me," he said, but knew he would love to see her with her guard completely lowered and with all inhibitions gone, but in private.

"The town council would love that news," she teased.

"I bet they would, especially Martin Ferris."

"Let's don't spoil our supper with talk of him," she entreated. All she wanted tonight was to think of T.J., to be with him, to be the only thing on his mind. She wanted and needed to know all about him and all about the wild emotions he stirred within her.

"Fine with me," he concurred, leaving the full glass of tequila near her plate. As he sipped his and ate his meal, he asked, "What do you plan to do when you retire? How long do teachers usually stay on the job and in one place?"

Carrie Sue unthinkingly took sips from the glass. She liked tequila, and it relaxed her tonight. It made her feel happy, weightless, and trouble-free. "I haven't planned that far ahead," she replied, her wits clear enough to realize he wouldn't buy Carolyn's story about a dress shop. "I have lots of good years left. You normally remain in the same place until you retire, unless there's a problem."

"Like the one you had in St. Louis?"

"Yep, or the one I might have here with . . ." She halted and sighed in annoyance. She downed the remaining inch of golden liquid in her glass. "It's your turn to do some talking, mister."

The smokey-eyed gunslinger refilled their glasses. "And say what?"

"When are you going after that man who used barbwire on you? And what mine are you planning to work for? Surely not Ferris's!"

"Nope, not his, but I haven't looked around yet. I'll hold off a while longer on my revenge; he's probably still watching out for me. First, I have to find the best way to ruin him, and catch him by surprise."

"If he's a rancher, snag him where it'll hurt the most. Cut his fences. Burn his barns and fields. Steal his payrolls. Rustle his cattle."

T.J.'s eyes widened. "Where did a gentle schoolmarm like you learn about such stuff? Most of it's illegal."

Carrie Sue pushed aside her drink and reached for her black coffee. "I read those ten-cent novels. They have some good ideas in them. The good man always finds a way to defeat his enemies, even bad lawmen and cattle barons and politicians. You have to take risks with enemies, or they'll get away with their crimes. Have you ever been tempted to become an outlaw? Didn't that gold tempt you to take it?'

"Yep, that gold was tempting, but not enough to challenge the law." He didn't add, what tempted me most was you, woman, but taking you captive was more dangerous than taking that gold.

Carrie Sue suddenly remembered something: he had been in this area "a dozen times," and he had worked for Francisco Carrillo once. She wondered if he had known Martin Ferris before she arrived here, but didn't ask. "Do you have family, T.J.?"

"Nope. How about you?"

She looked sad as she shook her head, believing her brother was lost to her if she remained as Carolyn Starns. "What do you plan to do when you retire from being a gunslinger and a drifter?"

"Don't know yet." He asked himself how a St. Louis schoolmarm had heard of him and why she'd said "campfire tales." He had to start paying closer attention to her words! That, he concluded, was nearly impossible with the stunning creature so near and inviting! He tried another subject, "You certainly had a tough time getting to Tucson.

I'm surprised you didn't turn back."

Tensed and lightheaded, the redhead remarked before thinking clearly, "That holdup and Indian raid weren't my only misadventures on the way here. The soldier's wife you saw at the station killed herself right in front of me. She was terrified of what those outlaws would do, so she grabbed a gun and shot herself before I could stop her. When I was on the Butterfield stage, it crashed outside Sherman trying to get away from outlaws. A Texas Ranger was killed. I only survived because the cavalry arrived in time to chase them away. It was scary. But I don't want to talk about that. Tell me about your travels," she encouraged.

"I've been lots of places, but none of them were special enough to entice me to settle down there. This hot box certainly doesn't."

"I know what you mean. I'm not sure I'm going to like it here." She dabbed at perspiration from the hot food, strong drink, and heat.

T.J eyed her intently, thinking how much he would enjoy a bath in a cold stream with her. He watched her dab at the glistening moisture on her face, and had the oddest urge to taste the salty liquid forming there. He shifted in his chair and warned himself to discard such thoughts. "What will you do if your opinion doesn't change?"

"Look for a cooler and prettier place to move. Maybe Colorado, or California, or back East. The South is beautiful and pleasant."

"I noticed that during the war, but I'm pretty much a Texan."

"A Texan?" she echoed, her voice sounding strained. What if he'd heard about that holdup near Sherman? What if he knew it was the Stover Gang? What if he thought it was odd that two redheads were involved? She was wanted in Texas, Oklahoma, New Mexico, and Kansas. But Quade's detective had not exposed her in Sante Fe or

Laredo, so no one in those towns could reveal her appearance. She had to chain her tongue and clear her wits!

The ebon-haired man had been furtively watching her strange reaction, and he became alert. "Most of the people I know best live there. Lots of jobs with high pay. She's a big state so it gives me plenty of room to stretch my legs."

"Which area do you like best?"

"The middle."

"Why?" she probed.

He chuckled. "I just told you why. You getting dazed on that tequila? Maybe I should take you home now," he suggested playfully.

Carrie Sue took his last words as a hint the wonderful evening was over. Yet, she teased, "Because you have other plans or because I'm being too nosey?"

He wished he did have other plans for tonight, other than taking this lady home after supper! But, she was a lady, so he could do no less without scaring her off or soiling her reputation, and he didn't want that to happen. He looked her in the eye and answered, "Both."

"Good, an honest man, and a brave one," she said with a smile. "I'm finished, so we can leave now," she said reluctantly. She didn't think he was trying to end the evening abruptly because he wasn't having a good time, but she knew she was making him apprehensive. A man like this one would value his privacy.

T.J. didn't want to take her home, but he was anxious about talking with her. There was little he could tell her tonight, and he didn't want to sit around in strained silence or fire too many curious questions her way. A few minutes at a time with her was what he needed, time enough to see her but not enough to get a probing conversation going about him. Lordy, she made him nervous, like a green soldier on his first Indian raid. Too, he made her awfully nervous, but why? She had him plenty confused!

They traveled to the boarding house without talking.

Carrie Sue pretended to observe her surroundings. "It's cooler tonight."

"Yep, it is." As he halted the carriage, he asked, "Is it all right if I come by tomorrow to show you a horse I've found?"

She smiled. "What time?"

"About ten, so you can ride him before it gets hot. I don't want the sun roasting that pretty head of yours."

"Thanks, I'll be waiting," she said as he helped her down. She realized he wouldn't try to kiss her tonight; he was too much of a gentleman, despite his rough existence. This contradiction in character and personality intrigued and delighted her. It also told Carrie Sue that he believed she was a real lady, and he was a hard man to dupe. That conclusion gave her confidence about succeeding in her new life here in Tucson.

T.J. wanted to pull her into his arms and kiss her but it was too soon to expose such hot desires, and someone might see them. He watched the moonlight dance on her tawny highlights and caress her face. He couldn't risk speaking again because his throat felt constricted with yearning. He smiled, tipped his hat, and left in the carriage.

Carrie Sue watched him ride away, thinking how tight-lipped he could get at times. She hadn't learned much more about him. Why was he so secretive? How could he expect to spend time with her without talking? Maybe he just didn't know how to deal with women, or maybe she made him extra nervous. At least he kept coming back to see her. Surely, she reasoned dreamily, that was a good sign.

When she went inside, Mrs. Thayer broke bad news to her: Martin Ferris had dropped by for a visit and one of the male boarders had told him she had left to spend the evening with T.J. Rogue.

"He was red-faced with anger. He's gonna be trouble, Carolyn."

128

"I was afraid of that."

"He said to tell you he'll call on you again tomorrow after dinner."

"It won't do him any good. I'm going riding with T.J. to try out a horse I'm considering purchasing. I need one to get around in this heat and he was kind enough to scout about for a good buy. He's coming for me at ten before it gets hot. Do you think I could take a picnic basket along so I won't have to return so early and confront Martin Ferris again before Sunday?"

"I'll prepare it myself," the woman answered happily. "You two look good together, Carolyn. I bet you're the first woman to turn his handsome head."

"I know he's the first to turn mine," the redhead confided. "But I'm hesitant about seeing him. My reputation's at stake."

"Don't fret over what people here will say. People gossip no matter how spotless your reputation is. Be happy, girl. They need a teacher badly so they won't fire you without good reason."

"If Martin Ferris has his way, he'll convince them my seeing a gunslinger is a good reason, or he'll make that threat tomorrow. You wait and see, Mrs. Thayer; I'll bet a month's rent on it."

"I ain't into losing a sure bet, girl," the woman concurred.

T.J. arrived on schedule the next morning with two horses. She met him at the corral, with a smile and a picnic basket. He told her the pinto was two years old and in excellent condition. "Do you know how to ride, Miss Starns?"

"Yes, Mr. Rogue, even schoolmarms have to get around."

As she stroked the brown and white mare and examined

129

the beast visually, he teased, "I thought ladies always used carriages."

"A mount is cheaper than a buggy horse and a carriage and harnesses, and much easier to take care of. I've had several horses in the past, so I know how to tend them."

"What about riding? You used to side saddle?"

"Side saddles out here are for genteel ladies and sissies."

"What about a gun? Do you know how to shoot?" When she stared at him oddly, he explained, "The West is a dangerous place, Miss Starns. You should know how to defend yourself. I'll give you some lessons today if you like. I even picked up a small pistol for you to try out, but we'll need to get a good ways out of town to practice. Sheriff Myers wouldn't like us shooting up his town and scaring his folks."

Carrie Sue became edgy. He was asking some alarming questions. Had he heard of the hold up by the Stover Gang near Sherman? Had he put two and two together? Or had he been suspicious of her all along? Was he trying to test her skills with a horse and a gun? Should she play dumb? No, that pretense could make it worse.

"You afraid of guns, Miss Starns? They aren't dangerous if you learn how to fire them and take care of them properly. I'd feel better about leaving you here if I knew you could protect yourself in a scrape."

"My father taught me how to protect myself before he was killed. I've even been hunting with him. But as you told me on the trail, if you pull a weapon on a man, you have to be prepared to use it."

"Some men back down when threatened."

"And most men won't, especially the really dangerous ones."

"You're saying you couldn't shoot a man even if your life's in peril?"

"Have you forgotten what happened on the trail? Yes, I could shoot a man, but I'd prefer to wound him. We do have lawmen to protect us and our property."

"Like they did on your way here. Johnny Law isn't always around when you need help, and sometimes he's as bad as the villains."

"That's true," she murmured, recalling the evil Ranger.

"Well, you want the infamous Rogue to teach you to shoot?"

"If the . . . legendary Rogue will join me for a picnic," she coaxed. "My pursuer came by last night and was furious to find me out with you. He's dropping by again at high noon. If you don't mind, I'd rather not return until later today. How's a bribe of fried chicken, biscuits, and canned fruit sound to you?"

"If you throw in riding and shooting lessons, it's a deal."

"You drive a hard bargain, Mr. Rogue. It's a deal."

Carrie Sue mounted agilely, and T.J. nodded approval. He slid sideways on his saddle and scooped up the fragrant basket. "Move 'em out, partner," he announced and led the way out of town.

Martin Ferris watched them ride away, then scowled with suppressed fury. . . .

Chapter Seven

They rode out of town to the west. A dirt trail led toward hills not far away which rose up from the harsh flat landscape. The ground was dry, sandy, and rocky, and scattered ravines were cut into its surface. The cacti were thick in this direction, especially the taller variety. Red or white flowers topped many of the towering cactus plants were birds darted amongst the sharp spines to collect bugs or to enter abodes they had made in the green giants. The further they rode, the higher the hills reached skyward. Huge boulders with clusters of small rocks were situated at intervals as if they'd been dropped from heaven by a mischievous spirit. They didn't see any water, but dry washes snaked over the rugged terrain to remind them this area wasn't always dry.

They had left town at a slow pace, then settled into a steady gallop. T.J. was pleased about how well she rode and how she treated the animal. As he slowed his pace, he asked, "How do you like Charlie?"

Carrie Sue laughed. "Who named her Charlie? She's a mare."

"The man at the stable said a rancher nearby left her with him to sell. He's had some hard luck and needs money."

The redhead lovingly stroked the pinto's neck. She gathered part of the white mane into her hand and studied it. She leaned forward and checked the animal's eyes. "How

132

much is he asking?"

"One-twenty-five. She seems well-trained and in good condition."

Happy to find a good getaway mount, the redhead added, "She has strong legs and a sleek hide. Her teeth are good and she has healthy hooves. And her eyes are clear. She's worth it."

T.J. was impressed by her knowledge and skill, but they increased his curiosity. She sat the pinto and handled her as if she'd been born in a saddle. If she'd been a rancher's daughter, he could understand such traits, but how did a schoolmarm know so much about horses?

"I love riding," she murmured dreamily. "I did it all the time back home. The horse I had in St. Louis was too old to make the trip here. I'm glad you found this one for me to buy. She's special."

"I'm glad you like her," T.J. replied, telling himself to relax or he wouldn't get any additional information out of her.

"I love her," the daring desperado corrected. "I'm going to buy her."

"You planning to change her name?" he teased.

"No. Charlie sounds good for a bright-eyed pinto. You ready to eat? I skipped breakfast and I'm starving."

T.J. guided her into a ravine where small bushes and squat trees along its eastern rim provided shade in the narrow, winding gulch. He dismounted and went to help her, but she was off the animal's back with noticeable agility. He put the basket on the ground and spread his blanket against the gully wall. "Let's eat, woman."

Carrie Sue sat on a blanket near T.J. and unwrapped the chicken and biscuits. She handed him a cloth and said, "I didn't want to risk breaking any of Mrs. Thayer's dishes on the trail. She's a wonderful woman. We've become good friends."

As they helped themselves and began to eat, he remarked, "It was smart of you to get up early to fry chicken and bake biscuits."

The redhead grinned and confessed, "I didn't. Mrs. Thayer insisted. She likes you, but she doesn't care for Martin Ferris at all and likes to help me avoid him."

He stopped eating to question, "Why?"

Carrie Sue decided to be completely honest on the matter. "Helen Cooper used to live at her boarding house. Mrs. Thayer didn't like the way Mr. Ferris treated the woman," she disclosed. "She doesn't believe Miss Cooper's death was an accident."

"Why do you think he killed her?"

Carrie Sue eyed him intently. "You sure she wasn't a friend of yours? Did you visit her when you came to town?"

"Nope. I didn't know her." He reached for another chicken thigh.

"Then why are you so interested in how she died?"

He drank from his canteen and offered her some water. "Because of you, Carolyn, your safety. Why do you think he did it?"

She was glad he cared enough to worry about her. "I think she was pregnant and he didn't want to marry her or create a scandal."

Surprise registered on his face. "What makes you think that?"

"Mrs. Thayer told me she was sick every morning just before she died. She also said Martin would summon her every few days and she didn't want to go, but seemed afraid not to mind him. He was probably threatening to fire her and she was terrified of him and losing her job."

"You aren't scared he'll do the same with you?"

"No, because I won't let him get to me," she vowed with confidence. "I would like to avoid any problems with Martin Ferris, but that's up to him. Can you open this can?" she asked, handing it to him.

He drew his concealed knife and complied. "He's gonna be plenty mad when he discovers you gone with me again."

"That's too bad because I can't let him control my new life and I can't hide from him every day. The last time I tried, I nearly got stung by a scorpion." She related the perilous incident at the school.

T.J. was amazed again by her courage and wits. This woman was not an ordinary schoolmarm, or an ordinary female! "You're a mighty brave and clever woman, Carolyn."

She handed him a fork and placed the can between them. "Thanks, but I have to be. My parents taught me to be independent. I've had to learn to take care of myself. I just hope I remember how next week."

After he took a bite of a peach, he asked, "What happens next week?"

She put her chicken biscuit aside. "The Mayor is giving a party for the so-called important people in town. I have to attend."

"Have to?" he stressed evocatively.

"Unless I want to offend everyone. Haven't you ever had to do something you didn't want to do, but felt you must to avoid trouble?"

"I try my damnedest to do as I please." He chuckled. "You know Ferris isn't going to leave you alone. He wants you, Carolyn, and he goes after what he wants. He can be sly and deadly."

Her purply blue eyes widened and her lips parted. She licked her dry lips. "You've met him before during your visits here, haven't you?"

He realized he had to tell her a few things about himself for her to keep opening up to him, and he wanted to know all about her. Besides, she could learn about his connection to Ferris from the man himself. "Yep. The problem I settled for Carrillo was over a land dispute with Martin Ferris, mainly water rights. You must realize how valuable

135

water is out here, and Ferris wanted it all. Carrillo paid me to make sure his cattle got water until the court settled the matter, which went in Carrillo's favor. Riled Ferris pretty badly."

"Merciful Heavens, you two are old enemies! That makes my seeing you worse for him. I bet he's burning like a wildfire about now."

"You care if it riles him to see me?"

She considered the dilemma. "I guess not. I can't live my new life worrying about pleasing a ba . . . beast like that. Either Tucson will work out for me or it won't. I can always move on to another town."

T.J. wondered why she kept saying "new life" and why she almost slipped into rough language ever so often. "Become a drifter like me?"

She stared out over the desert terrain. "No, I want to settle down this time. I'm getting too old to move around so much."

"Too old at twenty-one?" he jested.

"No, I'm . . ." Carrie Sue focused her attention on the food in her lap. "I'm just ready to grow some roots. I haven't had a real home since . . . back East."

"You women want and need homes, don't you?"

"Doesn't everyone, T.J., at some point in their lives? Wouldn't you like to shake the dust from your boots? Wouldn't you like to have a nice place to run to instead of bad ones to run from?"

T.J. forced himself not to look at her. Carolyn affected him in a curious way, a potent one. He was wary, though, because she was the kind of woman who would insist on love, commitment, and marriage from a man: things he had no time for at this point in his life. Lordy, he wanted her badly, but his surrender held a big price. Yet, he absently murmured, "Someday."

"This is my someday, partner. I was hoping it would work out, but I'm afraid Martin Ferris will mess it up for me."

She looked sad and frightened for a moment, which tugged at his embittered heart. He was responsible for the deaths of Arabella and Marie because he had asked them to meet him in Fort Worth where they could become a family and settle down, where he could carry out his responsibilities to the woman and child. Fate hadn't allowed him to become a husband and father, to perform his duty, to find peace and happiness. Now, he wanted Carolyn Starns to settle down with because she made him feel comfortable and enlivened, because she respected him and accepted him as is, because she created a white-heat in him which burned throughout his mind and body. Yet, he was afraid such an entrapping blaze would consume him and destroy her, and he despised fear and weakness. By seeing her, he was endangering her, especially where Ferris was concerned. The moment he left her side, Ferris would be on her like a starving bee on an exquisite flower! "You want to hire me to make certain he doesn't?"

Carrie Sue fused her gaze to his. He wasn't smiling. "Are you serious? What could you do to get him off my back? Legally."

"Don't want me breaking the law for you, huh?" After she shook her head, he suggested, "We could find a way to pin that woman's murder on him."

"It happened too long ago. We'd never find any evidence or a witness against him. That's one crime he'll get away with."

"What about pinning that attempted holdup on him. It was a secret, so he had to be behind it. Rumor said he wasn't responsible for the gold until the shipment was in his hands. If it never reached him, publicly that is, he has the gold and his silver. Quite a clever scheme. He probably knows I suspect the truth."

"Aren't you afraid he'll come after you?" she questioned anxiously.

"He's too smart to challenge me."

Carrie Sue knew he wasn't boasting, just confident in his skills and wits. "How can we prove he was involved?"

"I'll give it some thought." He wanted to have Martin Ferris out of the way before he left her here alone.

They ate silently for a time, then she asked, "Which side did you fight on in the war?"

"I fought with a man named Grant. He's President now."

She looked shocked. "You sided with the Union?"

"I reckon so. I saved Grant's life once. This man called Sharpe was playing on both sides of the fence and nearly got Grant killed. It happened in August of '64 at City Point, Virginia. Some Confederate spies got into camp and set off explosions. Stuff went flying everywhere, and Grant just sat there calm as could be."

"But I thought you saved his life."

"I did. One of the spies tried to shoot him before escaping, but I shot the careless Reb first. From then on, I was Grant's bodyguard till the war ended and I returned to Texas."

"Why did a Texan fight for the North?"

"I didn't start out on either side, just went there to look around. Since I hated slavery and the South favored it, I put in with the Yanks."

Carrie Sue didn't want to argue the reasons for the war, as she believed both sides had been in error, partially from misunderstandings. She had detected a coldness, a bitterness, in the way he said *slavery*. How curious for a gunslinger to have such strong feelings about it!

"What happened after the war?" she inquired pleasantly.

He shrugged as he put away his fork and napkin. It wouldn't hurt to relate things she already knew or seemed logical. "Nothing much. I was always getting into trouble. I didn't seem to fit anywhere. Maybe that's why people think I'm so tough; I had to be to survive. I lost my entire family at age seven, so I had to learn to be independent while I was

138

still a snot-nosed kid. I guess I grew up too fast and too hard. I had a reputation as a gunslinger before nineteen, so my path was marked."

"Were you ever in trouble with the law?" she inquired. If he had, then perhaps he could understand where and how she had gone wrong.

"Yep. That priest who helped raise me was murdered, but not before he told me who shot him and why. It was a crooked deputy. I went after him and killed him. The law didn't take much to having a starred man shot, so I was put in jail. I can tell you, woman, it ain't a good place to be. You could say that's why I've always stayed just over the line; I don't want that experience again."

Her heart pounded. Her lips were parted and dry. Her respiration was erratic. She hung on every word he spoke. "It must have been terrible."

"Try being a legend without your gun. Every prisoner in there wanted a piece of me, and every guard too. I'm lucky I survived to be released. Make sure you watch your step 'cause it's worse for women, especially one who looks like you. Those guards would devour you like dessert."

If the truth about her came out, at least he could understand why she wanted to avoid prison at any cost. When she had gotten entangled with the law, she had been young, reckless, and bitter. She had been blinded by hatred for the Hardings and misguided by love for her brother. She had thought only of the present, the punishment of her parent's killers, not considered or foreseen her future as an outlaw. Yet, even a man like T.J. Rogue had managed to stay on the right side of the law. Would he blame her for not doing so? "How did you earn a pardon?" she asked eagerly.

"I didn't. I told them everything when I was arrested. There was one lawman who wanted justice done so he tracked down the truth. If not for him, I'd be dead. 'Course, that same lawman will track me down and stick me in prison the moment I walk crooked." He reflected on

139

his friend Hank Peterson, but didn't mention his name.

"You were lucky, but you were innocent."

"Lots of innocent men filling up prisons, Carolyn."

"I suppose that's true. What about men who've made mistakes but want to go straight? How do they earn pardons?"

"Don't ask me. Never heard it done before, not to anybody I know." T.J. watched her eager anticipation alter to sadness and misery. He wondered if she knew someone in that predicament, someone special.

"That's a shame. I'm sure lots of men would do it if given the chance. Life on the run must be awful. Didn't it make you feel wonderful to do something good, like when you saved Grant's life?"

He looked at her oddly. "You know what I mean, T.J.," she explained nervously. "Don't you like doing things which improve your reputation?"

"I don't have a good reputation to worry about."

"You could have if you worked at it. You aren't as cold and hard as people say. Why don't you let people see the side of you I've seen?"

He stared at her. His body temperature was rising by the second, and not from the sun. Those periwinkle eyes were softly caressing him; those full lips were enticing him; and her gentle, hungry spirit was reaching out to him. Lordy, self-control was nearly impossible to maintain! He felt as if he were in a hot oven being baked by that smoldering gaze and fiery aura. "What side is that, Carolyn?"

She noticed how long he had observed her and how his body was responding to her intentional allure. She had to know what it was like to kiss him, to be in his arms. She had to help him learn to relax, to trust, to find peace, to yield to love. How wonderful it would be to learn those things together. If he came to love her and want her, her dark past wouldn't matter to him. "You're kind and gentle and courteous. You have a sensitive, generous nature, Mr.

Rogue, but you try to hide it. Why?"

"Traits like those make a man look weak, and weak men get themselves killed out here. I'm not as nice as you think," he remarked, praying she would halt her innocent attack on his warring senses. If she didn't in a few minutes, he would lose his head and be all over her!

Carrie Sue shook her head. "You'll never convince me of that. You're too hard on yourself, T.J."

He looked away and teased, "Then I'll let you remain stubbornly mistaken, woman. The food was good. Thank Mrs. Thayer for me," he said, changing the subject.

She accepted his clue to back off for now before she scared him too much. "Maria helped her, so I'll thank both of them."

"Maria?" he echoed, his gaze narrowing and chilling. The name reminded him of the deaths of Arabella and Marie. He swore once again to track down and kill the gang who attacked their stage and murdered them, just as soon as he killed a man who was to arrive here soon.

"You know Maria Corbeza at the boarding house?"

"No."

"She's the Mexican girl who helps Mrs. Thayer with the cooking and cleaning. She's very nice, but shy and quiet." She had noticed his reaction to the female's name. He was now moody and silent, and rapidly packing up the remains of their picnic so they could leave. She tried to draw him out by asking, "Which mine are you going to try?"

"None soon. I have business to finish here first."

"What about my shooting lessons?"

"Another day."

"Is something wr—" Gunfire cut off her question.

T.J. tossed aside the items in his hands. He grabbed her head and shoved her face down on the blanket, shouting, "Keep down and still!" His gaze followed the line of fire to a large pile of rocks near the curve of the deep gulch. He concluded that the men—just out of pistol range—were either bad shots with rifles and were only trying to scare them, or pin them down beneath the blazing sun which was overhead by this time of day.

"Can you see anyone?" she asked, her voice muffled by her position.

"Looks like three men in the rocks over there. Stay put while I get my rifle," he ordered. But when he tried to move in the direction of the horses, more bullets splattered the dry earth around them like a heavy rainfall. "We can't stay here in the open; they have a clear shot at this ravine. I'm going to push you up the bank on three. Get behind those bushes and lie flat on the ground."

Carrie Sue readied herself to scramble up the steep incline. When he reached "three," she struggled with the sandy bank and finally conquered its rim with T.J. pushing on her rear and feet. She stretched out her hand toward him and shouted, "Hurry!"

He threw her one of his revolvers as he commanded, "Get down, woman! Don't worry about me!" He raced for the horses and yanked his rifle from its saddle holster before vanishing around a bend in the gully. He wanted to use the hill nearby to get a closer view and better advantage. By the way the men opened up rapid fire on him after Carolyn was out of danger, he knew the men were after him and she would be safe for a while.

Carrie Sue realized what T.J. was trying to do, get behind their attackers. But their foes would make the same conclusion and be prepared to thwart him. She aimed T.J.'s pistol and fired toward the men to check its range. Gunfire wasn't returned. The bullet struck short of their foe's hiding place. It was rifle range, and she didn't have one to help her partner. She studied the landscape between her and their peril. Several smaller piles of large rocks were between them. Since the men seemed to have their full attention on T.J., she decided she could move closer and get into pistol range.

The redhead peered around the bushes to plan her path to the rocks, which included dodging cactus, scrubs, and spiny yuccas. She brushed the dirt and grit from her bloody hands and gripped the butt firmly, noticing the "T.J.,R." carved into it. She was wearing a split-tail riding skirt which reached the tops of her boots, so she needed to be careful of the bushes and cacti snagging it and delaying her progress. She took a few deep breaths, then raced for the rocks. Three warning shots were sent her way, but no man was that bad of a shot, she reasoned.

Carrie Sue remained low for a short time, then peeked around the edge of the largest rock. Her gaze scanned for T.J. and she saw him sliding forward on his belly just behind a rise of the hard ground. To give him time and cover, she fired two shots at their foes, nicking one in the arm. Suddenly she heard a sound which made her freeze. Without moving, her gaze searched the rocks for the rattler she had disturbed.

If T.J.'s gun had been fully loaded when he gave it to her, she had three bullets left. She dared not lift the pistol to check her ammunition, as movement would antagonize the already annoyed viper. Since he was shading himself during the heat of the day, he didn't want to move, and he was making it loudly known that he wanted her to do so.

The redhead knew she could not shift her legs to rise without being in the rattler's striking range. She hurriedly gave the manner serious thought. If she used her bullets on the snake, if the gun contained more, she would be defenseless against the villains nearby. So far, the men seemed interested only in T.J., but she couldn't be certain.

The ebon-haired man began firing at their attackers from his new position. Carrie Sue had faith in his prowess, so she fired twice at the rattler who was coming her way to make his threatening point. The wounded viper thrashed on the ground, fighting death to the last moment.

Her shots confused T.J. and he shouted, "Carolyn,

143

what's up?"

"A rattler, but I got him! I'm fine!" she yelled back to him.

The three villains rushed to their horses and galloped away, a hill protecting their escape. T.J. ran to where she was sitting, as he knew the men would be out of range before he could pursue them. He glanced at the snake, then at her. "You're a damn good shot, woman."

"We had snakes in . . . Charleston, too. Sorry I wasn't any help."

"That was a stupid thing to do. You challenge danger like you have nine lives. They got away, but two of them are wounded. Not badly enough to suit me. Let's get moving before they come back."

The flaming haired fugitive knew the attackers wouldn't return, and knew T.J. didn't think so. "What about my lessons?"

His smokey gray eyes looked her over, then he replied, "From what I've seen, you don't need any shooting or riding lessons. You hurt?" he asked, noticing bloody spots on her skirt.

"Just scuffed hands. I'll tend them when I get home. What do you think they wanted?"

T.J. stared in the direction of the villains' flight. He was intrigued by the skill and ease with which this schoolmarm handled a gun. But he had other matters to consider at this time. He suspected that Martin Ferris was behind this reckless attack. Obviously the cattle baron hadn't forgotten their run-in years ago and didn't like the relationship with the woman he'd staked out for himself. Ferris probably wanted to show Carolyn that she needed the protection of a wealthy and powerful man once her rescuer was gone. But if Ferris wanted to make him look weak in front of Carolyn, it hadn't worked, as his hirelings would report soon. Or maybe Ferris wanted him dead.

"Well?" she hinted. "What do you think?"

"Probably was Ferris trying to scare me off his woman."

"I'm not his woman," she protested.

"We know that, but he doesn't. I'll check on those men after we reach town."

"Did you get a good look at them?"

"Nope, but two wounded men can't hide easily. Let's go, Red."

"Don't call me that!" she stated harshly.

"Sorry, Miss Starns, no insult intended."

Carrie Sue lied to cover her slip, "When I was a child, that's how I was teased. I hated it, but I didn't mean to snap at you."

"Don't worry about it. I understand."

They gathered the remains from their picnic and mounted their horses. In silence they rode for town.

Carrie Sue reflected on the despicable detective who had tracked her down twice for Quade Harding. He had loved calling her "Red." If given half a chance, he would have discarded Quade's reward and orders to take her for himself! She hated both of those evil men!

T.J. furtively watched the woman nearby. Something was eating at her, something she tried to keep under control. She was such a compelling mystery. The more she related and exposed about herself, the more confused and ensnared he became. She had been so relaxed with him, but her guard was up again and he wondered why.

At the boarding house corral, Carrie Sue asked T.J. if he would tell the man at the stable she was buying Charlie on Monday when the bank opened. "Do you think he'll mind if I keep her until I pay him?"

"I'll pay him today, then you can repay me on Monday when I bring you the sale papers. A rough livery stable is no place for a lady."

Carrie Sue wondered what a gunslinging drifter was doing with so much money and why he was willing to handle the transaction. She smiled and thanked him for his

145

many kindnesses. He didn't mention the gun he had taken along today for her to try out, so she didn't either. She watched him leave, then went inside to see Mrs. Thayer.

The woman listened to the redhead's tale and frowned. "I bet Martin Ferris was sending you a message to keep away from Mr. Rogue or he'd kill him. You two be careful," she urged.

Carrie Sue also frowned, as she hadn't taken the attack in that light. If Martin Ferris was as dangerous and determined as she believed, then he would have T.J. slain without another thought. A famous gunslinger's death would entice a great deal of attention and gossip, but that wasn't why she wanted to protect the ebon-haired man. She cautioned herself to rethink her situation, her desires, her perils.

T.J. saw three men go out the back way to Ferris's office. They were wearing different clothes. One man was rubbing the edge of his shoulder like he had a flesh wound there, and another had something thick beneath his right sleeve, the size of a bandage. He trailed them to a saloon and watched them go inside. He carefully approached their horses at the hitching post. Two saddles displayed fresh drops of dried blood. He had an answer to the question of who was involved. He just didn't know the real motive yet. Without evidence the sheriff could use for arrests, all he could do was antagonize them into a showdown to punish them. He warned himself against calling out the men today and exposing his hand. But before he left Tucson, Ferris and his hirelings would pay their debts to him.

Carrie Sue went to church again Sunday morning with Mrs. Thayer. They made certain they sat on a pew which didn't allow room for Martin Ferris to squeeze into when he arrived shortly after them.

She paid little attention to the preacher's sermon as she was ensnared by deep concerns. She wondered if she should try to get a message to Darby to let him know she had arrived safely and had been accepted here as the schoolmarm. She didn't want her brother distracted by worry over her. She was also distressed over Martin Ferris's attack on T.J. Rogue. She asked herself if she should not see him again before his departure to protect him from further attempts on his life. She also needed to protect herself against suspicion and dislike once he was gone, and she never doubted he would leave town soon. Even if he was as drawn to her as she was to him, their bond wasn't strong enough to hold him here or to bind him to her yet. When and if he realized and accepted the truth about them, hopefully he would return to her.

After the service ended, Carrie Sue and Mrs. Thayer tried to leave quickly. Her ploy to avoid Martin Ferris didn't work. He hurried after them, calling her name. She had no choice but to halt and speak.

"I need to talk with you privately, Miss Starns," he said sternly.

"We can talk tomorrow at the boarding house if you like."

"This can't wait," he persisted, taking her arm and excusing them to walk a few feet away from the dispersing crowd and Mrs. Thayer.

"What is it, Mr. Ferris?" she inquired innocently.

"I don't think it's wise for you to be seeing that gunslinger socially. Some friends saw you two out to supper the other night and are gossiping about it. You have to be more careful with your behavior. You two were alone on the road after that attempted holdup, and people might think bad things about you if you continue seeing a common drifter. You have to be above reproach as our schoolmarm. I wouldn't want you getting fired over a rash friendship with a gunslinger."

"That gunslinger saved my life, Mr. Ferris, and I like him."

Martin frowned. "I've already rewarded him for saving your life and my gold, and you've thanked him; that's sufficient for a man like him. That little picnic yesterday was most foolish. What do you think people will say about you two taking off into the wilderness alone?"

"I didn't know there were any restrictions on my private life, Mr. Ferris. I'm unaccustomed to being told with whom I can make friends or see socially, as long as I conduct myself like a lady, which I have."

"It isn't ladylike to spend time alone with a man like Rogue."

"Do you know him personally?" she asked.

He shifted and glanced at the ground. "Not well, but I know his type. I know he's handsome and exciting to you women, but he has a bad image. Men like that take advantage of good women and ruin their reputations. I'm giving you a friendly warning, Carolyn; he'll cause you trouble here. Considering your example to our children, especially to the young boys who are duped by colorful legends, I must insist you don't see him again. If you need a horse, I'll gladly furnish one for you. If you're too proud to accept one as a gift, I'll make you a good price and let you pay me off a little each month."

"That's very kind, Mr. Ferris, but unnecessary. I purchased one yesterday, a beautiful pinto from a local rancher. Mr. Rogue found her for me at the livery and I was trying her out today."

"I see. You will consider my warning before the town council hears about this offensive manner and summons you for a serious meeting."

"Of course," she responded in a casual tone. "But I don't like justifying innocent actions to strangers. If they feel they must interfere in my personal life, I may have to reconsider such a demanding job. Good-bye, Mr. Ferris. I'll see you in church next Sunday."

"I'll pick you up Saturday night at six-thirty for the party at Mayor Carlson's. You haven't forgotten about it, have you?"

"Certainly not. I'll be ready. Thanks for the kind escort." Carrie Sue walked off while he was gloating over his minor victory. She would accept a ride with him to the party. Maybe that would keep him sated for a while! One thing, she knew he had lied to her, had exposed himself without realizing it: Mrs. Thayer had not told him about the picnic, she told him Carolyn was out looking at horses with T.J. Rogue. There was only one way he could have known about the picnic.

Carrie Sue completed her bath. She had been sweaty and dusty from a windy walk with Mrs. Thayer and other boarders after supper. She had spent a quiet afternoon in her rooms, studying lessons. It was nine o'clock and most of the guests were in their rooms for the night. She left the water closet and returned to her room, bolting the door.

She leaned against the door and sighed heavily with her eyes closed. The sitting room was dim, as only one oil lamp was burning low. She sensed a presence. Her eyes opened quickly. Her hand rushed to her right side as she shifted rapidly to check out the front corner of the room.

Chapter Eight

Carrie Sue didn't know what to say to the handsome man who was lazing in the corner as if this was his room, or theirs. One elbow was resting on the chair arm, causing that shoulder to rise slightly. His other arm was laying across his flat stomach. His head was leaning against the back of the chair. His long legs were stretched before him and were crossed at the ankles. Yet, he didn't look totally relaxed as his negligent position implied. He didn't move or speak. Nor did she.

The dim light cast a rosy glow in the room and on T.J.'s face. He kept staring at her. She struggled to break the tight hold of his gaze, and finally succeeded. His gunbelt was draped over the chair at the desk, where his hat was placed. She looked back at him. His shirt was unbuttoned to his heart, exposing a hard and hairy chest. His smokey gray eyes were locked on her face.

She felt tension in the room, within herself, exuding from T.J., but it was a strange suspense and excitement. It was almost as if they were communicating on a mental level. Each seemed to be summoning the courage to say and do something important.

T.J. stood and walked to her. Their gazes fused. He was aware of her state of dress, a nightgown and wrapper. She was barefooted, fresh from a bath. Damp wisps of fiery hair clung to her face, the remaining blaze of glory cascading down her back. Her periwinkle eyes were entreating. She was hesitant, but unafraid of him. This time, she did not avert her gaze when he aroused her.

His fiery gaze traveled down her face to her throat where he watched the pounding of her heart revealed at her pulse point. Lordy, sneaking here to speak with her was a stupid thing to do! If he didn't get out of here pronto, he would complicate her life and his, and the tasks before him. Right now, he had nothing to offer her, at least nothing she needed in her unpredictable existence in this new town. He lowered his gaze to where her chest was rising and falling erratically beneath her cotton garments. *Get out fast, Rogue!*

Carrie Sue knew she wanted and needed this man. He would be leaving soon, and she couldn't bear that, not without having him first. She had to let him know how she felt about him, about them, and hopefully that knowledge would lure him back to her one day. Her hands cupped his jawline and she lifted his head to lock their gazes. "It's all right, T.J.," she murmured, then kissed him.

She was pressed to the door by his strong body and ardent response. His hands went into her hair and pulled her mouth more tightly against his. The kiss exposed their deepest longings, their fiercest desires. His mouth roamed her face, his lips tasting the sweetness of her flesh and savoring its soft texture. Each trembled.

"Lordy, how I want you and need you, woman," he murmured.

Fires licked at Carrie Sue's body. She kissed him greedily, her mouth seeming to ravish his neck and upper chest. "I'm glad you're here," she whispered against his muscled torso.

After several more stimulating kisses, he gathered her into his arms and carried her into the other room to lay her on the bed.

They embraced, caressed, and kissed for a long time, even though their aching bodies were screaming for release. It wasn't necessary to whet their appetites or to enflame their senses; they had wanted this moment since meeting that morning at the home station. It just seemed natural to tantalize each other and themselves. His lips brushed over her features, and her hands caressed his lean back. His fingers trailed down her neck, and hers wandered over his shoulders. His mouth followed the path his fingers had burned down her chest, and her lips pressed against his ebony hair. He unbuttoned her gown, and she let him continue without protest.

Carrie Sue shifted to assist him with the removal of her garments. She finished unbuttoning his shirt and he yanked it off with eagerness to rejoin her, flinging it to the floor. He pulled off his boots and removed his jeans, then snuggled with her again.

He wished he could see her, but the room was too dark. Yet he remembered every line and curve on her face and body. He closed his eyes and thought of the prettiest sunset he had viewed. She was even more beautiful, more tranquil, more colorful, more inspiring. Her hair flamed like the rich reds and golds of a setting sun in the hottest of summers, or like the sleek hide of a wild sorrel racing across a sunny landscape. Sometimes her eyes reminded him of the purplish blue shade of the sky at dusk, or the periwinkle haze over the mountainous horizon. Other times her eyes were like two violet-blue flowers which bloomed in spring and demanded he gaze at them. Her flesh smelled like a morning rain, fresh and clean and scented with wildflowers. Her skin was soft, and golden where the sun had kissed it. Her body was lean, yet supple and stimulating. Pressing their naked bodies together made him shudder with need.

As he caressed her and kissed her, Carrie Sue felt like

honey warmed and softened by a brilliant sun, as if she were so limp she would melt into the bed beneath them. His hands were strong, yet fondled her with amazing gentleness. His kisses were urgent, but tenderly stirring. She loved the feel of him, his hard muscles which were honed to perfection, his downy soft skin, his lithe limbs which moved with agility, the rises and falls of his shapely frame where her bold fingers wandered. She loved his smell: masculine, clean, invigorating. There was such a strength about him, such an aura of confidence, such a fiery glow which spread to her. She savored the way he made her feel, the way he worked so lovingly, so leisurely, so skillfully on her body. She had never felt this way before and she wanted to burn every moment into her memory.

"You've been driving me crazy with hunger, woman. I don't think I could have resisted you another day. This is loco, but I can't help myself," he admitted hoarsely as he nibbled at her ear. She was exciting and mysterious. She was intelligent, but never made others feel inferior. She was gentle, sensitive, hard-working. She had a compelling strength and courage about her. Yet, she could be bold and stubborn and impulsive, a feisty spitfire.

Consumed by desire and ravenous for him, she replied, "Neither can I, T.J., neither can I."

His lips and tongue drifted to her breasts and stimulated her to writhing passion. When his hand roamed lower and touched her where no man ever had, she arched her back and inhaled sharply. With patience and gentleness, he aroused her until she cried out for a blissful end to this madness which had her engulfed.

T.J. entered her womanly domain, knowledgeable enough to know this was her first time. Joy and pride surged through him when he realized she had chosen him for this special moment. He was very careful not to move too swiftly or forcefully. Once she adjusted to his size and presence, he set a steady pace to carry her back to the fiery heights of passion's peak which she had left briefly.

Carrie Sue seemed to know instinctively what to do. She curled her legs over his and responded to his thrusts and withdrawals with a matching pace and pattern. She returned his kisses and spread her own over his face and neck. His back was moist and her fingers ardently slipped along its surface, admiring its feel and labor beneath them.

T.J. couldn't believe this was happening for him. Lady Luck was finally smiling on him. This fiery treasure had been dangled under his nose for twelve days but he never thought he could claim it and enjoy it, or be allowed by cruel fate to do so. Maybe she was his good luck charm, the woman to change his life, his means of escaping his troubled past. She was here with him, joined to him as no other person had ever been, responding to him as no female ever had. It wouldn't have worked out with Arabella; Carolyn was proving that at this moment.

He didn't know much about love, but he had heard enough to know what he was feeling for this woman had to be love, and that she was responding to him because she felt it, too. But how would she feel about him tomorrow? Next week? Next year? He had vengeful promises to keep, promises made before this mute one to her. How would she feel when she discovered he was little more than a hired killer? A man who used his guns and skills to solve other's problems? She would hate him when he walked away from her soon, hate him for misleading her tonight. And he had misled her by allowing her to believe this action would lead to marriage, for she was that kind of woman. He couldn't marry her until he settled some old debts . . . if he survived. By then, since he couldn't explain anything to her, she would be lost forever. Maybe that was why he had needed her so badly tonight, maybe why he had taken this perilous risk. For some reason, he didn't have the strength to leave Tucson without knowing her this way.

Passions built higher between them, taking away his fears and worries. His mouth covered hers, his tongue dancing wildly with hers. He felt her tense and arch, her nails digging into his back but not as painfully as the barbwire had done.

Over rapture's peak they fell together, riding on ecstasy's powerful waves. They came together blissfully, almost savagely, until they were drained of all tension. They lay nestled together on the damp sheet, reluctant to move apart, reluctant to speak and break the magical spell around them.

Carrie Sue's head rested on his chest and she listened to the thundering of his heart which surely beat with the same emotions that filled hers. She loved him and he belonged to her now. She had wanted him; she had staked her claim on him. She had branded him with her love and he could never run free again like the wild mustang he had been. By coming to her tonight, he had surrendered his freedom, he had torn down the wall around him, he had exposed his feelings for her.

T.J. heard her sigh peacefully as she snuggled closer to him. He wished it could be this way forever for them, but it couldn't. Should he tell her the truth about their situation? No, he didn't want to spoil this special night, or hurt her so soon after it. He would tell her tomorrow, tell her as much as he dared.

When he realized that the woman in his arms had fallen asleep, he gingerly shifted her to the other pillow to keep from awakening her. He rose from the bed and dressed. A dim glow entered the door from the lamp in the next room. He looked down at the dark form in the bed and his heart pained him deeply. She had been so honest and giving with him, but he had not done the same with her. She had let down her guard to allow him to enter her life, but he couldn't back away from his destiny. He retrieved his holster and hat. He locked the door from the outside and shoved the key under it into her room. Stealthily he left the boarding house without being seen or heard.

Carrie Sue stretched lazily and yawned. She felt wonderful, rested, happy, free. She knew T.J. was gone, else she would have sensed his presence and inhaled his manly odor the moment she awoke. Her hands moved over the bed where she had first experienced blissful love. Yes, love, she vowed peacefully. No matter what happened to her now, she loved T.J. and he loved her. They would have each other.

Carrie Sue bolted upright in bed. No, she warned herself, she couldn't be so dreamy-eyed and naive. Fate always stepped in and ruined things for her! She had to walk slowly and carefully this time. Making love was not the same as being in love. What if T.J. didn't feel the same way? At least not yet? And if he did, what should she tell him about herself? When should she expose the dark truth? Would it change things between them? What if she remained as Carolyn Starns and told him nothing about her criminal past? If she was never unmasked . . . No, she argued with herself, she couldn't continue her lies into their future. If he learned the truth weeks or months or years from now, it could damage their relationship.

"You're riding too fast down an unfamiliar path, Carrie Sue. First, you need to discover his intentions before you mark your trail for him to follow."

The daring desperado remembered something else: she hadn't told T.J. what she had learned yesterday from Martin Ferris. Perhaps she could go to the bank, withdraw the money for Charlie, then head for the stable to see if her love was there checking on his horse. If not, she could . . . wander to the place he was staying and see him under the public pretense of eating there.

Carrie Sue bounded eagerly out of bed. She used the water pitcher and basin to remove the sights and scents of rapturous lovemaking. She quickly checked the sheets, relieved to find no telltale blood there. She donned one of the prettiest dresses in her closet and a matching sunbonnet, bravely allowing her tawny red mane to flow freely down her back. She felt aglow, as if nothing could go wrong today. After speaking briefly with Mrs. Thayer, she was off to the bank and the livery stable.

Sheriff Ben Myers was in the bank. He smiled genially and greeted her. Carrie Sue did the same with him. Recalling that the rewards were one thing keeping her love in Tucson, she inquired innocently, "When do you expect the rewards for those stage bandits to arrive? I'm certain Mr. Rogue wants to get them before he leaves town."

Sheriff Myers's left brow lifted quizzically. "Did he forget to share with you, Miss Starns? I paid him that day you two arrived. The bank always keeps a fund for rewards so bounty hunters and the likes won't have to hang around waiting for them. When they come in, I just replace the money I withdrew. Is he cheating you out of your part?"

"Oh, no, sir," she vowed. "I told him I didn't want any of that blood money. I just wondered why he was hanging around so long. Drifters don't usually do that, do they?" Carrie Sue hoped she didn't sound like a blithering idiot.

"No, ma'am, they don't. I think he just wants to rest up a spell before heading out. He ain't been into no trouble here, so I leave him be. Men like to do heavy drinking and gambling when they get unexpected money in their pockets."

They chatted for a few more minutes before Carrie Sue left with the money to pay for Charlie, from Carolyn Starns's account. She fretted over T.J.'s lie, but did she have any room to fault him when she'd concealed worse things from him? Maybe he had only used that excuse to explain why he was lingering here because he hadn't wanted her to know how he felt about her.

The beautiful redhead reached the livery stable which was within walking distance from the bank. The smithy met her at the door as he was leaving for his midday meal. When she asked if T.J. Rogue had paid him for Charlie, the dirty but amiable man nodded. She thanked him for finding the pinto for her and asked about Nighthawk's injury.

The burly man who had more muscles than wits sent her a cordial grin. "Rogue's black stallion is fine, Miss. He ain't got no injured leg."

"A stone bruise under his front hoof," she clarified.

He scratched his greasy head and replied, "Nope. He was in perfect shape when Rogue got here, and he's still thataway. 'Course he needs a good run. Rogue's been renting a horse from me for some crazy reason. That black stallion is strong; he don't need no rest."

Carrie Sue laughed at what appeared her mistake. "Perhaps I misunderstood. I thought his horse must be injured since he was riding a strange one. Anyway, thanks for helping me find Charlie."

"You want me to give Rogue a message if he comes by?" he offered.

"No thanks. I'll have someone take the money over to his hotel. Since the bank was closed Saturday and I didn't want to risk losing Charlie to another buyer, he loaned me the payment."

"You got a good deal. That's the best horse in the territory. I told Bill I wouldn't show him to nobody but a good buyer."

Carrie Sue headed for the boarding house to get her dirty clothes to take to the laundress before she went shopping for a saddle. She was baffled by T.J.'s two lies. If Nighthawk wasn't hurt and he had received his rewards, what was keeping him in Tucson? If he had needed a woman, there were plenty for sale in the saloons, and he had plenty of money in his pockets. Had he stayed because of her? For what reason? Because she was irresistible as he had claimed last night, or because he knew or suspected who she was?

Surely the famous T.J. Rogue, a Texan, had heard of the Stover Gang, and might have met some of its members. But he wasn't an outlaw and he seemed determined not to become one. She knew from gossip that he was a trouble-shooting gunslinger who hired out for pay, but he wasn't a cold-blooded killer or a bounty hunter. At least she had never heard of him doing such things. He had to move around a lot because she had never run into him.

Maybe her lover was on a secret job here, but he couldn't or wouldn't tell her about it. Maybe he'd been paid by the Garret line or someone else to protect that gold shipment, which would explain why he hadn't stolen that yellow treasure after the attempted holdup and why he was so resolved to get it to Tucson safely. That would also explain why he'd been close enough to the stage to give assistance. Or perhaps he had gone into the bounty hunting business and had been after those men who tried to rob the stage.

Or perhaps he was after Martin Ferris again. He did ask a lot of questions about the slain schoolmarm. Maybe he was working for her family or a friend of Helen Cooper's. Maybe Martin Ferris had made enemies with someone else or was harassing Carrillo again. Something had happened between the two men long ago and perhaps it hadn't been settled to T.J.'s liking. A horrible thought entered her warring mind, surely Martin Ferris wasn't the one responsible for that barbwire incident! If so, it was a good reason for Martin to fear T.J. and want him dead. Or, want him slain for intruding on his affairs years ago. T.J. was interested in Martin and asked plenty of questions about the offensive man. If he was after Martin again, that told her why he kept warning her away from the vile beast. And if that was the case, she needed to avoid becoming entangled in their private war and drawing attention to herself.

But none of those possibilities revealed why T.J. gave her the impression he was hanging around Tucson for a crucial reason, as if he was waiting for something to happen or someone to arrive. Half the time she felt as if she were being watched, but by whom? By Martin Ferris for personal reasons or because of her tie to that handsome Rogue? By T.J. for personal reasons or because of her association with Martin Ferris? Perhaps she was being used by either or both men to get at an old enemy. Whatever was between the two powerful men, she must not get involved!

In the beginning, she had warned herself that T.J. Rogue could be perilous to her future. He could unmask her by accident, or by intention. She had been rash to get this close to a man like him, especially so soon after meeting him. But she had fallen in love with him and couldn't help herself. Merciful heavens protect her if T.J. was pursuing the Texas Flame! And heaven help him if he had duped her! She would never let him take her in or lead him to the Stover Gang!

Back off from him, Carrie Sue, and see what happens. If he makes no threats or intimidating moves, you'll know he isn't after you for your reward. If he is after you for yourself, he'll fight to keep you. But if he's trying to get to Darby, he'll slip up and expose himself.

"Carolyn," Martin Ferris called out from behind her.

Carrie Sue gritted her teeth before she turned to speak with the man. "Good day, Mr. Ferris."

"You busy?" he asked, looking her over appreciatively.

"I have some chores I'm tending," she replied, not in the mood to banter with him this afternoon.

"What if I tag along and we can chat?" he coaxed.

"Some of them are personal, Mr. Ferris. I have a great deal to do before classes start in two weeks. I hope you don't feel it's necessary to warn me a second time against seeing Mr. Rogue."

"You're a smart woman, so one warning is sufficient. Have you seen him again?" he questioned boldly.

Carrie Sue met his gaze without smiling. He was dressed and groomed immaculately, but he was beginning to sweat and flush. "Do you have the right to ask or to interfere?" she responded coolly.

He sent her a falsely rueful smile. "I'm afraid I do. The town council asked me to handle the problem."

"I wasn't aware there is a problem, sir."

He withdrew a handkerchief from his pocket and mopped at the beads of moisture on his face and the backs of his hands. "If you persist in this repulsive friendship, I assure you there will be."

"Explain why that's true," she coaxed in a demanding tone. "Why is Mr. Rogue so disliked and disrespected here?"

"Because you're a respectable lady and he's a no-count drifter."

"Are you certain of your facts, sir?" she challenged.

Martin Ferris looked shocked by her behavior and words, then annoyed. "Why are you so determined to see a man like that?"

"You misunderstand. That isn't the point. I just don't like being ordered about by anyone. I'm not a slave here, sir. I was hired to teach school, and I'll do it efficiently. As far as I've witnessed, Mr. Rogue is a kind and polite gentleman. I've met many so-called upstanding citizens who aren't as nice or as good as he appears to be."

"That's part of your trouble, Carolyn, you don't know him or his type. Every time he comes to town there's trouble. His business here is finished, so he should move

161

on. He won't as long as you're keeping him company, and the good folks of Tucson don't want his kind around."

Carrie Sue laughed. "Mr. Rogue isn't hanging around because of me. He's his own boss. He comes and goes as he chooses. I'm not enticing or encouraging him to remain here. He's smart, so he knows a prim schoolmarm and a gunslinging drifter can't mix. As far as I know, he's planning to get a job at a mine nearby or further north."

"Rogue ain't no miner," he refuted peevishly.

"A job as a guard or freight-wagon driver. You own a silver mine. Perhaps he'll check with you about a job."

"He'd be wasting his time! I don't want any hired guns around here."

The redhead decided to do a little detective work. "Somebody does because we were attacked by three gunmen while we were out riding Saturday. I was nearly killed."

"Who would shoot at you?" he asked skeptically.

"I don't know but it was a cleverly planned ambush, not a robbery attempt. They made certain not to get too close."

"Maybe they were after Rogue. He attracts trouble."

"Then why were they shooting at me after we got separated?" She noticed the surprise and vexation which flared in his dark eyes, telling her she hadn't been the intended target. "To make it worse, I was nearly bitten by a rattler while hiding in the rocks for Mr. Rogue to flank them. I couldn't move because they were firing at me. So you see, sir, he's saved my life more than once. If Mr. Rogue does have enemies here, they're fools to attack him. He's the best shot and smartest man I've met."

"If someone is after him, that's another good reason to keep your distance. You could get hurt or killed in the crossfire."

Carrie Sue pretended to consider his last words. "You could be right. No matter, I have too much work to do to spend time with him or any man. I'm sure he'll be moving along very soon."

At the same time, the lovely desperado and the man beside her saw T.J. leaving the telegraph office down the street. Without turning her head, she glanced at Martin Ferris who was scowling, his brown eyes cold and his jawline clenched. T.J. saw them and halted on the plankway. He walked toward them.

Carrie Sue didn't want to confront him while standing with Martin Ferris. "If you'll excuse me, I must tend my chores." She turned and headed for the saddlery shop, making it obvious to both men that she was leaving because of Rogue's approach.

Martin Ferris stopped T.J. from walking past him in pursuit of the rapidly departing redhead. "Leave her be, Rogue. She ain't your type."

"How would you know, Ferris?" the ebon-haired man taunted.

"She's too nice to tell you to keep away from her, so I'll do it for her. You're making trouble here again, and I don't like it. The town council wants her to stay clear of the likes of you. If you don't want to cause her problems here, then get out of Tucson today."

T.J. chuckled, vexing his foe. "The town council wants me to keep my distance, or you do?"

"Both," Martin replied coldly. "You could never get a woman like her, so give up before you harm her image."

T.J. scoffed casually, "You people can't boss her around."

"We hired her as a respectable schoolmarm, so we can fire her for unladylike conduct. We both know what people will say and think about her if she keeps seeing you. She needs this job, so don't make her lose it over gratitude to you for saving her life."

"You asking or telling?"

"Both," Martin replied again, his brown eyes narrowed.

"Sometimes I don't hear so well, Ferris," he teased pointedly.

"This time, you better clean out your ears because you won't irritate me again. I'm going to make certain that young lady gets a good start here, even if that means challenging you again."

"Like your hirelings did Saturday?" he hinted.

"Is that what you told Carolyn? It's my bet they were friends of yours trying to fool her into thinking you saved her life again."

"Is that what *you* just told her?"

"I didn't have to. She's beginning to doubt you. Didn't you see how she ran from you just now? She's tried to be nice to you, but she realizes you're taking advantage of her kindness to lost pups."

"Don't tell her any lies about me, Ferris," he warned.

"She's opening her own eyes, boy, but I'll help her any chance I get."

"I just bet you will," T.J. sneered. He had noticed the look Carolyn had given him, and it worried him. From the window in the telegraph office he had seen them standing here, talking like old friends. There was something odd about that woman which he couldn't put his finger on. Surely she wasn't leading him on for Ferris, hadn't lured him on a picnic so his men could kill him. She did probe him a lot about Ferris, but was it to see how much he knew about the man? No way, he decided, could that vixen be working for this man!

Martin gave a final warning before strolling away, "Keep your distance, Rogue, or you'll be sorry."

T.J. glanced in the direction Carolyn had taken, but she wasn't in sight. Should he go after her to see what was wrong with her today? What could he tell her to soothe her worries and fears? Maybe she had guessed the truth about the impossibility of their situation and was angry with him for tempting and seducing her, angry with herself for yielding to him last night. Maybe she was scared she would be exposed and sent packing. Maybe she did need this job, or want it. Once he told her he didn't have marriage in mind and would be moving on soon, things would be worse between them. Maybe it was best to let her cool off, or to let her believe the worst of him to make their parting easier for both.

Carrie Sue hurried to where T.J. was staying. She left the money and a note with the woman who had waited on them that night. In her message to T.J., she had asked him to leave her alone before she got into trouble here. She wrote that it was impossible and dangerous for them to be friends. To protect herself from gossip and an impulsive relationship with no future, they couldn't see each other again. She entreated him to understand and comply with her request. She did not mention what she had learned from the sheriff and stableman.

Afterwards, she returned to the boarding house and gathered her laundry. She delivered it to the woman for washing and ironing. Then, she went to the saddlery shop and purchased a saddle. The man was delighted to assist her and have her sale, and promised to have it delivered to Mrs. Thayer's barn before the day ended.

Carrie Sue went to a small mercantile store on a back street and purchased supplies for the trail, just in case she had to make a run for it. She returned to her home and concealed the supplies in Carolyn's large trunk which she had placed in the corner of her bedroom.

She hated mistrusting T.J., the man she loved and had given herself to just last night. Yet, she was afraid to trust him fully. He was so mysterious and could be so dangerous, even though he had revealed a few things about himself. Still, she realized he had related nothing which wasn't common knowledge or couldn't be true of any man like him. She had to be wary of everyone until her life was settled.

The following day, Carrie Sue remained in her room studying except for taking her meals downstairs. She told Mrs. Thayer she wasn't to be disturbed by anyone, and she explained her misgivings about a friendship with T.J. to the kind woman. Mrs. Thayer had seemed to comprehend her dilemma and agreed with her decision to avoid him.

On Wednesday, Carrie Sue realized she needed ammunition if she were forced into a fast escape. She hadn't seen or heard from T.J. or Martin Ferris. She prayed she wouldn't run into either man when she went out to make her purchase at that same small store. She also prayed that her purchase wouldn't seem strange to the owner. No matter, she had supplies, a horse, a saddle, and weapons ready for quick use, but she needed bullets and a rope and a rifle holster.

Something inexplicable was nagging at her. She felt overly tense today. She felt as if some threat was hanging over her head like a storm cloud. Usually she was right when she got such ominous feelings, and that worried her. Kale Rushton had trained her to trust her instincts, and she did. Yet, it was hard around that disarming Rogue. Her heart kept beating swiftly and her respiration was labored. Her skin tingled and felt flushed. She was edgy and insecure. Her instincts were telling her something, but she didn't know what!

Maybe it was an aching for T.J., or maybe it was the anxiety of wondering why he hadn't tried to reach her, by note or in person. They had slept together, then she had spurned him. Didn't he care? Didn't he want to resolve the trouble between them? Why hadn't he contacted her and asked for an explanation of her crazy note after their passionate night together? How could he take possession of her, then walk away as if she meant nothing to him?

Her heart argued, *Maybe he's scared and uncertain too. Maybe you hurt him with your demand for distance. Maybe he's staying away because you asked him to. Or maybe he's giving you time to change your mind and come to him.*

Her keen mind shouted, *Or maybe he got what he wanted from you and he's left town! Or he doesn't want a green girl again!*

Carrie Sue's heart and mind ceased their argument the moment she saw Curly James walking toward her. Her lips parted and her eyes widened. A feeling of intense apprehension washed over her. The blond gunslinger had ridden with her brother's gang, until he kept getting them into lethal trouble. Curly had always been an uncontrollable, cold-blooded bastard and Darby had told him to pack up and move on one day. Curly was boastful and arrogant, but there was no wanted poster out on him, as far as she knew. Surely there wasn't or he wouldn't be walking calmly down the streets of Tucson.

What, she wondered frantically, was he doing in Tucson? What if people saw them talking, as the man was grinning broadly and heading straight for her? He knew who she was! Merciful heavens, if anyone recognized him and put the clues together, she was in deep trouble!

Chapter Nine

The ruggedly handsome gunslinger halted before her and looked her over from head to foot. "How kin you git more beautiful ever' time I see you, Carrie Sue? What are you doin' here? Darby tol' me you'd left the gang. You think it's safe to be out in the open?"

"You've seen Darby?" she asked anxiously.

"Yep, he's in Texas. You remember that hideout in the mountains. He was camped there when I passed through."

"I thought he was heading for Oklahoma to lay low for a while," she said to draw out information. She didn't like this particular man knowing such perilous facts about her and Darby's gang.

"The trail was too hot for 'em. They're holed up in the Guadalupes. I plan to join 'em when I leave here in a few days. Darby said I could."

Carrie Sue recalled the hideout in the mountains which were half in Texas and half in New Mexico. Her brother was now closer to her if she needed help. Yet, she doubted his claim that Darby would hire him again, but Curly didn't appear to be lying; that worried her. "Is Darby all right?" she asked nervously, glancing about to see if anyone was watching them, but sighted no one. She had to hurry.

"Tough as ever. Why'd you run out on him?"

"I was getting too old to gallop all over the countryside a mile ahead of a posse. No one here knows who I am, Curly. I've been hired as a schoolteacher by the name of Carolyn

Starns. Please don't give me away. I'm trying to start a new life for myself."

He leaned against a post and rolled a cigarette. "That might be hard since Darby's gang has wanted posters out on 'em, exceptin' yourn don't have no good picture. You're lucky, 'cause I doubt anybody can recognize you from it. If he'd gotten out of Texas like I warned him, they'd all be safe. I tol' him to leave that Hardin' fellow alone. He's one mean bastard. I did some work for him, but he'd a killed me afterwards if given the chance. I got my pay and took off."

"You took a job for Quade Harding?" she asked disdainfully.

"I needed money and I couldn't do nothin' illegal. The law was breathing down my neck as it was and watchin' me like a hawk over a slow rabbit. I can't let my face git on one of them posters. I been hirin' out as a gunslinger and bounty hunter. I got me a good paying job here. Then, I'll be riding with Darby and the boys again."

"You've turned on your old friends?" she asked fearfully.

"Naw, only cheap outlaws we never met. I got to eat."

Carrie Sue wondered if this sly outlaw would turn on her.

Curly James grinned and shook his head, as if she'd asked the question aloud. "I'd never hurt you, Carrie Sue. You was always nice to me. I was hot-headed back in the ol' days, but I ain't no more. That's why Darby's givin' me another chance. I sure am glad. You'll be safe here, if Hardin' don't come after you."

"You wouldn't tell him where to find me, would you, Curly?" she asked, her tone pleading.

"Naw. Fact is, I may have to kill the bastard myself. Those other two who helped me with his job turned up dead. It's my thinkin' Hardin' got rid of 'em and plans to git rid of me if he can. They was to meet me in El Paso and head here. They never showed, and I heard they was killed. Made me too late for one job, but I got another. I figured I might as well earn some dollars while the boys are laying low. From what Darby said, they plan to laze around for a month or so."

Curly's expression and tone seemed odd to her, but she didn't show it. "Stay clear of Quade; he's an evil man." she warned. "If it weren't for him and his father, Darby and I wouldn't be in this mess. I'm trying to break away from my old life. People believe I'm this schoolmarm. If this doesn't work out, I'm either dead or in prison. Help me, Curly."

"Don't worry none about me, Carrie Sue. Honest," he vowed.

"I believe you," she lied with a radiant smile. She knew Curly James couldn't be trusted. Money—especially a reward as large as hers—had a way of blinding a man. But, she mused, what could she do about Curly? He could turn her in to the law or to Quade Harding. When his money ran out, he would, and she knew it.

She knew the word *give* was a mistake with a bastard like this villain, so she said, "If you need any money, Curly, I can loan you some or tell you where a large gold shipment is stashed."

His eyes brightened. "Where?" he asked eagerly.

"In Martin Ferris's safe. It won't be hard to find his office; he's a big man here." She didn't care if he robbed that vile man, and gold would make her reward less appealing. She noticed the instant glimmer of disagreement and disappointment in his gaze. "You know him?"

"I went on his payroll today. That's why I'm here. I did some jobs for him before, and he sent for me again. I guess he likes my work."

Carrie Sue felt weak and shaky. "Why? he's as bad as Harding!"

"To git rid of a snake named Rogue for him."

"Why?" she asked again, her heart drumming in alarm.

"Two reasons." He took a deep drag off his cigarette.

"Like what, Curly?" she pressed in a panic. If she warned T.J., he would wonder how she got her information. If she

170

didn't . . .

"Like I'm gittin' paid good to do him under and it'll be great for my reputation. Rogue's notch on my gun will set me for life."

"Please don't do this, Curly. He's good, damn good." She told him about the attempted stage robbery and how T.J. had saved her life. "You know I've seen the best guns around, Curly, and they're nothing compared to him. He's lightning fast and cold-blooded. Don't challenge him for any amount of money or glory."

"I kin beat him or any man to the draw."

"Did Martin Ferris tell you he'd already sent three men against him at the same time and they failed? I was there, Curly, and I wouldn't lie to a friend. Please, back off this time."

"I can't. I done took the money and gave my word, and Curly James don't run from nothing or nobody."

Carrie Sue realized that the blond didn't want to back down from a gunfight with T.J. Rogue, even if he wasn't being paid highly for it. The handsome fool honestly believed he could beat T.J. to the draw.

"You got problems with Ferris?" the man asked.

She tried to dupe him, win him over to her side. "He took a liking to me the day I arrived and he hasn't left me alone since then. He's been trying to force me to become his sweetheart. When his charm didn't work, he tried blackmailing me with my job. The town council does what he wants, Curly, so he threatened to get me fired if I wasn't nice to him. He thinks I'm friends with Mr. Rogue because the man saved my life and he fears Rogue will protect me against his pursuit."

"Zat true?"

She lied convincingly, "Mr. Rogue likes me and saved my life, but there's nothing more between us; I swear it. The real war is an old one between them and they're putting me in the middle of it. If you get rid of Rogue, I'll be at Martin Ferris's mercy. If I fight Mr. Ferris, he might learn who I am and use it against me. Please, Curly, let this one pass; I beg you. You can get Rogue another day in another town when I'm not involved. He'll be leaving here soon."

She dropped the disturbing subject for a time to ease her worries on another subject. "Is Darby laying low or working?" she asked. If the gang didn't stay on the opposite side of the neighboring territory, their presence could endanger her. Darby had promised not to come near Arizona Territory. She hoped he kept his word.

The blond eyed her intently. "Mostly layin' low. You want me to take him a message when I leave here?" he offered.

"Just remind him to stay out of Arizona or I'm done for. I'd better get along before someone sees us together. I'll contact you later."

Curly caught her elbow to halt her and suggested, "If you help me git that gold and stay with me a few nights, I'll drop off Ferris's payroll and forgit about Rogue."

Carrie Sue knew she couldn't do as he demanded, sleep with him, not after Rogue, not for any reason. She mused, what to do? If she coldly spurned him, all was lost. If she sought T.J.'s help and confessed the truth, all was lost. If she duped Curly, he would expose Darby's location and get her captured. Desperately she replied, "Give me a day or two to work out the details. Make sure we aren't seen together again or someone might get curious about both of us."

Curly James grinned at the prospect of laying his hands on a golden treasure and a fiery one. He had wanted this woman for ages, but Darby always kept the men away from his sister, even his friend Kadry Sams. Now she was in a bind as snug as wet rawhide and had no choice but to lean his way. If she liked him in bed, maybe she would take off with him after he finished his business for Ferris, which he had no intention of dropping, especially with Rogue sweet on her. He didn't want that gunslinger tailing them because of her. Of course taking Carrie Sue would rile his boss Harding

172

something terrible, but he would betray any man for lots of gold and the Texas Flame, even dangerous men like Harding and Ferris. He had planned to do Ferris's job while waiting for Darby to surface again to join him. After finding where the gang was holed up and learning their plans, he knew he had time to complete it before going back to work for Harding again. Now, he wouldn't need Harding's job. "It's a deal, Carrie Sue."

She cautioned, "Don't call me that again or someone might hear you. I'm Miss Carolyn Starns, schoolmarm, here. I'll contact you soon. Where are you staying?"

"The Morris Hotel, room ten. Let me hear from you by Friday."

"You will. It's a promise, Curly. Thanks." She smiled and left.

T.J. witnessed the curious interaction between the beautiful woman he loved and the violent outlaw he was waiting here to kill. He had seen Curly James in town this morning and had been dogging him for a chance to cause a *legal* showdown. He wondered what they were talking about and how they knew each other, as their conversation seemed too friendly to suit him. Had they met while she was passing through Texas, where Curly was from? Didn't she know who and what that blond was? Something wasn't right here. . . .

T.J. intentionally bumped into Curly James. The sunny-haired man gaped at him, recalling where and how they had met. T.J. was aware that Curly's fingers were stroking his gunbutt and the man was tense.

Martin Ferris walked up and commented, "I see you found him, Mr. James. This man has been looking for you, Rogue."

T.J. noticed the look of astonishment which filled Curly's eyes.

The outlaw swallowed hard and tried to master his infuriating rush of fear. "You're T.J. Rogue?" he finally asked, wondering why Quade hadn't told him that fact before he barbwired this man to a tree. If he had known, he could have killed Rogue that day.

"Yep. We have some old business to settle, don't we?" he said with a cold smile.

"You two know each other?" Martin inquired, baffled.

"We've met before, but we weren't properly introduced. Were we, Curly?" There was a steely edge to T.J.'s voice and gaze.

"Why don't we step into the street and git it done?" Curly sneered, his false courage having returned. He mentally cursed Quade for getting him into this bind. He had heard that Rogue was good, but hatred made an opponent even more dangerous. Curly thought of his Brownwood boss and chuckled. Quade would be the one in a tight bind when Curly didn't carry out his part of their bargain!

"You calling me out?" T.J. asked loudly for the witnesses who had gathered around them.

"If you ain't no coward, Rogue, you'll give me satisfaction."

"I guess I'll be obliged to send you back to your maker below. You'll count for us, won't you, Ferris?"

"I'll be more than happy to," Martin answered with a grin. Curly had been too late to do that stage job which had caused him problems, but not too late to rid him of this intimidating foe.

The two gunslingers stepped into the street. Martin counted off the paces and the men halted. Slowly they turned. "On three!" Martin shouted, rubbing his hands together in eagerness.

T.J.'s left hand was hanging loose at his side. His right one was poised near his waist as if he were planning to use it, and he knew Curly James would watch the wrong hand. He waited.

Carrie Sue had seen the action beginning from the store

window. She had hurried to the doorway and listened to the men's conversation. How, she mused worriedly, did T.J. and Curly know each other? Yet, Curly had looked shocked to learn the black-haired man was Rogue! Who had Curly believed he was? The hatred between them was thick and black like mud in the bottomlands. What was the "old business" to be settled between them? It looked as if Curly was going to try to do his job for Martin Ferris, which she hadn't doubted for a moment, but not this soon. Was the Rogue as good as legend claimed? She dearly hoped so.

Martin counted to three and a flurry of action took place. T.J. drew his left revolver, fired twice, and replaced it before Curly's gun cleared its holster. Suddenly Curly lay in a heap on the dusty street. Never had she seen a man pull a gun, fan the hammer, and shoot as swiftly and accurately as T.J. Rogue had done. If she had blinked, she would have missed everything! She asked herself if Curly James was the reason for T.J. coming to Tucson. Had he been waiting for this "old business" and showdown before leaving? Did he know Martin Ferris had hired Curly to slay him? It was terrible, but she was relieved by the outcome of the gunfight, because now Curly couldn't betray or blackmail her, and T.J. was uninjured. Her peril was over for now. Yet, she wished she had asked Curly if Darby had told him she was here. And, she wondered if the other job he had mentioned was the foiled holdup. That would have given her evidence against Martin. Then, she realized she couldn't have used it.

The sheriff came running down the street. Ben Myers went to where T.J. was standing beneath the sun, calm as a windless day. The two men chatted for a few minutes, then shook hands! Wariness filled her. Why was T.J. always gunning down outlaws? Had he lied to her about being a bounty hunter? Or was he something else? Carrie Sue wondered what was going on. . . .

Carrie Sue walked rapidly toward the boarding house to do some serious thinking, but T.J. caught up with her.

"Wait just a minute, woman," he ordered sternly. When she turned to face him, he read doubt and fear in her gaze. "I saw you back there."

Carrie Sue misunderstood his hint. She alleged, "He wanted directions and information, but I told him I couldn't help him because I was new here. He started flirting with me, but I set him straight. I told him I didn't like gunslingers. You surely do a lot of killing," she murmured in an attempt to focus the attention away from her.

T.J. knew she was lying and he needed to learn why, but later. "I meant, I saw you during and after the showdown. I'm sorry you had to see something like that. What else could I do, Carolyn? He called me out in front of witnesses. If I'd backed down, he'd have kept pushing until I got riled and fought him, or I'd have gotten a reputation as a coward. Besides, he's one of the men who barbwired me to that tree in Texas. We had an old score to settle. Myers said there's a reward out on him now, so he wasn't as smart as he believed he was. He was thanking me for taking him on 'cause the sheriff's old and slow with a gun. Curly James would have killed him in a showdown."

"Was Curly James the reason you were lingering in Tucson?"

Rogue knew she had learned the truth about the rewards and his horse, and he guessed those were the real reasons behind the note she'd sent him. He had left her alone since Monday afternoon, but had planned to see her tonight to straighten out the misunderstanding which he had created to explain his continued presence. She did not want him to leave her alone, he had reasoned, and she was not that afraid of Ferris, the town council, or of losing her job here! She had been angered, hurt, and alarmed by his lies. She had to wonder why he had duped her and others, and she had to question his honesty about his feelings for her. But, why hadn't she confronted him about those deceits? She was a brave and forthright woman, but a proud and cautious one. No matter her reasons for spurning him and for writing the seemingly desperate note, he had to earn her trust and respect again.

He replied carefully, "Yep, but I couldn't tell you I was lying in wait to kill a man. I caught up with his friends and they told me they were to meet him in El Paso to head here for a job. Their tongues got real loose after I barbwired them back-to-back. I was afraid Curly wouldn't show up when they failed to meet him as planned. It's my guess Ferris hired them for that holdup, but Curly got waylaid somewhere. You can bet he's worked for Ferris before, because men like Ferris don't use their own men for dirty work and risk exposure. I'm sure he hired Curly to kill me for thwarting his plans for that gold and you." He breathed deeply before saying, "You already know I didn't tell you the truth about those rewards and Nighthawk. Is that why you're mad at me?"

"After what Curly and those men did to you, I don't blame you for making them pay. I suppose you'll be moving on now."

She didn't answer his last question, and he didn't press her. That telegram had told him Curly was on the way, and Darby was on the move again. He had to get to Texas. "I'll be pulling out at dawn, but I'll send word where you can locate me in case you have trouble with Ferris and need my help. I hate for that bastard to outdo me, but you know we can't prove he was behind that robbery attempt or that he hired Curly to gun me down. Seems he made a mistake there, one he won't take lightly. I best move on to prevent trouble for both of us."

Carrie Sue realized she had to let their relationship end here in the open, not in her room tonight. She wanted him badly, but it would only make losing him more painful. His business was done and he wasn't hanging around because of her, so she needed to keep her pride and wits intact. "You've been a good friend, T.J., and I wish you luck wherever you

177

go. Good-bye," she said and shook his hand.

T.J. clasped it snugly between his and met her gaze. "I wish it could be different for us, Carolyn, but it can't. You understand?"

Carrie Sue forced herself not to break their visual contact and expose the pain which was tearing through her soul. "Yes, I understand."

"You sure you'll be all right here?" he asked, his gaze tender.

She smiled and jested. "Of course I will be, Mr. Rogue. After seeing you in action today, Martin Ferris will be too scared to harm me."

T.J. mentally added, *Especially after I get rid of his three hirelings tonight.* "Would you like to have a farewell supper tonight?"

She shook her head. "That wouldn't be wise for either of us."

"You aren't sorry, are you?" he asked, needing to know.

"No, only sorry we are too different to make it work."

T.J. breathed a deep sigh of relief. "If either of us ever changes—"

Carrie Sue squeezed his hand and interrupted, "Don't say it because we won't change, T.J. We can't change and survive. Go celebrate your victory—the men in the saloon will be drinking to you all night."

"You're one unique woman, Carolyn Starns," he murmured.

"Be careful, T.J.; Martin Ferris hates you." She told him about the man's slip about the picnic. "Watch your back, Rogue. An enemy like that doesn't give up easily."

"I'll be careful, woman, and you do the same."

She smiled radiantly and left him standing there. She was glad he had come after her to explain, to apologize, and to say good-bye. That told her he did care about her.

T.J. exhaled forcefully. Lordy, he hated to leave her behind, but he couldn't ask her to go with him. And it wasn't fair to her to try to see her tonight. By the time he finished his next task, maybe he would be ready to give up this wild life and settle down. And maybe she would still be willing to give him a chance. But that was months away.

T.J. was sprawled on his bed, trying to get some sleep before dawn. He wanted to sneak over to see his woman, but he didn't want to make his leaving any harder than it was on her. He had read the pain and disappointment in her gaze, and he was feeling the same way.

A knock sounded softly at his door. He came to alert. Surely it wasn't Carolyn taking such a risk to see him one last time! He opened the door. A man hurried inside and bolted it. T.J. eyed him inquisitively. "What are you doing in Tucson?"

"Trying to protect your cover, Thad. Captain McNelly got your telegram and sent me to see you about it. I was in Tombstone tracking down the Kelly boys, so I rode here as soon as I got his message. None too soon from what I heard tonight about your run-in with Curly James today. Now that's over, you can move on to the Stover case. I've been ordered to partner up with you."

T.J. stared at Texas Ranger Joe Collins, an old and close friend. Joe was one of the few men who knew his real identity, and they had worked together many times in the past. "Captain McNelly has agreed to let me take it on? He's been fighting me on it. I told him if he didn't relent I was going to resign and take it anyway."

Joe Collins replied, "He thought you were too personally involved to keep a clear head. He didn't want you getting yourself killed. He thinks you've probably settled down by now. If anyone can get to that gang, it's Thaddeus Jamison. Curly was one of those men who did that barbwire number on you, wasn't he?"

T.J. glanced down at his scars and said, "Yep, the last one

179

except for Quade Harding. Are Will Clarke and Captain McNelly still having Harding watched?" T.J. asked, referring to a Texas sheriff, and to Capt. L.H. McNelly of the Texas Ranger Special Force — one of his bosses. When he was in that trouble over killing a deputy, President Grant had come to his rescue with the offer of exoneration if he'd go to work as an undercover Special Agent and U.S. Marshal. Thaddeus Jerome Jamison had accepted the entwined jobs and been at them for years. As a cover, he had used the reputation of a famed gunslinger and the name Rogue, which he'd chosen because he'd often been called a savage rogue during his orphanage days. Two years ago he had added Texas Ranger to his jobs, a position that gave him all the authority he needed anywhere and any time to accomplish the most difficult and dangerous assignments, if he couldn't carry them out as Rogue and remain undercover.

Joe replied, "They know the Hardings are gobbling up land illegally. All they have to do is get evidence against them. You can't work on them again because they know your face. Besides, you can do more as T.J. Rogue than as Thad Jamison, Ranger," he remarked.

Half the time all he felt like was a hired killer who was paid and ordered to clean up the dirty West. "Yep, I can kill off lots of scum as Rogue. Just make sure they get Harding for me, or I'll have to give it another go," he warned. "Before you join me, Joe, contact Charlie Shibell. Have him check out a man named Martin Ferris. He owns a big ranch and silver mine." T.J. related the facts and his suspicions about the attempted holdup of the gold shipment and the probable murder of Helen Cooper which he wanted the Pima County Sheriff to investigate. "I thought it would look odd if Rogue contacted an Arizona lawman. Since I couldn't use a coded telegram, I was afraid Ferris might get hold of my message to him. I planned to wire Charlie after I left town."

"You had trouble with Ferris years ago when you worked on the Carillo case. He still after you?" Joe inquired.

"Yep. But he's after a friend of mine more, Carolyn Starns. She's the woman I rescued on the stage and we've gotten pretty close. Ferris has his mind set on getting her, like he did on Helen Cooper. I want Charlie to make certain he doesn't harm her. Handle it for me while I get a lead on the Stover Gang. Headquarters is keeping a file on their attacks, watching for a pattern. I need to learn what they've done since that Forth Worth job Monday. I haven't been asking about them 'cause I figured it might entice me to head after them before I finished this task. After you see Charlie, join me in El Paso at Mitch's."

"That's why I'm here. That holdup Miss Starns survived near Sherman was pulled by the Stover Gang. She might be able to give us some information about them. Your friend Jacob was killed on that stage, so McNelly wants that gang as badly as you."

"They murdered Arabella and Marie in March. Now they got Jacob. If they give me any trouble, I won't bring them in alive."

"I know, Thad. I'm sorry about your family and friend."

"Me, too. I hadn't seen Tim since I was seven. When I heard the name Major Timothy David Jamison, I couldn't believe he was still alive. Those Mexican bandits got him before we could be reunited." He gritted his teeth.

Joe Collins thought about T.J.'s three badges: U.S. Marshall, Department of Justice for President Grant, and Texas Ranger for L.H. McNelly of the Special Force. Few people knew about Thad Jamison, but plenty were aware of the legendary gunslinger named T.J. Rogue. Thad took on secret missions, reaching far and wide, ignoring perils and hardship to solve crimes and stop criminals. Thad did those jobs other men couldn't handle and didn't want. Joe didn't like, respect, or trust any man more than this one.

"Old man Harding is the one who's offered the biggest rewards for the Stover Gang's capture. They used to harass him all the time. Quade's the one who furnished the names and descriptions for their new posters, claimed he got them from a detective he hired to track them down. He wants them real bad, even Darby Stover's sister. But there's something strange going on there — her poster says "Alive Or No Reward." He's raised it to ten thousand each for the sister and brother, and he's even offering five each on the others. That Texas Flame is a real beauty, Thad. Flaming red hair to her waist and strange blue eyes. I brought along one of her new posters; it has a different sketch. Take a look," he said, withdrawing the paper from his pocket and unfolding it. "Did you ever see prettier eyes or hair? She looks as innocent as an angel. 'Course we know she isn't. A real shame she went bad."

Before he even glanced at it, T.J. had a terrible feeling in his gut. Carolyn had been on a stage robbed by the Stover Gang, a sole survivor, a flaming redhead with violet-blue eyes. She had appeared the same time the gang had dropped from sight. Everything about her flashed through his mind at lightning speed. He stared at the beautiful face of Carrie Sue Stover, and grimaced. It all made sense now.

T.J. reflected on what he knew about the mysterious outlaw. The early reports had listed a flaming haired female who rode with the gang but rarely participated in their crimes. Many had assumed she was one of the bandit's sweethearts or a female who lived with and worked for all of them. Later, she had ridden with them all the time, but always hung back, probably to avoid being recognized. She was an expert shot and rider — he knew from witnessing her skills. Yet, she seemed so gentle, such a lady, when she wasn't a little spitfire! She had almost fooled him. Yet, there was something about her which didn't add up, but she was one of them. She was one of Arabella's, Marie's, and Jacob's killers. He was heading after that notorious gang. The time had come and Carrie Sue, guilty or not, was in his path.

T.J. kept staring into those exquisite eyes as he reminded

himself of who and what she was, allowing his anger to mount so he could carry out his unpleasant task. "I'll get on their trail first thing in the morning, Joe. Tell McNelly this case is mine, all mine."

The Ranger looked at the sullen man and said, "They're laying low right now. Until they surface again, we can't get a lead on them."

"Yes, I can, through her," T.J. replied moodily.

"But how can we locate her?"

T.J. flung the poster on the bed. "I know just where to find her. She's pretending to be Miss Carolyn Starns, the new schoolmarm here. T.J. Rogue will help her escape to her brother, then I'll get them all. I have to do this alone, Joe. Do me a favor and see if you can get her posters destroyed. I'd like to carry out this mission without looking over my shoulder for bounty hunters and wild posses."

"She's the woman you telegraphed Captain McNelly about? This Carolyn Starns is actually Carrie Sue Stover?" he asked incredulously, and T.J. nodded. "She's a reckless one to live in the open like this."

"It wasn't reckless until this sketch was released. It's my guess they killed Miss Starns, and Darby's sister took her place. I'm going to dupe her into leading me to his gang. She could be here to wait for her brother and his men to arrive, could be staking out the town. She knows about Ferris's gold shipment and she's gotten familiar with Tucson. This could be their next target and she's the scout."

"It's a clever plan using her like that," Joe murmured.

"That Darby's a real snake. I should have known she wasn't what she claimed to be; she acted too wary and strange. Lordy, she can be mighty convincing. I'll have to keep a sharp eye on her."

"Can you trust her, Thad? She could lead you into a trap."

"Once she sees that poster, she'll have to trust me and that's all that counts. I want the Stover Gang dead."

"I'll have to get permission to recall her posters. I can say they were a mistake. I'll handle it tomorrow. Keep in touch if you can."

After the men made further plans, Ranger Collins sneaked from T.J.'s room. The ebon-haired man threw himself on the bed. Fury surged through him. He berated himself for getting involved with Carrie Sue Stover. He felt as if she had betrayed him. He loved her and wanted her, but that was impossible now. "Lord help you for doing this to me, woman."

The heartsick lawman seized the wanted poster and stared at the lovely image printed there. Was it possible she had left the gang and was trying to begin a new life? Was that why she had said they were too different to make a go of a future together? She had let down her guard for him, but why? He remembered how hard she had worked at the school and how she had tried to avoid Martin Ferris. If she was scouting Ferris out, she wouldn't be spurning him. She had been studying books and planning lessons as if she honestly intended to teach there. Maybe something in the past had compelled her into a life of crime which she didn't want. Maybe she had gotten entrapped by her brother's deeds. Maybe she really was trying to escape her old life.

"If you're for real, Carrie Sue Stover, I'm sorry because I need you to lead me to the others. This time, I'll be the one betraying you."

T.J. realized the danger he would be placing her in on the trail, but she wouldn't be any safer here with those posters around. He was thrice a lawman. Could he let her slip through his fingers after he had the gang in sight? Could he capture her and send her to prison, knowing what it would be like for her or any woman? Could he watch her hang? What else could he do? His hands were tied and her fate was marked because she was an outlaw, a member of the gang he had sworn to destroy. This wasn't a mistake and she wasn't working undercover. She was just as guilty and wanted as they were, and he had to do his job.

Carrie Sue returned to her room after breakfast to find T.J. waiting for her. "I thought you would be gone by now," she said, her gaze softening as it roamed his features. She walked toward him and halted. She knew something was wrong because he was oddly quiet and seemed to be in deep thought. Maybe he wanted and needed to leave town, but couldn't because of her. An air of uncertainty exuded from him. Her fingers touched his taut lips as she asked, "Are you sure you can't stay in Tucson a while longer? I'm not afraid of what Martin Ferris will do to me after you leave. I want you, T.J., at least a while longer. I'm not pressing for a commitment. I'm just afraid we'll never see each other again after you leave. There's so much I wish I could share with you, but I can't. If only we were other people," she murmured sadly.

T.J. clasped her hand in his and lowered it. This choice was hellish for him, especially after her stirring words. He inhaled deeply as if making a difficult decision, then said, "Get some things packed, Carrie. You're leaving here with me."

She paled and trembled. Her misty gaze locked on his piercing stare. He was armed, and she wasn't. He had the advantage, as she hadn't suspected treachery from him. Her energy and joy drained away swiftly. "So," she murmured, "you are a bounty hunter and you know who I am. I should have known better than to trust you or any man. Every time I do, I get into more trouble. Damn you."

Her gaze and expression sent pangs of guilt and anguish through him. "No, Carrie, I'm not a bounty hunter. But they'll be on your trail soon if you don't get out of here with me." He unfolded the poster and held it before her face. He watched her face pale even more and her eyes enlarge with panic. "Quade Harding released your real description. It says so at the bottom. When the mail came in, I was at the sheriff's office to sign papers to collect the reward on Curly James. Myers had to fetch my payment from the bank. While he was gone, I got nosey and opened an envelope from Texas because I always like to know what's going on there. The Sheriff's supposed to print up lots of these and post them. I stole it, so he doesn't know about you yet. He will soon, so you won't be safe here anymore."

"If those posters are out everywhere, I won't ever be safe again. Dammit!" she scoffed bitterly. "I thought it was over this time. Everything was working out fine for a change, except for Martin Ferris. Why can't they just let me disappear and start over? If they'd leave me alone, I wouldn't cause them any more trouble! I should have known Quade would pull this trick when he got impatient. I was stupid to think this ruse would work. I just wanted out so badly. Heavens, ten thousand dollars in gold. That'll be the end of me."

"I don't want to see you hurt, Carrie. I don't know what happened back in Texas to create your troubles, but they can get you shot or hanged before you can straighten them out. You have to get out of here and lay low for a while. And you need someone you can trust to guard your pretty backside. I'm more than willing," he offered.

"You can't help me, T.J. — no one can. I'm in too deep. Merciful Heavens, if I could go back to '69 and take a different trail, I would. I guess you realize this is what I couldn't share with you, T.J. This is why I was so edgy half the time. I have to get moving, fast."

"You don't stand a chance traveling alone, woman. I'm going with you and I won't take any lip from a cornered wildcat. I mean it."

"You don't understand what you'd be getting yourself into! I'm an outlaw. I'm wanted in four states. I have more charges against me than a dog has ticks! That bastard Quade Harding is responsible for everything that's happened to me. I should have killed him long ago, and his cold-blooded father. He'll never leave me alone."

T.J. had to know why his foes were so hot on this girl's trail. "Why do the Hardings want you so badly? Alive?" he asked. "That's a pretty big reward and a crazy demand. Where did he get your sketch?"

Carrie Sue met his gaze and told him the truth. "Why are you willing to help me escape? You don't want to become a wanted man."

"You know why I have to help you, Carrie," he replied tenderly, his hand lifting to caress her anger-flushed cheek.

She was scared; she was wary; she was emotionally torn between a loving faith and an instinctive mistrust. "What about my big reward?"

He captured her forearms and shook her lightly. "Listen to me good, woman! If I wanted money that badly, I would have stolen Ferris's gold. I took the rewards for those varmints I killed because it would have been silly not to, but I could never sell you to the law like a piece of prized meat. Surely you've been around me long enough to know you can trust me. I've been more open and honest with you than anyone else in my life. And it scared the hell out of me! Lordy, Carrie, I know what jails and prisons are like; I can't let you get caught."

His sincere words and gaze worked; they duped her. "Don't you understand, T.J.? If you're caught with me, you'll be in as much trouble as I am. I can't let you mess up your life for me."

He assumed his next cunning question was a safe one to ask. "All I have to know is how did you get Carolyn Starns's identity? I have to hear you say you didn't kill an innocent woman for a new life."

Carrie Sue inhaled deeply, fighting back unusual tears. She explained about the coach accident and her impulsive action. "I could have been a good teacher, honestly. It was like I was being given a chance to break free from the gang, and I took it. But Quade has tired of his cruel games and released my sketch. What now?" she murmured to herself.

"They'll be looking for me everywhere."

T.J. knew she might get suspicious of him if he suggested taking her to Darby for protection. "We'll figure something out later. Right now, we need to get out of Tucson, fast. Get packed, woman. We're wasting valuable time arguing. You're stuck with me."

"I can't let you ruin your life," she protested weakly, needing him.

"It's my life, what there is of it. If anything happened to you, it would be my fault. Like it or not, I'm going to help you get through this. Now, get in there and get ready to leave. Move it, woman!" Carrie Sue rushed into the bedroom to follow his order. She changed into a riding skirt, boots, and a cotton shirt. T.J. joined her. She retrieved her weapons from the hiding place in her closet and her supplies from the trunk, on which T.J. was now sitting and watching her.

She stuffed clothes into a small satchel. Suddenly a voice spoke to her from outside the bedroom door, inside the front room.

"I'm Charlie Shibell, Sheriff of Pima County. I'm here to arrest you, Miss Stover. Stay clear of those guns," Joe Collins warned. "I saw you in town the other day. When I got this poster, I remembered you. I want to get you out of Tucson and into my jail before bounty hunters see those new posters and try to take you away from me."

T.J. motioned to her to keep silent about his presence in the corner. When the Ranger entered the room, T.J. hit him over the head with his gunbutt, as planned. Joe had glanced his way, as planned. "He saw me. Let's get out of here. We're in this together now."

"He isn't dead, is he?" she asked frantically. "I don't want you to kill anyone because of me, T.J., please. I'd rather be jailed or hanged than make you an outlaw."

T.J. checked his friend, and wished some of her words and looks weren't affecting him so strongly. "Nope, just out cold and will be for some time. Let's ride, woman. I'll get the horses saddled."

"No," she protested. "You sneak out of here and meet me at the southeast edge of town. I'll take the backstreets from here and you leave from the livery stable. I don't want us seen riding out together. If that sheriff dies, I don't want anyone else knowing about your help. If he doesn't, it's your word against his, later. Don't act rashly. I don't want you on the run. It's a terrible existence."

He reasoned, "What if you run into Martin Ferris? He'll get suspicious and try to stop you."

"I'll handle him. I'll meet you on the road we came in on by stage, five miles beyond the last house."

He realized he couldn't argue with her. "I have supplies at the livery stable with Nighthawk. Be quick and be careful. If you try to protect me by not showing up, I'll track you down. Until you're safe, you need me to guard your back and I fully intend to do a good job."

"I'll be there soon. Now get out of here, Mr. Rogue."

After T. J. left, Carrie Sue checked the sheriff to make sure he was alive. She took the poster from Joe's pocket and stuffed it inside her satchel. She wrote Mrs. Thayer a quick note telling the woman how much she appreciated everything she'd done for her and how much she would miss her new friend. She said she was in trouble and had to leave town in a hurry, and that the woman would understand why very soon. She revealed that she had been trying to start a new life here in Tucson, but her wicked past was preventing it. She left the note on the desk, gathered her things, and sneaked out the back door. After saddling the pinto, she rode northward out of Tucson along the backstreets, even though the stage had entered town from the southeast.

Chapter Ten

Carrie Sue hadn't ridden far before she realized she was being followed. The redhead pulled out her fieldglasses and stared at the rider trailing her. It was T.J., and she sighed in relief. She waved to him to let him know she had sighted him, and she waited for him to join her.

She laughed and accused, "You don't trust me, Mr. Rogue? You're supposed to be on the other side of town waiting for me. You've ruined my brilliant strategy. I wanted to be seen leaving town northward, alone. If anyone saw you, they'll know you're with me."

He frowned at his bad decision, then grinned. "Don't worry; they'll think I was on to your ruse and was dogging you for capture. I was worried about you. I was scared you'd skip out on me to protect me."

Now that they were out of Tucson and could easily make a run for it, her tension had lessened. She felt safer in a saddle, out in the open, away from strangers, and heavily armed. She was with her love and he was determined to protect her and help her, to be with her. If his feelings were as strong for her as hers were for him, perhaps they could escape and make a future together. She would give him a few days to prove his love and commitment, then she would suggest her stirring plan. She merrily admitted, "The thought crossed my mind, partner, but I remembered your threat to hunt me down. I certainly don't want to get on T.J. Rogue's bad side. I have enough troubles as it is."

He liked seeing her relaxed and confident. He teased, "I'm glad you decided not to dupe me, woman. I would hate to think I clobbered that sheriff and got into real trouble for no good reason."

"You still have time to back out. Maybe he didn't recognize you."

"He knows me all right. We had a foul disagreement one night in a saloon. If I recall him accurately, he won't tell anybody about us too soon. He'll want to track us down so he can say he captured the Texas Flame and the notorious Rogue. And he won't want anybody to know we skunked him."

She sent him a playful grin. "At least we have male pride working on our side. Let's go before he comes to. I was going to tie him up, but I might need my rope for something else."

T.J. was glad she hadn't bound and gagged Joe Collins because that would be hard for the Ranger to explain. "Where to, Carrie?"

"I'm called Carrie Sue, but it doesn't matter. Let's ride for New Mexico. It's fairly secluded and I know some places there we can hide."

"As long as we're partners, it sounds fine to me."

They exchanged smiles and headed across country to avoid the public road south of their location. They traveled for hours through wild fields of saguaro cactus and into the Rincon Mountain range. They steadily pushed onward until the sun seemingly burned into their skulls and dampened their clothes. When they found a couple of taller trees, they dismounted and relaxed in the shade. While Carrie Sue strolled around loosening up her stiff muscles, T.J. poured water from one canteen into his hat and let the thirsty horses drink.

"I can tell I've been out of the saddle for weeks," she remarked, rubbing her lower back and flexing her shoulders. Her hair was twisted and tucked beneath her hat to keep her cooler. She sipped water from a second canteen and handed it to her handsome partner.

He took several deep swallows, then pushed up his hat with his thumb. "I wonder what Ferris will say and do when he finds you gone."

Carrie Sue laughed and retorted, "You mean when he discovers who I really am. Can't you imagine his face when he sees my wanted poster? He'll probably be relieved he didn't try to attack me."

He replaced the top on the canteen and hung it over the saddle horn. "I know what I thought and felt when I saw it."

Carrie Sue met his engulfing gaze and asked, "What was that?"

His smokey gray eyes enlivened as he grinned and eyed her head to foot. "How it didn't do you justice. You're one beautiful woman. I haven't been able to get you off my mind since we met."

She smiled and asked, "Was that all that came to mind?"

"Nope. I realized you were in deep trouble and would need my help to survive, if I could convince you to accept it. We've spent a lot of time together, Carrie Sue, and I think I know you by now. You may have done some things you're wanted for, but not all of them, and not because you wanted to do any of them. Isn't that right?"

"I guess a man like you would know that half the stuff said and written about people like us isn't true, or it's greatly enlarged. It all started out so innocently, T.J. All I wanted was justice and revenge. The Hardings killed my parents and took our land, but the law didn't do anything to them. I was bitter, and too young to know any better. So was Darby. Somewhere along the way, everything got out of control and there was no turning back. Twice before I tried to start fresh, but Quade's detective always found me and sent me on the run again. Sometimes I wished it were over any way possible." She leaned her head against the tree and closed her eyes to relax.

T.J. observed her profile and mood. He hated tricking her like this, but it was necessary. He had sworn personal revenge on the Stover Gang, and it was his lawful mission to defeat them. To get to Darby and his men, he had to strengthen the bond between Carrie Sue and himself so she would trust him completely and lead him to those murderous bastards. If this beauty was telling the truth about her entanglement with her brother, he would try to find a way to help her when this matter was settled, though it wouldn't be easy. After all, she was guilty, was an outlaw. If the crimes against the Hardings were the only ones involved, he wouldn't have a problem getting her a pardon. There were countless other charges, including three murders he needed to avenge. He knew she hadn't killed anyone, but she was an accomplice. She knew what those bastards were like, but she had stayed with them.

T.J.'s keen gaze scanned the horizon in all directions. If anyone remembered this redhead on the stage, and who could forget a beauty like her, other men were probably on her trail right now. He had to be careful until those posters for her were withdrawn, if Joe could get them pulled out of circulation so he could do his job. But something else troubled him—her acting skills. He had fallen for her ruse just like everyone else, and she hadn't confessed anything even after their passionate night, until today when she was forced to do so to escape. Even now, she was on guard, and that worried him. Had she tried to sneak out of town and lose him? To spare him from a criminal life because she loved him? Or to flee to her brother alone?

He glanced in her direction and she appeared to be dozing. Lordy, she looked so innocent and vulnerable. But he had witnessed the spitfire in her and he was aware of her reputation. He had observed her skills and he knew a desperate person was the deadliest of all enemies. What if she was fooling him more than he was fooling her? What if she was suspicious of him and was pretending she wasn't? What if she was letting him tag along only until she could elude him? Worse, maybe he was duping himself, being dreamy-eyed, because he wanted to believe her story, wanted to trust her, wanted to help her survive so he could have her later. But could he, after betraying her and using her? Would she be able to understand and forgive him?

Carrie Sue sensed powerful emotions in the air. Now that she was on the trail again, her instincts were alive. Merciful Heavens, how she wanted and needed to believe T.J., but could she afford to do so? She felt guilty about making him prove himself, but her life depended on it. She sighed heavily and stretched.

T.J. revealed, "I may as well confess something right now. Quade Harding is the man who had me barbwired to that tree. When he hears you're with me, he'll be furious. One day, I'm going to kill him. He'll pay for what he did to both of us." He smiled when she moved closer to him. "You know something strange? We have the same enemy and our lives have been similar. We both lost our parents and we both got into trouble, and we both wound up in the same place at the same time. It's almost like some force has been pushing us toward each other."

"Maybe that's why we find each other irresistible," she jested.

"Could be, woman. Let's get moving before Shibell tracks us here."

They journeyed until it was nearly dark and made camp in a treed area near the bank of the San Pedro River, about six to ten miles north of the road between Dragoon Springs and Tucson. Fortunately, the river—which could often nearly dry up—was flowing tranquilly at this time of year. T.J. tended the horses while Carrie Sue built a small fire to prepare a meal of canned beans and coffee. The moment they were ready, Carrie Sue doused the fire.

Along with the biscuits which Carrie Sue had sneaked from Mrs. Thayer's kitchen on her way out, she and T.J. ate the simple beans and drank black coffee. For the first time, trail food didn't seem so bad or—each decided—maybe it was the company they were with tonight. He washed the dishes in the river while she refilled their canteens. In case a swift start was needed, everything was repacked. The horses were nearby, watering and grazing contentedly, and the serene mood encompassed T.J. and Carrie Sue.

"You want to take a swim and cool off before we turn in?"

She smiled at him and answered, "I always say take advantage of water when you're near it. We'll probably sleep better afterwards."

T.J. grinned at her, a grin which said he had more in mind than a late night swim. "I'll meet you in the water."

Carrie Sue knew what she wanted tonight, him, and she was quivering with anticipation. Maybe this situation was crazy and dangerous, but she had to have him! In view of her stormy existence, they could be parted or slain at any time. For now, for a while, she couldn't leave him or resist him. Yes, that made her vulnerable, but she had to take this risk. She headed for the river's edge and undressed near a tree. She knew, and so did he, that no one should ride by this spot this late at night. She stepped into the cool water and submerged her body to her neck. She liked the feel of the sand under her feet and the sensuous splashing of water against her bare flesh.

T.J. surfaced before her, within inches of her body. She gasped in surprise and bolted upwards, the water striking her above her waist. Her eyes were transfixed on his handsome face where moonlight was playing over his solid features and enhancing his good looks. Just a glance from him seemed to awaken every sleeping emotion within her and whetted her appetite for the loving only he could give. His eyes seemed to burn into her very soul, into the core of her being, to ignite her senses into flaming desire. "I couldn't tell you were there."

"Old Apache trick," he jested with a devilish grin, his gaze

195

caressing her as his hands yearned to do. She had really gotten to him and he ached to possess her. No blaze of passion could burn brighter or fiercer than his for her. She had kindled a flame within him the first moment he sighted her, and he doubted that the ensuing wildfire could ever be doused. But that was a problem he would deal with later. "You're even more beautiful than I imagined you were beneath that simple dress at the home station." His arms encircled her waist and he sank slightly in the water to nestle his right cheek against hers, crushing her supple curves against his broad chest. He closed his eyes and inhaled the sultry scent of her salty body. Except for her infamous reputation, he knew little, if anything, about this mysterious and irresistible vixen. He wanted and needed to know everything about her, but he had to move cautiously.

Carrie Sue's fingers came up to rest lightly on his shoulders. Her naked breasts pressed against his collarbone, her stomach snuggled to his taut abdomen. Despite the cooling water around them, she felt aflame with blazing desire. She trembled as his lips nibbled at her ear and trailed slowly across her jawline to her chin, before they sealed over her mouth. She had promised herself never to trust another man, not after her grim experiences with them. But how could she not trust this man she loved and craved? Merciful Heavens, could she even trust herself?

They touched lightly, questioningly, leisurely. Their bodies ached to be joined, but neither wanted to rush this moment. His mouth was soft and smooth and stimulating as it claimed hers. They shared numerous kisses which increased their hunger. Their lips parted and they gazed at each other: hesitating, longing, burning.

Her fingers slipped through his dripping hair, brushing it away from his face. His hair was full and thick, nape length, as black as a moonless midnight. Her eyes slid over his features, and her fingers followed the trail of her gaze, encouraging her lips to join the stirring journey. She felt him

196

stiffen a moment, then relax as a moan escaped his throat. The midnight sun glowed on his torso and was reflected in his smokey gray eyes. He was like a wild stallion, an unbroken mustang, who allowed her to approach him and ride him. His frame was sleek and hard, yet supple. No ounce of extra fat detracted from his magnificent form. She traced the hairy path over his hard chest.

T.J. pulled her toward him. He had to feel her, taste her, inhale her. She couldn't be a vicious outlaw, not this proud and gentle creature. His mouth found her cheek first, then her lips, nibbling at them and mutely inviting her to do the same with his. His kisses were deep, greedy, pervading, and she responded in the same manner. His tongue enticed hers to mischievous play. His hands left her waist and drifted up her bare arms, delighting in the wet slipperiness which enlivened his senses. He sent them roaming over her shoulders and down her chest. Her wet skin was silky to his touch, responsive to him. His hand cupped her breasts and gently kneaded her taut nipples as his mouth labored tenderly down the silky column of her neck.

A tingling chill raced up Carrie Sue's back, which arched toward him when he lowered himself into the water so his mouth could taste the sweet rosy brown buds that were blooming beneath his toiling lips. His mouth seared over her tingling flesh with a white-hot heat which threatened to drive her mad. He was so warm and so tempting, so pervasive. His touch was tantalizing on her sensitive skin and it aroused every inch of her being. His tongue skillfully fluttered over her breasts like a delicate butterfly's wings. His hands shifted to her buttocks and pulled her tightly against him. Her head was spinning with pleasure and happiness. Countless sensations washed over her. She felt hot as a boiling pot, taut as a calf-rope during branding, and as giddy as a child at Christmas.

T.J. stood before her, eight inches taller than she was. His quivering hands untied the bandanna around her head and loosened her fiery mane. He spread the blazing glory around her shoulders and admired it as his fingers savored the texture. The flaming locks seemed to hint at Carrie Sue's leashed sensuality, her fiery nature, her imprisoned soul, her secret self which had been jailed with all men except him. Only from love could she have given herself to him. Without a word, he lifted her in his strong arms and carried her to the blanket which he had spread for them before entering the water. He lay her on it and gazed down at her, his hungry eyes traveling her full length. She didn't appear the least bit shy or inhibited with him. She reached for him and drew him down to her, boldly, possessively, enticingly. His heart pounded, sending fiery blood racing through his veins.

T.J.'s mouth fastened to hers and his hips pressed against hers. Carrie Sue felt his manly hardness and it heightened her desire to feel him within her. His ebony hair fell forward and grazed her face. Beads of water dripped from him and trickled down her face into her hair. His caresses were amazingly soft, yet urgent. His respiration was erratic, and it excited her to know how aroused he was. She thrilled to his masterful touch, his titillating kisses, his caring mood. He gently stroked her breasts, then suckled them without mercy.

Carrie Sue was breathing fast and shallow; her heart was thundering. His mouth and hands seemed to be everywhere at once and she was awash with searing passion. Stirring moans kept reaching her ears, some of them hers and some of them his. She pressed against his body; she clung to him; she ached for him to be inside of her. She shuddered, and so did he.

The Texas Rogue entered her slowly and sensuously, and the blissful sensation tore away her light restraint as she gasped for undizzying air. She clutched at him savagely as he gently set his pattern and pace. It was as if they were melting into each other like slabs of butter beneath a hot sun. They were one, joined in spirit and need. Her head tossed and her body writhed as if she would perish if he didn't feed her ravenous hunger soon. He moved deeper within her, his movements strong and skilled. The daring desperado caught his rhythm and responded feverishly.

T.J. wanted to surrender himself to Carrie Sue's spell, but he would lose all control if he didn't concentrate. He pushed himself deep within her as the beautiful redhead wrapped her legs around him, pleading for a race to passion's summit. Their bodies were locked together and moving rapturously as if one. He needed to withdraw a few minutes to cool his torrid flesh, but she wouldn't release him even for a moment.

Carrie Sue squirmed beneath her handsome Rogue as his lips brushed her breasts. She knew his restraint was stretched tightly, but she couldn't control herself as he filled her with wonderful strokes. She clasped his head between her hands and lifted it, wanting to stare into those smokey depths when that special moment of ecstasy arrived. She fused her gaze to his, as snugly as her body was sealed to his. She smiled when he kissed the tip of her damp nose. Then, the explosion came, long, deep, achingly sweet, powerful.

As she cried her victory aloud and meshed her mouth to his, his strokes became swifter and more forceful. His mouth feasted ravenously on hers as his body shuddered with his own release. His face moved to her neck as he gasped for air and continued his movements until he was fully sated. Her fingers stroked his dark, wet head and she smiled as she felt the throbbing pulsations cease within her.

T.J. rolled to his back and carried her along with him. His breathing was labored and his body was drenched with sweat. He was totally exhausted, a wonderful and thrilling fatigue.

Neither spoke nor moved as they shared the closeness of this serene aftermath. They listened to the songs of nocturnal insects and birds and the rush of the nearby river. They inhaled the sweet fragrances of the flowers that bloomed around them. The trees overhead were still, as no breeze stirred them at this peaceful moment. The night was cooling steadily, as was their flesh as it dried. Their respirations slowed to normal and their bodies relaxed fully.

T.J. knew this proud woman couldn't demand, and probably wouldn't request, a commitment from him. Her hazardous existence didn't lend itself to one. But she was the kind of strong woman who would not compromise over love, over trust. She would settle for nothing less than the one man who unleashed her inner soul and bound his heart to hers. When he stroked her silken body and experienced the overpowering force of their raging desire, he knew he was the one man who could earn her love and share it forever, even without marriage. He was the one man who could fulfill her, and she could do the same for him. But he was also the one man who could hurt her the worst, who could selfishly use and then cruelly destroy her.

He couldn't run away with her, no matter how badly he wanted her or how much he loved her. He couldn't become a hunted man, always looking over his shoulder. He couldn't let the Stover Gang continue their crimes, or get away with the murders of Arabella and Marie, or of Carolyn Starns and that Texas Ranger, a man he had known and worked with in the past. He had to stop them; he had to punish them. And this woman was the only path to victory.

Carrie Sue sighed peacefully and sat up. She gazed down at T.J. who was resting with one hand behind his head. She smiled and said, "I'm going to take a bath and get dressed. It's getting cool and we might have to take off in a hurry. I'll be back shortly."

He caught her hand and kissed her palm before letting her rise to leave his side. He watched her naked body as she headed for the river. A curious loneliness chewed at him. He closed his eyes and imagined his life without her, then dreamed of what it could be with her at his side forever. He had experienced so many bitter times. He had endured such misery and loneliness. He had been so empty, so hard, almost unfeeling in many ways. He had found his brother, only to lose him again before their reunion. He had lost Arabella and little Marie to brutal deaths. Now, he had found the one woman who could change his life, but he was going to lose her; it was inevitable. Bitterness attacked his gut. Why did that flaming redhead have to be Carrie Sue Stover? Why couldn't she have been born Carolyn Starns? Why had taunting fate thrown them together after her life was ruined, when she had little hope for survival and freedom? Why couldn't they have met years ago when her only criminal deeds were against Quade Harding?

He wanted to help her, but how could he? She had dug a pit and cast herself inside, and he didn't have a rope to haul her up with and couldn't think of how or where to obtain one. What a stupid thing for a lawman to do, to fall in love with a fugitive!

Catching the Stover Gang had seemed hopeless until he had met Darby's sister. If he could spare Carrie Sue somehow, he wouldn't use her to get at them. But he couldn't pardon her or get her a pardon, not after the things she'd done; so he might as well let her unknowingly help him get his task done quickly. Maybe, in the eyes of the law, that would make up for some of the wicked things she'd done.

He had come a long way from that quiet and terrified kid who had been kidnapped and half-raised by Apaches. He had come a long way from the white Apache warrior he had become before age thirteen. A boy grew up fast and hard under such harsh and demanding conditions, or he didn't survive them. He had come a long way from that "half wild rogue" at an orphanage in a San Antonio mission. He had traveled even further than the tough and embittered youth who went off to war, where he met the man who had become President of the United States. His journey had carried him through days of trouble and into the jail from which he was rescued by President Grant and befriended by several unique lawmen. Their trust in him had changed him forever. He couldn't look the other way when such malicious crimes had happened. He couldn't betray Grant, McNelly, Collins, Peterson, Clarke, and others close to him. He couldn't betray himself and what he knew was right and just, not for a woman he couldn't have.

Most people didn't know it and few would probably believe it, but he did have a code of honor, one instilled by his parents and the Apaches, and fortified by the good men he knew. He could hold his own against any man, match his skills and prowess against the best, and that wasn't boasting. He had traveled far and wide during his missions, and had left behind him a reputation as a legendary gunslinger. He sometimes wished people knew the truth about him so he would have their respect and acceptance. But he couldn't get his vital tasks done if people knew him as Thaddeus Jerome Jamison, Special Agent to the President, or U.S. Marshal, or Texas Ranger.

He was obligated to defeat criminals, especially the Stover Gang. But he hadn't bargained on this beautiful complication. This was a desperate situation which would force him to battle everything he was and all he believed in; yet, he couldn't hold back or retreat. He was honor-bound to seize victory any way necessary.

Lordy, last night seemed ages away from this one. After his shocking talk with Joe Collins, he had hunted down Martin Ferris's three henchmen and slain them. He hoped Charlie Shibell, the Pima County Sheriff and his good friend, would be able to get evidence against Ferris so the man couldn't give them trouble on the trail. He wanted Ferris to pay for his many crimes. T.J. realized that Martin would send men after them the moment they were discovered missing, even if he did or didn't know the truth. But once he saw Carrie Sue's poster, the Tucson mineowner would be determined to possess the fiery-haired vixen who

202

had duped him and enflamed his desire.

Strange, but reality seemed distant and unimportant at this moment. All he wanted at this maddening time was the redheaded vixen at the river. He would have to keep reminding himself of who and what she was.

Carrie Sue completed her bath and dried off with her dirty shirt. She washed it and tossed it over a branch to dry by morning, along with the cotton riding skirt and undergarments. She needed to keep her clothes and body washed whenever possible, as she couldn't always count on having water for such chores. She donned a deep blue shirt and snug jeans, and braided her golden red hair. She had been so calm and limp when she began her bath, but it had stimulated her. Now, she was strangely tense and alert. Perhaps it was her garments, braided hair, and being on the trail again which altered her from the lovestruck woman to the wary desperado.

As she gathered her things to rejoin her lover, Carrie Sue's mind was in turmoil. She had been given time to think, time for her fear to be leashed, time for her wits to come to full strength. T.J. had her confused and agitated. He was the only man besides her brother and Kale that she had trusted, to whom she had gotten this close. But she had lied to him, and he knew it. She was a valuable prize, and he knew it. She was a notorious outlaw, and he wasn't. She admitted she needed his help in escaping, as she couldn't imagine how many men were chasing her at this moment. Prison or a hanging was staring her in the face and, yes, she was scared. Only a fool wouldn't be!

But was it fair to involve her love in such perils? There was no future for them, and she didn't even know if T.J. Rogue wanted anything permanent with her. Wherever she went, someone would know about her, would have seen her poster, would endanger any new life she tried to begin. She couldn't get him killed. Bounty hunters would be eager to track her down for ten thousand dollars, and lawmen would be anxious to arrest the Texas Flame just for glory.

But something else was nagging at her. T.J. hadn't questioned her about her brother, his gang, and their past actions. Wouldn't any man, particularly a lover, want to know what she had done and why? He had stolen her wits and heart as easily as drawing his revolver. He had sneaked to see her Sunday night to unleash her passion for him, conveniently in time to seal their bond before this trouble began. Too, she had seen him leaving the telegraph office in Tucson. Why?

But there was more to worry her. That sheriff had sneaked into her room just as they were escaping, to compel T.J. more tightly into her hazardous life. The handsome Rogue had been at the home station for an *accidental* meeting and had *accidentally* been around when the stage was attacked so he could rescue her. Then, shortly after her talk with past gang member Curly James, T.J. had gunned him down.

What if it all was a clever ruse to get at her? What if T.J. wasn't who or what he claimed to be? What if that poster he had shown to her was false? What if he had printed it and shown it to her to send her on the trail toward Darby and his gang? What if he had been using his cunning to get close to her before tricking her? What if he was using her to get to Darby? And what would her brother say if and when she turned up with T.J. Rogue?

It was terrible not trusting a man under such conditions; yet, she had trained herself to be wary. Before she made her final conclusions, she had to discover the truth about her love. If he was after Darby and the Stover Gang, once she told him where they were or led him there, their love affair would be over and she would lose him. Perhaps she would have to kill him for betraying her. Carrie Sue returned to camp to find two bedrolls stretched out.

T.J. grinned and said, "If we're going to get any sleep

tonight, it has to be separately. I won't be able to leave you alone if I'm touching you. We have a long, hard ride tomorrow."

"Yes," she concurred, "we do, Mr. Rogue."

They rose at dawn, ate quickly and quietly, and were on the trail shortly after sunup, T.J. and Carrie Sue rode as swiftly as the rugged terrain and heat would allow, not wanting to overtire or overheat the animals and themselves. She watched the landscape become hilly and rolling. The flatlands were lost for a time, as were the numberless yuccas and variety of cacti—except for occasional prickly pears which fanned out on the dry earth, often to cover spaces of three to five feet. Trees were taller and mesquites were rarer. Loose boulders formed piles of rocks which seemingly spread out for miles on both sides of them. It made her nervous because there were so many places where they could be attacked and entrapped; yet, they continued.

The beautiful fugitive and the handsome gunslinger covered less distance that day than on Thursday. They camped in the Little Dragoon Mountains in a small valley between towering rock formations where lush grass was growing and a shallow seep was located, making the fatigued redhead glad her lover was familiar with this territory.

They had talked little during their arduous journey that day and in camp that night. They both knew their silence was not totally due to their exhaustion. Yet, they watched each other furtively and smiled when their gazes met, and they shared the few chores genially. Even though the rock-enclosed valley was off the nearby road, they were careful to watch and listen for stages and riders as they took turns sleeping.

Again, they arose early. As they headed out Carrie Sue

couldn't help but wonder why T.J. did not bring up the questions she thought should be asked. At least he should try to discuss why they were riding toward the very states in which she was wanted! He should want to know if she knew where to find her brother and if she was heading to rejoin the Stover Gang! As the day progressed, her worries, fears, and doubts increased.

T.J. guided them safely past Dragoon Springs and the Butterfield Stage station. He told her they needed to travel swiftly through this area which was so close to her last known location. He promised they could halt for rest for a few days in the Chiricahua Mountains: a day to a day and a half beyond them.

The air was hot and dry, too arid for cooling perspiration to form on her body. The blazing sun seemed to penetrate her shirt and jeans and sear her flesh, and she knew from experience that even clothed flesh could burn badly. She felt as if her hat was doing little good, as if her brains were being cooked slowly. She stayed thirsty, but knew the danger of drinking too much water too quickly; it was safer to sip frequently than to guzzle large amounts. She also didn't want to use up their water supply before reaching the next source. She concluded that the desert was wildly beautiful, but deadly. As the landscape of boulders and deep ravines continued on both sides of them, the daring desperado's apprehension mounted and she struggled to remain alert in the dazing heat.

Just after their midday break, they rode into the midst of concealed Indians who rapidly surrounded them. Carrie Sue paled with fear. T.J. held himself erect and proud.

"Don't touch your weapons; they're Apaches." he warned. "That's the infamous Geronimo coming toward us. Keep silent and let me get us out of this. If you speak, woman, they'll be insulted and very angry."

206

T.J. lifted his hand and greeted the renegades with the correct Apache words and signal. He touched his chest and revealed, *"Biishe, nagushnlti-ye Cochise, shitaa' daalk'ida."* The ebon-haired man told them he was "Nighthawk, adopted son of Cochise, his father long ago."

Carrie Sue did as her lover ordered; she kept still and silent. Yet, she was amazed by T.J.'s knowledge of the Apache language and signals, and she was baffled by how calm he seemed around warriors who had slain his parents years ago. There was something he hadn't told her. . . .

A stocky warrior approached them. Slowly the Apache circled the white couple and looked them over thoroughly. He said, *"Benasi'nldal,"* which meant Nighthawk had forgotten about him.

"Duuda," T.J. refuted. He explained that he had needed to return to *keeya',* his homeland to search for his family. In Apache, he continued, "I needed to learn of the white man and my history. I have never forgotten my Apache brothers and history. I have never turned against them or battled them."

"Andi," a second warrior replied as he left his hiding place and joined them, saying T.J.'s words were true. "Nighthawk told me of his hungers before he left our camp and my father's side."

207

T.J. smiled and nodded at Naiche, the second son of Cochise who had become chief after his father's death, a blood chief who was being compelled to share his power with the notorious Geronimo. For the benefit of Geronimo and others, T.J. said, "I heard of our father's death and it saddened my heart. He was a great leader."

Geronimo scoffed, "The white man forced him to a reservation, and it killed his spirit first and then his body. It is evil!" *"Ntu',"* he stressed coldly and bitterly.

"But he wished peace and survival for his people. It was wise."

"Naagundzu!" Geronimo shouted, meaning they were at war again.

T.J. kept his attention on his blood brother. "It is bad to begin the raids and warfare again, Naiche. You must find a way to make peace so your people can survive, as our father wished. The whites are many and powerful. They will hunt down your people."

Geronimo stated belligerently, "The bluecoats try to corral and tame us like wild horses. They track us as animals!"

"Because you prey on them as wolves after helpless sheep," T.J. reasoned softly. "The white man is here to stay, so you must make peace or your tribe will perish under his advance and guns. He does not understand the Apache way; he must be taught to do so."

Carrie Sue intently observed the two Apaches closest to them. The younger one was nice-looking. His dark eyes were shiny and alert, filled with intelligence and courage, and noticeably lacked any glint of hatred and danger to her and her lover. The only thing which detracted from his looks was his slightly drooping right jawline which caused the left corner of his mouth to lift slightly as if he were always half-smiling. He was clad in a striped cotton shirt, tan breeches, a knee-length loin drape, and the distinctive leather boots which could be drawn over the knees to protect them against cactus and other prickly plants. A red cloth was rolled and tied around his black hair, making a sharp contrast in colors. It reminded her of Kale Rushton who was half-Apache and wore his black hair long and wore a red sash around his forehead. The other man was much different.

He looked to be middle-aged, but it was hard to tell because his skin was so darkened by the Arizona sun. His features were nearly harsh, as was his piercing gaze. His hair, which was parted down the center of his head, only fell to his shoulders, unlike the long hair of the other Indians. His nose was large, very full at the bottom. His mouth appeared a mere slit across his face, a line which turned downward at both ends as if set in a permanent frown. Furrows cut into his forehead and between his brows, but she didn't know if they were due to the sun's glare or his ill-feelings toward them.

Carrie Sue's attention was drawn to the older man's deep-set eyes beneath overhanging brows. They were small, and glittered with powerful emotions. His gaze and expression hinted at a man who was short-tempered, suspicious, tough, a man with an unyielding spirit and fierce courage. She didn't need to be told this stocky man was Geronimo. She wished she could understand what the men were saying, but she didn't know a word of Apache; Kale had never tried to teach her.

Cochise's second son and chief of this band of renegades said, "You know why we have taken to the warpath again, Nighthawk. They invaded our land and made us prisoners. They force those on the reservations to work for them as slaves. Women and children are given a metal penny to gather hay for their horses, but this white money buys little. We were told to gather piles of cottonwood and mesquite, but were allowed only small shares for our campfires. We were forced to make a line to claim rations of flour and beef as the treaty promised if we halted our raids. Seven days' supply the Army said, but it was gone in four.

Yet we were forbidden to hunt game on lands which have belonged to us since Grandfather made them. Men must dig holes in the body of Mother Earth to do what is called irrigation so we can grow evil things within her belly for the whiteman to eat. Apaches are not farmers and we do not care for such foods. If we refuse to cut into the earth, we have nothing to do but drink, gamble, and repeat tales of past glories. Many warriors have become scouts for the bluecoats so they can ride free. We grew restless and escaped."

T.J. inquired patiently, "What of Tom Jeffords, Naiche? Can you not trust him as our father did? Can you not make a new treaty with him for the sake of your people?"

"The whites sent him away because he sided with us. Jeffords forced the whites to give us our sacred mountains as part of our reservation, but they have taken back their words and our lands. He was with my father before he left Mother Earth. They were friends. He is gone now and can no longer help us battle the evil whites."

T.J. knew that Cochise had died on the day and the hour he had told Indian agent Tom Jeffords he would. His people had painted his body yellow, black, and vermilion, had shrouded him in a red blanket, and had taken the chief's body into the sacred mountains and buried it in a secret place where it would never be found.

For the last two years, Jeffords had maintained peace, but Cochise's death had made it difficult. When Geronimo and other leaders began raiding across the Mexican border, trouble had begun.

T.J. hadn't been in this area in some time, but he always found ways to keep up with the local events and the tribe which had raised him. He hated the thought of the Apaches being wiped out, but there was little he could do to help prevent what seemed to be their grim fate. For the past few months, things had gotten worse.

The Mexican government had insisted that Jeffords and

the American authorities halt the Apache raids in their country. One bitter incident in March had brought the conflict to a head. It had been rumored that the marauding Indians had stolen gold and silver along with horses and cattle. Two white men had sold the Indians whiskey and gotten them drunk so they would reveal where the treasure was hidden. When the Indians refused to comply and the treacherous whites wouldn't give them more whiskey, the inebriated Indians had killed them. The taste of blood had brought back memories of olden times and sent the Apaches to raiding locally. Jeffords and the Army had tried vainly to capture the renegades and halt their attacks, and all Apaches had been blamed.

In April the *Arizona Citizen* of Tucson had declared, "The kind of war needed for the Chiricahua Apaches is steady, unrelenting, hopeless, and undiscriminating war, slaying men, women, and children, until every valley and crest and crag and fastness shall send to high heaven the grateful incense of festering and rotting Chiricahuas." The outcry of the Arizonians and Governor Anson Safford had been heard in Washington, and Tom Jeffords had been fired. The decision had been made to dissolve the Chiricahua reservation and to transfer its people to the San Carlos Reservation which was shared by over four thousand Apaches of all tribes. Geronimo had gotten wind of the offensive plan and fled, enticing four hundred followers to do the same.

T.J. had learned of Jeffords's firing and the intent to move the reservation; he had protested both actions to the President, knowing how the Apaches would react. But Grant had many problems and pressures at the time and couldn't relent to T.J.'s request, suggestions the special agent had known would prevent plenty of bloodshed on both sides. Now, it was too late to influence the President; war was on.

"There is nothing more I can say to you, my brother. You

must ride the path you know is best for Naiche. Will you allow us safe passage through your territory?"

"Who is the woman?" Geronimo asked, staring up at her.

"Kada'ultan," T.J. replied, telling him Carrie Sue was a teacher. *"Shiisdzaa,"* he added, claiming she was "my woman."

Both Apache leaders looked her over again, making her nervous.

"She must be brave and smart to be the woman of Nighthawk," Naiche remarked. "We need more women. Is she for trade or sell?"

T.J. grinned and shook his head. *"Duuda."*

"Lltse 'i'nagu 'akahugal," Naiche told him, inviting them to return to their camp to talk and eat before they left this area.

Geronimo shouted, *"Duuda!"*

The two leaders argued for a time, alarming Carrie Sue who couldn't understand what the heated debate was about, except for the constant motioning to her and her lover. Finally, Geronimo relented, if they were blindfolded on both trips, to and from their hidden camp.

T.J. nodded acceptance of the requirement. He told Carrie Sue, "They want us to go to their camp to eat and spend the night to prove we offer them no harm. They'll release us in the morning. If we don't agree, they'll be insulted by our mistrust and scorn."

The redhead eyed the two chiefs. "Will we be safe?"

The smokey-eyed man replied, "Yes, I know this leader. His word is his honor. We'll have to be blindfolded first. Don't be afraid."

Carrie Sue glanced at Naiche again. "I'm not. His eyes say he speaks the truth. Besides, they could have captured us or slain us here if they wanted to. I sense no danger from him. Who is he?"

"The second son of Cochise and my blood brother. I lived with the Apaches from seven to thirteen. My Indian name is Nighthawk."

Carrie Sue stared at him. Was he telling the truth? She gazed into his blackish gray eyes and glanced at his midnight hair and dark tan. Had he been raised as an Indian captive? Was that why he had reacted so strongly to slavery and why he had sided with the Union? Or was he half-blooded and didn't want to tell her? Could he be Cochise's son with a white woman? Was the leader before them his half-brother? Was that why it would be safe for them to enter the Apache stronghold? "I see."

"Does that bother you, woman?" he asked after her intense study.

"No, I have nothing against Indians. In fact, I can't blame them for what they're doing. If we'd treat them fairly, we could co-exist peacefully. You have good and bad Indians, just like you have good and bad whites. I won't have a problem with them unless they declare themselves my enemy just because I'm white. I don't even care if you're half-Indian, which you could be with those eyes and hair. I'd still feel the same way about you."

Naiche wanted to grin, but that would tell the white girl he understood her words. For a while, it would be nice if she didn't know.

But T.J. knew and he was glad she answered as she had.

Carrie Sue and T.J. were blindfolded and led away. The group rode across open land which soon became scattered with mesquites and scrubs. The land was relatively flat and grassy so the riding — despite the blindfold — was easy. They entered a protective rampart of granite domes and sheer cliffs. They headed for the natural fortress where Cochise had made his home and from which he had carried out his stunning raids. Years ago, Cochise's lookouts had stood on towering pinnacles of rock to sight their enemies or targets in the valley below, a stronghold from which the Apaches could swoop down without warning to attack wagontrains and stages and other travelers.

Carrie Sue missed seeing the awesome rock formations of the Dragoon Mountains and the concealed entryway to a narrow, six-mile long canyon which suddenly opened up into a forty-acre valley where water, grass, and security were seemingly provided for the Apaches by some Higher Being who desired their survival.

The blindfolds were removed so the redhead and ex-captive could dismount. There were numerous wickiups and rope corrals located in the valley. She was amazed by how many Indians had escaped the reservation. They were escorted to one of those dome-like abodes made from canvas which had been stolen from wagontrains and the Army.

T.J. told her they had been ordered to remain there while the men had a meeting. "About us?" she probed.

"Nope, survival strategy. Relax, woman, they won't harm you."

Carrie Sue needed some answers. "I take it you were more than their prisoner long ago after your parents were killed. Why do they treat you so well? Why weren't we disarmed?"

"Because Cochise took a liking to me and adopted me. I earned their respect and was allowed to join them, until I left at thirteen."

"You weren't rescued by soldiers?"

"In a way."

"What does that mean?" she asked, confused.

He revealed, "I was out with a small band when soldiers sighted us and attacked. I had one hand tied behind me to prove my skills at hunting, so the soldiers thought I was a captive who'd gotten one hand free trying to escape. I let them believe it so they'd send me back to Texas. That's what the Army did with white boys they rescued so they wouldn't be tempted to return to the Apaches and the only life they knew."

She removed her hat and fanned herself with it. "Did you

want to come back to them? Did you ever try?"

"Nope. I wanted to search for my older brother. He'd been taken by Mescaleros right after our captures. Since their territory was New Mexico and eastern Texas, I figured if my brother got free or was rescued, he'd be sent to one of those Texas missions."

She noted the haunted look which filled his eyes and darkened them, and she felt empathy toward him. She knew what it was to lose family, to lose an only brother. "Did you ever find him?"

"I checked all the missions when I got older, but no one had heard of him. I got news of him last winter by accident, but he was killed by Mexican bandits before we could catch up with each other again."

Such bitterness filled his gaze and tone that she questioned him no further on that subject. "I'm sorry, T.J.; that must have been hard for you to accept."

"Yep, fate was determined to defeat me, but I wouldn't let her."

"The Indians don't seem mad at you for escaping and never returning. What did you tell them back there?"

"Naiche and Cochise knew I would leave one day. The braves who escaped told them I was taken by the soldiers. They knew I would seek my own path and they accepted my hunger for the truth."

Still something didn't add up right. She inquired, "How could you accept the tribe who'd killed your parents?"

T.J. glanced at her, comprehending her confusion. "They were soldiers at war, and innocent people get in the way sometimes. They aren't the only ones who kill women and children during battles." He told her about the newspaper article and the events which had spurred this outbreak from the reservation.

That wasn't what baffled her. "But you're a Texan. How did you get to Arizona to be captured? If you were thirteen when you left, how could they remember you after so many

215

years. I'm confused."

"It's been sixteen; I'm twenty-nine. Are you forgetting I've been in and out of this area lots of times? I've seen them plenty since my departure. I left as a friend, and I always return as one."

She noted that he said "departure" not *escape*. She waited for him to continue.

"The Chiricahuas were helping the Mescaleros battle the whites. They knew if the whites got past their brothers' territory, they would advance here next. We were heading for El Paso to sell cattle, and the stock was needed by the Indians. It was the first time papa had taken all of us along on a cattle drive. If he'd let the Apaches have the cattle without a fight, they'd be alive."

To get off the painful past, T.J. started another subject to distract her. He explained how boys were trained for cunning and toughness, the two most important traits for survival in a harsh landscape. He told her how they were taught trickery as a better strategy than raw courage. A leader and his band were more highly praised for stealing a few horses or goods with no losses of life rather than stealing an abundance of them and incurring many deaths and injuries.

T.J. stood and looked toward the mountains to his left. He related how boys were forced to stay awake for long periods to learn how to thwart fatigue. They were compelled to run through miles of harsh terrain, carrying a mouthful of water all the way. If the boy spit it out or swallowed it, he must do the four-mile run again and again until he succeeded. A grown warrior could run seventy miles a day over any landscape. "We trained with arrows and bows and slings and rocks. We acted out battles and raids. We were shown how to use the land to conceal ourselves. We had to learn to survive using only our shields, wits, strength, and prowess."

He took a deep breath and continued, "By the time a boy

was twelve, either he was ready to become a warrior-in-training or he had to go through pre-training again from the start. To prove yourself, you were taken miles from camp and told to find your way back within a few hours, without being captured by braves in hiding."

"You made it, didn't you?" she asked, but knew the answer.

He nodded. "Yep, I had to. I was white so I had to prove myself more than worthy of being Cochise's adopted son."

"They're finding lasting peace hard to achieve, aren't they?"

"Yep. After the war, countless soldiers were assigned out here to string telegraph lines, build roads, protect settlers and miners, and control the so-called hostiles. The whites didn't realize how tough it would be to battle the Apaches. They're experts at striking from ambush; they can hide right before your eyes and you wouldn't see them. They know this terrain; they know how to live off of it and how to fight on it. The whites were at a big disadvantage out here. Until they got more fighters and better weapons than the Apaches."

A beautiful Indian girl called T.J. out to speak with her. They laughed and talked for nearly an hour. Carrie Sue felt her temper rising as she watched how the dark-haired beauty looked at and touched her lover, and how T.J. was behaving in return. Surely thirteen year old warriors didn't take girls to marry or to bed! Or did they?

When T.J. rejoined her, she asked, "Who was that?"

"Windsong, an old friend. She's grown into an eye-catching filly."

"Is she married?" Carrie Sue inquired, trying to sound calm.

"Not anymore. Her husband was killed a few months ago, from whiskey and a whiteman's disease."

She watched the woman vanish inside a nearby wickiup. "What was she doing, trying to entice you to rejoin them and take his place?"

T.J. eyed her with a mischievous grin. "Yep, but I told her I already had more woman than I could handle."

That jest did not soothe her ire. "I see."

He chuckled. "What do you see, my fiery vixen?"

"A roguish man playing tricks with me," she accused.

"Can I help it if a woman flirts with me? Made me feel good. I don't get much of that in the white world. Women are scared of me."

She frowned at him. "I could tell you were enjoying yourself."

T.J. sat on the blanket with her and tugged the red braid. "I'll remind you of your behavior when I act the same over another man."

"If we live that long," she murmured, feeling foolish.

"I told you they won't harm us," he comforted her.

"I'm not worried about the Apaches," she replied pointedly.

T.J. took her hand in his and vowed, "I won't let the whites harm you either, *Tsine.*"

"You shouldn't make promises you can't keep, Mr. Rogue. We both know my situation is impossible, just like the one with the Apaches."

"We'll figure something out. Trust me," he urged.

Naiche returned from the meeting, and he and T.J. talked in Apache for a time. Then, another warrior approached them. He spoke with T.J., pointing at her and making unknown remarks. She caught two of the words, but couldn't translate them: *"Naaki." "Tai."*

Coyote held up four fingers and said, *"Dii lii."* T.J. shook his head and smiled amiably. Coyote held up eight fingers and said, *"Tsaabi lii,"* and motioned eagerly at her.

"Duuda, Naaldluushi," T.J. responded genially.

The warrior eyed Carrie Sue and frowned at T.J. before leaving.

"What did he want?" she asked, knowing she was discussed.

T.J. laughed. "He wanted to buy you for his wife."

"Buy me!" she shrieked. When T.J. chuckled merrily, she added, "I hope you told him you can't sell what doesn't belong to you!"

"He went from two horses, to three, to four, then eight. That's a big price; you really captured his eye. I told Coyote he wouldn't want a sharp-tongued spitfire like you."

"And I wouldn't want a sa—"

T.J. hurriedly cut her off, "Calm down, *Tsine*. Women aren't allowed to be nasty to men in public. You don't want your hot temper and impulsiveness to cause trouble for us. If you behave like a rotten child, I'll be forced to spank you to save face and protect us."

"You try anything, Rogue, and I'll slit both your throats!"

Naiche remarked in English, "Her temper flames as brightly as her hair of fire, my brother. Why do you travel with such a defiant woman? Do you wish to borrow my lash to punish her?"

"Sometimes her mouth runs faster than her wits, Naiche, and she forgets how valuable she could be to someone who needs money for survival. She isn't usually so rude and forward. She's just tired and hungry. She'll tame down or else I'll punish her."

Carrie Sue caught the warning in his first sentence and fell silent. She must not offend these Indians, or enlighten them to her value. She hadn't realized Naiche could speak her language, but she should have been more careful. "I'll behave, partner."

Naiche and T.J. exchanged pleased smiles. They sat on blankets before his abode and consumed *ch'ilae'bitsi,* *'iigaa'i, 'itsa'ich'i'i,* and *lees'an:* roasted antelope meat, Apache cabbage, dried cactus fruits, and bread cooked in the ashes. The men drank *inaada*—mescal—while she had *tl'uk'axee'*—wild tea.

Afterwards, she thanked Naiche and smiled at him. The chief called Windsong over to take Carrie Sue to the river for privacy and a bath. She gathered her belongings and followed the Indian woman.

"She is very brave, my brother," Cochise's son remarked. "It was wise to use the blindfold to fool her. No outsider can see the hidden passage into our secret valley, not even your woman. But you have not forgotten it as Geronimo believes. It has been a long time since your last visit. Why have you returned?"

"I'm taking her back to her land. The dangers here are too many for her. Her brother is an evil man who causes the whites much trouble. People fear her and chase her to get at him."

"But you will protect her from them, as you tried to protect us from the evil whites. You lived amongst us when our father allowed the building of the Butterfield station near our mountains. He let the whites use our water and lands, but their greed increased. You were gone when the white man named Bascom destroyed the peace between us."

"I learned it was the Pinal tribe who caused the treaty to be broken, my brother. When they attacked white ranchers and stole a child, the soldiers had to ride against them. But they did not understand, all Apaches are not the same, of the same tribe. Bascom was eager for glory and he did not know the truth. I revealed it to them, but it was too late. No man can undo a past deed."

"Bascom insulted our father when he accused him of theft and lying. He shamed Cochise before the Indian and white man. He tried to hold my father and others captive for the black deeds of the Pinals."

"If Jeffords had been here in those days, the mistake would have been corrected before it led to war."

"Bascom hanged my uncle and his two sons. We were challenged."

"Was the new war worth the price, my brother? During the white man's big war against himself, he sent soldiers here with powerful weapons called howitzers. Do you wish them to return with such guns?"

"Have you forgotten what our father told you during one visit? He said, 'We kill ten; a hundred come in their place.' We destroy little weapons and they return with bigger ones with more power than our bows and lances. After you left, whites of all kinds poured into our lands like the summer rains. They do not wish to share; they wish to take. It cannot be."

T.J. knew the white population had grown to thirty-seven thousand by 1870, ten times larger than the Indian population. He recalled that Cochise had told him that he was intrigued by the white man's courage. That had been the great chief's reason for meeting with Tom Jeffords, a courageous man who became his friend for life.

"Four summers past, you talked the Great White Father into making peace with us again. Our father hunted and talked with General Howard for eleven days. Our father said, 'The white man and the Indian are to drink of the same water, eat of the same bread and be at peace.' He agreed to the treaty and reservation life until the Great Spirit called him two winters past. We tried to keep the peace, my brother; you know this. It cannot be. We will never go to the San Carlos prison."

As Naiche had said, there had been many times T.J. had tried to help make peace between the whites and the Apaches, especially after making contact with and going to work for President Grant in '70. But he could not change history or control an inevitable future. At times, he experienced bitterness over what both peoples had done to his life. But he had come to understand the Apaches who had raised him. They had taught him many things which had saved his life when threatened by man or nature. He had grasped their desperation to survive, to challenge the

221

people they viewed as invaders of their lands and destroyers of their people. The Indians had disciplined him, but never abused him; they had adopted him. They were simply different from the whites, a difference which prevented lasting peace.

Thad Jamison had been forced to accept the truth long ago about his past. He remembered the day his parents had died, his father while shooting at the Apaches and his mother from a stray bullet. He knew he and Tim had been separated only because white brothers would adapt better to new lives if they didn't have each other to whom to cling. Yet, he still sometimes felt resentment burning in his heart against the Apaches, and he knew that was only normal.

"When you leave this time, my brother, we will never see each other again," Naiche concluded.

"Your words are true, and it saddens me."

The chief offered, "If you wish to remain here with your woman for safety, no Apache will take your lives."

T.J. sighed heavily. "I cannot, my brother. There is something I must do. I will tell no one how to reach this stronghold. Your war is with the whites, not with me."

Naiche saw how troubled his blood brother was and knew the man needed to speak openly and honestly to someone he could trust. "Your word is your honor, Nighthawk. What bitterness eats at you?"

T.J. looked at his friend and replied, "What I must do is hard, Naiche; I must capture and slay the brother of my woman."

"She does not know this," the chief concluded aloud.

"No, and it will cause her much pain. My task will endanger her life. The whites wish her dead. By taking her back to lead me to her brother, she could be captured and slain by the white law."

"Can you do this thing, Nighthawk?"

"I must, for her brother killed my loved ones and friend. They ride as outlaws, murdering and robbing the innocent.

222

I have promised the Great White Father to defeat them. She must be my path."

Naiche knew the truth about Thad Jamison. "You are a powerful man with the white law. Is there no way to save her?"

"Long ago, she rode with her brother's gang. She is guilty by white law and must be punished. My powers cannot save her."

"Can you not let her escape after you capture her brother?"

"My word is my honor, Naiche. To do so I must turn my back on it. I swore justice and vengeance before I knew her. It is hard to deceive her and betray her, but it is too late to retreat."

"You must not leave the path marked for you, Nighthawk. You cannot show weakness and lose face for any reason."

"I know," T.J. murmured. "It is a dark and dangerous path I travel this time, my brother; it will demand much from me."

"If there is a way to bring light and safety to it, you will find it and use it. But do not weaken and betray yourself."

"Her pull is powerful, Naiche," he confessed.

"But you are stronger and more cunning. Have you forgotten how to make an enemy a friend? Have you forgotten how you hated the Apaches and swore vengeance on us? It was that strength and courage which caused my father to adopt you. Nighthawk found understanding. He became a son, a brother, a man. Use what you learned amongst us. If you could run seventy miles across the desert in the heat, surely you can travel this path. You found the way to become one of us. When you left, you found the way to become a white man again. Can you not find a way to save this woman who causes your heart to burn?"

"It's different this time, Naiche. She has made many

enemies."

"More than the Apaches have made?" he reasoned cunningly. "Yet we find ways to survive, to challenge our foes."

"Yes, Naiche, she has more foes than the Apache. They seek her everywhere. She has no stronghold such as this one. She cannot remain in hiding forever, for someone will find her. When she travels the land, she is in more peril than when you leave this place. You are a warrior, but she is a woman. How can she defeat such forces? How can she change what has been done in the past? She is like you, my brother; she is in a white man's trap."

"From your words, there is no way to save her. You must do what your honor demands. As with us, find happiness until death takes her. As with us, if you side with her, you will also die. You were sent from us to find the path you were meant to walk. Travel with her for a time, then ride on without her when she is lost to you."

"I have lost many things, my brother." T.J. told him. "I want this woman."

"As Apaches want survival and peace. Sometimes it cannot be."

Carrie Sue completed her bath under the curious gaze of Windsong who either couldn't or wouldn't speak to her in English. She sensed the Indian woman's irritation and intrigue, and she wondered what T.J. would do if she weren't with him on this visit. She had learned something new about her lover, his rearing and training by these Apaches and his adoption by the famed Apache chief who was now dead. Surely he felt a sense of loyalty to him, but how much? Which pull was strongest in a bind, the Indian or the white? And why, with his previous training and keen instincts, hadn't he detected their presence? Or had he? No doubt he had allowed their "capture."

She pondered the experiences and losses he had endured,

at least those she knew about, and realized what had made him as he was. And, there was no telling what else had happened to him over the years to create the legendary gunslinger T.J. Rogue. He had been forced to become a strong, self-reliant male, a loner, a man feared by people on both sides of the law. He was a man driven by ghosts, scarred and molded by events out of his control, urged onward in search of peace and respect: a story similar to hers. Perhaps that was why he had taken her side and was helping her.

But what had happened, she wondered, to him during the war between the North and South? Where had he gone? What had he done? How had he prevented becoming an outlaw, which usually happened to a man with his skills and nature?

If T.J. didn't seem to fit anywhere, what did he have to make his existence worthwhile? What did he want in life? Why couldn't he, if he loved her and wanted her, escape far away with her? What could possibly hold him to this area? And, why did she perceive that expectant air about him again, one similar to the one in Tucson?

There was, she decided, even more to this man than she had learned. But what were those secrets and how would they affect her?

Carrie Sue knew that T.J. loved her hair unbound, so she brushed it and let it flow down her back like a wild river of tawny red. She donned the one dress she had brought along, as she would have time to change clothes before they left this Indian hideout. She wanted to look as lovely as possible, to tempt him, she admitted.

Carrie Sue followed Windsong back to camp. It was nearly dark. T.J. told her to take a seat on a blanket near a campfire and to remain silent and respectful. She observed the ceremony of music and dances with awe. She watched the men drink mescal and talk, and she sipped the fiery liquid which her lover passed to her. She watched the women observe her, taking special note of her fiery mane.

The hour grew late, and she was exhausted. The drum of the music seemed to fill her head and chest; yet, she began to doze, to feel utterly relaxed, limp and warm.

"Why don't you turn in, Carrie Sue?" T.J.'s voice asked.

"Where?" she replied, too weary to argue or to be aroused.

"In Naiche's wickiup. We're his guests."

"Good-night," she murmured and headed that way. T.J. didn't follow. She fell on the bedroll and was asleep quickly.

T.J. finally joined Carrie Sue on the bedroll. She snuggled against him but did not awaken. He lay beside her in deep thought, musing over how their lives were so entangled.

Last summer Quade Harding had learned he was Thad Jamison, undercover Texas Ranger, from a careless officer who unwittingly had exposed his name and task during what the man thought was a private conversation in a Brownwood livery stable. T.J. had been investigating rumors about the Hardings and their illegal actions, but he had been compelled for the first time to leave a mission unfinished because of the man's rash slip, and that didn't sit well with him. Luckily the villainous bastard hadn't told his hirelings—Curly James and two friends—that secret when he had ordered T.J. Rogue's murder at the end of September. T.J. hadn't told Curly and his boys the truth either, as it wouldn't have changed what they did to him, unless entice them to murder him quickly and with certainty instead of leaving him to die a horrible death!

The Ranger who had been on the stage with Carolyn Starns had found him in time to save his life; now, his friend was dead at the hands of the Stover Gang. After healing, a vital mission had intruded on his search for Curly and his boys.

T.J. knew that Quade Harding assumed he was dead and there was no way the evil rancher would reveal his involvement with a Texas Ranger's death, so his secret identity was safe. If possible, he'd like to stay out of Quade's sight and hearing a while longer. Later, he would kill the snake for himself and his woman!

Bitterness chewed at the handsome lawman. It had been those cases which had prevented him from seeing his brother again. Actually Tim had been the one to hear of Thaddeus Jerome Jamison, a lawman who was heading soon to Fort Davis to work secretly on a case. Major Timothy Jamison had contacted Ira Aten of the Rangers and asked questions. T.J. had gotten the shocking news of his brother's survival and location in January, shortly before completing his mission in the Oklahoma Territory. Then, he had gotten wind of Quade Harding's cohorts, who were reported to be in Sante Fe. In February, Tim and his troop had been ambushed and killed by Mexican bandits who kept raiding over the border. T.J. had gotten the infuriating news a few days later, just as he was about to set aside his pursuit in order to visit his brother. The reports on Curly had proven to be wrong.

For a while he had been enraged and resentful. He had planned to quit his overlapping jobs for state, country, and President. He had intended to settle down with a lovely woman and her beautiful little girl, but the Stover Gang had murdered them in March. He hadn't quit his jobs; he had sworn revenge on the Stover Gang and Quade Harding. He had sworn revenge on the Mexican raiders, but the Army had done that task for him in late March. In April he had picked up clues on Curly's boys and tracked them down, to learn they were to meet their boss in El Paso on May first. Again fate had stalled him until May second. Assuming Curly had left El Paso, T.J. had gone to Tucson to await the bastard's arrival.

Along the way, he had met Miss Carolyn Starns, alias

Carrie Sue Stover. If his life hadn't been complicated already, it was now, for the woman who had stolen his heart and wits was connected to both enemies! And, she had known Curly James, a curious fact considering the blond gunslinger had worked for the Stover's enemy. His love certainly had traveled with some vile types. Yet, he knew for a fact she hadn't gotten cozy with any of those criminals. Didn't that say something important and good about the woman he loved and desired?

There was something else Thad Jamison wanted, his Texas Ranger badge with his name engraved on the back. He knew from reports that Darby Stover or one of the gang members was a collector of badges off the chests of slain officers of any kind of law enforcement, and his badge was among them. The Ranger who had been slain with Carolyn Starns during the holdup near Sherman had been keeping it for him until he completed a tricky case. That badge represented a lot to him, and he wanted it back! Soon, he promised himself.

When it was safe and the opportunity presented itself, he needed to telegraph his superiors on several matters . . .

He looked over at the sleeping vixen in his arms. *What the hell am I going to do with you, woman?*

His warring mind shouted back, *You mean, what the hell are you going to do about her, Thad?*

228

Chapter Twelve

T.J. awakened Carrie Sue so they could head out soon. With the flap down, she washed her face and hands and donned her riding clothes. After packing her possessions, she lifted the entry covering and joined the two men outside.

T.J. and Carrie Sue were served *itl'anaasdidze* and *banxei,* Apache mush and fry bread. They were given a supply of *tsguust'ei* and *bii bitsi,* Apache tortillas and dried venison, for the trail. When they finished eating, her lover went to bid old friends good-bye.

Carrie Sue asked Naiche, "What does *Tsine* mean?"

The Indian chief sent her a lopsided grin and responded, "It is what a man calls the woman he loves. You whites have many words for it, so it is difficult to translate. Do not tell my brother we have spoken of this word or he will be angry with me," he teased, hoping his revelation might help Nighthawk get closer to the woman and carry out his mission as quickly and painlessly as possible.

As T.J. and Naiche said their farewells, Carrie Sue wondered if the endearment had been used to fool the Indians into believing she was his woman to prevent problems, or if T.J. had meant it. Right now, her head ached from too much mescal to think clearly! She shouldn't have consumed any of the potent drink, but she had been so nervous last night not knowing how to act with T.J. here. She still wasn't certain of the Apache woman's role, and she didn't want to offend or insult any of them. Soon, she could relax.

Relax? her throbbing head scoffed. *When? Where? How? You're on the run again!*

In Apache, T.J. told Naiche, "I will send the Great White Father another message about Jeffords and the San Carlos movement. If I can change his mind about them, my brother, I will do so. It will take time for my words to reach his hands and ears. If he takes them to heart, it will take more time for him to respond and take action. Until that day, try to work with the new Indian agent for peace and a compromise."

Naiche replied, "I will give your words to the council, but I can make you no promises, my brother. While your words travel to the white leader and his words travel back to my lands, the whites and soldiers will not be at truce with the Apache. If they strike at us, we must defend our lives and lands."

T.J. coaxed, "Try to encourage your tribe not to raid on the whites from this full moon to the next. That will give time to make a new treaty to halt more bloodshed on both sides."

Naiche inhaled deeply, expanding his broad chest. "I will try."

"I can ask nothing more of you, my wise brother."

After a few more minutes of conversation in Apache, Naiche blindfolded them and led them out of the valley via the secret canyon. Miles away, the eye coverings were removed and they parted.

T.J. and Carrie Sue headed across a terrain of mostly yuccas, scattered bushes, and desert grassland. There were mountains in all directions, some distant and some close. It was fairly easy riding, except for her headache and excessively dry mouth.

They had traveled about twenty miles when he halted them for rest and water. T.J. knew she was in discomfort, but they needed to push on toward Apache Pass where he could conceal her in the Chiricahua Mountains while he rode to Fort Bowie to send critical telegrams. He had to complete his obligations to Naiche and his tribe before continuing his mission with Carrie Sue. He had to inform the President of what could happen out here if quick and fair decisions weren't made.

The lawman also needed to make certain the wanted posters on this beautiful fugitive had been withdrawn and that his superior knew all was going well on the Stover case. Too, he wanted to have an agent assigned to investigate her charges against Quade Harding. Since those events took place in June of '69, evidence would be hard — if not impossible — to find. But proving what had turned her bad was the only chance he had!

To give Carrie Sue more time to rest, T.J. said he was going to scout ahead for a short while. He told her to remain in the shade and to sip water slowly. He smiled when she simply nodded in her misery.

Carrie Sue watched the handsome Rogue leave, and frowned. She knew what he was doing, and it vexed her that it was necessary. She scolded herself for being so foolish last night. She knew that by nightfall the scorching sun would have sweated out most of the devilish liquid and she would feel like herself again.

She leaned her head against the tree and closed her eyes to shut out the sun's tormenting glare. She liked having T.J. be so caring and sensitive; she liked him calling her a romantic name, even if he didn't know she understood it. Before she reached El Paso and then headed for the Guadalupes where Darby was hiding — if Curly had spoken the truth — the matter of T.J. Rogue would be solved one way or —

Galloping hooves interrupted her musings. She jumped up, drew her revolver, and positioned herself for defense. T.J. came into sight, dismounted, and rushed toward her. She holstered the weapon.

"Trouble ahead, woman! I need you to hide here while I ride back to Naiche's camp and warn him. From those rocks, you can see miles beyond, even without fieldglasses. Several regiments of soldiers are coming this way with Apache scouts and Gatling guns. You know what that means. They'll be led straight to Naiche's camp and those Apaches won't stand a chance against those guns."

T.J.'s heart had pounded in dread when he had sighted those multibarreled weapons on their field carriages. He knew they could fire hundreds of rounds a minute. If the soldiers got into the secret valley or simply waited for the Apaches to ride out, it would be a slaughter. He had to do something to prevent such bloodshed, but he couldn't go reason with the Army. Without authorization, they wouldn't listen or change their minds, and his cover and mission would be destroyed for nothing. Besides, he had no proof he was Thad Jamison and he couldn't reveal that he worked for the President, who had given the order to move the Apaches to the San Carlos Reservation. Even if he told the Army he was trying to reach Grant to change his mind, they wouldn't back off on such weak words. "I have to persuade Naiche and his people to flee into Mexico until this current trouble settles down."

"How can you find their camp again?" she asked.

"They have guards posted who can see everything nearby. I know which direction to take. Remember, the sun was to our left, then at our backs. I can guess how many miles we rode and which way. All I need to do is be seen by them. They'll know something's wrong."

Carrie Sue didn't quite believe he didn't know the camp's location, but she didn't challenge his code of honor. "Does this mean your loyalty lies more with the Indians than the whites?"

"Nope, they're usually divided in matters like this because I know both sides. But I can't let a slaughter take place when I can stop it. There are women, children, and old ones in that camp, but those Gatling guns won't know the difference between them and warriors. If they'll just cross the border and lay low for a while, maybe things will cool down here with the new Indian agent in charge. At least I will have done the only thing I could."

Carrie Sue wondered why she wasn't surprised by his behavior. "Why would those Apache scouts help the Army track down their own people?"

"They're caught in the middle too. And it's the only way they can ride and live free of reservations. Besides, they're probably from other tribes and don't feel they owe this band any loyalty."

She wondered if, because of his troubled background, he had a penchant for helping the downtrodden or vulnerable. "Do you always help bad people like us when we're in trouble?"

"What makes you think that either side is totally wrong or bad?" T.J. asked. "You both got bad breaks in life and you have to accept them and deal with them. You can't believe that you or the Apaches are totally to blame for what's happened in your lives. Everybody makes mistakes and has flaws. Yours just multiplied before you could correct them. I think you and the Apaches are caught in other people's traps, but there's little I can do for either of you, except help you both survive until things change, if they ever do."

The redhead eyed him strangely. "What's in it for you, T.J.?"

He shrugged, then grinned. "With you, I'll get paid for my trouble and danger by getting to spend time with a beautiful and enjoyable woman. As for the Apaches, I owe them for what they've done for me."

She argued, "But you're breaking the law in both cases. I thought you always liked to steer clear of such perils."

"I have to do what I think is right and fair, so any more talk will have to wait until later. The Apaches only have a few hours to get packed and get away before those soldiers reach attack position. Right now the Army's camped during the heat of the day and, when they get going again, they'll have to move slowly with those heavy guns. Will you stay here until I return? I can move faster alone."

Carrie Sue realized he didn't want to leave her alone, but he wanted to warn his friends. She jested to cease his worry, "Without my protective partner, I have no choice but to await his return." Her expression and tone became serious when she added, "I'll keep hidden. You be careful, T.J., and please convince them to leave quickly."

"Be here when I return, woman, or I'll tie you naked to the first cactus I find after I recover you." The ebon-haired man pulled her tightly against him and kissed her with a feverish force that revealed his hunger for her, and his fear she wouldn't keep her word.

Carrie Sue caressed his cheek and jested, "Do you want to take my weapons along to prove I'll have to wait for you?"

"Nope, 'cause you might need them if another rattlesnake shows up, with no legs or with two of them. I'll get back as soon as I can."

Carrie Sue watched him ride off and she sighed wearily. At least this would give her time to relax and recover from her reckless drinking. She left her pinto concealed in the deep arroyo nearby, and she stretched out on her blanket beneath the low limbs of a shady mesquite.

Time passed as the day's heat, the lack of any breeze, the near silence of the terrain, and the soothing buzz of insects on the fragrantly flowering tree lulled her into a peaceful doze.

Suddenly Carrie Sue sensed danger and bolted upright, entangling her braided hair on a mesquite branch. Rapidly her hand had gone to her holster, to find it empty. As she freed her hair, she angrily watched the man who was squatting before her with a broad grin on his face. She realized what had aroused her from her too deep slumber—he had taken her gun. "What is the meaning of this, Martin?"

The cattle baron and silver mine owner chuckled. "So, I was courting a legend and didn't even know it," he mur-

234

mured. "I should have known you were too tough and sassy to be a schoolmarm." His brown eyes lazily walked over the beautiful redhead and he laughed again.

"I suppose you're here to arrest me so you can collect my reward," she said with a contemptible sneer. "How did you find me?"

"Arrest you, my famous Texas Flame?" he leaned back his brown head and laughed almost wildly. "No, Miss Stover, I'm here to capture you for myself. As for finding you so quickly and easily, I have my Apache scout to thank; he's the best around," he boasted, nodding toward one of two men nearby. "As soon as Ben Myers showed me your poster Thursday afternoon, I came after you. Naturally our old sheriff didn't want to call out such a famed gunslinger, even if she is a woman." He pushed out his lips in a silly pout and said, "But you had taken off with that Rogue. Were you two friends before that bungled holdup?" he asked, his tone now demanding and cold.

"We'd never met before, but I figured I could use his help in case trouble came along before I could convince everyone I was Miss Starns. Men are easy targets when they think they'll get something from you out of gratitude," she remarked, trying to sound poised and cold like he was. If she was going to control this situation, especially get out of it, she had to fool Martin Ferris, to pretend she was like him.

"What was that little schoolmarm act about?" he questioned.

Carrie Sue watched the sweat roll down his face, too much for even the dry heat to consume. His cheeks were flushed as red as blood, and his lips were trying to parch. He definitely was not an outdoor man! He looked miserable in his soaked and rumpled clothes. He acted as if he were surrounded by hell's flames instead of desert heat. And the holster around his waist looked totally out of place on him. She almost laughed at the comical sight, but knew that would be unwise, as he was a dangerous foe. She didn't think he would believe her story about starting a new life and it wouldn't matter to a villainous beast like him if he did, so she related what would seem obvious and credible. "I was staking out the town for Darby's gang. I was supposed to decide if there were any easy, profitable targets there. If Tucson looked good to me, I was to send him a telegram on June first. Seems I messed up this time." She laughed softly and curled her arms around her upraised knees, wanting to appear relaxed and confident.

"It was working perfectly until those wanted posters arrived, and I'm not fooled easily. How did you find out about the wanted posters before they reached town? You took off like you had been warned."

She sent him a sly smile before answering, "I was, by Curly James, before Mr. Rogue inconveniently shot him. He used to ride with my brother's gang. We were old friends. We bumped into each other only minutes before his death and he told me my description and sketch had been released and I best get moving. I took off at dawn the next morning, but Rogue saw me leaving and followed. I persuaded him that Darby would ransom me for more than my ten thousand dollar reward, so he agreed to escort me to my brother. Of course, I planned to elude him along the way, after he and his guns had served me well as guards on the trail."

Carrie Sue lowered her legs and curled them to the left of her buttocks so she could lean forward, closer to the man's face. After sending him an enticing smile and seductive gaze, she asked, "Well, Martin, what are you planning to do with your helpless captive?"

"I have a big ranch and it's mighty private. No one will find you there unless I want them to. If you do as you're told, you'll be safe with me. I don't care about your measly reward."

Carrie Sue watched his tongue lick his lips in anticipation of having her at his mercy. She saw the lust glowing in his eyes, causing his face to redden even more. She heard his breathing alter as he became aroused just by looking at her, being near her, and having control over her. Those were weaknesses of which she could take advantage if she were clever and careful. The intelligent woman knew what this lecherous and wicked man wanted from her, and she had to pretend she was agreeable. "Since I have either a rope or a cell staring me in the face, your offer sounds most appealing, Martin. In fact, very appealing," she added, moving closer to him. When T.J. sneaked up, which she hoped was soon, she needed to be close enough to grab the vain man's weapon. The only problem was, she didn't know how long her lover had been gone or when he would return!

Martin extended his hand and helped her from beneath the tree. "You made the right decision, Carrie. You will understand if I take precautions with you until we're home and I'm certain I can trust you?"

"Of course. What would a woman want with a stupid or reckless man?" she teased. "Where is your ranch? What's it like?" she inquired to stall for time for her partner to rescue her.

"You'll see," he murmured, eyeing the area between her throat and cleavage where her shirt was opened for air. "Where is Rogue now?"

Beyond where they were standing, she saw the Apache scout studying the signs on the ground. "He went scouting. There's a detachment of soldiers miles up that way. He was looking for the safest path around them. I was asleep, so I don't know how long he's been away," she informed him, trying to sound as if she were being totally honest with him. Besides, if these men had been tracking them or observing them, Martin Ferris knew the truth.

"Does she speak the truth?" Martin asked the Indian.

The dark-skinned man who was dressed half in white-man's clothes and half in Apache garments replied, "The whiteman rode in the direction she said. He returned and talked. He left again and rode toward the Dragoons. He left two hours past."

Martin Ferris already knew before reaching this makeshift camp which direction T.J. had taken and when he had left because he had been watching the scene with his fieldglasses from a rocky peak in the distance. He also knew from their tracking that the couple had been captured and released by the renegade Apaches, which he found odd. He just wanted to see what the redhead would say before and after the Indian's words. "Why would Rogue be heading for the Apache stronghold after he sighted those soldiers?"

Carrie Sue had sensed trickery in the man, so she was prepared not to look surprised or unmasked. "I wouldn't know, unless he wanted to warn them of danger. He didn't tell me he was heading back to their camp, and I'll be surprised if he can locate it again. I wasn't feeling well, so he told me to wait for him here. I assumed he was doing what he said, looking for the best way out of this area. He gave me a kiss and galloped off, then I took a nap."

"What do you mean he was 'heading back'?" Martin asked, though his tone and expression made it all too clear he already knew the answer.

Nonchalantly, Carrie Sue sighed. "The Apaches captured us on the trail, blindfolded us, and took us to their camp for questioning. They seemed to know who Mr. Rogue was and admired his courage, so they released us this morning. For all I know, they could be old friends. I was kept in a separate tepee, so I didn't hear or see anything to tell me otherwise. He could have made some trade with them for our freedom."

"I'm glad you're being truthful with me, Carrie," he remarked in a pleased tone. "Let's get moving out of this heat." He ordered the Apache scout to stay behind and ambush T.J. to prevent him from following them. "After you're done here, catch up with us on the road or meet me back at my ranch for payment. I want his guns for souvenirs," he added, but they all knew he meant he wanted them as proof.

Carrie Sue had no choice but to do as Martin Ferris ordered, and to pray that her lover wouldn't ride into the trap set for him. She had faith in T.J.'s keen wits and skills, so he should be fine. She thought she had this lecherous villain at least partially duped, and the odds would be only two-to-one on the road, which might aid her escape. She gathered her things and mounted the pinto.

"Sorry about this, Carrie," he said with a falsely rueful grin as he bound her hands before her and took control of her reins. "What the hell are you looking at, Jess," he scowled at the other man, whose eyes had been glued to her curvaceous form. Jess quickly looked away.

Her quivering hands clung tightly to the horn, relieved she was such a good rider, skills she tried not to reveal to the two men who rode on either side of her. That idea didn't work too well since the pace and terrain forced her to use them to remain in the saddle. If she were thrown off at this speed, she could be severely hurt. She wondered if Martin was testing her in some cruel way, or merely assumed she was an expert horsewoman.

They traveled fast for the perilous terrain and heat, but Carrie Sue didn't say anything to slow them. When the horses got winded and Martin became overheated, he would be forced to take it easier. She hated to push her animal this hard, but if she suggested a lesser pace, Martin might take it the wrong way and watch her too closely. She had to let him get over-confident where she was concerned!

They reached the road to Tucson and continued to gallop swiftly. She finally decided that Martin was afraid his Indian hireling might not kill T.J. and the handsome gunslinger would be dogging them any time now. They only halted twice for short breaks before reaching the San Pedro River at dark where they made camp in a sparsely treed area.

Carrie Sue was aware of how close they were to Tucson, one day's ride. By using the cleared road and swift pace, they had covered a great distance today. She wondered why they hadn't met anyone along the public road. Where were all the soldiers, renegades, stages, and solitary travelers? Was T.J., she worried, alive and chasing them?

She was annoyed when Martin Ferris refused to untie her hands so she could relieve herself more easily behind thick bushes not far away. Nor did he unbind her hands while she ate her helping of canned beans and stale tortillas, a sparse and untasty meal prepared by Jess. Her headache had eased up, but was not totally gone. She blamed the lingering discomfort on the hot sun and swift pace, but tried to ignore it to keep her wits clear. At least their fast ride had prevented any talking on the trail which would have kept her on alert for many strenuous hours. She teased him flirtatiously, "Is this necessary, Martin? You have my weapons, horses, and supplies. Surely you know I'm not going to escape into the desert without them. Besides," she hinted seductively, "we both know I'll be safer at your ranch than anywhere else."

"Apaches can use this land with ease, and a smart woman like you might have those same skills. I would hate for you to trick me, Carrie, and force me to hurt you. This way, you won't be tempted to act rashly during the night. Relax, we'll be home before sundown tomorrow."

It was apparent that Martin was exhausted from his uncommon exertions, too fatigued to even make any sexual overtures. No doubt he assumed he had plenty of time to tame her and use her.

After she was secured to a tree for the night, Martin and his man took turns guarding the camp, with Jess taking the first watch and keeping his lustful eyes on her. She assumed their caution had as much to do with marauding Apaches as with T.J. Rogue. She fretted over what Sheriff Ben Myers was doing and thinking. Had the Tucson lawman sent out telegrams about her presence in and escape from his town? Did the lawman know about Martin Ferris's pursuit?

Carrie Sue's turbulent mind would not allow her to stop thinking so she could get some sleep. She asked herself if T.J. didn't catch up with them on the trail, would he come to Martin's ranch to rescue her? Wouldn't her lover guess that was where she would be taken? Wouldn't he guess that Martin Ferris would have his men watching for his stealthy approach?

And what of dear Mrs. Thayer? What had the woman been told? How had she accepted the shocking news about Carrie Sue Stover? One day, she hoped to get word to the woman and explain everything. But right now, she had to worry about escape from this beast.

The night was strangely still and quiet, and a full moon eerily brightened the landscape which was wild and rugged. It was too quiet, she fretted, because she didn't hear any bird, animal, or insect stirring about or making noises in the bushes or in the distance! It was as if some evil force had every living creature imprisoned, as if some oppressive and eerie heaviness was covering the landscape. In every direction, tall cactus looked like large fingers or hands pointing heavenward. She glanced skyward and saw clouds increasing on the midnight blue horizon. Maybe, she mused, a storm was brewing. That suited her fine, as it would cool the air and her body and it would release her tension. It might offer a chance for escape and wash away her tracks from even that Apache's keen eyes.

The redhead tested the strength of the ropes again. Too tight, she decided helplessly. She wanted water, but she refused to ask Jess to come near her to bring the canteen. She was exhausted, achy, and hot. The way she was bound to the tree, she couldn't shift to get comfortable. All she could do was spend a tormenting night on a complaining rump.

As Carrie Sue reflected on her dire situation, she was amazed by Martin's pursuit without a large band of men behind him. No doubt the conceited rancher believed no harm could come to him, and he didn't want anyone to know she was in his possession. Else, the law would take her away from him. Mercy, he was so like Quade Harding!

She knew it was long past Martin's watch time when Jess awakened him. She feigned sleep to prevent any conversation between them. While pretending, she dozed lightly.

After allowing her to excuse herself in the near darkness, Carrie Sue's hands were untied for a short time so she could eat another sparse meal and rub her wrists. Neither man was close enough to permit her the opportunity to seize a weapon from his holster. She had to figure out a plan to get away and return to Darby. But first, she had to earn Martin's trust. Maybe she would be forced to remain at his ranch until an opening presented itself, if she could control his sexual demands! As she drank her coffee, she asked her cocky captor, "What did Sheriff Myers say when you told him you were going after me?"

The brown-eyed man chuckled. "I didn't tell him anything about my plans. Except I did warn him to telegraph the Texas authorities that you'd left our area long ago so those blood-thirsty bounty hunters wouldn't pour into Tucson. I believe he was going to tell them you were seen heading northward toward Colorado. Doesn't matter; we'll be at my ranch before news gets out and you're in danger."

"What about Mrs. Thayer? What did she say when you went to check on me? She was nice and I liked her. Does she know the truth?"

"She knows you were using her place to hide, and she was mighty surprised. You had her fooled. People don't like being fooled, Carrie."

The redhead doubted Mrs. Thayer was really angry with her. Now, her new friend understood the meaning of her letter. With luck, Mrs. Thayer would give her the benefit of explaining before she judged her too harshly.

"Mount up so we can get out of here," Martin ordered.

While they were talking, Jess had doused the fire, packed the supplies, and saddled the horses. Her hands were bound again, and off they rode at breakneck speed just as the sun was rising.

It was clear and hot, so Carrie Sue realized it wasn't going to rain. She noticed the air was very still again today, and she could use a nice breeze. She realized that T.J. would guess their pace from the condition of their tracks, and hopefully he would race to catch up with them. Yet, he had used a great deal of time riding back to Naiche's camp, so she couldn't surmise how long that trip would take. Then, he had to battle that Apache scout and track her. With this pace and so few stops, could her love overtake them? He and his horse would already be tired from their long ride, and he would probably doubt that Martin would keep such a fast pace on this terrain.

A terrible thought came to mind: what if Martin had ordered the scout to conceal their departure trail? What if T.J. didn't guess who the scout worked for, or withdraw clues from the Indian before slaying him? How would he know where to search for her?

Following that alarming talk with herself, the day went by sluggishly despite their rush.

A shot rang out from behind them, and Jess fell to the road. Carrie Sue twisted in her saddle to see who was coming. Her heart fluttered with excitement.

Martin guided his horse in front of hers, his hand extended backwards to hold her reins as he positioned her between himself and T.J.'s gunfire. She realized the Tucson rancher was making a desperate race for town while using her as a shield. They were near the Old Spanish Trail, making Tucson about twenty miles up the road.

Carrie Sue could not allow them to reach town. She took hold of Charlie's mane and leaned forward. When she had herself steadied there, she released her grip and struggled to loosen the animal's bridle. She forced it over the mare's ears and shoved it down Charlie's forehead. The animal instinctively opened its mouth and the bridle was yanked free.

Instantly the redhead caught Charlie's mane and tried to halt her swift gallop so she could turn around and ride toward her lover.

The moment her reins went loose in his grip, Martin pulled back on his own. Before Carrie Sue could gain full control over her startled mare, Martin was beside her, a revolver aimed at her chest. He shouted, "Stay back, Rogue, or she's dead!"

She and Martin were sitting sideways in the road. She saw T.J. stop. Nighthawk paced apprehensively, and her lover did not pull out his rifle. She knew Martin could not shoot T.J. with a revolver at that range, nor could her lover shoot her captor without his rifle. She wondered what was going through T.J.'s mind, as he was not a man to surrender or retreat. Her heart pounded with fear.

Martin backed his mount until she was between the two men again. He handed her the bridle and ordered, "Put this on!"

It was obvious to everyone that T.J. didn't have a clear shot at Martin. "I have to dismount first," she told the villain.

"Do it, and no tricks!" the annoyed and scared man shouted. "Go for that rifle, Rogue, and I'll fill her with bullets!" he warned.

Since Martin had his attention on her lover, Carrie Sue decided to use a clever dismount to get the upperhand. As she was moving her right leg over the saddle horn, she was muttering, "Jess should have put it on correctly, and he should have been guarding our—" Carrie Sue forcefully kicked Martin in the stomach and knocked him to the ground. She hurriedly put her boot back into the stirrup and galloped toward safety with her love, who was racing toward her.

"Get down!" T.J. shouted as he took the right side of the road.

Carrie Sue urged Charlie to the left and bent over the animal's neck. The moment she had attacked Martin, T.J.

had drawn his rifle and galloped toward them. She heard shots behind her, but didn't know if Martin was shooting at her or her rescuer. T.J. returned Martin's fire.

Carrie Sue gently tugged on Charlie's mane. When she turned, she saw Martin Ferris lying on the ground and T.J. approaching him. She guided Charlie back to the scene to find her captor dead.

She dismounted and stared at the man's bloody chest. Weariness and dejection filled her. "What now, Rogue? They'll surely hunt us down for this so-called murder of an upstanding citizen. No one will believe he wasn't taking me in for that reward. Merciful Heavens, another false charge against me!" she scoffed bitterly. "Now you're involved. I'm sorry."

This was one time the law knew she wasn't to blame for a foul deed, and T.J. couldn't help but wonder how many other charges against her were either false or exaggerated or self-defense. Her mood tugged powerfully at him. He reasoned to comfort her, "He was trying to shoot you in the back, not kill me, woman. I had no choice but to get him first. You had nothing to do with this shooting," he vowed as he drew his knife and cut her hands free.

Carrie Sue rubbed her chaffed wrists as she explained, "You don't understand, T.J.; it's another charge against me. They just keep piling up no matter what I do or where I go. I'll never get out of this mess alive; it'll never be over, for either of us." she glared at Martin's body and wanted to kick it in frustration. "I have only myself to blame. If I weren't an outlaw, things like this wouldn't happen to me. I wouldn't be forced to do the things I do and keep breaking more and more laws."

He argued, "He was trying to kill you; it was self-defense."

She sighed deeply. "In my position, nothing is viewed as self-defense. The law will say I murdered him while trying to escape capture."

"But I know better, woman."

"What difference does that make? They'll only charge you for siding with me. They'll say you're just as guilty and you'll be in as much trouble and danger as I am. This isn't fair to you, T.J. I shouldn't have dragged you into this mess."

"I'm in it, so it's too late. Forget it for now."

She asked, "How did you overtake us so quickly?"

"I met Naiche halfway back to his camp, so I wasn't away that long. He agreed to take his tribe across the border for a while. When things quiet down, he's going to try for another truce."

She smiled in relief and said, "That's good. How did you elude that Apache scout Martin left behind to ambush you?"

"I didn't. He's dead. When something's wrong, I get this crazy itch. I sneaked back through the rocks to take a look around before I whistled for Nighthawk. I got the drop on him first."

"And he told you who captured me?"

"Nope, and he'd brushed away most of your trail for a ways."

She looked baffled. "Then, how did you know where to find me?"

"An Apache can hide a trail real good, but not from another Apache, and I was trained by them. I turned his horse loose; he can graze until he's found by someone or he'll join up with a herd of wild horses. I hid his body, so no one will be suspicious of us." He chuckled. "I guess Martin forgot I'd seen his scout in town, so I knew who had you. I took a shortcut by Dragoon Springs and found where you'd camped for the night. Not a comfortable one I could tell. Besides, Nighthawk is one of the fastest horses alive."

"What are we going to do now, partner?" she asked again. She told him about Ben Myers getting the wanted poster and telegraphing she was gone. She also revealed what had been said and done between her and Martin.

"That's perfect, Carrie Sue. It'll give us time to rest before we get out of this area. I know a place we can use, a large cave off the Old Spanish Trail, not far from here. We'll hide the bodies and horses there. You'll feel better after you're rested."

She smiled at him and said, "This is the fifth time you've saved my life. Won't that become a tiring job?"

"Fifth time?" he said, surprised.

"During that holdup, during our picnic, with that sheriff in my room, with those Indians, because there's no telling what they would have done to me if you hadn't been along, and today. That's five."

He didn't expound on her remarks because those incidents had sapped some of her confidence. Yet, he had to point out how much she needed him to strengthen their bond. "You're a skilled, smart, and brave woman, but you can't take on every lawman and bounty hunter alone. I told you I was needed to guard this pretty backside."

She admitted he was right and she couldn't do it alone. "You've convinced me I need your help and protection, T.J."

To lighten her somber mood, he tugged on her braid and teased, "No matter what happens, I'll stick with you. I'm surprised you weren't worried about me."

"Why should I have been? You're the best."

He grinned in pleasure and gratitude. "I'm glad you have so much confidence in me, but you're downing yourself too much. You're just as good as I am in most areas. Are you forgetting you saved my life at that picnic? If you hadn't been there to shoot at them, it would have been three-to-one odds, and I might have been killed."

"You're only trying to swell my head, Mr. Rogue. I recall how you took on more bandits than that during the stage holdup. Besides, there wouldn't have been any danger to you if not for my presence."

He shook his ebony head and refuted, "You're wrong, woman. Martin did it because we're old enemies. If his men hadn't attacked me out there, they would have ambushed me another time."

247

"What's to stop those three men from coming after us now? They know who I am and probably know Martin came after me."

"They can't; I got rid of them before we left town."

Sadness troubled her mind and heart. "You've had to kill too many times to save my miserable life, T.J. It has to stop."

"I didn't kill anybody who didn't need killing or who didn't provoke it. You're not to blame, Carrie Sue," he murmured and caressed her flushed cheek. He wanted to yank her into his arms and kiss her soundly. Lordy, she was getting a powerful grip on him! "We can't stand here jawing. Somebody might come along and there's a storm brewing. Let's get these bodies loaded and get to the cave."

T.J. retrieved Jess's body and horse, then loaded Martin Ferris on his. He guided her to the Old Spanish Trail cut-off and headed toward the Rincon Mountains which were twenty-two miles from Tucson.

They rode for a few miles, then left the trail to head into the hills. It was an area of small trees and bushy scrubs, mostly mesquite and catclaw. Large clusters of prickly pear, yuccas with tall shoots, towering agave plants, and numerous saguaro cactus were scattered around them. The land was rolling in places, and many dry washes ominously cut across the terrain. They journeyed uphill where rocks ribbed the landscape. Finally, they reached the cave's yawning mouth which was almost concealed by rocks and brush until one was right on it.

They dismounted near sunset. T.J. pointed out the Sonora Desert, the highest crag of the Santa Rita Mountains, and peaks which were in Old Mexico. It was a lofty spot, a perfect hideout with a view of the surrounding area. They entered the hollow mountain, and she was surprised by how cool and refreshing the interior was with a temperature in the low seventies.

"Wait here at the entrance while I fetch some brush for a fire. We'll need light and something to cook over. I'm starved.

I haven't eaten since I took off after you," he confessed before leaving to gather wood. When he returned and unloaded it, he guided her to a large cavern not far into the hillside. He built a fire for light, then took the bodies into a side tunnel to keep her from having to look at them. After unsaddling the horses and hobbling them, he smiled and said, "I'll be back soon. I want to cover our trail and see if I can get some fresh meat to roast. Don't leave here. Understand?"

"I promise. Please, be careful," she urged.

Carrie Sue sat on a low ledge in the dancing shadows of the campfire, anxiously waiting for her love's return. She wasn't afraid of the darkness which engulfed the rocky tunnels in all but the area where she was standing. She was aware of every minute that passed. She recalled what he had said about a storm brewing and the area outside this protective cave was a flash flood location. She knew how treacherous dry washes were when they gushed with violent water.

Carrie Sue jumped when it thundered loudly. She grabbed a torch and rushed to the entrance. The storm broke overhead. The lightning and thundering seemed continuous, powerful, endless. The rain poured so heavily that she couldn't see outside to watch for T.J.'s approach. With visibility near nothing, how could he find his way back? What if he got injured in the obscuring storm?

Suddenly she realized he had known the storm was close! He knew the signs and dangers of this territory. Why hadn't he let the rain conceal their tracks? Why couldn't they eat the food from Naiche, or eat from their supplies, or from Martin's? She panicked again . . . .

Chapter Thirteen

Carrie Sue paced the entry tunnel from the opening to the first cavern. She knew T.J. was planning to return because he had left his supplies with her. But, she fretted, where had he gone and why? Had he ridden into Tucson to send a telegram to someone, perhaps the same person he had telegraphed last Monday? Who? For what reason? To let someone know he had been delayed by this grim set-back? Could he possibly be a bounty hunter who was after bigger game than her? Was he hoping to romance her into leading him to Darby and his gang? T.J. Rogue was a loner and a talented gunslinger, but a man who stayed just within the boundaries of the law, a man who made his own decisions and went his own way, not a man to become just another gang member, even to be with her.

The daring desperado admitted that ten thousand dollars was a lot of money, and the capture of the Texas Flame would bring any man a lot of glory. Why would a legendary gunman ignore both to help her? If he loved her, he hadn't said so. He seemed to be enjoying their wild and wonderful romance, but did he consider it a permanent one, a special one? Or something to pass the time? Although he was passionate and protective with her, he was also mysterious and guarded. Maybe what had her so anxious was that he was a little too glued to her for a loner like he was and a fugitive like she was! If he was so crazy about her that he was willing to put his life and reputation on the mark, why didn't he tell her? Why couldn't she trust him fully?

Carrie Sue had never surrendered her heart and body to a man before, and she prayed she wasn't wrong about him. Because of her lifestyle, she had been given very few opportunities to be romanced by any man except outlaws like Kadry Sams and Dillon Holmes. She trusted few people, and she feared she couldn't trust her lover or herself. Maybe that was the problem, the source of her apprehensions. Maybe she was trying to convince herself she didn't and couldn't trust him because she was afraid of what it would mean to believe and accept him.

She was so confused. By pushing him away, was she only trying to spare herself from a hard and painful choice? Was she only trying to prevent his possible betrayal? Or was she trying to keep him safe from the dangers that haunted her? She was scared to trust him and to yield fully, scared he wasn't for real, scared he wasn't as serious about her as she was about him; and she was scared he was for real and she would lose him or destroy him.

Her head was spinning from dismay. Even if she was mistaken about his good feelings and motives, would he soon tire of her and this unlawful adventure and betray her? She had to clear her wits because he was too disarming. He could be so gentle and persuasive, but he was also tough and hard, and something was eating at him. Yes, she was leery of this enchanting rogue and distressed by her own warring emotions. She hated these fears and doubts, but she couldn't seem to master them. Her next actions depended on what he said and how he acted when he returned to the cave. . . .

Carrie Sue walked to the ledge and took a seat again. She scanned her surroundings. The ceiling in this area was soot-blackened, no doubt from fires used by ancient people, Indians, outlaws, and others. She—

"Carrie Sue," her lover's voice broke into her musings.

She hurried to the entrance to find a drenched T.J. and Nighthawk coming in out of the violent storm. He handed her a pail and asked her to fetch rain water for the horses while he unsaddled his stallion and fed the horses the bound hay he was carrying. She noticed a lantern tied to his saddle horn. She questioned, "Where have you been, Rogue? You could have let the rain wash away our tracks."

"I know," he agreed, then chuckled. "But we needed something for the horses to eat because I can't let them roam outside and be seen. We needed light, and a pail to give them water. This cave is dry."

She followed him inside to get her answers. "A campfire would give light," she hinted.

"And use up too much wood. If it went out while we're sleeping, this cave gets mighty dark. We're camping way back in there," he told her, motioning to the tunnel to their right.

"Go back in there?" she murmured almost inaudibly, her eyes widening in astonishment as she glanced in that dark direction. "What if we get lost?"

T.J. set the lantern aside and removed his soaked saddle. He tossed it on the ledge where she had been sitting so it could drip. There was no need to hobble Nighthawk, so he guided the animal to where the others were standing. He cut the cord around the bundle of hay and spread it on the rock floor so they could eat.

"Did you hear me, Mr. Rogue? What if we get lost in there?"

"Sorry, woman, my head is getting dizzy from hunger and fatigue. We won't get lost. I've been here plenty of times. This was one of the Apache tests for entering manhood. You were taken way back into the tunnels, given a small torch, and told to use your wits and courage to find your way back before the torch burned up. The area we'll camp in is where boys were taken to spend the night waiting for visions. It's flat and sandy, and we'll be safe there if anybody shows up. Don't worry; I've camped, explored, and played here many times."

His confidence dispelled her worries. "Where did you get this stuff? Did you go into Tucson?"

He lit the lantern and began unpacking supplies. "Nope, too dangerous. I stole it from a rancher not far away. I also shot us a rabbit. Roasted meat," he murmured and licked his lips. He was honest on those replies. He hadn't dared enter Tucson to look for Joe Collins or to send telegrams to his superiors from Ben Myers's town. "I knew if I told you my plans when I left here, you would argue and worry."

"You're right," she concurred. "That was quite a risk."

He shrugged wearily. "The horses have to eat and drink, and we have to see. Why don't you fetch that rain water for them while I take some of this stuff to our camping area? I'll build a fire and be back shortly for you." He didn't want her to see the wood and supplies he had brought here early Thursday morning after his Wednesday night talk with Collins. Just in case they had needed to escape quickly and conceal themselves for a while, he had prepared things to camp here. If she noticed his preparations, she would wonder about them. "I'm sure there's plenty of brush back there from old camping trips, but I'll check while I'm gone." He loaded up and lifted the lantern to illuminate his path. Within minutes, he and the lamp's glow vanished.

Carrie Sue held the bucket outside and let the pouring rain fill it. She carried the pail to the horses and let each one drink. Afterwards, she refilled it again and placed it nearby. While she waited T.J.'s return, she stroked the pinto. As always, she mused, T.J. had logical reasons and credible explanations for everything. Either he was the cleverest man alive or he was being honest with her!

The redhead's partner rejoined her, without his shirt and boots. His wet hair curled in mischievous black waves, as did the hair on his hard chest. His saturated jeans clung enticingly to his hips and thighs, hinting at their strength and sleek shape. He was carrying two blankets over his left arm and a hunk of soap in his hand, and two lanterns.

T.J. nodded at the items and suggested, "Why don't we take turns getting a bath in nature's shower right outside the entrance? It'll be easier than poking holes in a pail and hanging it from a rope. After what we've been through during the past two days, I know it'll make me feel better. You wanna be first or last?"

"Last," she responded. "Where did you get the other lantern?"

"It was in the back. Somebody left it there, thank goodness."

She waited in the large cavern for T.J. to walk to the entrance, strip off his jeans, wet himself, lather up, rinse off, and return to her location. While he was busy, she stripped and wrapped the blanket around her to be ready to do the same task after he finished.

Before leaving him there, she admired his magnificent body clad only in a blanket around the hips. She smiled when he warned her to walk carefully, as the rock flooring was slippery when wet.

Carrie Sue dropped the blanket just inside the cave. She stepped outside and drenched her hair and body, aware that no one could sight her in the blinding downpour. She gingerly stepped beneath the protective ceiling of stone and lathered herself from head to foot. It felt exhilarating to scrub the dirt and sweat from her hair and flesh, and she savored the refreshing chore as long as possible. She let the water rinse away the suds before standing just inside the cave to dry off with the blanket. She shivered from a chill as a blast of wind blew rain against her.

Carrie Sue stepped further into the passageway and dried off again. She wrapped the damp blanket around her and tucked it snugly above her breasts. Carefully she made her way back to T.J. "It's getting dark and cool outside," she remarked as she squeezed more water from her long hair.

She shuddered again.

T.J. had placed one lantern on the rock shelf near his saddle, out of reach of horses' hooves. He doused the campfire and said, "That'll give them plenty of light and I won't have to keep checking on the fire. Let's get you to that warm blaze in back. Dry your feet good or you could slip on these rocks. Some of the pathway is steep."

As she obeyed, Carrie Sue didn't mention the two bodies in the side tunnel, but she remembered they were there in the darkness. Even though they were enemies, now that their peril was over, she hated to just discard them like unwanted trash. Yet, they couldn't turn the bodies in and there was no way to bury the two men. She gathered her clothes and boots and followed her love into the shadows.

They headed into the right tunnel, then rounded a sharp bend whose passageway led into a nice sized chamber. They zig-zagged left into an even larger chamber where draperies of stone looked like a frozen waterfall. T.J. paused for a while and moved the lantern back and forth so she could view the awesome sight.

In all areas the walls were mostly shades of brown — ranging from tan to chocolate hues — with a few shades of gray and white intermingled. Most of the side walls and flooring were smooth, almost slick, even when dry. It appeared as if a massive underground river had created this series of chambers and passageways and had rubbed them smooth over a long period of time. She was amazed by the wildly beautiful formations from the floor and the ceiling, which were sometimes unending like columns holding up a structure.

Here and there, they had to walk on sideways slants or down almost too steep paths of solid stone. On occasion, they had to duck low ledges with sharp and jagged tips. She noticed how some formations looked like the saguaro cactus set in stone. They passed areas where the flooring seemed to have ripples like stone waves on a strange sea. Many of the chambers were enormous, others small and cramped. The tunnels ranged from narrow and low to wide and tall. They followed the often snaking path through the darkness lighted by one lantern, which she prayed wouldn't go out. Merciful Heavens, she decided, it would be black as soot and scary as hell in there.

T.J. told her these passageways ran for miles in numerous directions. In one side tunnel there was a sink hole which had no doubt ensnared some unlucky explorers. They walked deeper into the crystal caverns until the path opened up into an oblong chamber where a cheery fire chased away more darkness. Even though a river had once eaten away at this underground area, it was totally dry now. A sandy bed had been left behind upon which T.J. had made their camp.

She glanced around, relieved this area was flat and large. She saw brush and wood piled in several places, and she saw evidence of old campfires. She looked at her lover when he put aside their things and told her to follow him again before she got comfortable.

They retraced their steps for a few feet. "This isn't far, Carrie Sue. When you reach this fork, go left and round this corner. This is the outhouse when you need it."

Without further delay or embarrassing words, he guided her back to their campground. "I'll start the rabbit roasting while you get that head dry and get on something warm."

Carrie Sue pulled a nightgown from her pouch, glad she had brought it along impulsively. Since no one could find them, she could be comfortable. As T.J. was facing away from her, she didn't turn her back to drop the blanket and pull the gown over her head. Then, she bent forward to dry her hair with the blanket. When she went to sit near the fire, she brushed and braided her flaming mane while T.J. prepared coffee and readied the Johnnycake mix of plain flour and water with a pinch of salt. She watched him cut strips of salted pork for obtaining grease in which to cook the flatbread, and he placed them in a small frying pan.

We've got your authors!

If you seek out the latest historical romances by today's bestselling authors, our new reader's service, KENSINGTON CHOICE, is the club for you.

KENSINGTON CHOICE is the only club where you can find authors like Janelle Taylor, Shannon Drake, Rosanne Bittner, Sylvie Sommerfield, Penelope Neri and Phoebe Conn all in one place...

...and the only service that will deliver their romances direct to your home as soon as they are published—even before they reach the bookstores.

KENSINGTON CHOICE is also the only service that will give you a substantial guaranteed discount off the publisher's prices on every one of those romances.

That's right: Every month, the Editors at Zebra and Pinnacle select four of the newest novels by our bestselling authors and rush them straight to you, usually *before they reach the bookstores*. The publisher's prices for these romances range from $4.99 to $5.99—but they are always yours for the guaranteed low price of just *$4.20!*

That means you'll always save over 20% off the publisher's prices on every shipment you get from KENSINGTON CHOICE!

All books are sent on a 10-day free examination basis, and there is no minimum number of books to buy. (A postage and handling charge of $1.50 is added to each shipment.)

As your introduction to the convenience and value of this new service, we invite you to accept

4 BOOKS FREE

The 4 books, worth up to $23.96, are our welcoming gift. You pay only $1 to help cover postage and handling.

To start your subscription to KENSINGTON CHOICE and receive your introductory package of 4 FREE romances, detach and mail the card at right *today*.

We have 4 FREE BOOKS for you
as your introduction to
KENSINGTON CHOICE
To get your FREE BOOKS, worth
up to $23.96, mail the card below.

FREE BOOK CERTIFICATE

As my introduction to your new KENSINGTON CHOICE reader's service, please send me 4 FREE historical romances (worth up to $23.96), billing me just $1 to help cover postage and handling. As a KENSINGTON CHOICE subscriber, I will then receive 4 brand-new romances to preview each month for 10 days FREE. I can return any books I decide not to keep and owe nothing. The publisher's prices for the KENSINGTON CHOICE romances range from $4.99 to $5.99, but as a subscriber I will be entitled to get them for just $4.20 per book or $16.80 for all four titles. There is no minimum number of books to buy, and I can cancel my subscription at any time. A $1.50 postage and handling charge is added to each shipment.

Name _____

Address _____ Apt. _____

City _____ State _____ Zip _____

Telephone ( ) _____

Signature _____

(If under 18, parent or guardian must sign)

Subscription subject to acceptance. Terms and prices subject to change.

KC0495

We have
4
FREE
Historical
Romances
for you!

(worth up
to $23.96!)

Details inside!

KENSINGTON CHOICE
Reader's Service
120 Brighton Road
P.O.Box 5214
Clifton, NJ 07015-5214

"You're handy to have around, Mr. Rogue. I could get mighty spoiled with all this attention."

"I thought all women were spoiled," he teased, grinning at her.

"Most men think we are." She retorted and laughed. A contradictory sensation filled her; it seemed strange being here with him, yet perfectly normal. It was as if they were the only two people in existence, or as if they had escaped far from grim reality. Primitive feelings were aroused by their simple and cozy setting and his state of dress. Dreamily she remarked, "With that blanket wrapped around you, if your hair was long, you'd look like an Indian."

"I'm glad you didn't say half-breed. That's a nasty name, and I sure was called it a lot after my so-called rescue by the cavalry. That and a savage rogue," he added unthinkingly. He caught himself before telling her that was how and where he had gotten his undercover name. He rubbed his smokey gray eyes and said, "Lordy, I'm tired."

Carrie Sue gazed at him and agreed, "You look it, partner. Did I thank you for losing all that sleep to catch up with us and rescue me?"

"Yep." His gaze met hers, and they stared at each other. He noticed the azure gown which flowed over her soft curves like sensuous waves, and his body warmed. He drowned himself for a time in the bluish depths of her engulfing gaze. He wanted to loosen her hair and let the red mane flow around her face and shoulders like a tranquil and inviting waterfall. He longed to caress that silky flesh of rosy gold. He wanted to run his forefinger over brows which matched her tawny red hair. He yearned to kiss her nose and full lips, her shapely cheekbones. He craved to trail his hot tongue along her collarbone, to tease it over the throbbing pulse in her neck, to dip it into the hollow at her throat, to send it between her breasts and down her stomach and . . . "You have the prettiest hair and eyes I've seen on any woman," he complimented her unexpectedly, uncontrollably. He shook

257

his head to clear it and his hand stroked his whiskered jawline. "I need a shave," he murmured as if suddenly feeling awkward.

Carrie Sue realized this secluded and intimate situation made the carefree loner a little nervous. She was certain he had had plenty of sex, but love and closeness were new for him, and no doubt intimidating. Tonight they were totally alone, so either they talked casually or they would create an uneasy silence. She was touched by his near loss of poise, and it enflamed her passions to witness it. Surely that told her how deeply and strongly he was affected by her. "Thanks, partner; I like your looks too. What do you want me to do to help?" she inquired, aware of the heavy sensual aura around them.

"Just sit there and let me admire you," he replied huskily, then cautioned himself to stop acting like . . . Like what, a lovesick boy? He had to get control of himself and the situation or he'd foul up!

His words, expression, and mood aroused her. "That's too easy. Give me something harder," she almost whispered in a strained voice.

He rubbed his jawline again and looked hesitant. His keen mind shouted, *Get on with your work and stop acting like an ass! She's opened the door, so jump in fast before she slams it again!* "Would you get mad or upset if I asked you about Curly James? I saw you two talking that day and couldn't figure it out. It didn't look like strangers meeting. How did you know a bastard like him?"

The ex-outlaw drew up her knees and banded her legs with her arms, interlocking her fingers. She wet her lips and answered, "I'll admit I lied to you that day, but you now realize I had no choice. I was pretending to be a schoolmarm, and I hadn't known you very long. Curly James rode with my brother a long time ago in Texas. He recognized me and wanted to know what I was doing in Tucson. I told him the truth and he agreed to keep my secret. To answer your

258

next question, no, I didn't believe him and I was wondering if I should leave town before he could trick me. You saved me from that choice and problem when you gunned him down. Curly never was one to be trusted. He was wild, reckless, and mean. He was always disobeying Darby's orders and getting the gang into trouble, so Darby asked him to leave."

He hinted, "I don't imagine Curly took that news well."

"No, but the other men agreed with Darby's decision." She told him what Curly had said about Quade and Ferris, and of her suspicions about both men. He agreed with her. Yet, she didn't tell him about Curly claiming to have seen Darby and his plans to rejoin the gang.

T.J. shifted his position on the ground. He cleared his throat and asked bravely, "Speaking of your brother, don't you think it's about time you tell me about him and your life with his gang? I've been biting my tongue to keep silent. I was afraid of making you nervous if I pressed for more information, but I need to know more about you, woman. I figured you'd speak up when you were ready, but you've stayed tight-lipped. I kept thinking you'd open up when you realized you could trust me. Why haven't you, Carrie Sue?"

She fused her violet-blue gaze to his entreating one and responded, "I was wondering why you haven't asked me those questions. Frankly, it had me worried. You're right; you deserve to know more. My brother didn't like killing unless it couldn't be helped. But Curly did a lot of shooting; then, he'd tell Darby he was forced into it. Darby knows that robberies and rustlings don't create posses the way killings do. Despite what people think and say about my brother, he isn't cold-blooded. Like me, he was forced into this miserable life and he can't get out of it. Mostly he uses the same six men, but some jobs called for extra guns. He was always careful about the men he let join his gang for a while, but sometimes he got fooled and let a bad one in. As soon as he realized his mistake, he corrected it."

T.J. wanted to ask if one of those *mistakes* was responsible for the deaths of Arabella and Marie and Jacob, but he couldn't, not yet. "You love him a lot, don't you?"

Carrie Sue's eyes softened and glowed. "Yes, I do. We've always been close." She told him about their Georgia farm and its loss to a wicked Carpetbagger, and how her father had obtained vengeful justice. She related facts about the Texas ranch and how the Hardings had taken it from them, killing her parents during the process, and how she and Darby had gone after revenge. She explained about her years with the gang and her attempts at new beginnings, chances always spoiled by Quade Harding, the man who had barbwired her love to a tree to die. She explained how her identity had been kept secret until Quade unmasked her with that new poster.

She went on, "In '73, Darby and a few of his closest friends tried to go straight. They bought a ranch near Laredo. We stayed there for eight months and everything was wonderful. I even had my twenty-first birthday there in April. Then, Quade Harding had us tracked down. We had to leave everything behind but the clothes on our backs and our horses. We hid out in Mexico for months. That's when Quade released the men's descriptions—I suppose to get a line on me. May of '74 was when he put out that bad sketch just to scare me. We've been on the move ever since, surviving the only way left open to us."

She talked about how people used to love Darby's legend—until false charges, mistakes, and sensational newspaper accounts had darkened his image. She admitted they had shot several of Quade's men during raids and pursuits, and shot other men in self-defense. She told him they had been accused of Quinn's accident, which was a lie. She claimed that their "groundless harassment" of the Hardings and responsibility for Quinn's crippling were the devious lies which Quade used to explain his large rewards.

Her story moved him deeply, but he had to ignore such

feelings to do what had to be done. Maybe she was telling the truth about Darby Stover, or perhaps she was blinded by her love for her brother. Either way, he had to capture the Stover Gang. He quelled his guilt to continue. "Your dealings with Quade Harding explain why he's so determined to capture you and get rid of Darby. Until now, he's held silent to get you back alive and safe. I guess he finally realized you're too smart to get snared. Maybe he's hoping you'll rush back to him for help and protection.

"Never!" she vowed coldly. "I'd hang first!"

T.J. understood Quade's obsession with this ravishing vixen. But he would go down shooting before he let Harding get his vile hands on her! As he turned the rabbit to roast the other side, he asked, "Have you ever been captured or tried to clear yourself?"

She sighed heavily, bitterly. "Yes, I was captured once. Darby busted me out of jail just before two deputies raped me. Another time, I turned myself in to a Texas Ranger. I had the drop on him, but I couldn't gun him down to escape. Besides, I figured if anybody could help me get a fair shake, it was a Ranger. He cursed me and beat me and nearly broke my arm before I wounded him and escaped. I wore a sling for two months. Then, Quade's detective caught up with me several times with his threats and abuse, but I always managed to get away. I guess that explains why I have trouble trusting men."

T.J. was shocked by those confessions, and he didn't doubt them. But he'd never heard of a Ranger capturing the Texas Flame. Considering her treatment by the tainted lawman, no wonder he'd kept silent! Later, he would get the man's name from her and take care of him! "Yep, I understand. I wish I could think of someone to help you, but I can't." Even if he did know some powerful men, he couldn't tell her at this time and he didn't believe there was anything his friends could do for her.

Carrie Sue smiled sadly, but gratefully. "There is nothing

and no one to help me, T.J. Darby and I got in too deeply and there is no escape for us. We'll have to keep running and hiding until we're jailed or hanged or we get far enough away to be left alone. When I locate him, I'm going to try to persuade him to head for Montana or California or the Dakotas. He thinks fleeing is useless because somebody finds us wherever we go, if we don't stay in hiding. We can't do that forever. We have to eat." She gazed at him tenderly. "I wish you could have met Darby before all this mess changed him. I'm worried about him. He's been forced to stay in a life of crime too long. I'm afraid it's going to make him hard and cold, and make him do things he doesn't want to do. If you want to know the truth, partner, I'm not as afraid of hanging as I am of prison. And that's probably what the law would do with a young woman. If only I could rub out my past as easily as you get rid of your trail or enemies, but I can't. Quade has forced me out of hiding again. After trying so many times to start over, I'm beginning to doubt it's possible. I suppose the only thing I can do is rejoin Darby."

"Do you know where to find your brother?" he asked.

Carrie Sue wished he had replied in another way, had offered a safe and happy life with him far away. Perhaps he didn't want that solution with her; or perhaps he hadn't thought of it yet. She responded carefully, "When we split up near Sherman, he was heading for Oklahoma to lay low for a while. I figured I'd head toward Brownwood and leave messages at our old hideouts along the way. It'll be hard chasing him with my poster nailed up everywhere. Maybe when he sees it or hears about it, he'll come looking for me. I know he won't come to Tucson because he promised to stay clear of this area to give me a chance to start over, and he knows I would take off the moment I sensed danger. While Quade was holding silent, Darby wouldn't attack him, to protect me and the boys. Once he learns what Quade has done to me, he'll go after him again."

T.J. noticed the way she'd hesitated before answering him. Fatigue and depression, he wondered, or planning a devious reply? Lordy, he had to convince her to be totally honest with him, for both their sakes! "That's why you want to head for Brownwood?" When she nodded, he asked, "That's too risky with Quade Harding searching for you. Don't you realize he'll be on the lookout for Darby's revenge?"

Carrie Sue lifted the frying pan and started cooking the Johnnycakes. "I guess you're right, but what else can I do?" She glanced at him and said, "I didn't want to drag you into this mess, and I'm sorry you're involved. It will be too late to change things if you don't back away from me and leave now."

When she reached for a fork to turn the pork strips, he captured her hand, compelling her gaze back to his. "It's already too late to back away, woman. I can't leave you until this matter is settled."

Settled how? she helplessly wondered. "If you have as much brain in that handsome head as I think you do, you'll get out while you can. If you don't, you'll get in as deeply as me and Darby. Once you're entangled with the law, T.J., there's no going back to your old life. This isn't the existence either of us wants for you. Nobody knows about you except that sheriff. It'll be your word against his, unless you can provoke him into a gunfight and get rid of the one witness against you."

"It's already too late to turn back. He's probably reported my actions by now."

"It'll be worth the risk to make certain you aren't on the wanted list. If I were you, T.J. Rogue, I would call his bluff. I'll be fine alone, so stop worrying about me and get on with your life."

Defiance clouded his smokey gray gaze. "I can't. You mean too much for me to desert you. I can't imagine you being an outlaw on the run forever, much less being the notorious Texas Flame. You're nothing like your reputation, Carrie Sue. If you give me some time, maybe I can think of a better way to help you."

"People do a lot of things when they have to. Don't waste your time and strength fighting my battle, T.J.; I lost it long ago."

As if angered and challenged by her loss of spirit, he argued almost harshly, "No battle is lost until you're dead, woman, and you have plenty of life and prowess left. If you want something badly enough, you'll find a way to get it, and you can with my help."

What she wanted most of all was the man sitting near her, that and a bright future with him, and her brother's survival. If only the three of them could leave the West and start a ranch somewhere together. But where would they get enough money? And where could they go where the law couldn't reach them? It was hopeless. "I'm starving, and I can't think straight anymore. Can we finish this talk later?"

T.J. saw how agitated she was becoming. "You've told me enough to know I made the right decision joining up with you. Lordy, I wish I knew of some way to get you out of this mess. About the only thing I can do right now is get you back to your brother for protection. Much as I hate to think it, Carrie Sue, that's the safest place for you because we can't hide out here forever, or hide anywhere long. If I don't find work by the time that reward money runs out, we'll be forced to commit crimes for it and dig ourselves in deeper."

"That's my point, T.J.; one bad thing leads to another. I was going to withdraw some of Carolyn's money and hide it for an emergency, but I forgot. I was too busy with the school and you and Martin. At least I did get a horse and supplies. Mercy, this will be dangerous."

T.J. guided them back to his mission. "I like your idea of getting Darby to go straight in some town far away; that's the only way you two can survive. When we find your brother, if I can help you convince him to take off for distant places, I will."

Carrie Sue realized he did not say he would go with her or with them. She decided this was not the time to ask him if he was in love with her and if he'd seek a future together. She wanted him to recognize those facts and make those decisions for himself without any pressure from her; that was the only way it would work between them. Maybe he hadn't confessed love and a hope for a life together because he was too honest or too proud to lie about his feelings for her, which could be nothing more than the passionate desire and kindness he had exposed to date.

She smiled and said, "Thanks, T.J.; I'll probably need your help."

Together they completed the meal and devoured every bit and drop. She helped him clean up the area, then he went to the entrance to wash the dishes and to check on the horses one final time. While he was gone, she spread out their bedrolls, on opposite sides of the cozy fire to prevent looking overly eager to spend the night in his arms. Since she didn't know for certain what he wanted from her, she didn't know how to act tonight.

T.J. returned and put away his belongings. He watched Carrie Sue take the lantern and vanish from the chamber for a while. When she came back, she sat on her bedroll. He had noticed instantly where she had placed them and took her unintended hint. Considering her emotional state tonight, he didn't want to press her romantically. He wanted her to realize he was with her for more than sex, and he didn't mean his case or his revenge. He wanted her to see that he could be unselfish and understanding. He wanted her to realize that he could be a friend as well as a lover.

Thad Jamison admitted to himself that he loved and wanted this woman in bed and out! All he had to do was figure out how to pull off the impossible feat of winning her and being able to keep her. He wasn't the kind of man who ran away from trouble like a coward, but he would leave his present life behind after this mission if he could save her and take her along with or without the law's permission. Much as he hated the reality of using and betraying his love, he couldn't turn his back on who and what he was. He couldn't become a weakling just to win her. He couldn't let that murderous gang go free any longer, and he was the only lawman with a path to them. With Carrie Sue involved, he couldn't turn the case over to another Ranger or marshal. Yet, once she realized what he was doing or had done . . .

T.J. dropped those troubling thoughts. He withdrew a bottle of whiskey from his saddlebag and offered her a few sips to relax her and help her sleep.

As she smiled and accepted the bottle, Carrie Sue wanted to shout at him that all she needed tonight was him, but she didn't. He looked exhausted, and he was jittery. Perhaps making love after their serious talk would intimidate him further. She needed for him to hold her, but she would settle for having him nearby and pledged to aiding her survival. Besides, she was tense too, tense over her tormenting confessions, tense over her doubts, and tense over the two bodies somewhere in this cave. Considering the twists and turns they had made between here and the entrance, Martin and Jess could be lying around that far corner! She almost felt as if Martin Ferris's eyes were on her this very moment and his evil mind was plotting revenge. She knew that was ridiculous and only proved how fatigued and clouded her mind was. She returned the bottle to her lover and thanked him.

"Get a good night's sleep, woman; we have a lot of lost ground to make up tomorrow. I don't want anybody figuring out to look in the last place you should be, still near Tucson. That poster's been out for a week or more, so there's no telling who's on your trial by now. I want us out of Arizona pronto."

"Are there any bats or slithery critters in here?" she asked to change the subject. She didn't like those flying and crawling creatures, but she wasn't afraid of them.

He caught her ruse and grinned. "Nope. Besides no food supply, this cave system is too dry and rocky, and too dark back in here for anything without a lantern. If you get scared, you can join me over here. I promise I won't let the fire and lantern go out."

All she could hear was their breathing and movements and words and the crackling of the fire. There was a curious aura in this secret place, a spiritual one, an eerie one. Maybe there were Indian spirits here, or ghosts of unlucky men or ancient people who had died in this place. She wasn't afraid, just uneasy.

"Did you hear me, Carrie Sue?" he asked, lifting his head and looking in her direction. "I won't let the light go out."

Without moving from her back, she replied softly, "Thanks, but I'm not scared. I was just wondering because I hadn't seen anything or heard any noises. It's so quiet, not even any echoes. I can't even hear the storm or horses."

"The storm's over. Most of the water should be gone by sunup. Those dry washes take it away quickly, what the ground doesn't suck up fast. You'll be surprised when you go out in the morning; you won't even be able to tell it rained, much less stormed like crazy."

"If the light did go out, would you be lost in here?" she asked.

"Nope. I could find my way out by feeling along the walls. I know which tunnels to take even in pitch black, and I know where the pitfalls are located, and believe me there are plenty of them. Don't you get up during the night and go roaming. There are sinkholes, bottomless pits, narrow ledges, and worse. You'd be lost in less than five minutes." He lowered his voice to a whisper as if relating a secret. "All through these caverns are trail markings, if you know where and how to look for them. With or without light, we're safe."

"So if we got trapped in here, you could douse the lantern

and guide us to safety or into hiding?"

"Yep, so relax and get to sleep before I have to pour more whiskey into you to settle down that pretty head and silence that tasty mouth."

Carrie Sue laughed before responding, "That's all I needed to know, partner. Good-night, T.J."

The redhead tossed aside her light blanket. She stretched and yawned contentedly. She rubbed her grainy eyes and sat up. Smiling, Carrie Sue turned to awaken her love.

Her smile faded rapidly and she paled. There was no bedroll across the small fire. There were no saddlebags or supplies in sight. There was no T.J. Rogue!

Carrie Sue jumped up and looked around in panic. Nothing except her, her bedroll, a campfire, and some brush was left behind!

The anxious woman frantically realized — except for her gown and bedroll — she had no clothes, no weapons, no boots, no supplies, no food, no water! Worse, she realized she was imprisoned in this hazardous labyrinth which would be Satan black when that pile of brush was used up within a few hours.

How clever, she ranted to herself, for him to leave her in the one place from which she couldn't escape! How had she slept so deeply as to not hear his treacherous movements? It couldn't have been anything in the whiskey because he had drank from the same bottle. She realized his wits and skills were far superior to what she had imagined, and she had imagined them to be the best. Where had he gone? Why had he left her here without even food and water? Was he fetching a posse? A partner? Was this a terrorizing tactic? A test?

268

Chapter Fourteen

"Damn you, you bastard!" she screamed as loudly as she could. "I hate you! I'll kill you when I get my hands on you!"

Her previous thoughts echoed through her mind, *In the one place from which she couldn't escape* . . . "Think, Carrie Sue. No man can outwit you or capture you if you keep your wits clear."

The angry fugitive realized she couldn't remain there and wait for the fire to burn up all the brush. She comprehended the perils involved in her decision, but she had to risk finding her way to the entrance. She closed her eyes, envisioned the cave opening, and mentally retraced their steps; first right, around a left bend, bear right after the first large cavern, pass a tunnel on her right, through that large chamber with the frozen waterfall, use last tunnel to left, horseshoe into this oblong chamber. All she had to do was reverse those directions and backtrack to safety; no, only to light.

Carrie Sue didn't know what she would do when she reached her entrance in only her gown, but she would be in the light there to make her next decision. She left her sleeping roll where it was. She tied the tail of her gown in a secure knot above her knees to prevent tripping over it. She grabbed the largest piece of wood for a torch and held it in the fire until it flamed on the end. She headed toward freedom.

Just as she reached the end of the sleeping chamber, she nearly crashed into T.J. Rogue who eyed her strangely, then set down his lantern. She glared at him and accused, "You bastard! You're lower than a sidewinder's belly. I should have known not to trust you. Who did you fetch to turn me over to? Will I be allowed to dress first?" she inquired sarcastically. She accepted the fact she couldn't pass the strong man who was blocking the tunnel, for now. She wanted to rave at him and tear into his handsome face with her nails, but she needed to conserve her strength for a better opportunity.

T.J. stared at her in confusion. "I heard you screaming while I was on my way back to awaken you for breakfast. What has you so riled? Did you sleep with burrs in your blanket? You cuss worse than I do when that temper flares. I'll have to change that bad habit."

Her violet-blue eyes narrowed and chilled. She balled her fist with the urge to strike him. "You filthy vermin! How dare you betray me, and leave me trapped here! Give me a gun and I'll kill you!"

The ebon-haired man was still baffled. "What are you talking about, woman? I was up front cooking breakfast, right where I said I would be. I haven't been anywhere, and you were never in any danger. I sneaked out to let you sleep as long as possible."

"Sneaked out with everything and left me here defenseless!" she scoffed. "That fire will be out soon, and I want my clothes!"

Was that, he wondered, the problem? She had panicked when she found him and everything gone? But why? Didn't she believe his note? "How else could I prepare our meal? I woke up early so I decided to save time by carrying our things up front and having our food ready. I figured you were exhausted because you didn't even stir."

Carrie Sue brought up the blazing torch in her hand to strike him forcefully across the head so she could escape this cunning rogue and cease his tormenting lies.

T.J. seized her wrist and wrestled the torch from her grip,

270

casting it aside. He grabbed her and pinned her against his bare chest, which was difficult with her fighting him like wild. "Settle down, you little spitfire. I left a note by your bedroll so you wouldn't panic before I returned for you."

"Liar! There was no note!" she shouted again, struggling to free herself from his powerful grasp. She couldn't, so she glared at him.

T.J. was mad, but he pretended to be angrier than he was. "I'm going to release you, you little wildcat, and you go look beside your bedroll. Go on," he ordered sternly, freeing her and pushing her in that direction. "Damnation, woman, I'm telling the truth and I can prove it!"

Carrie Sue calmed slightly. He was blocking the escape tunnel, so she decided to put some distance between them. Since he knew these passageways and she didn't, it was rash to flee in the other direction into the perilous darkness. She stalked to the bedroll and looked at the sandy floor around it. "Nothing here, Rogue."

"Look again!" he shouted back at her.

Carrie Sue picked up the blanket which she had tossed aside upon awakening. A note was lying there. She glanced at T.J. before scooping it up to read. Just as he claimed, the message said he was up front packing and cooking and would return for her soon. Had she accidentally concealed it? Or had he hidden it long enough for her to panic? She scolded herself for behaving like a fool and for instantly doubting him again. The vexed redhead crumpled the slip of paper and tossed it into the fire. She watched it burn before turning to face her sullen lover.

"Get your bedroll and follow me," he commanded without a smile.

Carrie Sue was still edgy, but she rolled it and secured it with the leather ties. "What about the fire?" she asked contritely.

"It'll go out soon. There's no danger of it spreading anywhere." He lifted the lantern and ordered gruffly, "Let's

271

go."

Carrie Sue followed close behind the moody man who wasted no time guiding them back to the entrance where a campfire was going and their meal was ready to be completed. It was easy to see he had spoken the truth, and remorse consumed her. The smell of freshly perked coffee filled her nostrils, as did the odor of horse droppings. She glanced that way and frowned, not at the odor common to her, but at herself for her impulsive behavior. The horses were saddled, and her clothes were lying on the nearby ledge.

As if reading her mind, he said in an unapologetic tone, "Sorry about that oversight. We can stand outside and eat where there's fresh air. What's gotten into you, woman? I was just trying to give you as much sleep as possible. Get dressed while I finish here."

Carrie Sue watched him kneel at the fire and begin working on their meal. She felt terrible about her behavior and words. "I'm sorry for what I said and did, T.J.; that wasn't fair of me."

Without turning, he replied in a cool tone, "No, it wasn't fair, woman. After our serious talk last night, I thought you were beginning to trust me, but obviously I was wrong and that worries me."

"Surely you can understand why I panicked when I found you and everything gone and didn't see that note," she entreated.

He halted his chore to look at her. "I know all your secrets and I trust you, so why do you find it so difficult to trust me? Have I said or done anything to make you doubtful?" His gaze returned to the fire.

She joined him on her knees, his profile to her. Her gaze slipped over his bronzed face, chest, and shoulders. She wanted to fling herself into his arms and beg his forgiveness. She released a deep breath whose intake she hadn't noticed. She said in a rueful tone, "No, but I find it difficult to trust anybody, especially a man, except Darby and Kale. After all

I told you last night, can you blame me?"

He didn't appear to soften and he didn't meet her troubled gaze. "Nope, but Darby's the one who got you into all this trouble, so why is he the only one you trust? Brother or not, he was wrong." He didn't mention the other man, but committed this information to memory.

She was miffed. "You can't blame him, T.J.; he didn't twist my arm. I agreed to help him battle the Hardings. You know why."

He briefly glanced at her to check her expression. "Yep, you agreed to help him get justice and revenge on the Hardings, but you didn't agree to become an outlaw, to do all those other crimes."

She reasoned, "Once Quade found out about us, which was my fault, we didn't have any choice in our actions. We had to survive."

He poured her a cup of coffee and sat it nearby. He refuted, "Yes, you did have a choice, Carrie Sue, just like I do every time I'm tempted to break the law or I run into trouble. If you'd gone to the authorities, perhaps you could have gotten it straightened out before your landslide came."

She looked stunned, hurt. "Who would have believed us over the Hardings? They wouldn't even investigate Darby's charges after our parent's deaths and the seizure of our ranch. Darby went to every law office he could think of, but no one would help us. We were young and scared and foolish. We didn't think about going straight because of Quade's pursuit and the crimes we'd committed. I'll even admit that the boys found their new lives exciting. They were reckless and daring, and having fun together. It was like being caught in a flood; things kept pushing us onward to a waterfall. Once we were carried over it, we couldn't fight our way upstream again."

T.J. realized he had to back down. "I guess you're right, but it riles me how you were ensnared in this trap by Harding and your brother and you can't get free. You shouldn't have to live like this."

Carrie Sue misread his meaning. She thought he was angered because she was unavailable because of her past, a past for which Quade Harding was responsible. He even blamed Darby for her predicament. She asked, "Why did Quade have you barbwired to that tree?"

He looked at her as if surprised by the change of subject. He shrugged. "We were in a poker game and I accused him of cheating. I caught him red-handed and he was humiliated. The bastard didn't admit he was guilty. He tossed his winnings to the table, got up, and said the money wasn't worth dying over and he wasn't about to call me out over a silly misunderstanding. He just strolled out of there, red-faced. I couldn't shoot him in the back, so I let him play the coward," he related deviously. "Nothing makes a foe quicker than humiliation, and nothing settles that offense except death."

"Then what happened?" she pressed when he fell silent.

As he worked on his task, he went on in a casual tone, "He didn't want to use any of his men and he didn't even use his brand of barbwire so it couldn't be traced to his ranch. Since you've ranched, you know how many kinds of barbwire there are and most cattlemen prefer a certain brand. Curly James and two of his friends were in town, probably smarting from being tossed out of Darby's gang. Quade hired them to do his dirty work."

"How did you know Quade was responsible? Is he your only enemy? And how did they get the drop on you? I wouldn't think that possible."

"Curly boasted about how much Harding was paying him to get rid of me, in a very slow and painful way, one to give me plenty of time to suffer and to pray for death." He paused a moment before saying, "I hate to confess it, but they took me by surprise while I was bathing. A woman helped them, so I have little reason to trust sly vixens," he teased pointedly. "While I was in the tub without my weapons, the girl who was supposedly helping me scrub and fetch

274

stuff, unlocked the door and made lots of noise while they slipped in."

"You let a woman bathe you?" she asked, astonished and jealous.

He chuckled and seemed totally relaxed by now. "I heard it was a real nice pleasure, so I tried it, and I'm sorry I did. They caught me with my pants down and guns missing. I was knocked unconscious, taken out the back way, and pinned to that tree with wire stickers."

"Does Quade know you're still alive?" she asked worriedly.

"I don't think so. No, I'm certain of it." He related what the Ranger had done, but as if he had taken that precaution. "I stole a drunk's body and dressed him in my clothes and put him in my place. I figured by the time Harding checked on me, if he ever did, wouldn't be anything left but bones and clothes."

"What if Quade went back too soon and realized it wasn't you?"

"If that problem exists, I'll deal with it later. We both have a debt against Quade, and one day I'll settle it for us when he least suspects it." He poured himself another cup of coffee and sipped it.

"Something I don't quite understand, T.J.: with your reputation, how would Quade not know that you're still alive?"

"Because I left the area right after I got loose and replaced myself on that tree. I've been tracking Curly and his two friends since I healed. I got them all, one by one, just like they deserved. I doubt Harding knows I'm still around and plotting revenge."

"If he does, he'll be sending someone after you. Quade doesn't give up on something he wants. Those detectives will track you down just like they tracked me down several times. As with me, Quade knows what you look like and can provide your description."

"Then maybe I'll have to take care of him sooner than I planned. In fact, I'll probably do him under when we reach Brownwood. I'll turn you over to your brother and I'll go after Harding. That way, he'll be off both our backs for good. It's a shame I didn't take care of him before he released your description. I was heading back to Brownwood after I finished off Curly James, but I met a distraction."

She smiled warmly. "I wish you had. Then, I'd still be a schoolmarm in Tucson. I'd have been free forever."

"I guess that's something else for you to hold against me."

She asked, "What do you mean by something else?"

His gaze locked with hers. "Evidently you've got something against me because you can't seem to trust me."

She caressed his smoothly shaven cheek and vowed, "I promise I won't ever mistrust you again."

"We'll see," he hinted, then returned her smile. "We have a long way to ride together, woman. I'm afraid the next time something strange comes up, you'll forget this promise."

She stroked his jawline with the back of her hand. "I swear I won't."

"I'll be counting on you, Carrie Sue, because there will be times when you'll have to get me out of trouble. I have to know I can depend on you like you can depend on me."

"You can, T.J. honestly." She leaned forward to kiss him.

He imprisoned her face between his hands and kissed her with a hunger greater than the one in his belly. Suddenly smoke and a sizzling noise caught their attention. They jerked apart to find their meal about to be ruined. They laughed and hurried to save it.

When they finished eating and cleaning up, T.J. repacked their supplies while she dressed nearby with her back to him. She pulled on jeans, boots, and a long-sleeved faded blue shirt. She strapped on her holster, checked her weapons as usual, and told him she was ready.

"We'll leave the bodies where they are. No better place for an evil man to be buried forever than in total darkness. We'll take the horses along for a while. If we release them here, they might find their way home or back to town. I don't want anyone in Tucson to be alerted to a problem and begin a search. By the time Martin Ferris and his sidekick are missed, we'll be long gone."

Carrie Sue agreed. She twirled her long braid and tucked it beneath her hat. Taking Charlie's reins, she led the brown and white pinto outside. T.J. joined her with Nighthawk and the other two horses. She noticed only bridles on them as she mounted.

"Let's try to put this area behind us again," he murmured.

They headed down the Old Spanish Trail. When they reached the road into Tucson, he didn't have to slow down because they could see for miles in both directions.

T.J. halted. He pointed southeastward and said, "You ride toward those mountains while I hang back to cover our tracks. Use the terrain to set your pace, and I'll catch up soon." He passed the two horses reins to her. "Keep your canteen handy. This ride will be slow and hot, and we don't want to halt until necessary."

Carrie Sue left the road and headed across country at a sluggish pace, weaving her way around mesquites and scrubs and cactus. It didn't take long for the morning sun to get high enough to cause sweat to ease down her face and slide down her stomach from beneath her breasts. Riding toward the sun created a glare in her eyes which was too low for her hat to prevent. Her eyes soon grew weary and red from the dryness and squinting. The terrain jostled her in the saddle, almost as badly as the stage ride had done weeks ago. Time passed, but she couldn't sight her lover when she halted a moment and twisted in her saddle to look behind her. She scanned the area in all directions and saw nothing moving. She continued, trying to ignore the heat.

She traveled alone for two hours before T.J. joined her. She smiled and said, "Everything all right back there?"

"Stop a minute while I take these coverings off Nighthawk's hooves. The Apaches taught me this trick to conceal tracks."

She watched him dismount, untie the leather squares, and pack them. He glanced up at her and grinned. "That should protect us for a time, unless somebody hires another Apache scout. Won't fool him."

T.J. took the reins of Martin's and Jess's horses. They headed off again, with her lover in the lead. They passed north of the Santa Rita Mountains and rode for the Whetstones. They halted there to rest and eat strips of jerky, which wasn't her favorite meal.

As if establishing a new rapport after the incident this morning, they talked little as they moved along beneath the blazing sun and through the difficult terrain. It was dark when they reached the San Pedro River and stopped to camp.

"When we head out at dawn, we'll leave Ferris's horses here near water and grass. Why don't you freshen up after that hot ride while I tend ours? It's cold beans tonight, woman, because I don't want anyone seeing a fire and coming to investigate."

"That's fine. Think a bath is too risky?" she inquired.

"Yep. It'll have to wait until we're camped in the Chiricahuas. Lots of water there, cool and pretty area. We'll stay there a few days to rest," he murmured as if visualizing a dreamy setting. "Stay dressed and ready to take off like a hare before a coyote. I'm going to take off the saddles, rub 'em down a bit, and resaddle them for a fast getaway. We can't take any chances tonight, woman."

Carrie Sue caught the underlying meaning of his words, no lovemaking. She followed his suggestions, knowing he was right.

The redhead removed her shirt at the riverbank, rinsed off, dried with it, then donned a clean one. The nights were cooler, sometimes chilly, so a clean, dry shirt would feel better tonight. She removed her boots, rolled up her pant

278

legs, and dangled her feet in the water. Afterwards, she dried them and replaced her boots on soothed feet.

Carrie Sue returned to where T.J. had lain out their bedrolls, side-by-side. She sat on hers and ate the beans, warmed only by the sun, and washed them down with water and one sip of whiskey to put a more pleasant taste in her mouth for the night. She tried to wash the dishes, but T.J. insisted on that task.

"I'm used to taking care of chores around camp, so I don't mind. Besides, I want to freshen up, too," he remarked, then peeled off his damp shirt and tossed it on his saddlebag. He headed for the riverbank.

Carrie Sue reclined. She commanded her heart to stop racing madly and her mind to stop thinking up reckless ways to seduce him tonight. She craved him fiercely, but lovemaking here was too dangerous. She eagerly looked forward to those cool and secluded mountains ahead.

She closed her eyes and fantasized about her irresistible partner. She reflected on their sensual nights together, and longed to repeat those blissful sensations. Maybe she could slow this trip to Darby and spend as much time with her love as possible before something parted them. The desperado could not imagine what her brother was going to say when she suddenly appeared in his camp, without or with her lover. T.J. was doing exactly what he had promised, defending and helping her, but she wanted more from him, so much more. Slowly she drifted off to sleep with images of them dancing peacefully in her head.

T.J. found her asleep when he reached his bedroll. He gazed down at her and intense longings surged through him. She was right about him tricking her with that note. He knew how brave and strong and smart she was, so he had to prove to her how alone and vulnerable she was without him. He had used that situation to scare her, to panic her, to push her closer to him. He had noticed how, even though she was righthanded, she always grasped her blanket and threw it aside with her left hand. And, even though the fire had been to her left, it was too far away to entice her to change her habit, as neither slept close enough to the fire for a spark to jump on their bedrolls.

Before they reached Darby's camp, he had to find other ways to eat up her remaining mistrust, which he was certain still existed. He had to make their bond so powerful that, if trouble arose for him in that outlaw's haven, she would side with him against those murdering bandits, even against her brother. He felt that she was falling in love with him and he needed to strengthen that bond. He planned to do just that while they were camped in the Chiricahua Mountains for days.

There were baffling parts of this mission which he needed to know, but it would create more suspicions if he probed them even casually. No matter what she said or thought about her brother's character and intentions, Darby Stover was a cunning outlaw who had to be stopped any way possible.

T.J. stretched out on his bedroll and tried to relax. He wished he could tell her the truth and obtain her help, but he doubted she would ever betray her only brother. Even if he could dangle a pardon beneath her beautiful nose, she probably wouldn't aid him.

A pardon for her aid, his keen mind stressed. He knew that wasn't possible, but should he pretend it was? If offered her freedom and a life with him, would she take his side and help defeat her own brother and his gang? T.J. asked himself if he could accept such rewards if it meant betraying and killing his brother Tim. He tried to put himself in her place, and Tim in Darby's. In all honesty, what would he do if his trickery meant earning a pardon and winning her? Could he live with himself afterwards? Would he come to despise himself, and her for tempting him to such treachery? Would it make a difference to him if Tim had killed her family? He couldn't answer.

Lordy, what was he doing in love with a woman like Carrie Sue Stover? How could she seem so innocent, so gentle, so kind and caring when she had been an outlaw for years? How could she not have been touched, tainted, by such a lengthy existence? Those big periwinkle eyes and rosy gold face appeared to glow with purity and warmth, but what if she had learned to use her special traits to her advantage? What if he was totally wrong about her? What if she was the one using and duping him? She had been ready and willing to kill him this morning! She had played Carolyn Starns with a skill to be envied by the best actress! Lordy, what if she was just like her brother?

You're grabbing for a dust devil, Thad, and it can't be captured. All it will do is dirty your hands and choke you. Forget this nonsense until your mission's over and you discover the truth. If she isn't guilty, you'll find a way to save her from prison and the rope, even if she refuses to forgive you and stay with you. But what in blue blazes will you do if she is guilty? Or if you get her killed by accident? He couldn't answer those questions, either. . . .

The following day, they traveled between the Dragoon Mountains where Naiche's camp had been and Tombstone, a town known for its savageness. Since that wild town was Ike Canton's domain, they didn't linger there. The ride was long and hard because T.J. was determined not to halt before reaching their enticing campsite.

After telling her it was sixty miles, he reminded her that an Apache warrior could run on foot under these same conditions to cover seventy miles in one day, so covering less by horse would be easier.

Many times they were allowed by the terrain to ride side-by-side at a leisurely gallop; other times, they were compelled to ride single file through scrubs and desert vegetation at a snail's pace. Often T.J. scanned all directions with his fieldglasses, as one could see for miles in this area. Even though they were far from the road, he didn't want to take any chances of their dust attracting unwelcome visitors.

The sun was behind them now. It beat down unmercifully on their bodies, urging them to continually sip water to prevent dehydration. They steadily journeyed, eating away the miles to their destination. Yet, they were careful not to overtire or overheat the horses.

Carrie Sue sensed her flesh burning beneath the garments. She couldn't remove her hat to cool her head or roll her sleeves to cool her arms as the sun would attack her fiercely. She rubbed her salty brows with the backs of her forefingers, and winced when the tiny balls of fire drifted into her eyes. When they teared, she blinked to help wash away the stinging sensation. She felt sticky all over, and a salty residue was left behind by her perspiration—moisture which dried almost instantly everywhere except on her clothes. She wondered if steam could rise from her head which seemed saturated by boiling liquid, as was her hatband. She wished she could pull off her boots if only for a few minutes and pour water over her scorching feet. She was miserable, but she never complained to her partner or slowed their progress.

At last, the baking sun lowered itself toward the earth, and the heat lessened. Soon, the Chiricahuas rose like magic from the Sonoran Desert. The lowlands drifted upwards into a cool forest of spruce, fir, oak, juniper, pinyon, aspen, pine, and cypress. The heavily forested mountains offered shady glens which were breathtakingly sheltered by massive and unusual rock formations. She noticed a variety of shrubs, mosses, flowers, and ferns set amongst the trees and rocks. They journeyed through the foothills, beside creeks, and through canyons. T.J. guided her toward a camping area which he remembered. When they arrived, she beamed with pleasure and relief. It was cool and lovely, and plenty of water was nearby in a stream-fed pond.

T.J. told her, "You rest while I scout the area. I want to make certain no one is around in any direction. We'll eat when I get back."

She watched him vanish from sight. She unsaddled her pinto and led the mare to water. Carrie Sue encouraged the animal to step into a shallow area where she could splash water on her sweat-drenched hide. She rubbed the pinto and talked softly to her. When the animal was cooled and relaxed, the pinto began grazing peacefully near the water's edge.

The redhead discarded her hat and weapons. She knelt and washed the salty surface from her face. The water was wonderful, inviting. Unable to resist the impulse, she stripped and went swimming. When her fiery body was refreshed, she fetched her soap and blanket to bathe leisurely. Her arms and thighs were pinkened by the searing sun and she rubbed them gently. She could tell the same was true of her back. She loosened her braid and washed her hair, ducking over and over to rinse it. Finally she left the stream-fed pond, dried off, and put on her gown. Carrie Sue sat on a rock and brushed her wet hair.

Dusk was nearly gone beneath the rising three-quarters moon when T.J. returned and wearily dismounted. He looked at the gown clad beauty on the rock who was nonchalantly brushing her fiery mane, and scowled. He gently caught a handful of drying hair and demanded, "What is this, woman?"

She laughed and teased, "My clean head, Mr. Rogue."

He chided, "Don't jest with me, woman. It looks more like a matador's red cape and this area could be filled with raging bulls. You were supposed to stay on guard until I returned. Taking a bath was a damn stupid thing to do while I was gone! I told you that's how I got snared by Quade's men. When I'm not around, keep a gun in your hand."

"I was miserable, T.J.," she explained. "I knew you'd—"

He irritably cut her off, "Miserable is better than killed,

raped, or captured! Do you even realize how tempting you are?"

"I hope I am, but only to you," she replied boldly.

T.J. glared at the beauty. "Sometimes you're too damn tempting and I can't keep my head clear for wanting you!"

She smiled. "Good, that makes two of us in that uncomfortable predicament. Besides, I like having you rescue me all the time."

He warned angrily, "One of these times, I might not get back in time to rescue you from one of these stupid stunts."

"But you always arrive in the nick of time, my handsome gunslinger. I've come to depend on you for everything. You've had very little sleep in the last few days; you're just tired and edgy. Why don't you get cooled off and relaxed while I prepare supper?" she suggested, calm as the wind in the secluded valley.

"That sounds like a perfect idea," he agreed. He unsaddled his horse and set aside their supplies. Nighthawk followed him to the water and was rubbed down before he joined the mare to graze. T.J. stripped and entered the soothing water.

Carrie Sue noticed his absence of modesty and grinned. She liked him not feeling inhibited or embarrassed around her, and that mood spread to her. She walked to the bank, lifted his holster, and called out, "I guess this means it's safe here?"

He glanced at her and replied, "From everyone but me, woman. I still might punish you for being so reckless."

Carrie Sue laughed softly and teased, "Be careful of the Texas Flame, Mr. Rogue; she may singe your hands when you spank her. What would you like me to prepare for supper, partner?"

"You," he answered without jest.

Carrie Sue stared at him in astonishment, then her face softened into a radiant smile. "Consider your supper ready and waiting, partner." She replaced his weapons, returned to their gear and laid out one bedroll.

In seconds, T.J.'s wet hands gripped her shoulders and turned her to face him. His smokey gray gaze locked with hers as he asked, "Did I hear right?"

In answer, Carrie Sue eased her arms around his neck and pulled his head downward to kiss her. Her breath was taken away as he possessively yanked her against his nude body, its moisture dampening her nightgown. There was a desperation in his kisses to which she readily responded. He was no longer elusive; at this feverish moment, he seemed so vulnerable, so susceptible to her allure. It had been a week since they had made love and she craved him wildly.

Overcome with a passion which had been restrained since last Thursday night, his fingers roamed into her wet hair and pulled her head more snugly against his mouth. He shifted them to capture her jawline so he could spread kisses over her face. He hugged her tightly, resting her head against his drumming heart with a quivering hand. "Lordy, you make me go crazy when I'm near you."

"But you're with me all the time," she whispered in a voice hoarsened by powerful emotions.

"I know," he murmured with his lips pressed to her head. "What am I going to do about you, woman?" he unintentionally asked aloud.

Carrie Sue mistook his meaning, but it thrilled her to learn what an overwhelming affect she had on him. Evidently, she concluded, he was panicked over his urgent feelings for her, especially in light of her situation. To relax him, she murmured, "You'll have plenty of time to decide, T.J.; there's no rush. We'll take it slow and easy until we figure out this crazy predicament. For now, just love me."

T.J. leaned back his head and looked into her arresting eyes. Nothing could be easier than to love her, emotionally and physically; and nothing could be more demanding. He was relieved by her lack of pressure and was enflamed by her unleashed desire for him. "You're the only woman who's wanted to understand me and accept me as I am. I don't have any experience in matters like this, so be patient."

She nestled against him and heard what she wanted to hear in his words. "I know what you mean, T.J.; it's scary as hell, isn't it?"

"Worse," he admitted. "I want you so badly I feel like an overfilled feed sack about to burst and scatter my existence in all directions. Lordy, these feelings make me nervous. I've never let anybody get this close to me and, when I do, it's . . ."

Carrie Sue trailed her fingertips over his parted lips when he halted. "It's an outlaw," she calmly finished for him. "Can't we forget about that problem tonight and just be together? Talking about it isn't going to change anything, only make us feel worse. While we're together, can't we just enjoy each other until we have to separate?"

He stared into her glowing gaze and asked seriously, "Can you accept that, Carrie Sue? It isn't much to offer."

She entwined her fingers in his hair and smiled encouragingly. "You're wrong, T.J.; it's the most I've ever gotten from anyone."

Guilt charged through him like a cattle stampede. Yet, he wasn't being totally dishonest with her. He wasn't lying about his feelings and desires for her, and he wasn't leading her to believe there was a future for them. "But we only have until—"

She silenced his weak protest with, "That's better than no time at all," and a passionate kiss. When her lips left his, her fingers replaced them as she coaxed, "Don't say anything else. I accept things the way they are between us, they way they have to be. For tonight and for as long as we have together, just need me and love me."

T.J.'s mouth slanted across hers in a tender kiss which answered her urging truthfully. As one kiss dissolved into another, the pressure of his lips varied from firm and demanding to tender and soft. His capable hands wandered up and down her back as if they were explorers trying to map every inch. His mouth journeyed down her neck and over her ears, driving her mad with uncontrollable cravings.

Carrie Sue wondered if her kindled body would burst into a roaring blaze and consume her if the rising heat within her was not doused soon. She yearned to feel her bare flesh against his. She wiggled her hands between their close bodies and unbuttoned her cotton nightgown to the waist. She pushed it over her shoulders and let it slide down her lowered arms and off her fingertips. She knew that T.J.'s eager hands had helped peel it over her shoulders and send it along its snaking way to curl around her feet. She pressed her naked frame against his, and both moaned at the tantalizing contact.

Her senses were alive and responsive to any and all stimulation. When Carrie Sue leaned her head backwards as T.J.'s lips roved down her silky throat, her long hair tickled the tops of her buttocks and caused her to arch toward her lover. As she moved her head back and forth, and she pressed her hips against his, he shuddered and returned his lips to hers to ravish her mouth with undeniable urgency.

T.J's body itched and tingled all over, and it begged for appeasement. His tension was mounting fast as he tried to move slowly and skillfully with her and he wondered if he could explode just from touching and being touched by her. Lordy, no woman had ever aroused him to such heights of hunger and to such a perilous strain on his control!

T.J. shifted his hands to her breasts and kneaded them with a gentle strength, feeling the buds grow hard beneath his fingers. His knees were weak and shaky, so he guided them to the bedroll. His mouth left hers to trail down her neck to the valley between her breasts before allowing his hot tongue to circle each peak and pleasure both. His left hand was sent down her ribcage, moving over each bone slowly and sensuously as if his fingers were counting them. His palm flattened against her stomach and shifted back and forth between the ridges of her hips, each passing taking him lower and lower.

Carrie Sue quivered in anticipation. When his fingers deftly caressed her, she squirmed in delight. She trailed her right hand over his shoulder and stroked his extended arm. She wanted him to continue this thrilling play of hands and lips, but her body yearned to have him within her. "Please, T.J., I can't take any more teasing. Love me now before I go mad. It's been so long."

T.J.'s mouth went to her lips and he moved his body over hers. He entered her slowly, delighting in her welcoming warmth. As passion threatened to overwhelm him, he moved with powerful thrusts, then paused a moment and lifted his head to take in several deep and steadying breaths. When she moaned in protest and her hands and hips urged his firm buttocks to continue their tantalizing movement, he revealed huskily, "Go easy, woman; I'm on the edge. Hellfire, I've been on the edge since I touched you. My control is about gone. Lordy, I want you so bad."

Carrie Sue pulled his mouth back to hers after telling him, "There's no need to control yourself, my love." She was already experiencing tiny waves of ecstasy. She wrapped her legs over his and arched toward him as he rocked his body against hers, causing those waves to build in force until they crashed over her and swept her away in their wild current. He stiffened and paused briefly, then pushed himself deep within her womanhood. She felt him throbbing within her and knew he was obtaining the same potent victory which she was enjoying.

He buried his face in her flowing hair and drove into her over and over until every drop of love's liquid had been drained from him. He held her tightly as he caught his breath and rolled to his back, carrying her along with him.

They lay there in each other's arms, sharing and savoring their closeness. A little less than a full moon glowed down on them and bathed their moist bodies in her romantic light. A mild breeze waved over their naked flesh and dried it. She sighed peacefully and snuggled closer as the fingers of his right hand drifted up and down her arm. His left arm rounded her back with a loving embrace and held her close to his side.

Dreamily her fingertips grazed through the field of black hair on his chest. They roamed a supple terrain of lean and hard flesh. They wandered over boney ridges and firm valleys. One took a mischievous dip in his navel pool of moisture. Suddenly her left arm banded his firm waist and she hugged him tightly. As she relaxed again, her fingers went back to their appreciative play.

A joyful smile slipped over T.J.'s face, for he grasped her serene mood and knew he'd given her great pleasure. At this time, not an ounce of tension troubled him. The most ravishing and unique woman in the entire world was lying in his arms and belonged to him. Whatever problems existed beyond this tranquil haven could be handled and considered later. He didn't want any troubling thought or mood to spoil this wonderful moment. He closed his eyes.

Twenty minutes passed and Carrie Sue believed her lover had fallen asleep from exhaustion. She was tired and sore and sensuously sated, but she was too hungry to drop off to sleep. She eased from his arms and bedroll to see what she could find to eat in his supply pouch. She moved quietly and carefully so as not to awaken him.

Just as she reached for the pouch, T.J. asked in an odd tone, "What are you doing?" He bounded forward and halted her action.

She looked up, his face shadowed by its lowered position and that of the moon's behind him, and replied, "I'm starved. I was looking for something to eat. I thought you were asleep. Did I disturb you?"

"I was just resting and giving you time to rest. I'm too hungry to sleep, too. I'll find us something quick and easy. Why don't you wash off and put on your gown?" he suggested, tugging playfully at her hair.

Carrie Sue did as he asked to prevent him from witnessing her reaction to his curious behavior. It was almost as if he was hiding something in that pouch. Of course, some people just didn't like others going through their belongings. Yet, he always was the one to unload and load the supplies, and usually the one to prepare them. Was there something concealed in his possessions that he didn't want her to see?

She stepped into the water and rinsed swiftly because its temperature and the air's had dropped since sundown. She dried off, donned her nightgown, and loosely braided her hair to prevent its tangling. She sat on the bedroll and waited for him to join her.

T.J. didn't build a fire. When he sat down beside her, he teased, "You almost spoiled my surprise. I've been saving these treats until we got here to enjoy them." He handed her a metal plate with several items on it. "Naiche gave these to me. This is saguaro fruit. It's sweet and delicious. The Apaches gather it in early summer. You can eat the fruits raw, or make thick cakes with them and store them for a long time. They also make a tasty juice."

"Saguaro? Isn't saguaro that huge cactus that only grows in certain parts of Arizona and New Mexico?" she inquired, eyeing one.

"Yep, try it," he coaxed.

She did, and smiled, "It's good. I wouldn't have thought about eating part of a cactus. I guess that's why the Apaches can survive in this desert; they know what to eat and how to get water."

"Try this," he urged, pointing to another item on her plate.

Carrie Sue lifted the vegetable which resembled an artichoke heart. It was warm from being in his pouch beneath the sun. She tasted it, and was reminded of a sweet potato. "I like it. What is it?"

"Parry Agave. You remember, those tall tree-looking

290

plants with clusters of yellow flowers."

"The ones tequila is made from?" she asked and grinned. "Is this going to get me drunk?"

"Nope. The Apaches used to spend four months a year gathering, roasting, and drying agave. Once its prepared, it lasts up to a year."

"How do they prepare it?" she asked, then continued eating.

"They gather the shoots and roast them over hot coals. Then, you peel 'em and eat 'em until your belly wants to burst. Tequila is made from the stalks, not these roots," he stated merrily and licked his lips. "Naiche's people dig up the roots, bake them for two nights and one day in stone-lined pits with the agave covered by hot rocks."

He chuckled and leaned closer to whisper in a roguish tone, "But he did give me a skin of tequila if you want some tonight."

"After the last time, I think I'll stick to whiskey when I have need of a sip of lively spirits." They both laughed in recall of that night in the Mexican cafe and in Naiche's camp, and her sufferings afterwards.

T.J. ate and drank from his plate and cup because Carrie Sue had her own now. He was impressed by the preparations she had made in case a swift flight from Tucson was needed, and it had been. He offered her jerky and almost stale Jonnycakes.

She rejected the dried beef strips, but ate two cakes. When he asked if she wanted him to warm some beans, she shook her head. "This is plenty for tonight, thanks. You're a good cook even when you don't cook, partner. I can learn a lot from you."

"How about starting your lessons another time? I'm ready to fall out on my feet." Carrie Sue handed him her empty plate and cup, and he put everything away. He spread her sleeping roll beside his.

They took their places, both choosing their backs. Just as

she closed her eyes, his hand found hers and squeezed it. She returned his gesture, and they drifted off with fingers entwined.

Breakfast — fried salt pork, flour gravy, Jonnycakes, and black coffee — had been cooked and eaten. The dishes were washed and stored. Both were dressed, and the horses were tending themselves.

T.J. told her to relax with that book he had seen her place in her saddlebag in Tucson, while he went to cover their trail from yesterday. He explained, "It was too late last night to conceal our tracks and set a false trail. I also want to do some hunting for fresh meat. You stay here and rest, but stay on alert, woman. Keep your pistol close and your ears open. I'll be back in a few hours. No bathing or swimming alone," he added as he mounted Nighthawk. He needed to do and learn a few vital things today, and she would be safe. A telegraph line was situated not too far away . . .

Carrie Sue waved and watched him leave. She glanced at the possessions T.J. had left behind. She wanted to go through them just as soon as she was certain he wasn't hiding nearby and spying on her to see if she could be trusted not to pry into his belongings or to desert him during his absence. She fetched her book and sat down to read, placing her revolver beside her. Soon, she would discover why he didn't want her looking inside his pouches. . . .

Chapter Fifteen

Carrie Sue pretended to read for thirty minutes while she reflected on T.J. Rogue and her situation with him. Sometimes he gave off an arrogant air, but — she concluded — it was only enormous self-confidence and his custom of being self-reliant. Sometimes he found it hard to be open with her, but that was due to his being a loner for so many years. He was a man resolved to fight all obstacles in his path, a man who could endure anything he encountered and survive. His experiences had toughened him and honed him into an undefeatable force, except for that one incident with Quade. There was a powerful strength about him: physical, mental, and emotional. She felt that until meeting her, he had been satisfied with his carefree existence; now, he wanted and needed more, and often didn't realize that fact or want to accept it.

Yet, T.J. Rogue could be vulnerable, susceptible to her pull, worried over the danger she presented to and for him, distracted and disarmed by her. Too, he was a man with a haunted past which still troubled and plagued him. He could be easygoing one minute and guarded the next. What, she wondered, drove him the hardest?

The redhead didn't sense any eyes watching her and decided T.J. wasn't spying on her from the rocks which surrounded this small valley. She lay the book aside and went to search his pouches. She didn't find anything unusual inside them. Then, she remembered he had taken his saddlebags with him. She frowned, then decided that might be only from force of habit.

Why, she asked herself, couldn't she trust him completely? Why did she sense there was something crucial going on inside his head, something which involved her? As far as she knew, they only had one connection, Quade Harding, and one bond—their mutual attraction. So, why did she feel as if there was more between them, something mysterious and dangerous? On the other hand, why should he trust her? That wasn't a common trait of a gunslinger or an outlaw. Yet, both wanted to believe the other; she was positive of that.

Tensed by her thoughts and actions, Carrie Sue strapped on her holster and went to gather wood. She jumped when she spooked a slumbering Whitetail deer and the animal fled swiftly. She remembered T.J. cautioning her about snakes in this region, particularly in July and August. "Stay alert," she warned herself.

The flaming haired woman used an extra knife to dig a fire pit and gathered rocks to encircle it. Afterwards, she took a walk to admire the scenery and to dispel her anxieties.

T.J. had described the northwestern section of these mountains and she longed to ride there to observe those magnificent scenes. He had drawn verbal pictures of the "Land of the Standing-Up Rocks" as the Apaches called that area. Maybe she could persuade him to take her there tomorrow.

She wondered what was taking her lover so long to conceal their trail and to shoot fresh meat. He had left early, and it was past midday. She was bored and restless. She didn't want to read, although she loved reading. Today, her concentration was missing.

She recalled the fishing hooks and string in T.J.'s pouch.

She fetched them and secured them to the sturdy limb she located. Taking his extra knife, she dug in the clumps of grass near the stream for several worms. While her pinto aimlessly grazed, she fished.

She laughed aloud when she snagged the first one, a little over a pound. Quickly she imprisoned the squirming creature on a thin rope by running it through his mouth and out his gill and looping the end. She tied the rope to a bush and dangled the fish in water so it would stay alive and fresh until she finished her task. She attached another worm to the hook and tossed it beneath the surface. It took her longer this time, but she caught another one about the same size. Excitement and satifaction filled her. If her luck held out, she could surprise her lover with a tasty meal tonight.

Carrie Sue caught one fish bigger and one smaller than the other two. She put away the fishing supplies and found a distant spot to clean her nice catch. Expertly she scaled and gutted the fish, then washed them in the lake.

From the sun's position, it was around three o'clock. She built a fire and let it burn down to smouldering coals. While doing so, she scouted for more rocks and placed a stack on either side to form two support ledges. She located four sturdy sticks and sharpened one end on each. Carefully she shoved a stick through each fish. Afterwards, she suspended the largest one horizontally between the rock ledges.

Considering the hour and the length of cooking time at that height over the coals, T.J. should return by the time the last one — the smallest — was ready to be placed over the pit. When the largest was done enough to meet her schedule, she positioned the two medium fish on either side of it.

She mixed flour and water and salt for fresh Jonnycakes. Added to the remaining agava roots, which she would warm soon on the hot rocks, T.J. was in for a special treat tonight. At last, she placed the last fish over the fire and turned the others once more.

She was getting annoyed with her tardy lover when he

rode up and dismounted. "No luck?" she hinted, noticing his empty hands and saddle.

He grinned as he eyed the beautiful vixen and feast before him. He replied, "Looks like I have plenty right here. How did you manage this?" he asked, surprised and pleased. He hunkered down opposite her.

"My father and brother taught me to fish and camp cook. It passed the time today," she remarked, sounding and looking as vexed as she felt. "I borrowed your supplies. I hope you don't mind."

"Of course not, woman. Feel free to use any of those supplies. You did better than me. Thank goodness or it'd be beans again tonight." He frowned playfully. "I'm afraid I didn't see anything small enough to shoot, and I don't like killing more meat than I can use."

"I'm glad. Senseless killing distresses me," she remarked as she began cooking the circles of bread in the edge of the fire. She placed the agavas on the other side to absorb heat. "You want to get the dishes and pour us some whiskey?" Carrie Sue stood and unbuckled her holster. She laid it aside.

T.J. eyed her intently and pondered her request for liquor instead of water or coffee. He asked, "You mad at me again?"

Her periwinkle eyes were cool when they met his smokey gray ones. "You've been gone since early morning. I was worried."

He knew she meant suspicious, not worried. He knew he had to dispel her mood quickly. "I backtracked a good ways and covered our trail. Then, I made several new ones in various directions to confuse anyone who comes along. Afterwards, I did some hunting, but we wouldn't want to eat the only small game I spotted: Apaches fox squirrels, lizards, coatimundis. That takes time, woman, lots of it."

The redhead realized she was acting oddly. She sighed and smiled. "I know, but it's sundown. What if something had happened to you? I wouldn't know how or where to find you so I could help."

He relaxed. "You're right. Just in case we get separated, we need a plan for joining up again. What do you suggest?"

"Since we're heading for Commanche, why don't I give you a map of where we're going and mark a few spots between New Mexico and there?"

"Commanche? Is that where you're to meet Darby?" he asked.

She shrugged as she continued her chore. "I'm not certain. After we parted near Sherman, he was heading for Oklahoma to lay low a while. If he knows about my trouble, he'll either head for a spot on the Pecos River or the cabin and hope to join up with me there. Since the river comes first on the trail, we'll check there before heading for Commanche. I'll draw you a map later."

T.J. wondered if she was telling the truth, or if she was testing him. If she suspected that he was after Darby and his gang, maybe she figured he would take the map and be done with her, one way or another. "I'll take the map, Carrie Sue, but we'll make sure we don't get separated. It's too dangerous out there for you alone, and you aren't familiar with this territory. If you want to call off your search for your brother, I'll guide you anywhere you want to go. What about it? You want to give a new life another chance? In your place, I would."

The desperate fugitive considered his answer, and what action he would take if she accepted his offer of escort. If he was after her and/or Darby, once she gave him a map and if he believed it was real, he wouldn't have any further use for her. If that was his motive, he certainly wasn't going about obtaining victory in a logical manner!

Carrie Sue didn't know what to think. If he loved her enough to go to such perilous lengths to help her, why didn't he want to remain with her, to run away with her? Perhaps he knew she wouldn't take his advice about escaping, so he was unafraid to use his offer as a clever ruse. And, perhaps he thought he had her in his control and could entrap all of them. "I have to see Darby first. If I can't persuade him to go straight some place far away, then I'm going to give it one last try. If your offer's still open after you get rid of Quade Harding, you can guide me some place wonderful and safe."

T.J. sent her a broad smile, one which brightened his eyes and softened his features, one which looked totally honest and sincere. "That's a wise choice, woman. I'm proud of you. I give you my word of honor to become your future escort. Just as soon as we finish with Darby and Harding, it's Montana or wherever you want to go. Who knows, maybe I'll stick around a while and get you started on this new life, make sure no Ferrises are around. Would that be all right?"

"More than all right, partner. Thanks. Our wonderful meal isn't going to be so wonderful if we don't pay attention to it," she jested.

"I'll fetch the dishes and drinks, Ma'am," he said, then bowed comically before doing so.

As she served their plates, he said, "I need to draw you a map of this area and all the way through New Mexico, just in case of trouble. I'll mark some places and give you some names of friends who might help if anything happens to me. I said, might help, Carrie Sue. I can't promise anything because of who you are. You understand?"

She looked at him, her gaze wide and her lips parted in surprise. "I understand, and thanks."

T.J. cunningly added, "Just so you'll know you can trust me, don't give me a map so I won't know where we're heading. When we get near Darby's hideout, you can take my weapons and bind my hands."

This time, total astonishment was exposed in her expression and voice. "That would look as if I don't trust you at all."

He shook his head. "Nope, it'll be the smart and careful

298

thing to do. In your place, I'd do the same. I don't mind. Just promise me I'll be safe when we reach him. I wouldn't want your brother acting like an irate father when he learns about us."

Carrie Sue laughed. "He won't. Darby trusts me to make my own decisions. He knows I wouldn't do anything foolish, and he knows I would die before endangering him. If I take you into his camp, he'll know you can be trusted."

T.J. smiled. "Let's eat before all your work is wasted."

After they devoured the fish, agava, and Jonnycakes and washed them down with sips of whiskey, they shared the cleanup chores.

T.J. suggested they take a swim before turning in for the night. When she agreed, he walked to the bank, stripped, and dove in. Carrie Sue did the same. They laughed and relaxed as they played chase-and-tag in the cooling water, and shared provocative kisses each time they touched. Their game lasted for over an hour until they were winded, and highly aroused.

T.J. left the water, dried off, and wrapped a blanket around his hips. He sat on a bedroll and leaned his back against a large rock. He watched Carrie Sue leave the water and dry off, delighting in the way the moonlight shimmered over her wet body. After she secured a blanket around her, he enticed, "Come over here and sit with me."

The redhead eagerly did as he said and sat on the bedroll between his legs. She snuggled against him and sighed peacefully. Her body was turned slightly to the left, one hip resting on the bedroll. Her legs were curved backward to the right and her ankles were crossed. T.J.'s left arm crossed her breasts and lightly captured her right arm near the elbow. Her left shoulder was under his with her fingers curled over his arm. Her weight was partially on his extended left leg, but his right one was raised and lying against her buttocks. His right fingers began to draw little designs on her right shoulder, and he bent his head forward to nuzzle her ear on that side. The position was so comfortable, so intoxicating, so perfectly meshed.

She dreamily entreated, "Tell me more about you, T.J."

He ceased nibbling on her ear and replied, "Like what? You know about all there is to learn about me."

She nestled closer to him and stroked the outside of his left thigh with her fingertips. "Like what you've been doing since the orphanage and war. Why haven't you found a place to settle down by now?"

His fingers began to trail up and down her bare arm. "A man like me hasn't needed a home and, when you travel around all the time, you make few friends. I've been a cowhand, a guide, a shotgun messenger, a guard for gold or silver wagons, a trail boss, and lots of other things. I guess I've had about every kind of job there is to make a few dollars. Between jobs, I rest and look around, and try to stay out of trouble, which isn't easy sometimes."

She laughed. She wondered if there was a special meaning to his words that he hadn't needed a home, as he hadn't said doesn't need. "I'm surprised that a man with your skills and prowess hasn't become a lawman of some kind. Have they ever approached you about one of their jobs?" She felt him tense, then relax.

He chuckled heartily, his chest movements shaking her lightly. "T.J. Rogue, a lawman? Lordy, woman, what office would trust me that much? Besides, I hear the pay is small and the perils large."

Although it wasn't a firm denial, she let it pass. "What about a bounty hunter? You could easily track down the worse criminals and earn big money."

Scorn filled his tone when he responded, "I feel the same way about bounty hunters as you do. My reputation isn't the best, woman, but I don't want it becoming any worse. Bounty hunters can't be trusted; they're cold-blooded and greedy. They shoot too many innocent men, or shoot men they could bring in alive. I've seen boys who couldn't be more than fifteen or sixteen strapped over their saddles, or men old enough to be grandfathers many times over with bullets through their heads. Nobody can tell me that's necessary, just easier for those snakes."

"What hunger drives you onward the most, T.J.?"

"What do you mean?" he asked, baffled by the deep question.

"Why do you stay in this unrooted and dangerous existence?"

"I don't know, Carrie Sue, but I will when I find it. I guess I just have a restless nature and I don't mix too well with regular people." As she fell silent, T.J. thought about the wires he had sent today. He hoped the President would heed his warnings and requests on the Apaches. He knew he couldn't risk using his operator key to tap into the telegraph lines again until they reached Deming, and that was a long time to wait to learn if her posters had been recalled by the Texas Rangers. At the same time, he would discover if the Stover Gang was on the trail again and where they were attacking. At least his office knew he was on the case and all was going as planned with Collins. Joe was to tell the Pima County sheriff of his lethal run-in with Martin Ferris. All of those messages had been sent in code.

T.J. stiffened. His hand covered her mouth and he strained to pick out a certain noise in the rocks to their left. "Stay here behind cover while I check on something," he whispered. After handing her a revolver, he vanished into the darkness.

He was back soon, grinning and chuckling. "Just a gray fox on the prowl. I scared him off. You ready to turn in?"

Without hesitation, she answered. "Yes."

"Would you like to sleep with me tonight?" he invited huskily.

"I'd like to sleep with you every night," came her bold response.

Looking into her moon-lightened face, he said, "Suits

301

me, woman." T.J. put the two bedrolls together and Carrie Sue lay down. He joined her, and placed a revolver nearby.

Their mouths met in a tender kiss which soon became a series of passionate ones. T.J. deftly loosened the blankets around their bodies, bringing their heated flesh into contact. She closed her eyes as his lips started a fiery trail down her throat, one which eventually covered her entire body. Soon, she irresistibly joined his bold adventures along new paths of lovemaking and she followed his hoarsely spoken instructions with eagerness and ecstatic delight. For hours they made love leisurely, uninhibitedly, blissfully, until they fell asleep cuddled together.

Carrie Sue jerked upwards when a rifle shot abruptly awakened her. She had slept late, as the sun was peeking over the tall peaks to the east. She looked around, but didn't see her lover. Quickly she wrapped the discarded blanket around her and grabbed her weapons. Then, she saw T.J. weaving through rocks and heading her way, carrying something. "What is it?" she shouted to him.

When he reached her, he held up the small animal and replied. "A javelina, small enough to be real tender and delicious after roasted. He must have gotten separated from his band. Usually they travel in herds of five to nearly thirty. Ever seen one? Or eaten one?"

Carrie Sue shook her head as she eyed the creature with small ears, a protruding snout, and almost no tail. He looked to weigh about fifteen to twenty pounds and was dark gray. "He looks like a pig with hair," she remarked, mischievously wrinkling her nose.

T.J. put down his burden and rifle. "You're right. The Apaches hunted them for their hides and meat, so I've eaten plenty, and killed plenty with a bow and arrows or a lance. These little boys usually nose around at night or real early in the morning, and get real mean if cornered or chased. When they send out an alarm to the herd, it's almost like a bark. They scare your pants off if you spook 'em. They chatter their teeth like the rattling of a sidewinder. I think you know what that is since you called me one in the cave," he jested.

Carrie Sue stuck out her tongue at him. She asserted, "You deserved it, partner, for scaring me witless."

T.J. chuckled merrily and teased, "Better watch it, Red, or I'll clip off that tasty tongue and cook it for my breakfast."

When he roguishly yanked her against him and brushed his lips over hers, she murmured, "Is that what you like best about it?" She flicked her tongue over his lips as her subtle words reminded him of how rapturously it had worked on his body last night.

"You're a woman of many surprises, Carrie Sue Stover."

As if it had been weeks since they had been together, they hurriedly undressed and fell upon the rumpled bedrolls, making love in an urgent and stimulating rush. Both were panting breathlessly when they finished and rolled to their backs to rest.

"Lordy, you keep me boiling all the time! But I surely do like how you cool me off. Shame that lack of heat doesn't last long."

Carrie Sue wiggled half atop him and teased, "I'm glad it doesn't. If you didn't crave me as much as I do you, I'd have to get the drop on you and force you to do my bidding at gunpoint."

He locked their gazes and said, "Yep, it's good we're matched."

She nibbled at his sensual lips as her naked body rubbed against his. "I like all the things you're teaching me, partner. I'm glad I brought you along. Just look what I'd be missing."

"There's plenty more to learn and experience, Red. Just make certain you don't use these facts and skills on anybody but me."

Carrie Sue gazed lovingly into his smokey gray eyes. She didn't care if she was naked in daylight with this man. She also didn't care that he was calling her "Red," because he did it in such a provocative and seductive tone. "As long as you're satisfied to remain my private teacher, I'll stay your devoted student."

"That's a bargain, my ex-schoolmarm. Right now," he said, capturing her in his arms and coming to a standing position with ease and strength, "let's get washed up and cook some breakfast."

T.J. carried her to the water and waded into it. They were waist deep before he placed her feet against the bottom. After kissing her soundly, he coaxed, "Get busy, woman. I'm starved."

Following their baths, they dressed and began their chores. While Carrie Sue gathered more wood, T.J. skinned and carved the peccary. She built a fire in the pit and made coffee as he took the unusable parts of the animal away from camp. She mixed Jonnycakes and started them while he cooked small strips of meat, the larger hunks to be roasted slowly to eat later. As he watched the cakes, she fetched their dishes and poured them coffee. They talked and ate.

Carrie Sue smiled after the first few bites and said, "It's good."

T.J. seemed utterly at ease this morning, smiling and chatting freely. He related some of his experiences during the war between the Northern and Southern states. He talked about some of the famous gunslingers and lawmen he had met over the years, and about a few run-ins with each. He told her about some of his adventures on the trail. Yet, everything he revealed, which could be checked out or might have been heard by her, was true about T.J. Rogue.

Carrie Sue enjoyed their conversation and rapport, which continued while they cleared the dishes and he put the rest of the meat on to roast slowly over the next few hours. They strolled around as she related more about her farming days in Georgia and her ranching days in Texas. She revealed more about her experiences with Quade Harding on the QH Ranch near Brownwood, below Commanche on a map.

When their talk came around to her brother, she spoke of their days growing up, not of their years on the trail as outlaws.

But T.J. did. "Money, cattle, and goods can be replaced, but a life can't. If you get caught, killings will be the hardest crimes to justify. I hope you don't get involved again." T.J. asked her about the killings they had been forced to commit.

Her bright smile faded and her sunny mood darkened. The lovely fugitive looked dismayed by the direction of their conversation. She admitted that killing was repulsive to her and to Darby and that they always tried to avoid it, unless it was necessary.

T.J. had to ask, "I know what makes killing necessary in my existence, Carrie Sue, but what makes it necessary in yours?"

She began to fidget as she explained, "Stages are always ordered to halt when bandits approach, but some drivers are reckless or cocky. Unless they tried to escape us, there never was any shooting. Or unless we were being shot at and our lives were at stake. You already know why we had to defend ourselves against Quade and his men."

Despite her unease, he continued, "What about the innocent victims of your attacks, the old men, women, and children?"

A haunted expression clouded her violet-blue eyes. "Can we skip over such a painful part of my life?" she entreated sadly.

He nodded and asked, "Who was the Texas Ranger who abused you?"

The flaming haired woman looked surprised by his unexpected question. Yet, she answered, "Virgil Ames. Why?"

"Well, I won't be able to teach him a lesson about how to

treat women, even women in your predicament. He was shot by Bill Longley. Ever heard of him or met him?"

"Heard of him, yes. Met him, luckily no. They don't come any lower or viler than Longley. He hates Negroes and kills one every chance he gets. I hear he wears a goatee which gives him a devilish look. Doesn't he do a lot of bounty hunting?"

"Yep, every time he's low on money. He's only about twenty-five, but he has at least thirty killings to his name. He's a wild and savage man. He's just lucky the law hasn't gotten something on him yet. If he comes after the Texas Flame, the law won't have to worry about him anymore; I'll take him coffin deep."

T.J. returned to the fire pit to check on the meat. He poured more coffee and leaned against a rock while he sipped the hot liquid gingerly. He smiled when she joined him. He resumed their conversation. "If Longley hadn't gotten Virgil Ames, the Rangers would have soon. I hear they don't like anybody, especially their own men, giving them a bad name. Ames gave me a hard time back in Texas, but I didn't let him provoke me into being reckless. I suppose he tried the same thing with Bill Longley and it didn't work. I don't exactly know what happened but the law didn't arrest Longley. That's one less revenge we have to worry about."

"That's a relief. I've always been nervous about running into him again. I knew that if that day ever came, I'd have to kill him and be in more trouble. You can't go around shooting Rangers, even with good reason. I have to admit, Virgil Ames was the only bad one I've met."

He concurred, "Yep, you don't run across many bad Rangers. Usually they're straight talking and fair. If Ames had been a good one, things might be different for you today."

"And we wouldn't have met," she added meaningfully. "I wonder which episode will prove best for me," she murmured evocatively.

He grinned and asserted confidently, "I will, naturally."

Carrie Sue smiled and relaxed again. "We'll see, Mr. Rogue."

"Yep, Red, we will," he replied, licking his lips.

Time seemed to move by swiftly today, too swiftly to suit either of them. Both were acutely aware of their plans to leave this tranquil haven at dawn the next morning.

Carrie Sue asked, "Will you take me to see that area northward?"

"Yep, let's saddle up. Grab your canteen and fill it."

Slowly they rode through the mountains located between the Sonoran and Chihuahuan Deserts. She saw and heard many bird species: busy flycatchers, Mexican chickadees, rufous-sided towhees who were scratching in the leaves, wrens with their laughing echoes in the canyons, raucous gray-breasted jays, and exotic-looking coppery tailed trogons.

There was a variety of plant life which seemed unlikely to grow in the same or nearby location, but it did. There were cactus in the lowlands; stunted oaks and pines, twisted alligator junipers, and cypress in the dense forests in the canyons; and scrubby manzanita, buckthorn, and skunkbush on the ridges. Forests of ponderosa pines, Douglas firs, and aspens filled the higher slopes. There were dry, sandy spots; there were lush grassy ones.

They reached their first destination, "the wonderful land of cliff formations." She saw hedgehog cacti with their red blossoms sprouting between rocks. There was an abundance of creeks, supplying plenty of water for the animals of this wondrous world. T.J. lead her from place to place, sometimes on horseback and sometimes on foot.

Extraordinary rock sculptures greeted her ever widening eyes. There were acres of pinnacles, organ pipe rocks, towering spires, massive stone columns, and enormous boulders delicately balanced on small pedestals. The incredible formations were a spectacular sight. The couple traveled the riparian trails through floral meadows, and cool woodlands, and along paths made by thousands of moccasined feet over the years.

T.J. escorted her to the area called "Heart of Rocks." There he showed her an echo canyon where she bounced words off the mocking stones, and a rock grotto which they could walk over, under, around, or through. She could see from the well-worn trail that it had been used many times in the past. They halted at Turkey Creek to rest and refresh themselves before heading back to their camp in the southern region of this splendid location.

When they reached their campsite, T.J. checked on the meat which was cooking in the fire pit. He asked later, "Do you have any kin back in Georgia? Some relative who'll take you in if you can get back there safely?"

Her gaze was locked to his. "No, I don't."

He clarified, "Once I get you back to your brother, if anything happens to Darby, you'll be all alone?"

"Yes," she responded, if she didn't have her lover at her side.

T.J. exhaled loudly. "That's something you have to think about, Carrie Sue. Considering the kind of life you two lead, he could get killed at any time. I'm sorry, but that's a reality you have to face. What would you do?"

She had faced that grim reality long ago, even if she hated to think about it. "If you mean what I think, T.J., I'm confused. I'd never stay with the boys if anything happened to Darby. I've already told you I'm leaving the gang after I see Darby once more."

"That isn't what I was asking. What would happen with Darby's gang if anything happened to him after I left you there to go after Harding? I mean, what would they do with you? How would they treat you? You're a beautiful woman, and they're violent outlaws. Would you be safe with them until you escaped or I returned?"

When she hesitated, he said, "I can see from your reaction that you aren't certain you can trust them."

Carrie Sue was thinking more of his words "violent" and "escape" than she was about his disturbing questions. She hated to spoil their lovely day with such dismaying conversation. She told him, "They've been with Darby since the beginning and are friends of his."

He pressed, "But that doesn't mean they're friends of yours, right?"

She frowned and answered, "I've been around them off and on for seven years, but they're not family to me. What's your point?"

T.J. was relieved to learn her only affection and loyalty lay with her brother, but he replied, "That worries me, woman."

Carrie Sue had never thought of being alone with the gang. Frankly, she didn't know how the outlaws would behave without her brother's guidance and influence, especially Kadry and Dillon. As for Kale, she would be safe with him. Yet, T.J. seemed to be probing her loyalties and affections for the men. Surely he didn't think she'd change her mind after seeing them again. Maybe he was only worried about one of them being too special to her, or worried that she would take their side if trouble struck. The gang members were all right, but she had avoided getting close to men who could die at any moment, except for Kale. She thought it best not to go into detail with her lover over that amiable relationship. She stated confidently, "Don't let it. If there's a problem, I can take care of myself."

"Against how many men, Carrie Sue?" he asked skeptically, slyly.

"The last time I was with Darby, he had six men, seven including himself. Sometimes for bigger jobs like robbing trains or rustling cattle or holding up a well-guarded Wells Fargo freight, he hires additional men for a week or two. I can trust Darby's friends, but I don't know about any others who might be in camp. Rest easy, love; the boys wouldn't harm me or allow anyone else to do so." Carrie Sue knew there were posters out on the Stover Gang, so she wouldn't be giving away any secrets by speaking the men's names. To let him believe she trusted him fully, she listed the gang members, "He normally rides with Kadry Sams, Walt Vinson, Tyler Parnell, John Griffin, Dillon Holmes, and Kale Rushton."

"A man would have to be deaf and blind not to have heard and read about them. Six expert gunmen are a lot for one woman to handle, especially one as desirable as you are, Carrie Sue. Any of them ever try anything with you in the past? You know what I mean."

"Why? You planning to challenge them to a showdown for my honor?"

"Nope, for your protection, if necessary."

"It won't be, partner. My brother takes care of me in camp."

"What if he isn't around or gets wounded or killed? Who would give you trouble? I'd like to look 'em over before I leave you there."

She wanted to drop the subject, but knew her lover wouldn't let her until he had the answers he was seeking. To appease him—but to lighten his grave mood—she continued in a playfully mischievous vein. "You promise no trouble you possessive male?"

"Not if they leave you alone and give you time to leave safely."

"The worst is Kadry Sams. He's Darby's best friend, so don't start anything with him or Darby won't take kindly to my bringing you along. Kadry never harmed me, but he was always after me in public and in private. His chase was worse when Darby wasn't looking or nearby, but he never succeeded. The other one is Dillon Holmes. He's the one I'll have to watch the most. He's sneaky around the others and bold around me, if I got alone with him, which I avoided like a chigger patch. Kadry is part of the reason I left so many times. He wanted to marry me and didn't want to be put off much longer. If I hadn't left near Sherman, it would have come to trouble between us."

"I'm surprised he let you go without a fuss. Why did he?"

She laughed. "He had no choice; Darby agreed with my decision. Kadry said he knew I'd be back soon, and it appears he was right."

T.J. cleverly hinted, "What if Kadry is the one who released your description to force you back into the gang, not the Hardings?"

"Friend or not, Darby would kill him," she vowed.

"If his deed ever came to light," her lover added. "I'm serious."

Carrie Sue contemplated his words, then shook her head. "No, Kadry would never endanger me; he wants me too badly. I could get killed and he'd never get his hands on me again. Too big of a risk."

"Isn't that also true of Quade Harding? Somebody betrayed you to the law, and it surely wasn't me. I didn't even guess your secret. If that poster hadn't come out, I doubt anyone else would have either."

"You worry too much," she teased, and he frowned. "I tell you what, partner; when we reach Darby's camp, you study Kadry and Dillon before you leave and tell me your opinion of them. If you're still available after handling Quade, you can take me far away."

"You have another bargain, woman. But what do you mean by if I'm still available?" he queried with intrigue.

"You said Darby could get killed at any time. The same is true of you, T.J. Rogue, my famous gunslinger with a highly coveted reputation. Even if you defeat Quade, he's not the only man after your handsome hide. You're more enticing to other gunslingers than nearly naked women hanging over saloon bannisters are to sex-starved cowpokes when they ride into town. Who'll be my escort then?"

"Don't worry about me or your escape, Red. I won't die

311

before getting you far away from your threat. If Darby is near Brownwood, after I leave you in his camp, you'll have one week to say good-bye while I finish off Harding. Then, I'll drag you away even if I have to face down Kadry, Dillon, your brother, and the entire gang." T.J. knew where he would go after dropping her off, to alert the Rangers and plan their captures, not to Brownwood after Harding.

"I guess that means you aren't planning to join the gang?"

"I doubt it. If I do, it won't be for long. 'Course, that all depends on if I'm a wanted man now. We'll decide later. It's time to eat supper. Coffee or whiskey? What do you want tonight?"

She was glad the subject was back to pleasant ones, and she intended to keep it that way for the rest of the evening! "Coffee with supper, and you later, if you don't mind my working you so hard. You're like water in this desert area, my handsome and creative teacher; I have to take every advantage of it when it's available, 'cause you can't ever tell when it won't be."

Chapter Sixteen

As they were packing the next morning to leave, Carrie Sue tested a suspicion of hers. She picked up T.J.'s saddle-bag and remarked, "I'll fetch some paper so you can draw me that map before we ride out."

The raven-haired man nearly yanked the bags from her and said, "I'll get it. You finish your chores. I have an Apache charm in here and it's bad luck for a woman to touch it. Besides, a lady shouldn't handle men's underwear." He chuckled to pass off his odd reaction.

"I've handled my father's and brother's many times."

"That's different. We're strangers," he reasoned playfully.

"Considering our relationship, Mr. Rogue, we're hardly strangers anymore. I know what you're hiding in there," she teased.

His head jerked in her direction and his expression was strange. To hide her suspicion, she jested, "You have keepsakes from your old conquests and you're afraid I'll get wildly jealous if I see them."

He laughed and retorted, "How did you know?"

With a seductive grin, she ventured, "Don't all men keep souvenirs of such victories? I'll have to think of something special to give you when we separate so you'll always remember this one as your best. Do the map, partner, while I finish with Charlie. I promise not to peek at your feminine treasures or order you to throw them away."

He chuckled and said, "Thanks, you're a wise woman, generous, too." When the map was done, he handed it to her and cautioned, "Don't lose it. It might save your life if anything happens to me."

"I'll keep it close to my heart," she replied and shoved it into her shirt pocket, more intrigued than ever about his saddlebag contents. How, she plotted, could she get a peek at them?

On the way to Deming, New Mexico, they passed more brown mountains on both sides, mountains which looked purple in the distant haze. Hills varied in size and height, many with rocky ridges and craggy protrusions which formed unusual shapes and gave the scenery a wild and rugged appearance. Some rocks were side by side like towering stone cactus which grew from the earth to the peak like sturdy walls holding back the tall mounds behind them. The terrain was covered by scattered scrubs and thick grassland. There was a large dry wash to their left, as they traveled near — but not on — the public road. The area had flattened out; the tall cactus and yuccas were gone for a while. It was almost like traversing a vast prairie.

They by-passed the rough settlement of Shakespeare, which was a mining town and a brief stop on the Butterfield and Garret stage lines. The quiet couple weaved through the Pyramid Mountains. They came to areas where no trees or bushes grew, where the mountains and hills were a great distance away, where the ground was sandy and dry. They crossed several playas where the desert terrain sent forth the mirage of water, of beautiful lakes and rivers which weren't really there, unmerciful illusions which played havoc with heat dazed senses. Occasionally clumps of grass were seen, but nothing more. It was a barren location, one which put them in the open for a long stretch.

Carrie Sue wondered if this area wasn't hotter and dryer than Arizona had been. She didn't like this valley, this lack of cover from the heat and from human perils. There was no place to hide, no cover for shade. T.J. told her they were about seventy miles west of Deming, and she eagerly looked forward to reaching that area.

They did very little talking because they needed to stay alert in the almost mesmerizing heat and glare of the blazing sun, and talking also dried their throats even more than the arid climate. Overhead were wispy clouds on a pale blue sky which offered no shade beneath their skimpy sizes, a trick often used by travelers in the open. Neither cared for this hazardous stretch of their journey which made them easy targets for attackers and the weather. Yet, it had to be covered.

Suddenly, a tree-lined dry wash seemed to spring miraculously from the barren earth to entice them toward it. Nearby was an abandoned shack and well. They halted to water the horses, refill their canteens, and refresh themselves. They only rested there for a short while because T.J. warned that other travelers could come along at any time.

Soon, they continued their ride, but the demands eased up for a while as small trees and bushy scrubs again dotted seemingly endless grasslands. Yet, the ground was still very dry, and Carrie Sue realized how hardy the plants must be to survive under such harsh conditions. She was amazed by the way the bushes and clumps of grass made the desert region look cool and green, almost inviting!

At last they halted, forty miles from their secluded haven in the cool Chiricahua Mountains of Arizona. The heat and terrain had been responsible for their slow progress today. The sun was setting and the western horizon was ablaze with shades of rich colors: reds, pinks, oranges, golds, and violets on an ever darkening blue backdrop.

T.J. chose a scrub-lined arroyo which put them out of sight of any late passerby. They unsaddled and tended the loyal horses first, then made camp. He warned against a fire, as smoke would give away their location and presence. He handed her weather-heated strips of peccary meat and a plate of beans, to be washed down with water as whiskey only made one more thirsty and sweaty in such heat.

The couple was tired from their demanding ride, so they claimed their bedrolls quickly, side by side. Neither mentioned lovemaking, as both knew it was impossible at this spot. It was even too hot to cuddle during sleep, but they did kiss good-night several times.

The ride was much the same the following day with landscape varying back and forth as with yesterday. It was hot on this fourth day of June in the year of eighteen-seventy-six. They were forty-five miles from Deming, where T.J. planned to make a stop for supplies.

Carrie Sue realized that the Tucson school was to have reopened for classes tomorrow. She wondered what Mrs. Thayer and Maria were doing and thinking. She wondered what the town residents, especially those who had met her on the streets and in church, thought about Miss Carolyn Starns turning out to be the notorious Texas Flame, a thought she did not find the least bit humorous. She wondered if Martin Ferris's body had been found, or if friends were searching for the mysteriously missing rancher at this moment.

The fiery redhead tried not to think about eager posses and greedy bounty hunters tracking her. She tried not to think about Darby's perils. She hoped he was resting in the Guadalupe Mountains which straddled the New Mexico-Texas border. She also tried not to let tormenting doubts about her lover gallop into her sluggish mind, but she couldn't master that runaway topic.

As she traveled near T.J. Rogue, she was plagued by doubts, fears, and worries. She wished she could halt such feelings, but she had learned to survive by her instincts, instincts which warned that he was trouble. She had just spent days making love to him and talking with him; yet, she distrusted the legendary Rogue! Loving T.J. was easy, irresistible, but believing him was difficult. Maybe that was the core of her problem; she was too emotionally involved with this peak of prowess to judge him accurately.

The desperado reflected on the *evidence* against him. Why had a loner taken to a proper lady, a staid schoolmarm, a passing stranger in a relay station? Even if he was attracted to her, men like him would have avoided her or believed her out of his reach. Yet, he had continued coming around her even before she appeared receptive to his pull. Perhaps it had been her connection to Martin Ferris which had enticed him to keep company with her; perhaps he had wanted to aggravate his past foe and provoke Martin into a battle. Later, he had been waiting for Curly James to arrive, and had seen them talking. Somehow, T.J. had always been around—as with the stage holdup and the attack during their picnic—always been there when she needed help, as if he had advance notice of trouble in the wind. Had those numerous incidents been coincidental or created by his design?

Then, he had just happened to be in Sheriff Ben Myers's office when her first poster arrived! He had just happened to be in her room to rescue her from that other sheriff. His questions in camp and on the trail could be normal or sly ones. Yet, he was asking plenty about Darby and his men, particularly about their skills and weapons. He had said it was information needed in case he had to defend and rescue her from that gang. Yes, he always had logical explanations!

Lately he had pressed her about her actions with the gang, wanting to know exactly where she had gone and what she had done over the years. He had wanted to know if she had spent most of her time in the gang's camp and if she had taken care of the men by cooking and cleaning and washing for them. He had seemed pleased when she had told him she had rarely been involved in the heart of crimes, and she didn't tend to the men's chores, only to Darby's.

The inquisitive male had wanted to know why no one had realized the Texas Flame was Darby Stover's fiery-haired sister and gotten her description out sooner. She knew she had explained that before, but she did so again. She also told him that the few men who had seen and met her face-to-face were outlaws who wouldn't or couldn't release information on her without incriminating themselves.

Since that night in the colossal cave and later in their romantic hideaway, T.J. had gone from refusing to ask any personal and probing questions to pouring them from his loosened lips! What worried her now was his main topic always seemed to be Darby Stover and his gang! And, there was the curious matter of what was inside his saddlebags.

On the other hand, she knew Martin Ferris had been behind that picnic attack. She knew from Martin that her poster had arrived in Tucson on Thursday, but after her morning departure. Had there been another one in the early mail as T.J. claimed, the one he had seen and stolen? Did he make it a practice of opening others' mail? Could it be true, as he claimed, that fate had guided his hand to that letter? Why two posters to Ben Myers, if that was where T.J. had gotten his copy? Who had released her new description: Quade or his father? Or T.J. to force her onto the trail with him? Had it been in his possession all along, with him waiting for the perfect moment to use it? Had someone tipped him off by telegraph, ordering him to speed up his ruse? Had he left during the night while they were at the cave? Where had he gone that day in the Chiricahua Mountains?

There were too many unanswered questions about her lover, too many *coincidences* and pat explanations. If only she dared to demand answers, but that would alert him to

318

her lingering mistrust. If T.J. Rogue was a threat to her and Darby, she was no match for his prowess at this moment. It was a quandary which only time and events could settle for her. Was it, she asked herself, wise to let T.J. keep forging a stronger bond between them, uncontrollably or intentionally on his part? She would make her final decision about her lover at El Paso. Merciful Heavens, she wished she could trust him completely, but she was afraid she couldn't. Until she was certain of him, she couldn't lead him to her brother. . . .

They neared Deming at dusk. T.J. showed her an excellent place to hide while he went into town for supplies.

"It's too risky," she protested his decision.

"I know a man here that I can trust. I'll get supplies from him. We have to eat, woman. And I'd like to get some news. We've been out of contact for days. I want to see if your posters are everywhere and if I'm a wanted man. I have a gut feeling that Shibell didn't let it be known you slipped through his hands and I got the drop on him. He's a proud and stubborn lawman. He'll want to correct his mistake without anybody learning about it. Trust me; I know what I'm doing."

"I'll go with you," she announced.

"You can't; that's definitely too risky. If I get chased, I can flee better alone. I'll work my way back to you after I lose them."

"If you aren't back by morning, I'm coming after you, Rogue."

He grinned at her defiant expression and warning. "I will be."

Carrie Sue and her pinto stayed hidden in the trees while she watched her lover ride off again. She was tempted to follow him, but knew he would catch her and it would cause trouble between them. She glanced at the possessions left behind. No saddlebag was among them. If they were careful, they had enough supplies to get them to Mesilla where he had another friend who had a place they could use. Without a doubt, he had another reason for going into town!

She withdrew the map from her pocket and studied it. She read the names and locations of T.J.'s friends, and wondered who—no what—they were. The one in Mesilla was Hank Peterson, but she'd never heard of him. Nor had she heard the name Mitchell Sterling who was in El Paso. One owned a cantina and the other owned a mercantile store. The map ended there because T.J. knew she was familiar with Texas. Whatever happened, she'd never look up strangers for help.

The flaming haired fugitive remained there, fretting, until T.J. returned. He grinned lightheartedly as he served her fried chicken, biscuits, and steamed vegetables which were rolled inside a clean cloth.

"Good news for me, woman," he said, "but I'm afraid you aren't as lucky. Your poster's up all right, but they don't know about me. Shibell kept his mouth shut just like I presumed."

She tried to pass him some food, but he shook his head and said he'd already eaten with his friend. She wished she could see one of those wanted posters and compare it to the one in his possession. If they weren't alike, that would answer one question for her! Somewhere and somehow, she had to get a look at one of those *real* posters. As she ate, she listened intently to his words.

T.J. sipped tart tequila as he reluctantly related his devious tale to cover his trip into town to use the telegraph. He hoped she would credit the unusual tone of his voice to the strong liquor, not as the effect of his guilt and deceit. Many times he had fooled people easily, but he found it hard to look at her while lying. "Matthew Grimes, that's my friend, saw a marshal today and he learned a lot which he passed along to me. You were reported last seen in Tucson, but nothing was mentioned about me escaping with you. The law assumes you left town Wednesday night before your posters reached Ben Myers on Thursday. They figure by now you're either heading north to safety or you're back in Texas with your brother. His last strike was two weeks ago near Fort Worth, and Monday after our picnic. That means he isn't laying low in Oklahoma. Either he has to be near Brownwood or the Pecos River, like you predicted. You must know Darby well."

Rapidly she figured the distance and time involved in Curly leaving her brother at the Guadalupe hideout on May eighteenth and Curly's arrival in Tucson on the twenty-third against Darby's being able to reach Fort Worth to commit a robbery by May twenty-second. Darby would have to have left the hideout immediately—after telling Curly he was staying there for a while—ridden hard and fast, known his target ahead of time, and carried off the deed in less than five days. She knew from experience that schedule was impossible, and Darby never struck a target without careful preparation and observation!

Who, she mused worriedly, was lying? T.J. to trick her, or the law? If it was the law, was the reported charge a mistake or a sly trick to lure her there for capture? If it was T.J., did her lover expect her to panic and refute the information, then rashly disclose the whereabouts of Darby's location? It could be that another gang was impersonating them; that happened sometimes with them and with other well-known bands!

"What's wrong, Carrie Sue?" he questioned her moody silence. Excluding his remorse over his ruse, he felt wonderful; the Rangers had withdrawn her posters as requested, claiming it was a sketch of the wrong woman. That compliance should reduce her peril during his case. He yearned to tell her she was safe for a while, but he couldn't without exposing himself and his mission.

The keen-witted outlaw realized her lover wasn't fusing his gaze to hers as he spoke, and his voice was strange despite the scratchy tequila. He seemed an odd mixture of joy and tension. He seemed alert and wary, a little too edgy for an unwanted man. "What did Darby hit?" she asked, trying to look and sound sad at his so-called news.

He answered honestly, "A Union Express office. Got away with a big haul of greenbacks. Maybe he's planning on trading them for gold like the President promised. Paper is easier to carry off than heavy gold."

She frowned, not at his unamusing assumption, but at his or someone's chosen target. Unless Darby had changed his mind since they parted, her brother never struck at Union Express, which was too heavily guarded. Darby Stover wasn't one to get desperate enough to be reckless! She noticed how many times her lover unconsciously wet his lips and dried his sweaty palms on the knees of his jeans, and she observed how the pulse point in his throat exposed his rapid heartbeat. These, combined with his odd anxiety, unnatural tone of voice, and curious expression, were signs of dishonesty that any astute and intelligent person could read, as Kale had taught her. Anguish seized her, but she concealed the reason. "I wonder if he knows about my trouble. If he's working near a big town, then I would imagine so. That also puts him nearer Brownwood than West Texas. Still, we should check there first as we pass by."

He sensed that something was wrong, but he couldn't surmise what. To draw her out, he said, "Once we reach Texas, we'll have to be more careful than ever. It's about seven to ten days from the border to Commanche. You still determined to see your brother?"

Carrie Sue realized another peril. What if they—the law or her beguiling lover—used her reported capture to lure Darby into a trap? If her brother didn't know where she was, he might fall for such a clever ruse. She nodded and replied, "I have to. There's no way I can reach him to let him know

I'm all right and what my plans are. I want to convince him to join me; that has to be done in person."

"You think he'll listen?" T.J. probed.

She sighed heavily and shrugged. "He'll listen, but I can't decide what he'll do afterwards. Darby thinks he's trapped in this miserable life; Quade saw to that with his action near Laredo. And he knows how many times I've tried to go straight and my description wasn't even out. I'm not sure I can persuade him we'll be safe anywhere. But I'm going to try my hardest. I don't want my brother killed or hanged or jailed, T.J.; he made a mistake which carried him away like a flood. He kept getting pulled down by currents he couldn't fight. It isn't fair! It's all Quade's fault. If you don't kill him, I will. That bastard! He's going free while his victims are on the run!"

"Don't worry this pretty head about Harding; I'll take care of him. All you have to think about is getting to Darby, talking to him, and escaping before the law closes in on you two. I'll help, Carrie Sue."

She looked at him and smiled faintly. If he loved her, why wasn't he insisting she leave the hazardous West immediately? He was tough and strong, so why wasn't he binding her and dragging her far away? He was smart and careful, so why wasn't he trying to convince her that searching for Darby Stover was too perilous? He wasn't a wanted man and didn't plan to become one, so why wasn't he more worried about the enormous price on her head and the countless men who were pursuing her at this very time? His words and actions didn't make sense!

Yes, her warring mind argued, it did make sense if he was after Darby Stover! In light of his many contradictions and curious behavior, it certainly seemed that way to her, much as she hated to accept that grim fact. The questions were: who did he keep contacting, and why did he want her brother so badly, and when would he betray her?

Not wanting her to watch him defeat her brother, T.J.

suggested desperately, "Since I'm safe for now, Carrie Sue, why don't you conceal yourself and let me take a message to Darby? You can use one of your old hideouts and tell me how to locate him. If you put something in your letter that only you and Darby know, that'll convince him I came from you. I can tell him it was too dangerous for you to travel and I can bring him back to where you're camped. You know, with him in the open again, the law and bounty hunters are going to be everywhere. Please let me go after him alone while you stay safe," he urged.

"Even with a lock of my hair and all our family secrets written in a note, Darby Stover wouldn't believe you. He'd think those things were tortured out of me. He knows I would never, under any circumstances, reveal his location. He'd probably kill you!"

"It was worth a try, Red; I don't want to see you harmed."

She smiled, wanting to believe that last statement. Maybe it was true; maybe he had fallen enough in love with her to forget about capturing her; maybe all he wanted now was the Stover Gang. But didn't he realize she could not betray her brother, even for him? And if he loved her and wanted her afterwards, didn't he realize that could never happen if he was responsible for Darby's capture and death? How could she ever surrender her heart and body to the man with her brother's blood on his hands? She couldn't.

Carrie Sue comprehended his worry over her, and that teased warmly at her heart. She would let T.J. Rogue use his prowess and wits to get her to El Paso safely, then she would take off on her own. She could easily find Darby's hideout from there. If her lover tried to stop her from leaving him . . .

"Quit frowning, love; everything will be fine soon," he murmured tenderly and stroked her lined forehead.

She focused misty eyes on him. "I'm not sure, T.J.; I have this terrible feeling something is going wrong somewhere."

"What, love?" he asked. "I'll protect you with my own

life. No one is going to harm you again. Once this is over," he paused a moment before continuing, "you'll be safe and happy forever. I swear."

Tears, which were unlike her, gathered in her eyes as she thanked him. He had called her "love" twice. Why? And why did it seem as if he was being totally honest at this moment? If he knew how much his betrayal would hurt her, and the sharp-witted male had to know, why would he continue his ruse? Why was he so resolved to capture her brother? And, surely he was. For a man to have such consuming bitterness and determination and to be willing to sacrifice anything for a particular victory, there had to be a good reason. What was T.J.'s?

Merciful Heavens, if only she could demand the truth! If she did, he would either lie or he would end his cruel ruse or he would jail her and continue his trek after Darby Stover. No, she couldn't let him know she was on to him! She had to reach her brother first and get him far away from peril. Then, she would seek the truth about her devilish Rogue . . .

Chapter Seventeen

Early the next morning, almost before dawn, they broke camp and headed for Mesilla and another of T.J. Rogue's friends.

Before pulling out, T.J. had questioned her silence. She had told him she was worried about Darby being on the move again. If he was captured or slain before she could reach him, her brother wouldn't stand a chance of having a new beginning, and he deserved one. She told T.J. she had a horrible feeling that she had seen her brother alive for the last time, that some unknown threat was stalking him.

T.J. had replied, "A man who lives by his guns expects to die by them. You aren't responsible for his fate, Carrie Sue, and you can't halt it. Whatever happens, I'll take care of you."

As they traveled, she considered her dilemma for the seemingly hundredth time. How could she love a man she distrusted? Yet, she knew it was far more than physical attraction for him, and she suspected it was the same for T.J. Rogue. The only thing she didn't doubt was the fact they were in love and wanted to be together for keeps!

T.J.'s grudge against Darby had to be vitally important to him. What, she pondered, could it be? Had one of their victims been his father or brother? No, one was killed long ago by Apaches and the other had died at the hands of Mexican bandits. Or so her lover had claimed. What if the Stover Gang had killed his brother? What if they had killed his best friend? For a man with so few friends, each one would be precious to him, worth dying for while seeking revenge.

Yes, she concluded, T.J.'s motive had to be personal revenge. That would be the only thing important enough to sacrifice their new and unexpected love and to risk his life and hers. Who was the victim?

Maybe T.J. had had other family, members he hadn't mentioned to her, members left behind on that ill-fated journey into the Apaches' hands. Perhaps a baby brother or sister, she mused. The possibilities were endless and frustrating. For all she knew, one of the men riding with Darby could be T.J.'s long-lost brother who'd gone bad. The ages of most would figure out correctly, and her lover was mighty interested in each one. No, she protested, that was too far-fetched.

But something else wasn't. If another gang was impersonating them, why couldn't another gang have killed this person whom her lover wanted to avenge? What if Darby and the others were innocent of T.J.'s mental charges? What if her love was after the wrong killer?

Darby Stover and T.J. Rogue were the only people in the world that she loved with all her heart and soul. If it came to a choice between the two men, and Darby's life was at stake, she would have to take her brother's side. Merciful Heavens, what would she do if it came to a shoot-out between them? If Darby had to die because of his wicked deeds, she prayed that it wouldn't be at her love's hands.

Those agonizing thoughts finished making her decision. Trust him or not, there was no way she could lead T.J. to Darby's hideout. The two special men in her life must never meet and battle. Besides, she couldn't endanger T.J.'s life by delivering him into the hands of his unsuspecting enemies, skilled gunmen who made the odds seven-to-one against him! And, since he wasn't a wanted man, she couldn't be the one to ensnare her love in a life of crime. Guilty or not of her mental accusations, she had to part ways with T.J. Rogue in El Paso.

After leaving the Deming area, the landscape was back to dry and sandy terrain which was pancake flat. On occasion it drifted into scrubby spots that abounded in snakeweed, a bushy plant which appeared globular in shape and gave off stinky black smoke when burned. The "matchweed" was known to be poisonous to some stock, but fortunately its foul taste kept them away from it. Most were densely crowded into scattered patches and were covered in clusters of yellow flowers, adding green and yellow coloring to the pale brown earth.

Suddenly an exquisite section filled their vision, and she was amazed anew at how rapidly and unexpectedly the landscape could alter. All around them thousands of yuccas in full bloom were sighted and enjoyed. The patches were thick and beautiful, appearing like countless white torches held skyward by skinny green hands. Carrie Sue twisted in her saddle to take in the view from all directions.

Amongst the cloud white abundance were mesquites and cacti. Along the dry washes they passed, blue paloverde edged the rims. She wondered why the tree-like bush was called blue, when it was covered in masses of yellow blossoms! In locations where there were plenty of them, it looked as if the desert washes were lined with a golden trail. She knew that paloverde was Spanish for "green stick" and referred to the bark color. This display of life and beauty distracted her for a time from her troubles. She cleared her mind and let Mother Nature entertain and relax her.

They were less than forty miles from Las Cruces, a large town adjoining the smaller one of Mesilla. Northward, she could make out the Robledo Mountain in a whitish blue haze which made it appear a ghostly outline against the distant horizon. Southward were the Potrillo Mountains. Eastward — their direction — were the Organ Mountains, before which was spread Las Cruces in a tranquil valley.

T.J. remained on alert, knowing there would be bounty hunters and lawmen who hadn't gotten the word about withdrawing her posters from circulation. And, there would be some men who wouldn't believe the posters had been a mistake. He had to be careful. Wanting to reach Mesilla with its protective cover by nightfall, he urged them onward at an increased pace which wasn't too demanding on the horses.

At their mid-way break, they finished off the chicken and biscuits which had been left over from last night. They rested quietly for thirty minutes, then hit the trail once more.

Carrie Sue didn't realize the land wasn't flat ahead until they reached the edge of a downward slope which entered the valley where their destination was located. She reined up and looked at the sight of Las Cruces snuggled at the base of the large mountains. "This is a perfect place to build a house," she remarked to her companion.

T.J. lifted himself in his stirrups and looked around, smiling and agreeing, "Yep, this is some pretty view, woman." He glanced at her and asked, "How does a bed sound for tonight? We're almost there."

"Sounds wonderful, partner. That and hot food and a cool bath. Lead on, my faithful Apache scout," she jested.

They crossed a narrow section of the Rio Grande, which miles ahead formed the boundary between Texas and Mexico, and bore south. The area was shrouded in shadows by the time they reached the outskirts of Mesilla. Beneath a half moon, T.J. guided her to his friend's house.

For a brief moment as they dismounted, Carrie Sue was consumed with panic and wondered if his betrayal would come here, tonight. No, he needed her to lead him to Darby.

The trees were larger in this area of adobe homes and Spanish structures. As he put their horses into a small corral, fed and watered them, T.J. related how La Mesilla had started as a Mexican civil colony in eighteen-fifty with around eight hundred Hispanos. He told her that one of the buildings had housed the territorial capitol of the Confederacy. Not too far from his friend's house was a plaza, to its right was his friend's saloon, near the La Posta.

He led her inside the Mexican-style house and put her things down. "You rest while I go tell Hank we're here. I'll bring some food back and help you prepare a bath. Stay inside and out of sight, woman; we don't know what's waiting out there," he cautioned.

Carrie Sue nodded wearily, took a seat, and removed her boots. She flung her hat into another chair and leaned back on the comfortable couch. "Take too long, partner, and I'll be asleep," she murmured. She watched T.J. flash her a breathtaking smile, toss his saddlebags over his shoulder, and depart. Without delay or hesitation, she grabbed a colorful poncho from a chair and wiggled it over her head, settling the blanketlike cloak over her feminine body to conceal it and her weapons. She seized a sombrero from a wall hook and stuffed her braid beneath its tall crown. She slipped out the back way to follow him. She peered around the house and edged toward the front.

Carrie Sue looked in both directions and located her lover's retreating back as he headed down a narrow street. She waited until he rounded the corner and, sighting no one, she hurried that way. She was careful not to make any noise, and her bare feet aided her.

She saw him enter a fancy cantina on the next street near a long, cream-colored building which was marked "La Posta." So far, he had told the truth. She heard the music and laughter and voices from her concealed position, but she couldn't see inside the swinging doors. She had to get closer! Cautiously she crept toward her destination.

When two men came outside, she flattened herself against the wall behind her, and her heart pounded in alarm. Fortunately they headed in the other direction and vanished soon. She made it to the side of Hank's place and peered through a window which looked dirty enough to prevent anyone from sighting her face. It was a large room with wooden tables and chairs, much like most saloons. There was a lengthy bar at the other side, and a hazy glow filled the room from lantern and cigar smoke. Men were drinking, playing cards, and chatting. Mexican girls waited upon the customers, smiling and teasing them. Then, she spotted her lover; he was speaking with a man shorter than he was, an American in a Mexican settlement. . . .

The redhead studied the stranger. He was dressed in a white shirt, a black and gray striped vest, and dark trousers. She supposed he looked authentic for a gambler and saloon owner. He wasn't wearing a visible weapon, but most men like him carried smaller ones concealed. His graying hair had once been blond and his face was tanned from hours beneath the sun. Odd, she mused, for a business man who kept late hours and spent so much time inside during the day? Nothing really to go on, she concluded.

She watched them head into a back room and close the door. She worked her way around the building, but the only window was too high for observation or eavesdropping. She frowned, wondering what was being said inside the room she was leaning against.

A door opened nearby and a woman walked outside. She glanced in Carrie Sue's direction and asked in Spanish, "What do you want there?"

The daring fugitive ignored her and quickly left the scene before the woman summoned her boss and she was caught red-handed. She hurried back to Hank's house and replaced the borrowed items. Removing her gunbelt and laying it aside, she half-reclined on the couch.

In twenty minutes, T.J. was back, carrying a meal of floured tortillas, enchiladas oozing with sauce, and other Mexican dishes. He smiled as he placed the food on the table. "Ready?" he hinted.

Carrie Sue pretended to drag herself wearily from the

couch. "Did you find him?" she asked as she sat down at the table.

"Yep, he'll be working a few more hours. You'll have to meet him in the morning, my exhausted vixen. After we eat, you're getting a bath and turning in." He dropped his fork and leaned to recover it, taking a look at her feet. As suspected, they were dirty. He grinned, aware she was the one sighted by one of Hank's woman. He also realized that either his guard was down too low or she possessed more skills than previously believed, as he hadn't seen or heard her!

As if reading his thoughts, she remarked, "I checked on Charlie and Nighthawk. We pushed them hard these past few days. I think I got a stone bruise; I should have put on my boots."

"It'll feel better after you soak it a while. Be glad it isn't a cactus spine; they're hell to remove. How's the food?"

"Delicious, Mr. Rogue, even better than what we had in Tucson. Or I'm twice as hungry." She laughed and took a few bites before asking, "What did your friend say about you bringing me here?"

"I trust Hank Peterson. He understands your problem. I told him you're going straight, so he's willing to help by hiding us tonight."

"Why?" she probed, observing him more closely than he realized.

"Why what?" he asked, looking baffled.

She clarified, "Why is he willing to aid a criminal and endanger himself? And why do you two trust each other so much? I'm valuable property, remember?"

Enlightenment brightened his smokey gray eyes. "We've worked together several times in the past. He's one of my best friends, and he feels the same about me. We've saved each other's lives a few times, so we're close and tight. He knows I wouldn't be taking this risk unless I trusted you and believed you, and had good reason."

"Which is?" she prompted before sliding a forkful of

enchilada into her mouth and licking the mischievous sauce from her lips.

He stopped eating to gaze at her across the table. "Don't you know the reason by now, Carrie Sue?" he asked in a quiet tone. "Isn't it the same reason you let me tag along and have allowed me to stay?"

"If that's a sly way of asking me how I feel about you, Mr. Rogue, I think I've pretty well exposed myself in that area. Like it is with you and Hank, I think we're tight and close. You did say your friend has to work late, didn't you?" she hinted audaciously.

Passion darkened his eyes and his respiration altered as his heart speeded up with anticipation. "Yep, lucky for us," he murmured.

They finished their meal quickly, each continually glancing at the other and smiling in suspense and eagerness. T.J. fetched a metal tub and filled it with tepid well water while she cleared the table. As she bathed inside, T.J. stood at the well in the moonlight to scrub and rinse himself. When he went inside, she was waiting for him in the bed which he had pointed out to her. He approached it, and she lifted her arms in summons.

T.J. released his blanket and it dropped to the floor. He joined her on the bed and gathered her into his arms. "Lordy, this feels good."

"The comfortable bed or me?" she teased.

"Both, but you best of all," he murmured, closing his mouth over hers. His hands wandered over her body, caressing here and fondling there. He was glad he had asked Hank to give them some time alone tonight, and that his friend had understood their need for privacy. Yet, Hank Peterson was worried about the relationship between them and how it might affect T.J.'s judgment and mission. T.J. was too, but it couldn't be helped. He loved this woman and needed her. He thought she had come to trust him almost fully, but evidently he was wrong. Her following him tonight proved she possessed lingering doubts, and it had been her in Hank's poncho and sombrero.

T.J. couldn't blame her for being cautious, even suspicious of him. After all she was a famous outlaw with a large price on her head and she was guiding him to one of the most notorious bands in the West, which was led by her brother. Yet, she needed him for protection and aid, so she wouldn't pull any tricks any time soon. Perhaps tonight was one last test to make certain of his loyalty, and he had passed.

Carrie Sue's fingers drifted over her lover's back and shoulders. She liked the smooth texture of his flesh and the hardness of the muscles beneath the bronzed covering. She was stimulated by the contact of their bodies and their mouths. She was painfully aware this could be the last time she ever made love to T.J. Rogue, as El Paso was their next stop. She clung to him and kissed him urgently, feverishly.

T.J. trailed his lips over her face, returning time and time again to her insistent mouth. He tried not to nuzzle her face and throat too roughly as he hadn't shaven in his rush to fuse their bodies into one wild and blissful union. His mouth roamed down her chest and his hand traveled down her sleek side. Gently he teethed the rosy brown buds on her breasts, and deftly his fingers tantalized her to squirming desire.

Carrie Sue closed her eyes as she absorbed these rapturous memories which might have to last a lifetime. Her fingertips traced little patterns on his shoulders as she mentally marked the splendid territory as her own private possession. She felt as if she were drifting on a cloud and being pleasured to the fullest degree by the only man she had ever and would ever love.

T.J. adored this woman, this gentle creature who filled his life with joy, this wild vixen who challenged him to risk all to have her, this prized lover who made his body ache with hunger and his heart sing with happiness. Carrie Sue Stover was one helluva woman! She was his woman, and he would do whatever necessary to keep her safe and with him.

As they rested in the golden afterglow of lovemaking, Carrie Sue suspected that her lover knew about her mischief, so she slyly murmured, "I didn't tell you the truth earlier. I followed you to the saloon. I wanted to see who you were meeting. I'm sorry."

T.J. hugged her tightly as he revealed, "I know what you did, and I understand. You can't be too careful, love, even with me. Luz, that's Hank's woman, told us she saw someone outside wearing Hank's poncho and sombrero. You see, my sneaky redhead, that poncho is a special design, a one-of-a-kind, which Luz had made for him."

Carrie Sue giggled when T.J.'s fingers played over her ribcage. "I never thought of that angle. Snared by a lover's gift."

"That was a stupid thing to do, woman," he chided softly. "You could have been seen and captured."

"I'll be more careful in the future, and more trusting."

"Good. Now, we need to get cleaned up and turn in. Hank insists you use his bedroom. He and I will bunk down in the other room."

Carrie Sue protested that hospitality, but T.J. held firm. They rinsed off, emptied the tub water, cleared away their things, and she went to bed in the back room with the door closed.

Hank and T.J. stood near the corral the next morning and talked. The graying blond asked, "How are you planning to handle this case once you locate them? You can't take on seven men alone, and you know she's going to kick up a ruckus when she realizes she's been duped."

T.J. glanced at the ex-Ranger with whom he had worked many times, a good friend whom he trusted fully, a man who still served as a contact for Rangers on the trail. "I just want to discover their hideout. Then, I'll alert the Rangers and let them take care of the problem. I'm going to try my damnedest to keep from being the one to take out her brother. She'd never forgive me if I killed Darby."

"What about her, Thad? You know you can't get a pardon for her. I gave you the answer to that question last night. The President understands your feelings, but she's an outlaw, has been for seven years. Even if she helped you capture her brother's gang, that wouldn't make up for all she's done. The law says she has to pay."

T.J. began to fidget; that wasn't the answer he had wanted and prayed for from his superiors. "I'll think of something, Hank. I can't let her go to prison or die. Lordy, man, I love her."

Hank Peterson's faded blue eyes settled on Thad Jamison's pained expression. "I never thought I'd hear such words from those lips. You've really settled down over the past two years and I'm proud of you. I just hate it that she's on the most wanted list, and that she's as guilty of breaking the law as a rustler caught with a hot branding iron in his hand. If you don't cool your head and heart, my friend, you're in for one tough time when you have to arrest her."

"I can't do that, Hank," T.J. revealed sadly, stubbornly.

"You'll have to, Thad; this is your case, by your choice and insistence. You can't back away now; it's too late. You're too close to her and she's the only one who can end this madness by that gang. Like I told you last night, their last few crimes have been vicious."

"From the reports I've been getting along the trail, it doesn't sound like the same man she describes as Darby Stover. I wonder . . ."

Hank reasoned with a clear head and keen wit, "What do you expect from her? She's his devoted sister. Rest assured, it is the real Stover Gang on the rampage again. They're smart and fast and real mean, Thad. The only way we're going to stop them any time soon is through her. You have to do this, for justice and yourself."

T.J. caught the implied hint. "I haven't forgotten what they

336

did to Arabella and Marie, nor to our friend on that stage. I'll stop them, but I won't let her get harmed."

"There's no way you can prevent that from happening, Thad."

"There has to be a way, some legal crack she can wiggle through."

Hank shook his head. "I've asked a lawyer friend of mine to look for it, but he doesn't think one exists either, not for the Texas Flame. I'll let you know what he uncovers. Keep me alerted by telegraph."

"Don't forget to send those coded messages this morning after we leave. I'll pick up the answers in El Paso. That'll probably be my last contact for a while. I don't want her getting suspicious of me again. I just earned her trust, though Lord knows I don't deserve it."

"Don't be hard on yourself, Thad; you didn't expect to fall in love with her. By the time you were on to her, it was too late. It took some doing and lots of telegrams to get those posters on her recalled. You can bet your boots there are still some around or people who haven't gotten the news, so be careful." Hank passed along other facts, "Quade Harding and his father were furious about it. We've tried to quiet them down, but they suspected something is up. We told Quade that poster he released wasn't the Texas Flame and he could get an innocent woman killed. He was ordered to stop interfering in our affairs. Harding claimed he put out that recent sketch to protect Carrie Sue Stover, to get her taken alive and delivered to him so he can help clear her of the mix-up. He says he knows she isn't the Flame, but others believe she is so she's in great peril. Of course, we don't buy that story; he's up to mischief. We told him his poster on Carrie Sue was illegal, so he agreed to pull it and cancel his reward on her. That'll help maintain our secrecy. The newspapers were forced to print retractions. I doubt you've seen the stories about her; the papers gobbled up news on that sketch and big reward. They're using that old picture again, which

337

doesn't pose a threat to her or you. Dave's still working on the Harding case."

T.J.'s smokey gray eyes darkened with anger. "You know Harding's the one who forced her into a life of crime. Dave better get him."

Hank Peterson conceded, "What she and her brother did against the Hardings was justified, but their crimes since then aren't. Don't deny that truth to yourself."

"I don't, but it riles me how she got entrapped."

"I know, but they've become hardened criminals over the years."

"Not Carrie Sue. You'll see when you meet her."

"A person can't live that kind of life without being affected by it."

"She was affected, but not in a bad way. That's why she kept trying to escape that existence, but Harding wouldn't let her."

"We'll get Harding: don't worry."

"If you don't, I will, one way or another," he vowed coldly. "You did send that messenger to Mitch last night?"

"Yep. He'll be ready to play along with your deceit. We'd better get inside and get breakfast going. She should be awake by now. I'm eager to meet this woman who stole your heart."

Carrie Sue finished dressing in a clean blue shirt and jeans. She brushed her hair and let it hang free, knowing that style made her look innocent. She wanted to meet and impress Hank Peterson. She packed her things, made the bed, and left the room.

The two men were in the kitchen. She joined them, timidly smiling first at her lover, then at his friend. "Good morning, gentlemen. That was the best night's sleep I've had in days. Thanks for the loan of your bed, Mr. Peterson. I know that we're putting you in danger by accepting your many kindnesses; you're a good friend to T.J."

He looked her over and entreated, "Please, call me Hank. You ready for some coffee, bacon, eggs, and biscuits?"

"Sounds marvelous. Thank you," she replied, licking her lips.

Hank studied the ravishing beauty whose shapely figure was displayed by her snug garments. Those large periwinkle eyes stunned him with their color and expression. She looked as pure as a newborn babe. Her hair was like a golden red halo about a glowing face which could halt a runaway train on its tracks. Her skin was downy soft and unmarred. Her voice was cultured and musically appealing. She had real breeding and good manners. She was exquisite and delightful, not what he had imagined.

Carrie Sue realized the man was impressed with her, and surprised to see she wasn't some terrible monster. She wanted those thoughts and feelings to continue. She was extra careful with her words, looks, and behavior. She offered politely, "I can prepare breakfast while you two have your coffee and talk over old times."

T.J. said, "We've already talked for an hour and had two cups of coffee while you were snoozing, woman. The biscuits and bacon's about done. Scrambled eggs all right with you?"

"If you cook them good and done," she replied with a bright smile.

"Good and done it is. The dishes are there," he remarked when she looked around for them to set the table.

"Sometimes I think you read my mind, T.J. Hank, you should tell him how dangerous it is to do that with a woman," she teased.

Hank laughed and agreed, "She's right; it gets you into trouble."

As they ate, Carrie Sue remarked, "T.J. told me you two have worked and traveled together many times."

"Yep," he responded like her lover would. "We've pushed cattle, ridden a dusty trail, guarded strongboxes, branded stock, got stages in on time, hauled freight, and done a passel of odd jobs together over the years. I got too old and retired here with my cantina. Ever so often, . . . T.J. stops by to see me. I miss those old days, but I like being settled down when winter and bad weather comes around."

Carrie Sue caught his hesitation over her lover's name and wondered what it meant, if anything. She smiled warmly and said, "I know what you mean. Trail life can be rough, unbearable at times. Is there anything you want to ask me while I'm here?"

"Nope. The less I know about you, the better for all of us."

"Thank you, Hank. I just didn't want you thinking so badly of me, or of T.J. for helping me. Sometimes people aren't as bad as their reputations make out."

"Now that I've met the beautiful woman he described last night, I believe it." He saw her blush. He was astonished, moved. "Of course, from knowing T.J. Rogue, I realize reputations get colored."

The redhead didn't know why or how she had blushed, but she was glad, as it had a nice affect on Hank Peterson. "I'm lucky T.J. came along when he did. He's saved my hide several times. He's a very special man, Hank, not many would do what he's doing for me."

T.J. teased, "Don't go telling my secrets to Hank. He thinks I'm a tough and cold son-of-a-bitch. You'll spoil my image, woman."

She laughed merrily and added, "You're special too, Hank, but you'd have to be to be his friend. I know how tempting it must be to have a ten thousand dollar prize sitting across the table from you and you can't collect on it."

"It isn't tempting at all, Carrie Sue. A man would have to be a fool to sell out a woman like you. I think T.J.'s right to help you; I just hope he doesn't get into any trouble being so kind and reckless."

"I promise to do my best to protect him," she vowed.

They finished off the food and cleared the table.

T.J. looked at Hank. "I hate to say it, old friend, but we have to get moving. I'd like to make El Paso by nightfall."

Hank shook Carrie Sue's hand and said, "It was good meeting you. I hope everything works out just fine. T.J., you let me hear from you."

"I will, Hank," the ebon-haired man replied, affectionately slapping his friend on the back and giving him a bearhug.

The lovely fugitive observed the scene with interest. It was clear their friendship was not a pretense, and that warmed and relaxed her.

As they mounted, Hank said, "You two be careful."

T.J. and Carrie Sue replied simultaneously, "We will."

Hank scratched his head as the couple waved and rode off, skirting the town. Nope, he concluded, the girl was nothing like her reputation. In fact, he couldn't believe she was an outlaw, and he'd met plenty. Now he understood how and why Thad Jamison was in love with her.

Shortly after dusk, Carrie Sue and T.J. entered El Paso at the base of the Franklin Mountains and situated on the Rio Grande River. Here, she realized, she could escape across the Mexican border if there was trouble. They worked their way to another friend's home: Mitchell Sterling, who owned a large mercantile store in town.

The man greeted them at the back door. T.J. grasped his hand and said, "Good to see you, Mitch. Thanks for the help. Hank said he'd send you a telegram to expect me and a guest."

The brown-haired man of about forty replied, "I got it this morning. I sent my wife and children to visit kin in the next town so we'd have privacy. If there's one thing I owe you, friend, it's plenty of favors. All you have to do is ask for one. I take it this is the lady who needs protection and privacy?" When Carrie Sue stepped forward, his eyes widened in exaggerated surprise. Then, he looked at his friend oddly.

T.J. smiled at him. "Yep, she's the one in the papers and on those wanted posters, but it's a mistake, Mitch. She isn't the Texas Flame. I got to know her in Tucson; we're good friends. When those posters came out, I helped her escape. I'm getting her to Ranger Headquarters in Waco so we can straighten out this crazy error. I knew I could trust you to help us and keep quiet. We have to be real careful until we clear up this mess. Her name's Carolyn Starns; she's a schoolmarm. Somebody mixed her up with Carrie Sue Stover after that holdup near Sherman. Probably because there aren't many flaming redheads around these parts and some people are eager to get their hands on that big reward. We'll talk more later. We're starved."

Mitchell Sterling shook hands with her and said, "Pleased to meet you, Miss Starns. You two come in. I held supper for you."

Carrie Sue loved the big house, but wished she didn't have to put this family man on the spot. She wondered what her lover had done for Mitchell Sterling to earn such respect and loyalty, and why her love would take unfair advantage of the man's generosity. Over dinner of a beef roast with fresh vegetables, she received her answer.

"I don't suppose T.J.'s told you what all he's done for me." When the redhead shook her head, Mitch filled her in after a genial smile. "About a year ago, I had some bullies giving me trouble at the store. The law couldn't catch 'em and stop 'em, but T.J. did. Those ruffians had me and my family terrorized until he came to town and took over. They cost me plenty of money, but T.J. here refused to take payment. Said he didn't like their kind and enjoyed sending 'em on their way."

After a few bites, Mitchell added, "But that wasn't the first time he saved my life. We met during the war and served together for a year. I'll admit I was pretty scared, but T.J. always looked out after me. He's a man who takes care of his friends."

"I'm glad to hear that, Mitch, since I'm a new one. I hope he can help me solve my problem as well as he solved yours," Carrie Sue said.

"If anybody can help you, it's T.J. Rogue," Mitchell asserted.

T.J. chuckled and pleaded, "Come on you two, stop praising me or my head will swell and my hat won't fit anymore."

They chatted lightly for a while longer, then cleared the table. They retired to the parlor and sat down. Mitchell served them an after dinner wine and they all relaxed as they sipped it.

"From experience, I know you like to keep your business private, T.J., so I won't ask anymore questions about her troubles. I'm sure you'll find a way to solve them." He turned to the topic to politics. "I've been hearing some interesting things about our commander during the war. I'm sure you remember President Grant since you saved his life once. Word is, he's eager to run for a third term, but his Republican friends can't get the nomination for him. The majority's afraid of this upsurge of Democratic strength and the third term issue."

"You can't blame them, Mitch. Grant's been surrounded by scandals for eight years. Guilty or not, soot around him has to blacken him. But he'd get my vote if he's listed again. He seems to be running the country as well as anyone else before him. I haven't forgotten him. He taught me plenty during the war. He was a damn good commander."

"Word is, if they get another candidate, they might lure those Liberals back into the Republican Party. Looks like it'll be that Hayes fellow from Ohio. He was a Union officer with a spotless record. He's been a congressman and the Governor of Ohio three times, so he knows plenty about politics and government. It doesn't hurt any that he's a champion of civil service reforms. I surely hope they choose him over that Senator Blaine who's been linked to one of those railroad scandals."

343

"Who do you think the Democrats will push?" T.J. asked, worried about his friend Grant's loss of power and distraction when he needed the President's help in the Stover matter.

After taking another sip of his wine, Mitchell surmised, "I think it'll be Samuel Tilden of New York. He's the Governor and doing a good job at it. Made lots of powerful friends with plenty of money."

"Never heard of him, but I miss lots of papers and news on the trail."

"You been near Pine Springs lately?" Mitch asked. T.J. shook his head.

Carrie Sue had sat quietly listening to the two men and observing them. Her ears perked up when Mitchell Sterling mentioned the area near the Guadalupe Mountains, her destination! Coincidence? she mused, then told herself that was possible. Curly James hadn't told T.J. anything before dying, and no one else knew where to look.

"That damn Salt War is boiling like a wild kettle again. We had trouble there in '63, then again in '67 and '68. Charles Howard and that fiery-tempered Italian Don Louis Cardis are at each other's throats again. And that Mexican Padre Borajo in San Elizarie isn't helping matters. It could get real dangerous at Salt Flats and here. Borajo is siding with Cardis and trying to stir up his people against Howard and the Americans. The Padre was ordered by the church back to the Mexican interior, but he refuses to go. I don't like the smell of the air, T.J. Both sides have been taking salt from those flats for years. I don't see why anybody has to go and claim them and try to charge everyone else for what's lying free on God's earth. Governor Hubbard is keeping a keen eye on the situation, but I think he's holding back too long. He needs to get soldiers or Rangers in here immediately to handle matters before there's killing. If you asked me, I think it's coming to a silly war over that white powder. You stay in touch with me, after you finish with the little lady here, in case I need your help protecting my property. Borajo is inciting his people against all Americans in this area; that worries me."

T.J. leaned forward and propped his elbows on his knees, clutching the glass between his hands. "Don't worry, Mitch; I'll let you know where I can be reached when I complete her job. What do you read on King Fisher? Is he still operating near Castroville and Eagle Pass?"

"He surely is, and I hope he stay there. Papers say a Ranger called Captain McNelly is pursuing him. If I were him, I'd be mighty careful. Reports say Fisher has one hundred outlaws terrorizing the countryside down there. Fisher boasts publicly he's seizing control of the entire area. I surely do hope he never takes a liking to El Paso."

T.J. had one answer he needed, where Captain McNelly was and how he was doing with his case. He knew from Hank Peterson that Rangers Jones and Steele were entangled by the range wars caused by the introduction of barbed wire in '74. With the inventions of barbwire, the well drill, and the windmill, ranchers were spreading across the previously unusable grasslands and fencing off rangelands and waterholes, which created a whole series of problems for the law. He needed to learn who was available to assist him when the time came for action against the Stover Gang. Later, he told himself. He teased ex-Ranger Sterling, "I believe the King loves Mexico and the border area too much to take on your town. I met him once. He's a real mean cuss who's provoked easily. I surely would like to avoid another run-in with him, especially with all his boys around. A gun can only hold so many bullets at a time."

Mitchell Sterling, who still lent the Rangers—especially his close friends like Thad—a hand when needed, poured himself and T.J. more wine. Carrie Sue politely refused another glass. "You heard any interesting news recently during your travels?" he questioned T.J.

The ebon-haired male leaned back in his chair and stretched out his legs. "I hear tell the train is extending its tracks this way soon. That should help your business. Makes

345

goods easier and cheaper to get."

The man scowled. "Yes, but it lures train robbers into the area. If there's anything we don't need, it's more trouble over this way."

"What do you mean?" her dark-haired companion inquired.

Mitch began their ruse. "That Wes Harding's kicking up his heels all over, and the Stover Gang's raiding again." He glanced at the redhead and asked, "You mind if we talk about them, Miss Starns?"

Without flinching, she replied, "Certainly not. Since it involves me now, T.J. and I need to learn all we can about that gang."

"Maybe they'll catch the Texas Flame before you two reach Waco. That'll make it easier for you to clear yourself. They hit the Union Express Office in Fort Worth a few weeks back, a bank in Hillsboro on the twenty-fifth, and did some rustling near Eastland on the thirtieth. Then, last Saturday, they struck a stage near Big Spring. Since you weren't around and T.J. can vouch for your whereabouts, that should prove your innocence. Everybody knows he tells the truth, so they'll accept his word. We've been warned to keep our eyes and ears open because the law thinks they're heading toward El Paso. They're probably on their way to New Mexico or Arizona where there's plenty of gold and silver, if they don't ride for San Angelo and circle back toward Waco. The soldiers from Fort Davis are on the prowl after 'em. They're real mean cusses, T.J. I hope they get caught real soon. Been lots of killing on this spree, and lots of boasting like they want everybody to know they're the best outlaws in the state. Nearly every day the paper reports some new crime."

Mitch retrieved a small bundle of newspapers and handed them to T.J. "I kept them; so if you'd like to take them along and read them on the trail, you're welcome to them. You can't ever tell who you'll cross in the road, so you'd better keep up with where the trouble is. That story about you is in there, Miss Starns. It says you were hiding out in Tucson as a teacher. The law thinks a Martin Ferris helped you escape because he vanished at the same time. They think you two headed further west or northward; that's where they're searching." The ex-Ranger knew that story had been retracted or corrected, but that was one paper he hadn't included in the bundle to keep her in the dark. He also knew his friend would prevent her from seeing it anywhere. By the time they hooked up with the Stover Gang, if Darby knew about the weird incident, the bandit leader would hold Harding responsible.

T.J. sent her a keep-quiet look. "Good. That'll give us time to clear you and get the truth out." He rose and said, "I think my partner's exhausted, Mitch. Why don't you show her where to bed down for the night. I'll bring her things along."

Mitchell Sterling glanced at the beautiful redhead and said, "I hope we haven't talked your ears off, Miss Starns. Kind of rude of us to leave you out of the conversation."

Carrie Sue smiled genially and said, "I enjoyed listening to such intriguing subjects, Mitch. If you don't mind, I'd like to read those papers tomorrow and catch up on the news."

"Sure thing. I'll leave them in the parlor." He led her to a small room near the back of the house. "Will my daughter's room be all right?"

"Yes, thank you, Mitch. I'll see you in the morning." She smiled again and shook his extended hand.

After Mitchell returned to the parlor, T.J. sent her a rueful smile and said, "I'm sorry about what he said, but he believed our story."

"We're placing him in deep peril. That isn't fair or right, T.J., not even from a friend who owes you a mountainous favor."

"I know, woman, but we needed a safe place tonight and a chance to get supplies. Even if Mitch knew the truth, he would help. I just think it's best not to let too many people in on our secret. It makes things awkward for them."

347

"When the truth comes out, he'll know we deceived him, used him. Nothing is worse than to betray a loved one or a friend."

"If I ever see him again, I'll say you gave me the slip along the way. He believes you're Carolyn Starns and a terrible mistake's been made, so he'll think I believed you, too. Your life's at stake, woman; we have to fool Mitch and others. I don't like it, but it can't be helped."

She replied wearily, "I understand, T.J., but I hate doing this. Our being in his home can get him arrested as an accomplice. You'll have to tell him those other lies so he won't get into trouble later or feel betrayed by you."

T.J. said, "I will, honest, as soon as we reach a safe place where I can send him a telegram. Get some sleep. We'll rest here tomorrow and take off before dawn on Thursday. From here on, it'll be more dangerous for you than before."

He caressed her cheek. "We'll talk more in the morning. Afterwards, I want to do some scouting around, see what I can pick up about your brother. He may be nearer than we know. Try to think of any places around here where he might hide. We'll check them out when we leave day after tomorrow."

As T.J. walked down the hall, he was worried about this new outbreak of crimes by Darby Stover and his gang. The message last night had told Mitch to reveal anything he had heard recently in front of Carrie Sue, but he hadn't expected that enlightenment to include so many crimes! He wondered if the gang was indeed heading this way, or if they would turn south toward the Davis Mountains or Mexico to hide. Considering the number of targets they had taken in the last few weeks—which wasn't like Darby Stover—surely they wouldn't strike at the other towns near Brownwood. Maybe, he surmised, Darby had a new style, or a sly plan to work around Brownwood and Commanche while awaiting news of his sister, or her arrival. His flurry of criminal activity could be to let her know where to look for him. He wondered if

Darby knew about the posters, stories, and retractions, and what the outlaw thought about the crazy incidents.

From the window, Carrie Sue watched T.J. Rogue and his friend walk down the street together, talking seriously. She shook her head in mounting sadness, for Mitchell Sterling was a terrible liar. She hadn't fallen for their clever pretense tonight, not even surrounded by all that genial and masculine talk. Mitch had been prepared to deceive her; no doubt Hank had sent him a detailed message last night while she was sleeping in his bed. Mitch had known who she was before her arrival, and not from posters or newspaper stories. Mitch's conversation about her brother had been carefully planned. Mitch couldn't be trusted, nor could those false newspaper accounts.

Far worse, T.J. Rogue could not be trusted at all. A man like him would never bring her here and dupe his good friend, and they could have gotten plenty of supplies in Mesilla from Hank. There was a crafty motive and keen mind at work. If T.J. was bringing others into his duplicity and they were obliging, something terrible was at work around her. Obviously Hank and Mitch were two of the men he had been contacting in Tucson and along the way. And, for all she knew, that man in Tucson wasn't a lawman, just another one of her lover's accomplices. But what did these men want from her? Merciful Heavens, could it be the sixty- six thousand dollars in gold and paper money? Maybe it was more now if the gang's big targets had contributed to their reward offers. Would her lover do this to her?

349

Chapter Eighteen

After breakfast, Mitchell Sterling headed for his mercantile store, leaving T.J. alone with Carrie Sue. He told them he would pick up food for dinner from a local restaurant and be home about six-thirty.

Carrie Sue had observed Mitch closely this morning. It might be crazy, but he didn't seem like a treacherous man, nor had Hank. Maybe T.J. had duped them into willingly helping their friend. Maybe her lover was the only one of them who was being deceitful. She didn't doubt that Mitch knew who she was, but he was following T.J.'s request to pretend he didn't. Perhaps her love was afraid she'd skip out on him, so he had asked Mitch to scare her with those false reports.

T.J. said, "I'm going to do some scouting around town today and see what I can learn. I'll get a newspaper and see if there's any current news on your brother; you can read those other ones while I'm gone and maybe draw a clue from the reports. I can always pick up information in saloons from drifters, gamblers, and cowpunchers passing through town. Men get real talkative over a drink and card game."

She clasped his hand and stroked its back with her cheek. "I'll make sure no one sees me here at Mitch's. I hate putting you in this awkward position, T.J., and I appreciate all you're doing to help me. When we leave town tomorrow, we'll head for a spot where the gang's camped lots of times when we needed rest and distance. It's where the Toyah Creek joins with the Pecos River, about three days from here. If they didn't head there after that holdup at Big Spring, then we'll ride for Commanche. There's a cabin north of town which can't be found easily."

"It should take us about eight or nine days to reach the first town between here and there, so we'll need a pack horse and additional supplies to get us to San Angelo. I'll buy one while I'm out today. Do you mind if I trade Charlie? That pinto could be recognized and give us away," he suggested with reluctance, knowing she liked the animal.

Her eyes and voice were sad. "I think that's wise, but I hate to lose her. In eleven days, we should be near Brownwood and hopefully so will Darby so we can settle this matter. I wonder if people, especially lawmen, think it's strange the Hardings want us so badly. I mean, it's been years since we harassed them. In fact, I think it's odd that Quade Harding put his name at the bottom of my poster."

"Not really," T.J. asserted. "That's to let everyone know who's offering the highest reward. It's much more than the government's two thousand each. He also wants to make certain you're captured alive and delivered to him. Who would claim two thousand when he can get ten by taking you to Brownwood and the QH Ranch?"

"Is that legal?" she inquired.

"Yep, he can have you taken to him for payment, then he can turn you over to the law for their reward. Lawmen don't like it, but there isn't anything they can do about it. I would imagine the law's keeping an eye on the Hardings over this suspicious affair. I would be."

"But if it isn't illegal, what good would spying on them do?"

"A man who bends or breaks one law, usually does it with others. If I were a lawman, I'd think he was up to no good, and I'd watch him. If we're both lucky, Quade will do something wrong and get caught. Then, we won't have to worry about endangering ourselves for revenge."

"Don't count on it, partner. He's been evil for years and never been caught. I'll admit, Quade's as clever as he is mean and wicked."

"Very few men get away with their crimes forever, love."

Carrie Sue stretched and yawned. "Merciful Heavens, I'm tired. I didn't sleep well last night. I think I'll read those papers and get plenty of rest before we hit the trail again. You be careful today."

"You need anything before I leave?" he asked.

"You can hold me and kiss me," she answered, knowing where their contact would lead, but she needed him one last time.

T.J. pulled her into his arms and covered her parted lips with his. His heart ached for this secret breach between them to be destroyed. His body yearned to fuse with hers. His mind pleaded for peace.

Carrie Sue feverishly kissed and caressed T.J. as she peeled off his shirt, and he did the same for her. Their chests touched, then they swiftly pressed together to remove any space between them. He scooped her up in his arms and carried her back to her borrowed bed. They both hurriedly removed their boots and jeans. She flung aside the covers and they fell entwined upon the bed.

They made love with a tender and tantalizing urgency which neither understood in the other. Their lips and tongues meshed in a wild and stirring dance. Their arms and hands embraced and caressed. Their bodies united as one. And afterward, they remained locked together, kissing, touching, holding, savoring, until a tranquil glow relaxed them.

T.J. arose and rinsed off in the basin nearby. He said, "I'll wait to trade Charlie as we're leaving, just in case her description is out. You take it easy today, and I'll see you about six. Don't unlock the doors for anybody, or stick this beautiful head outside."

She stretched and yawned again. After a radiant smile, she said, "I plan to be wickedly lazy today, partner, while you get our chores done. After my bath, I might not leave this bed until dinner time."

T.J. bent forward and kissed her on the nose. "I wish I could join you all day, but one of us has work to do."

"We'll have plenty of time on the trail for other . . . business," she teased guilefully in a seductive tone.

As her love reached the bedroom door, she called out, "T.J., please be careful out there. I don't want you forgetting about that sheriff we clobbered in Tucson. And don't get into any trouble in those saloons. You stay away from those fancy dressed gals there!"

"You don't have to be jealous or worried, love; I have all I need right here. Relax today; I'll be safe and careful."

"If you're not, partner, I'll thrash you good after I rescue you."

T.J.'s gaze fused with hers for a moment, and both smiled as each felt as if they had the other exactly where wanted. . . .

Carrie Sue noticed that T.J. didn't take his saddlebags with him, but she couldn't locate them during a brief search. She did find a Mexican blouse, skirt, and sandals in Mrs. Sterling's closet. She took them to use as a disguise to get her out of town. She packed enough supplies for a two day trip, careful to use two canteens to give her and her horse plenty of water between creeks. She clipped out the newspaper articles on Darby's false raids and packed them.

She knew her brother hadn't committed those robberies and rustlings, but she couldn't decide if another gang posing as them had. That was something she needed to discuss with Darby. Either it was a ruse to draw them into the open, a trick to lure her into the area, or they had a serious problem of impersonation.

She wrote T.J. a carefully worded note. In case their paths crossed again, she didn't want him to know she was suspicious of him.

She clipped a lock of her hair and bound the end with a blue ribbon. She placed both on her pillow. Using extra blankets, she formed a body roll and covered it, making it appear she was asleep if her lover returned earlier than planned and looked in on her. She drew the heavy curtains over the lace ones to darken the room and aid her ruse.

Carrie Sue donned the Mexican garments and covered her head with a colorful shawl, normally used to ward off the sun's heat, but one which would conceal her fiery hair. She carried her things to the barn behind Mitchell Sterling's home. From recall on their arrival, she knew the merchantman had around ten fine horses in his corral.

"Sorry, Charlie, but you have to stay behind this time," she murmured as she stroked the pinto's neck. "That hide of yours is too easily recognized." She chose a sturdy sorrel and saddled him. Taking one of Mitchell's saddles, she placed it where hers had been and hoped it wouldn't be noticed as the wrong one until she was long gone.

She secured her saddlebags, bedroll, and supplies behind her cantle and looped the canteens over her pommel. She mounted, tossed the shawl over her head, and left the barn. The daring desperado left the area by the back way, hardly enticing any notice in her disguise, which made her grateful this town was populated so heavily with Mexicans. Once El Paso was behind her, she kneed the reddish-brown stallion into a gallop toward the Guadalupe Mountains, northeast of town.

Carrie Sue knew the Hueco Mountains would come first, then the Cornudas, Salt Flats, and Guadalupes. She wasn't worried about the Salt War which Mitchell had mentioned last night, but she would be on alert for any threat in that region.

Outside of town, she encountered scattered scrubs and

grass clumps on dry and sandy ground. Sometimes the land was flat; other times it was covered with rolling hills, deep ravines, and shallow dry washes. She could make out the Huecos in the distant haze. Above her the sky was a rich blue shade, unlike the pale blue of Arizona. The clouds were large and billowy. A rider could take refuge under them from the blazing sun. She loved Texas and found its climate and landscape less demanding than Arizona's and New Mexico's desert terrain and soaring heat.

She journeyed steadily, aware that T.J. would head southeast to search for her when her disappearance was discovered this evening. She took the time to cover her tracks for a while. Yet, if his Apache training was still in full force and his investigation into her escape paid off, it wouldn't do any good to conceal her trail from his keen wits.

After a few hours, she located a safe place to change her clothes and don her boots, packing the stolen ones in case they were needed another time. She took breaks only when her mount needed them. She wanted to put as much distance as possible between her and El Paso as quickly as possible. Too, she wanted to reach Darby soon. Besides, her appetite was missing as she reflected on T.J. and Darby.

The riding was easy in this less rugged region. The grassland and scrubs were green this time of year and following a recent rain. She always saw mountains, or hills, or mesas, or buttes in the distance on all sides. Often the hills appeared to be covered by green fuzz which she knew was shortgrass. She was familiar with this area, so she didn't worry over getting lost.

Her Remington revolvers were strapped around her waist and to her thighs, the forty-fours giving her confidence and a sense of security, as did her enormous skills with them. Her Henry rifle, a fifteen-shot repeater with lever-action, was close at hand if needed. She missed her lover something terrible, but she could take care of herself. Still, she hoped and prayed she wouldn't run into anyone who'd seen her poster. She hated the thought of killing someone to defend herself, but ten thousand dollars would make a life-and-death struggle for anyone.

Despite what she had told T.J. about a lack of sleep last night, she had slumbered fairly well under the circumstances. She watched the sunset's reflections on the clouds before her. They were shades of pink against a backdrop of intermingled blues, grays, and lavenders. It was a serene sight, but it didn't relax her. She remained on guard as she continued her slowed pace after dark, as she intended to go on for a few more hours before napping.

When T.J. returned, he stabled the pack horse before he fed Nighthawk and Charlie, then put their supplies in the barn, which he packed and readied to move out early in the morning. He checked to make certain his saddlebags were still where he had concealed them, and noticed they hadn't been disturbed. He smiled in pleasure, not wanting her to find the telegraph key, picture of Annabelle and Marie, and his badges. He walked to the house and found it quiet.

T.J. went to the back room and eased open the door. He saw the shapely form lying in the darkened room. He smiled again, and decided to let her rest a while longer. Mitchell had gotten a late supply of goods and wouldn't get home until seven.

T.J. returned to the parlor and fetched himself a drink from the sideboard. He relaxed in a chair and called to mind the telegram he had received two hours ago, telling him of Darby Stover's raid on a Wells Fargo office in Brady, a good day's ride from Brownwood, eleven days from El Paso. That told him where the Stover Gang was operating and where he and Carrie Sue needed to head in the morning.

He hadn't learned much at the two saloons, only heard more about President Grant's problems with the election later this year and more about the Stover Gang's movements. T.J. wondered if his position would be affected by the election of a new president. Currently he could come and go anywhere as he pleased with his three badges. They came in handy if a certain mission took him out of Texas into other states. They always gave him more jurisdiction, authority, and power than local or state lawmen, if the undercover T.J. Rogue was forced to become Thaddeus Jamison. He used whichever badge was needed for that time, place, and task. Sometimes he ran into bad or stubborn lawmen and had to pull rank on them with one or more of his badges. Yet, he always tried to work as Rogue so few knew him as Lawman Thaddeus Jerome Jamison, especially in Texas.

Actually, he liked being a Special Agent for the President, a United States Marshal, and a Texas Ranger. If he ever had to chose one job and rank over the other two, he didn't know which one it would be. He only wished the possession of so much power could help his love, but it didn't. He sipped his drink and sighed deeply.

When he realized it was nearly dark outside, he decided to awaken Carrie Sue. He lit a lamp and carried it down the hallway. He opened the door and approached the bed. His hands reached out and pulled back the covers.

T.J.'s eyes widened, then narrowed as he angrily scooped up the lock of golden red hair and the folded note. He sat down the lamp and read it:

Dear T.J.,

Please forgive me for deserting you like this. Since you aren't a wanted man and we keep endangering your friends, it's best if I continue alone to Commanche. I know bounty hunters and lawmen will be searching for me, but I have to take those risks without involving you further. I can't keep using and duping your friends. And I can't allow you to be killed because of me.

The newspapers are wrong about Darby. He never

strikes Union Express and he never gives his name boastfully. He never makes that many hits so close together. Another gang must be using his reputation and name or it's a trick by the law to lure us out and capture us. If he doesn't know what's happening, I have to warn him. I have to let him see for himself that I'm fine, in case the papers tell more lies and claim I've been captured to entrap him.

Thanks for everything. When I'm settled somewhere far away, I'll contact you through Hank Peterson because you trust him. I took his address, so I'll write or telegraph you as Sue Starns. I love you and will miss you dreadfully. Please be careful and don't come after me. I would die if you were slain trying to help me. And I couldn't bear it if you were sent to prison because of me.

I know where Darby is hiding. Curly told me that day in Tucson, but I had to keep it from you. I am certain Darby is lying low for a month or two like he told Curly, so he can't be guilty of all these suspicious attacks.

I swear to write you later and hope you'll want to hear from me and come to see me. I've left you a souvenir on my pillow from the Texas Flame. I hope it's the only one in your collection with real meaning. I can't wait until we're together again. I'll try to make it happen very soon. Forgive my new ruse. I love you, T.J. Rogue.

C.S.S.

T.J. sank to the bed, staring at the shocking note and worrying over her reckless action. He had to find her, and fast! But how had she gotten away? Charlie was still in the barn. He realized she must have stolen one of Mitchell's horses.

The distressed lawman hurried to the corral. He had

studied his friend's horses earlier and decided which one to trade for Charlie. He had to smile when he saw that the chosen sorrel was missing. It was obvious she had good taste in horseflesh. He checked the saddle near his, and grasped that clever precaution. He hadn't noticed it wasn't hers when he was in the barn earlier. He checked their old supplies, to find some missing and two canteens gone. At least she would have plenty of water and food. And, she was well-armed and skilled.

He returned to the house, impressed with her preparations, wits and courage. He couldn't track her at night beneath such a scanty moon, and it was too late to question possible witnesses. He went to her room and admired her handiwork there before making the bed. In the parlor, T.J. took a seat to think.

Mitchell came home with their dinner. He smiled and greeted his dark-haired friend. He sensed T.J.'s sullen mood and questioned it.

T.J. informed him, "I've got bad trouble, Mitch. Carrie Sue took off right after my departure this morning, so she has a good headstart on me." The intelligent lawman related what the redhaired fugitive had said to him last night and this morning and most of what her note had revealed. "Lordy, Mitch, where is she heading?" He paced anxiously as he made his plans. "I'll head for Brownwood to see what's happening there. Maybe Dave has some news by now. If she's right about her brother's innocence in these crimes, where is Darby Stover and who's to blame? If Carrie Sue honestly believes her brother headed for Oklahoma to lay low, could she be riding in that direction?"

T.J. sighed. "I just can't decide what's she's thinking and doing. Telegraph Dave in the morning, then send word to me in San Angelo. I should get there in a few days. Maybe we can meet in Commanche. I'd like to know what I'm riding into before I reach Brownwood."

The ex-Ranger asked gravely, "Do you think he's being

framed?"

"Lordy, I don't know. From what she's told me about Darby, it doesn't sound like him, and he's surely changed his pattern. If anyone should know how he thinks and operates, it's his sister. But if she's mistaken or Darby's changed and she's heading for Brownwood, she'll be riding into danger with all that's going on in that area. Even with her poster recalled, she could get snared by accident."

Mitchell remarked, "At least we know why she wants to see him in person. I can't blame her. She's a real prize, T.J., and I don't mean reward-wise. Frankly, I like her and believe her."

T.J. jumped up to pace nervously, which was not like him. His smokey gray gaze was somber and his body was taut with unnatural fear. "I wish you were still working with me. We've solved some tough cases together and I can use your help and wits on this one. Lordy, I'm too closely involved with her to think straight."

"Sorry, old friend, but I'm enjoying my retirement and family. But I'll do whatever I can to assist you from here. You think she would listen if you confessed the truth? Would help you with your mission? If she truly loves you, it's got to be real tough on her being in this mess."

T.J. halted and looked at his friend. "She would never betray her brother for any reason or any person, including me and a pardon, which I can't arrange. Even Grant refuses a presidential pardon for her."

"That shouldn't surprise you. She's an outlaw. And he's trying to secure a third term. He won't do anything to cause more doubts about himself. He's already been accused of doing illegal things for his friends."

"I understand, but it riles me to be so damn helpless!" T.J. revealed, "She took those newspaper clippings to show Darby. Lordy, Mitch, much as I hate the man and want to see him punished, I hope she doesn't find out those reports are accurate. It'll crush her." T.J. inhaled deeply and let the spent air out loudly. "Maybe Darby Stover wants to go straight and he's desperate to get enough money to take off to parts unknown. Or maybe he wants enough money to send his sister far away to safety. I just can't figure it out yet. I need to locate her and meet this clever brother of hers."

Mitchell questioned, "What if Curly James lied to her about seeing Darby on his way to Tucson? What if she's riding into a trap? Didn't you say he worked for Harding in the past? I think I'll check to see if he telegraphed anyone from Tucson and betrayed her."

T.J. whirled and gaped at Mitchell Sterling. "Lordy, I overlooked that angle! What if that bastard was still on Harding's payroll? Curly knew exactly where Carrie Sue was at and maybe where Darby was camped. He used to ride with the Stover Gang, so Darby wouldn't be suspicious of him. Curly could have alerted his old boss to their locations for those rewards. You're right; we need to learn if any messages were passed between them. Check the office here, too. If Curly saw Darby before he reached the Texas border, he might have contacted Quade from here. This is where he was to meet his boys before I got to them."

"I'll handle it first thing in the morning and wire you in San Angelo," Mitchell promised. "I'll also wire Dave in Brownwood and let him know you're on the way and what's going on. Check with him when you arrive."

"Damn!" T.J. swore irritably. "If only I'd arrested Curly, then I could question him or have him questioned. Revenge stinks this time!"

"That would have broken your cover, Ranger Jamison. At least he's out of the way and can't do more harm to her. You want me to wire Hank to tell him to be on the alert for news from her?"

"Yep. Thanks. I'll keep in touch with you and him. At first light, I'll do some scouting and questioning. Surely someone saw a beautiful redhead leaving town. I need to know which direction she took. Damn that Curly! There's no telling where he sent her! Or to whom. . . ."

"Just hope it's toward her brother so she'll have some protection."

T.J.'s eyes brightened and enlarged. "You know something, Mitch? If Darby's gang is being framed, Curly was the perfect one to let that other gang leader know Darby was out of reach for weeks so they could impersonate him and his men. With Darby laying low and out of touch, the law would put the blame on the Stover Gang. I wonder . . ." He paused to contemplate the matter. "What if there's more to this alleged frame than money? What if someone wants Darby in deeper trouble? Make it so he can't go anywhere without being hunted? Maybe even force Darby to seek revenge to halt his imperiling intrusion? Make it too dangerous for Carrie Sue to approach and rejoin her brother?"

"Quade Harding?" the astute Mitchell hinted.

"Damn right!" T.J. shouted angrily. "If there is a frame and has been for years, that means Carrie Sue and her brother might not be responsible for all the charges against them. And if Quade Harding is in the middle of this mischief, we'll get him for sure this time."

"You're overlooking another point, my friend; they are still outlaws and they're guilty of plenty of crimes. Taking a few away won't help her much, if any," Mitchell warned.

"I know," T.J. murmured and clenched his teeth. He withdrew the fiery lock from his pocket and passed it beneath his nose. The hair was soft and fragrant and brought her image to mind. The words in her note raced through his head. Was love, he pondered, her real reason for deserting him? What did she think he would feel and do after discovering her escape? Had he done anything to arouse her suspicions against him? Anything besides his crazy behavior over his saddlebags? He had to admit everything about their meeting and relationship was curiously coincidental. As smart and instinctive as she was, Carrie Sue had to realize most of those incidents were strange. No wonder she couldn't dismiss her lingering doubts!

T.J. thought about their lovemaking this morning. She had known she was running out on him soon. *Lordy, her emotions must be in turmoil.* She had exposed love and urgency, a desperation he now understood.

Mitchell queried him on his plans, and they discussed them in detail. Except for his Ranger badge, T.J. left the others and his papers with Mitch for safekeeping and secrecy.

T.J. told his friend about the stolen horse, which had been traded last night for the pinto. "I'm glad she was smart enough to change mounts; that mare is probably associated with her by now. You best keep it in the barn and sell it across the border real quick."

"Don't worry; I'll take care of it tomorrow."

T.J. fumed as he tried to eat the chilled dinner in his highly agitated state. He didn't like not knowing what and whom he was up against. He was worried about his love's safety. How could he calmly eat dinner when she was out there somewhere alone, facing no telling what? He had to find her quickly. Yet, all he could do was head for the area in which Darby Stover was supposedly working and hope to get a line on her. If it was another gang as she believed, he'd be no closer to her there than he was here tonight. *Damnation, you frustrating vixen! If this case gets any more dangerous or complicated, I might have to expose my identity and rank to solve it without you getting harmed.*

It was nearing dusk Thursday afternoon when Carrie Sue reached the salt basin. It had been a grueling two day journey. She had eaten, slept, and rested very little along the way. Rocky ramparts seemed to leap skyward in the distance to present a harsh, but majestic, view. The Guadalupe Mountains were starkly barren when approached, but they concealed many hidden meadows, forests, canyons, and streams. A variety of life filled the interior, ranging from desert to canyon woodland to highland forest varieties: yuccas, cacti, rattlesnakes, scorpions, the poisonous desert scorpion, agaves, walking-stick chollas, sotol, coyotes, mule deer, mountain lions, pines, firs, maple, ash, walnut, aspen, chokecherry, elk, racoons, wild turkeys, and sometimes black bears. It was a primitive area whose trails into the highcountry were rough and steep, whose inner canyons rimmed shady glens and cool creeks. The precipitous cliffs and surrounding desert belied the beauty and tranquility of the inland, except when late summer thunderstorms violently attacked here.

El Capitan peak loomed before her and over the sparse settlement of Pine Springs. She skirted the tiny settlement of Salt Flats, knowing that a lone rider at that distance wouldn't attract much attention or interest, and her sex couldn't be detected that far away.

The sun-bleached salt flats looked pearly gray this late in the afternoon. They seemed to stretch for miles on either side and before her. It was a dry terrain, one of value to many people. Yet, she found no trouble crossing that trouble-torn region. She weaved through the Patterson Hills and passed the sentinel peak. She slipped by the Pine Springs area and The Pinery, where a Butterfield stop had been situated since '58. The exhausted redhead halted at Manzanita Springs for her horse to rest and drink.

She had ridden a little over a hundred miles and had about ten to fifteen to go, if Darby was camped in McKittrick Canyon as Curly James had told her. The freshwater springs were cool and inviting. She removed her boots and dangled her feet beneath the surface. She splashed her face and arms and took long drinks.

The sun's heat was gone. The temperature was in the comfortable seventies. She was glad it wasn't spring, as high winds with forceful gusts often lashed unmercifully at this area.

She knew this area was frequently the base for the Mescalero Apaches, but she wasn't afraid. Those Indians knew who she was. They liked and respected Darby Stover and allowed him to camp here whenever he desired, as her brother was truthful with the Apaches and always brought them many gifts of friendship and gratitude. It helped that one of Darby's men—Kale Rushton—was part Apache and was admired by the Mescalero tribe for his harassment of the whites.

The Apaches made their camps to the far western side of the mountains, so they rarely saw the Indians when camped here. Usually Darby and Kale Rushton went to visit them when they reached this area to let the Apaches know they were at their campsite in the canyon. Since most whites feared the Apaches, Darby's gang didn't have to worry about being located in this secluded and peaceful region.

Knowing now that T.J. Rogue had been raised by Apaches, she wished she had met them and learned their language. She wondered if the Mescalero tribe in these mountains was the one who had captured and raised his brother. She hadn't been able to speak that question in fear of giving away a vital clue about her destination.

Carrie Sue reached the eastern entrance to McKittrick Canyon and headed along the winding trail. She followed the perennial spring-fed stream whose banks were edged by grey oak, velvet ash, bigtooth maple, willows, and lacy ferns. In the rapidly fading light, she admired the beauty of prickly pear cacti, alligator junipers, and the sparkling water. She inhaled the mingled scents which surrounded her, noticing the pines and madrones most of all. She saw a mule deer browsing at the edge of the woods, and other creatures scampering home for the coming night. She noted the rapid and stealthful movement of a coyote, a misunderstood animal who was no threat to man. She experienced the solitude of this vast wonderland, but wished it weren't getting dark so quickly.

She knew her way blindfolded, but accidents did occur on shadowy paths, and the moon was nearing its crescent stage of little light. She made certain her rifle was cocked for use, just in case a mountain lion challenged her or a spooked elk charged. She knew that Darby always posted a guard at the entrance to the canyon, but no one had called out to her or presented himself. The weary redhead hoped that wasn't a bad sign. She had about two to three miles to ride to reach the rough cabin, located at a spot on the stream where the canyon split north and south, making two escape routes over the ridges if ever needed. Yes, Darby Stover was too clever to box himself into a trap!

Carrie Sue tossed back her hat and loosened her hair to let the fiery mane glow in the receding light to reveal her identity. Still, no one joined her. Darby had trained and ordered his men to be careful, but only a stranger wouldn't recognize her as the Texas Flame, his sister. Even so, her hair should alert an unknown guard to her identity.

She halted and listened as she looked around, but heard and saw nothing but movements of nocturnal animals, insects, birds, and other creatures. She sensed no piercing eyes or threatening presence. She wondered if Curly had lied or if her brother had left this area and was—

Carrie Sue mentally scolded herself for thinking such ridiculous thoughts for even a moment. Darby Stover was a natural-born leader of men, too bad they were outlaws. She knew why the regular gang followed him, trusted him, would die for him. Darby had the kind of personality which made people like him and want to be around him. He was clever, fearlessly brave, coolheaded, and highly skilled with physical and mental prowess. He always had a crafty backup plan. He never got caught. He was never reckless and impulsive. He was a smart planner. He wasn't arrogant or cocky. And he had a smile which could melt the coldest woman's heart, a smile which made his eyes glow on a tanned face with white teeth and handsome features, a dazzling and boyish smile which relaxed, charmed, and disarmed even men. He always robbed companies, not people. He always tried never to harm innocent bystanders. For those two reasons, he hadn't been feared like a common criminal, and many had considered him an admirable rebel, until the last few years.

At least Darby Stover had been that way. Over the past months before their separation, she had watched him changing, watched him accepting his life and reputation as an outlaw, watched him decide to become the best and most well-known bandit leader in history. Life had made it too hard for him to stay on the right side of the law, so he'd quit trying. What happened to him at the Laredo ranch had changed him, made him believe he could never escape his trap, so why delude and punish himself? The posses never gave him time to halt long enough to go straight, unless he vanished from sight as when he came here. But the moment he was seen anywhere, the maddening and exhausting chase was on again. It was like a grim challenge he had to meet.

When her brother and his men were younger, their bloods had been boiling for excitement and adventures, for conquests and riches. After a taste of money and suspense, none of them had wanted to work hard for a meager salary from sunup to sunset and be too fatigued to care if life was passing them by. Those early days of battling Quade Harding had been fun and profitable for them, but their first killing had turned the tide, had provoked more than the Hardings after them.

Carrie Sue sighed heavily. Maybe T.J. was partially right. Maybe she did have a rosy, inaccurate view of her brother. Maybe he had become hardened and chilled by his lifestyle. Maybe it was too late for him to change again, to change back to that happy-go-lucky boy who had taken on a powerful enemy with the hope of obtaining justice. Those admissions hurt. Yet, at last, she had to face the truth.

She had given Darby the benefit of the doubt. She had

loved him and followed him into great perils. She had ruined her life doing so. Maybe she had refused to look at him and their lives with an unbiased mind. Maybe she hadn't wanted to believe what they both had become. Maybe she inwardly resented the gang because Darby wouldn't be in this mess without them, still in this existence without them. She would give anything if the only charges against them had to do with the Hardings, charges a good lawyer might be able to argue successfully.

Following the deaths of innocent victims in March and April, she had suspected the truth and desperately fled it. Now, she was riding back into the hopeless situation she had escaped. The redhead was too tired to deceive herself. She loved Darby and wanted to see him. She prayed she could talk some sense into him, but she doubted it. No matter what happened, she had to get far away as soon as possible. She should have done so long ago, after leaving the Harding Ranch.

She would reach the campsite soon, but she realized Darby wasn't here because no guard had been posted at the entrance. She hoped no one else was using the crude cabin tonight. She would rest, then decide how to locate him safely. How she wished T.J. was here to help, comfort, and understand—

Someone leaped on her horse behind her and banded her chest tightly with his arms, preventing her from drawing her weapons or battling him. In his right hand he held a shiny blade near her face. Her heart pounded in alarm as she suddenly wondered if Curly had someone waiting for her, and she berated herself for being so careless.

He said in Spanish, *"Hola, chica. Que me cuenta?"*

Chapter Nineteen

The man reined in her horse, dismounted agilely, and assisted her to the ground. She angrily pounded his hard, bare chest and scolded, "Damn you, Kale Rushton! You scared ten years off my life!" She wasn't amused by his joke and, even though she was not a young girl anymore, he continued to call her *chica* as he had since seventeen.

Kale chuckled and looked her over in the waning light. "What's wrong with you tonight, *chica?* I've been trailing you since you entered the canyon. You're guard's much too low, *mi belleza.* I might have been a hungry *leon* and gobbled you up in two bites."

Carrie Sue relaxed and grinned. "I'm exhausted, that's what's wrong," she replied, softening her tone. "I've been on the trail for two days with hardly any rest. I'd about decided you all weren't here."

"How did you know?" the half-Apache asked, his black eyes alert.

"Curly James told me. He came to Tucson and got himself killed there in a showdown. We've got trouble, Kale, but we can discuss it in the morning. I need some sleep badly before I collapse."

The twenty-seven-year-old man with flowing black hair past his shoulders smiled and nodded. Kale Rushton was half Spanish and half Apache, and was an appealing male of good looks and a virile body. His hips were clad in snug jeans and his ever present red sash was secured around his head. Kale was

369

only four inches taller than her five-seven height, but he was solidly built. He had been with Darby since the Quade Harding affair. She liked Kale because she always felt she could trust him. "It's good to see you, *amigo*."

"*Lo mismo digo,*" he murmured, saying "the same to you."

"Is Darby all right?" she asked worriedly.

"*Si,* only restless to be on the trail again. Why are you here, *chica*? What happened to drive you from Tucson?" he asked, perceptive.

"I was exposed and had to flee for my life."

"You came all this way alone?" he queried, his gaze widening.

"Let's talk about it later," she coaxed, yawning and flexing.

Kale suggested, "Why don't you bed down where I stand guard? If you enter camp this late, it will disturb everyone and you won't get any rest for hours. I'll be on guard until dawn."

"That's a good idea, *amigo*. Let's go before I hit the ground."

They mounted double-back and returned to a grassy area near the entrance. Kale unpacked her bedroll and spread it out for her. As he unsaddled her horse and tended the sorrel, Carrie Sue drank cool water from the stream. She stretched out on the bedroll and closed her eyes.

When Kale took his place nearby, she lifted her head and looked at him, asking, "How long have you been camped here?"

"For weeks, why?" he questioned, sensing there was an important meaning to her query.

"I thought so. See you at dawn, Kale," she said and went to sleep.

Kale Rushton withdrew his knife and stone. He began sharpening the already incisive blade, a habit when he was in deep thought. The half-Apache observed the redhaired beauty for a long time, deciding something terrible had driven her from her new life, something which would affect all of them. Patience was one of his best traits, so he could wait until morning to discover that reason. If danger was close, she would have aroused the others.

Kale removed the fiery red sash from across his forehead. He grasped his long black hair and bound the flowing mane at the nape with it. His Apache hairstyle was his badge of honor, his pride in and acknowledgement of that part of his heritage, a sign of his rebel spirit.

He had met Darby Stover during a saloon brawl in Brownwood, shortly after Darby's parent's deaths and a week before his new friend went on the vengeance trail against his enemies the Hardings. Kale remembered those days clearly. The twenty-one-year-old Darby had been suffering badly over his parent's deaths and the loss of his property, and the law's refusal to punish those responsible. Darby had needed a friend, a helper, a confidant, a comforter. As for Carrie Sue, the young beauty had no place to live and no money for support, and jobs were few for seventeen year olds with her looks. Besides, Darby hadn't wanted his sister to slave for strangers, and Kale had agreed.

Even at twenty, Kale had done plenty of gunslinging, horse thieving, and cattle rustling. Because of his looks and mixed blood, he had endured lots of trouble, hatred, taunting, and challenges—incidents which had made him into a tough and self-reliant gunman who enjoyed getting the best of his physical and mental attackers. Men who gave him trouble or ridicule found their properties burned or stolen, but no one had ever been able to pin one of those deeds on him.

Kale had been the one to suggest revenge on the Hardings, telling Darby he should do similar things to Harding as punishment. He was the one who had taught Darby many Apache tricks, trained the youth in how to pull off crimes and get away with them. He owed Darby Stover his life and loyalty, as Darby had saved his life during that saloon brawl when a man was going to shoot him in the back. He and Darby had taken an instant liking to each other and become fast friends.

Kale had worked with Walt Vinson, Tyler Parnell, and John

"Griff" Griffin many times in the past. He was the one who had introduced Darby to them and suggested they form a gang to harass Quade Harding. Knowing they needed another couple of men, they had observed prospects in saloons, gunslingers and drifters passing through town. They had met Kadry Sams in a saloon following a showdown with a famed gunslinger. They had picked up Dillon Holmes while visiting Miss Sally's brothel in San Angelo, after witnessing a fight between Dillon and another customer who favored the same "soiled dove."

Kale knew he preferred following Darby, helping with the plans and suggestions, and teaching his friend all he knew, but he didn't care about being the leader. Too, the half-Apache realized that Darby Stover was a natural-born leader. He liked and respected his friend, and nothing Darby did turned Kale against him. He also liked being a member of the famous Stover Gang.

Kale knew he was the most loyal outlaw in the band. Except for Kadry and Dillon, the other men weren't as smart and skilled as Darby and Kale and they just naturally followed along behind a superior leader and expert warrior. Kale knew that Kadry Sams would like to be a leader, but he would never go against Darby Stover, nor would the rest of the gang back him. But if anything happened to Darby, Kadry would be the one to take control of the gang.

Kale Rushton liked Kadry, but he realized the light-haired bandit with impenetrable sky blue eyes was more conniving, cold-blooded, and harder than any of the others. Kadry was also more daring than Kale and Darby, almost to the point of being recklessly brave.

Over the years, Darby had let other outlaws or gunmen join their gang for certain jobs, but never for any length of time. It was obvious to the seven men who composed the Stover Gang that they had a special rapport, trusted each other, and liked each other.

Kale loved this life. It was exciting, stimulating, challenging.

They were always seeking a bigger haul, taking on a more dangerous target, getting away quicker and cleaner, outsmarting the law and their targets, and moving from place to place. Kale knew he was part of the reason why Darby and the gang had done so well and why Darby had remained in the outlaw business so long. He was aware that Kadry was a little jealous of his tight bond with Darby, but not to the point of leaving the gang or going against Darby. Sure they had had occasional squabbles, but nothing serious. Disagreements sometimes arose under the conditions in which they were forced to survive and work. Sometimes they got edgy and nervous during lengthy pursuits or during long periods of laying low. But mostly they lived in close and tight rapport like a family of brothers with Darby as the father.

The only thing Kale Rushton didn't like was Darby bringing his younger sister into this dangerous and difficult existence. Kale trusted Carrie Sue, and had confidence in her skills, but he didn't believe a woman like her should endure this kind of life. He also didn't like Kadry Sams pursuing her hotly. His only quarrel with Darby was that his friend didn't see that such a relationship couldn't work; yet Darby wouldn't discourage it.

Years ago when Carrie Sue learned of their plans to destroy the Hardings, she had demanded to help seek justice and vengeance. Kale had warned both they must be careful and that they needed to know more about Harding's business and schedule. Since the villainous bastard had offered her a job several times, she had taken it to be the spy whom they needed. When Harding figured out their plot and gave her false information to entrap them, their task had fallen apart, but the gang had gotten away without deaths or injuries. After Harding confronted her, she had managed to use her wits and skills to flee the beast. Ever since that day, she had ridden with them off and on.

Darby hadn't been too worried about Quade's threats because Quade wanted her too badly to endanger her; his refusal to give out her description over the years had proven it. Yet, the harassment of Quade had been halted to protect her, something which still riled Darby.

Kale Rushton knew Quade Harding would never give up trying to possess Carrie Sue Stover. Quade was like a ferocious badger with his teeth locked into a delicious piece of meat; he would hang on until he wore her down and devoured her, unless he was killed.

Kale was worried about her return to them tonight. Things had gotten hot for them all over the territory. That was the reason why they had been unable to make it into Oklahoma and why Darby had suggested this distant place for resting and keeping out of sight for a while. Nowadays, they were chased everywhere they went by wild posses and bounty hunters and eager lawmen. Yet, this far from central Texas where they usually operated, they were safe in this Apache place.

The ruggedly handsome bandit glanced at the sleeping woman. Evidently something had gone wrong in Tucson because she had been determined never to ride with the gang again. Kale decided to persuade Darby to get her plenty of money so she could get further away from the hazardous West. Maybe next time she could find success.

As dawn approached, Kale nudged Carrie Sue's shoulder and awakened her. Softly he murmured, *"Chica,* it's time to stir your blood and clear your head before Griff comes to take over."

The drowsy redhead sat up and flexed her sore body. She smiled and said, "I'm getting too old and stiff for this kind of life, *amigo.* I'm going around the bend to take a quick bath and change clothes." She gathered her things and left him sitting there.

When she returned, she was clad in the Mexican skirt, white blouse over a camisole, and sandals. Her tawny red hair was flowing about her shoulders. She greeted Kale with a bright smile. She looked rested, fresh as the pleasant summer morning which surrounded them.

"I'm starved, but food needs to wait. I trust you most of all, Kale, so please convince Darby to do what's best for all of us when you hear my news later. First, I need to speak with him privately. Can you fetch him for me and keep the others in camp?"

Kale nodded. "The boys will be stirring soon. I see smoke which means coffee. I'll send some to you with Darby. Watch the entrance for me." Kale headed toward camp at a steady run which would take him ten minutes in his well-honed condition.

She guessed accurately, for Darby came into sight within fifteen minutes, riding bareback. In his excitement, he hadn't even buttoned his shirt or donned his boots. He leapt off the horse and embraced her.

He held her away from him and studied her with affection and intrigue. His eyes were soft like warmed chocolate and sparkled like the sun-lit stream nearby. A broad smile revealed white teeth and deep grooves at the sides of his mouth. His face was perfectly shaped, as were his features. Yes, she concluded in love and pride, he could stop a woman's heart or cause her to stare and stumble.

"What are you doing here, Sis?" he asked, eagerness brightening his dark eyes even more than before. "I thought Kale was teasing me."

Carrie Sue's fingers combed through his mussed dark auburn hair which was shaggy on the sides, but didn't conceal his ears. Sideburns crept to his lobes and brought attention to his strong jawline. The nape curled boyishly at his collar and she playfully fluffed that area. "You need a haircut, Darby Stover, and a shave," she added merrily as her hand teased over two day's growth of dark whiskers.

"Surely you didn't come here to make sure I'm taking care of myself. How did you find us? Why are you here?"

"Did Curly James pass through here recently?" she asked.

Darby sent her an odd look. "Yep, why?"

"On the eighteenth?" she probed.

"Yep, he had business in Tucson. He was coming back to join up with us again for the next few jobs. I'll need some extra men 'cause I'm planning to hit some big targets. I know he was hard to control, but he promised no trouble or killing," Darby asserted when she frowned.

"Did you tell him I was in Tucson?"

"No way, Sis. I was hoping he'd miss you. What's going on?"

"What business did he have in Tucson?"

"Don't know. Give, Sis," he demanded, getting impatient. "All Kale told me was you arrived late and slept here."

Carrie Sue sat down on her bedroll and patted the area next to her to indicate he was to sit there. "We need to have a serious talk, big brother. We've got lots of trouble." She told Darby about running into Curly James on the street and what passed between them, letting him know that's how she located him. When she related news of the showdown with T.J. Rogue, her brother's eyes widened in astonishment.

"Curly challenged Rogue? Is he crazy?" Darby scoffed.

"Not anymore. Rogue had him on the ground before his pistol cleared his holster. Ever met him?" she inquired.

"Met him, no, but heard plenty about him. He's taken down more gunslingers than I've met, killed more men than a dog has fleas. So, what are you doing here? Did Curly cause trouble for you?"

"Not really, but I didn't trust him to keep his promise to me. Not with my new poster out. It has an accurate picture of me, Darby. I found out just in time to get out of town before I was arrested. The Hardings have upped our rewards to ten thousand each, and five each on the boys. Add that to the law's offer of sixteen, and the gang is worth sixty-six thousand. That makes us real tempting to everyone, big brother. I've no doubt Curly would have collected on mine if Rogue hadn't killed him."

"Damn that Quade Harding! I didn't think he'd ever do this to you! Wasn't killing Papa and Mama and stealing our ranch enough for the bastard? I know he wants you badly, Sis, but this can get you killed."

Hurriedly, Carrie Sue went over her experiences in Tucson and her problem with Martin Ferris. Then, she related her many rescues and adventures with T.J. Rogue, omitting their love affair. She told him why T.J. killed Curly and about T.J.'s helping her flee Tucson. She went over her plights on the trail and admitted, "I deserted him in El Paso, but I feel awful about deceiving him after all he's done for me. I didn't want to get him into trouble by tying in with us." She did not tell her brother about her suspicions of T.J., in case the two men ever met. She didn't want Darby gunning down her lover if he wasn't guilty, and there was a slight chance he wasn't.

Darby eyed her intently. "You're in love with him, aren't you?"

Carrie Sue licked her lips and nodded. "Crazy, isn't it?" she jested.

Darby scowled, but replied, "Not after what he's done for you. He's got quite a reputation, but he isn't an outlaw."

"I know, but he was willing to do anything to help me."

"That means he probably loves you, too. What about Kadry? He loves you and wants to marry you. This'll bust him up badly."

"You know I don't love Kadry. I've tried to tell both of you that many times. Love isn't something you force, big brother; it either happens between two people or it doesn't. It just isn't there for Kadry. Besides, I'm leaving again to give it another try farther away. I can't see Kadry as a husband, father, and rancher."

"What about Rogue? Do you see him that way?" Darby asked.

"I don't know, but I'll let him know where I am once I get settled."

"You trust him that much?"

"Yes. And it won't endanger you if I'm far away when I contact him. I had to see you in person, Darby. I had to let you

377

know I'm all right in case the law tries to trick you by saying I've been captured. Once I leave, don't believe any stories in the newspapers." She reached for her saddlebag and withdrew the articles. "Read these and the dates."

"What the hell?" Darby exploded in disbelief as he scanned the reports of *his* crimes on May twenty-second, twenty-fifth, thirtieth and June third. "I wasn't anywhere near those places! This isn't the first time we've been accused of the wrong crimes!"

Carrie Sue urged, "You have to give it up, big brother. It's too dangerous out there. Either the law is boxing you in with lies, or trying to lure me into a trap, or some gang is playing yours. If you're being framed, it has to be Quade Harding, with Curly's help."

"Curly's help?" he echoed, baffled.

She reasoned, "How else did this other gang know you were out of touch so they could operate freely as the Stover Gang? I knew you weren't responsible, so I had to warn you. I know your style and I know you, Darby Stover. You don't go around killing people on every job or telling your victims they've been taken by the Stover Gang. Besides, Curly worked for Quade in the past. He and two men barbwired T.J. to a tree to die slowly for Quade; that's why T.J. killed Curly and wants to go after Quade. We have a mutual enemy."

"You believed that tale? Rogue getting ambushed by Curly and his boys? From what I hear, he's the best gunman around; you don't snare a man like Rogue easily."

"I saw the scars, and he told me that story before he knew who I was. I'm certain it's true, Darby."

"Or you want to believe it is 'cause of how you feel about him."

Carrie Sue related the incident as T.J. had told her. "When Curly saw T.J., he went white. He did that because he recognized him as the man he'd hired out to kill for Quade." She moved closer to her brother and clasped his hand in hers. She entreated, "Please, let's ride for Montana while it's safe. We can buy a ranch there and be happy and free. This other gang has stirred up everyone against you, and your large reward is tempting even for friends. Ten thousand dollars in gold, Darby, that's more than most of our takes. Give it up, please."

Darby jumped up to pace, agitated by this unexpected turn in events. He argued sullenly, "We don't have enough money for a ranch or anything else, Sis. Give it up to do what? Live how? Like dirt farmers or poor cowpunchers? We'd never make enough to have any kind of decent life. Always looking over our shoulders? Never able to relax or feel safe? I don't hanker to be strung up to a cottonwood and have my innards dump themselves down my legs while I dangle on that tree and people gape and joke and have a good time like they was at a Sunday picnic."

He continued at her silence, "They'd never put me in jail and, if they did, I couldn't stand being locked up forever. Our faces are known everywhere, and Harding won't quit hiring detectives and bounty hunters until he has our bodies! It's too late to turn back, Sis. But I want you out of this mess for keeps. I'm going to get you plenty of money so you can get away. Alone, you stand a chance of making it. I don't want you getting killed and I don't want you around when that last bullet strikes me down."

"Don't say that, Darby!" she shrieked at him.

"It's coming one day, Sis; it can't be stopped. Accept it and get out while you still have a chance to survive and start over. You deserve a home and a family. You ought to have them by now. If Rogue is the man you want, find him and convince him to join you. I'll stake you two," he vowed.

Carrie Sue tried another angle. "What if Curly told Quade where you're hiding? If Quade's your framer, he won't come here or send anyone after you while he's blackening your name. But if he isn't, he could be on his way here now, with a large posse. Curly didn't have time to betray me, so Quade can't know where I was."

Refreshing that treachery in his mind, Darby cursed,

"Damn that bastard Curly! If Rogue hadn't killed him, I would! He's fooled me twice, and I don't fool easy! Looks like Harding's given up on catching you first and wants you dead if he can't have you."

She ventured, "Or he hopes I'll figure out his ruse and rush into his arms and save you and myself."

"You think that's his motive?" Darby asked.

"I don't know, big brother. Too much has happened lately and my wits aren't clear. What else could he want from this ruse? If he's the one behind it," she added, but somehow knew he was.

"Let's get back to camp and talk with the boys. We'll need to pull out in the morning. Just so there won't be any trouble with Kadry, let's keep quiet about this romance with Rogue."

"How did you guess the truth?" she teased.

"I've always been able to read you, Sis, so don't start keeping secrets from me. How far has this romance gone?" he asked gravely.

Carrie Sue lowered her lashes a moment. "I'm a grown woman, big brother; I'm twenty-four and that's private."

"That far, huh? Oh, well, I can't say much. I've had me plenty of women and I didn't love any of them. At least you love this man."

"No more than I love you, Darby Stover."

The outlaw leader helped her to her feet and hugged her tightly. "I got you into this mess, Sis, and I'll get you out. Soon, I promise." He eyed the poster and clipping about her. "With these around, you're in big danger, Sis. You'll have to stick with us until I get you away."

They gathered her things and rode to the cabin. It was a crude structure made of oak logs from the area. There was no stove, so all cooking was done outside, near the stream. The cabin backed up to steep rocks, and trails led off to its right and left and traveled into the interior of the mountains. From there other trails snaked into New Mexico and into western Texas, providing many escape routes.

Carrie Sue saw the boys sitting around the campfire drinking coffee. As they approached, all except Kale came to greet her.

Tyler Parnell, a simple man of thirty with light brown hair and hazel eyes, helped her down and said in a thick Arkansas accent, "Shore good ta have ya back, Miss Carrie Sue. We done missed ya."

She smelled the ever present hint of whiskey on Tyler, who towered over her at six-feet-two inches. When he hugged her, his short beard and wiry mustache scratched her cheek. She glanced at his first cousin Walt Vinson who was a man of thirty with medium brown hair, hazel eyes, a shorter beard but softer mustache, and about Tyler's height. She smiled and nodded hello. As always, those two men reminded her of brothers because they looked and talked so much alike with their rough country tongues. Walt fingered his gunbutts and nodded in return. Neither had changed their habits she realized.

John "Griff" Griffin shook her hand energetically and said, "Yes'm, good ta have you back, Missy Stover. It dun been quiet without you."

"Thank you, Griff," she remarked to the black man with a cleanly shaven jawline and a long black mustache. Griff was thirty-one, the oldest of the group. His obsidian eyes sparkled when he grinned. He jammed a stick in his mouth and began chewing on it, as always.

Dillon Holmes grabbed her and hugged her and kissed her on the cheek, but only because she turned her head when he boldly went for her mouth. As usual, he smelled of aromatic cigarillos from Mexico. At six feet, the twenty-nine-year-old man had dark brown hair and intensely green eyes. His hair was straight and, from a side part, fell across his forehead in a haphazard manner. "Hello, Dillon."

"You're one sight for sore eyes, Carrie Sue," he murmured in his heavy southern drawl from Mississippi. "Glad you're home again."

Kadry Sams parted the group with his six-one frame. His sky blue eyes trailed over her leisurely. He habitually finger-combed his wavy hair which was a mixture of dark and sunny blond. At twenty-eight, Kadry Sams was a handsome man with a splendid physique. She dreaded the confrontation, but smiled genially and said, "Hello, Kadry."

"Ye been gone tae long, me beautiful lass," he murmured with a Scottish burr. He captured a lock of her hair and teased it under his nose. "I been awaitin' ye return. Canna git ye anything?"

"Coffee, please," she replied.

"Ye wish is filled, me bonny lass. Gie me ae moment. 'Tis ae fine day fer ye tae return home. I've missed ye." He went for her coffee.

Walt asked, "Whatcha doin' back, Miss Carrie Sue?"

"Did dat Tucson turn out a bad place?" Griff added.

"Let her catch her breath, boys," Dillon drawled.

While Carrie Sue sipped the hot liquid, Darby related the news to his gang, who were just as shocked and vexed as her brother was, except for Kadry Sams whose blue eyes burned with jealousy.

Kadry hinted, "Sae, ye met tha famous Rogue, did ye?"

"I wouldn't be here now if he hadn't saved my life a few times," she replied, bravely looking at the blond while speaking.

"Why dinna ye bring him along?" Kadry asked, fingering his hair.

"Why should I?" she asked in a flippant tone.

Kadry eyed her suspiciously and shrugged. "Nae reason."

"What'll we do, boss?" Tyler asked.

"I don't lack nobody playin' usins," Griff said.

"Naw, me neither," Walt added.

Dillon's mysterious green eyes remained locked on Carrie Sue as if he weren't listening to the important conversation. Kadry nudged him, and glared when Dillon glanced his way. Dillon grinned and shrugged. Carrie Sue realized with annoyance that a new challenge for her had been given and accepted. Nothing and no one had changed. She frowned at both men, then returned her attention to her brother.

Darby caught the interaction. He warned sternly, "Settle down, boys. We gotta think this through." He showed them the clippings.

Kale Rushton remained quiet and alert, sharpening his knife.

While the men were passing around the newspaper articles with the false stories, Kadry whispered to her, "Ye best stay with us frae nigh on, lass. We should hae seen ye poster comin'. Old Quade willna e'er gie up on ye."

Carrie Sue recalled what T.J. had suggested about this man possibly being the one who had released her description to force her back into his reach. No, she concluded, there was no way he could have done it. Not that it wasn't a clever and daring idea, but Kadry hadn't been given the opportunity to pull off such a dangerous ruse.

She divulged, "I'm not staying long, Kadry. I only came to warn Darby and to let him know I'm safe."

"Wha' mean ye, lass?" he asked, staring at her.

"I'll tell you what she means," Darby answered for her. "I'm getting her plenty of money, then she's hightailing it far from here. I'm sending her to Montana to buy a ranch, or a hotel, or store, or something. If all goes well, we might even join her in a few months."

Carrie Sue's head jerked in her brother's direction. She returned his broad smile which made him look so boyish. "You will?"

Darby caught her free hand in his. "I ain't making no promises, Sis, but I'll think about it. For sure, you're getting your butt out of this area. We'll pull out at dawn tomorrow. We need to make a big hit to let folks knew we didn't pull those other ones. We'll head for San Angelo, supply up there, and make a strike a few days later. We can head for Miss Sally's Parlor House and get some news from her. She always protects

383

us and she knows everything."

The men agreed, as always. As breakfast was being cooked by Walt and Tyler, Kadry and Dillon surrounded Carrie Sue.

"Dinna worry, lass; I'll take care o' ye."

Dillon's heavy southern voice refuted, "I do it best. I'm the one who took a bullet in the shoulder to save you."

Carrie Sue didn't want any trouble, so she said, "You're both good friends and I'm grateful, but I can take care of myself."

Kadry's blue eyes darkened. "I'll kill him with me bare hands!"

"If I don't get the sorry bastard first," Dillon remarked.

Trying to make light conversation, Carrie Sue said, "I think he's the one framing us, but how can we prove it? Even if we catch him red-handed, who'd believe us?"

"Just kill the sorry trash and be done with him and his troubles."

"Ye make that sound easy, Dillon. How canna we do it?"

"Yeah," Tyler agreed. "He's been a pain in our arses fur years!"

"We can't risk going after Harding," Darby told them. "He'll be on the lookout for us. It's too dangerous for Carrie Sue. Us, too, if we want to live much longer. Nope, we can't be reckless or stupid."

"I lack Montanee. Sounds good ta me," Walt murmured.

Tyler teased, "Ya ain't never been there, Cuz, so how'd ya know?"

"Well, I heared it was great," Walt retorted with a grin.

Griff hinted, "Yes'm, a man could git lost up thar."

Dillon murmured dreamily, "I like the idea of settling down. We been at this for years. I'm tired of running and hiding and having nothing. I may get me a wife, and home, and children up there."

"Dinna go ae lookin' at her, Dillon. She be mine."

Dillon chuckled and replied, "That's up to Carrie Sue, isn't it?"

Darby wasn't one to deceive his friends and he saw trouble was brewing over his sister, so he revealed merrily, "Stop it, boys. Carrie Sue has her sights set on T.J. Rogue, so you're wasting your breath."

Carrie Sue wasn't totally surprised by her brother's disclosure as he lived with these men like brothers, and it would halt their sieges.

Kadry's blue eyes narrowed. "Wha' be this, lass?" he demanded.

"My private business," she responded in a cool tone, glaring back.

Tyler asked, "Will Rogue be joinin' us, boss?"

"I wouldn't mind having him, if we run across him."

"Rogue ain't no outlaw. We couldn't trust him," Dillon argued.

The leader explained, "He's an expert, boys, and he saved her life."

"Dinna matter tae me who or wha' he is. He canna steal her."

"Shut up, both of you," she commanded. "I'll choose whom I'll see and not see. I like you both as friends, but nothing more. Get it?"

Kale spoke up for the first time since returning to camp to announce her arrival, "When we leave, we'll have plenty to do, so let's stay limber and alert. We have that other gang to worry about."

Walt suggested, "If'n Miss Carrie Sue rides with us, they'll know we're th' real Stover Gang. The other un don't have no Texas Flame."

Kale instantly said, "No. It's too dangerous."

Dillon concurred, "I agree. She stays in camp."

Walt said, "I didn't mean no harm. I just want 'em unmasked. Them stories in th' papers are gittin' us in trouble lack she says."

Carrie Sue grinned. "I have a better idea on how to unmask those pretenders. It's dangerous and we might get caught, but it could work."

Chapter Twenty

"What do you mean?" Darby asked as the men gathered around to hear her suggestion.

She reasoned, "Since they're using the newspapers against us, why can't we use the papers in our favor? When we reach San Angelo, you can kidnap a reporter, bring him to our hideout, and we'll give him the facts. Any newspaper man would die for exclusive interviews with the Stover Gang, and every paper in Texas and probably in other states will carry his story on us. We'll tell him our backgrounds and how we got ensnared in this business. That should put Quade Harding and his father in the boiling pot. Maybe other victims of theirs will step forward to give evidence against him. Or get the law to looking in his direction. Quade will be too busy defending himself to give us much trouble. Maybe our story will flush that other gang into the open or make them stop framing us. And . . ."

She paused for affect before adding, "It should make the law get suspicious of who and why we're being framed and start them to investigating the situation. If Quade's involved, it could get him caught and punished. It's worth a try since we can't get near him to avenge Mama and Papa. After reading the truth, most everyone will have sympathy for us and it'll brighten our reputations. People used to like us, but bad stories and lies have hurt our image. We need to win over the people again. If we get caught, a friendly jury would be a

big help. Besides exposing Quade, it may get his huge rewards withdrawn. If so, those two thousand dollar government ones won't look as good to our pursuers."

"You think it'll work?" Darby murmured, eagerness filling his eyes.

Carrie Sue smiled at her brother. "We'll tell the reporter
they can be certain of any jobs we pull because we'll give our
target a lock of the Texas Flame's hair. Before I leave, I'll cut
off a few inches and make ribbon-bound curls. Very few
people have hair my color, so this false leader won't be able to
hand out convincing locks. It's simple: no golden red curl, no
Stover Gang responsible. Without locks of my hair, that
other gang can't pretend to be us anymore. This way, the
Stover Gang will get blame or credit only for the jobs you
pull."

Kale grinned. "You are one clever woman, *chica*. It's
good."

"Does this mean we won't haveta shave, boss?" Tyler
asked.

When Carrie Sue glanced inquisitively at Darby, he explained, "We got new horses and planned to disguise ourselves so we could move about safer. Tyler, Griff, and Walt
were going to shave off their beards and mustaches. Me,
Dillon, and Kadry were going to grow some here before
leaving. Kale's got too much Indian blood to grow more than
a faint shadow," he jested. "We planned to do our hair
different, too. Except Kale; he refuses to cut his, but he said
he'd tuck it under his hat and stop wearing that red sash."

Carrie Sue didn't ask why the three men involved hadn't
begun their facial hair yet, probably the habit of shaving
wasn't noticed or they had planned to stay here a long time.
"That won't be necessary now. You want people to recognize
the gang. Don't wear masks anymore so they can see that
your faces match those on the posters. Your crimes aren't
doing the gang as much damage as those pretenders' are.
They're killing people and hitting reckless targets. Those big

companies will fight back harder and meaner than our usual targets. They have the money and power to hire large bands to hunt us down."

"Damn those Hardings!" Dillon shouted and lit a cigarillo.

"Are ye sure 'tis him?" Kadry asked.

The redhead replied, "At first, I thought the law might be tricking me or endangering the gang with false reports by turning everyone against us. They know we have people who give us aid sometimes. Then, I decided those stories are true, just not about us. Who, but Quade Harding, has the motive, money, and guts to pull this off?"

Kale concurred, "She's right. Good thinking, *chica.*"

Walt queried with a frown, "Won't it be dangerous ta steal a reporter an' show 'im our hideout?"

"Darby can learn from Sally who's the best one, where he works, and where he lives. He can take one of you to help him abduct the man from his home or office. You can blindfold him and lead him around in circles to disorient him. He'll be too excited to be scared or reluctant. This will be the biggest story of his lifetime. He'll be plenty willing to oblige us with printing the truth. I'll give him a lock of my hair to use for comparison in future jobs. Think what a famous man we'll make of him. He won't turn us down."

"You're right about that, Sis. It's a damn good idea. It'll work. We been laying low for weeks. We're getting restless. This is the perfect first job to pull. Before a week's out, we'll have that other gang in a stew. This is gonna be fun. We head for San Angelo at first light. You boys get plenty of rest today, and get everything packed."

Carrie Sue added, "If Curly was the one tipping off Quade, his boss will be in a terrible fix when he isn't warned we're on the move again and he pulls a job at the same time we do."

Late that afternoon, Carrie Sue took a walk with Kale Rushton after his lengthy nap. Kadry was on guard duty, and Dillon wouldn't approach her while she was in the half-Apache's company. Walt, Griff, and Tyler were playing poker with Darby. She had talked over old and future times with her brother, a conversation which made her restless.

"Kale, how is Darby these days? He seems different since I last saw him. He's quieter and moodier. What's wrong?"

"Seven years is a long time to be chased around the countryside, *chica*. I think he misses what he lost, a home and a family, and he's missed you like crazy. A long time ago, we could ride into towns for fun and rest. Nowadays, we can't. What good is money if you can't spend it somewhere and enjoy it?"

"Then, why is he so reluctant to go straight some place?"

"He doesn't want to admit it, but he's getting worried about how long he can survive and when he'll make his first mistake and get us all killed or captured. This kind of life gets tiresome, *chica,* for men like them. Me, it's all I've ever known. 'Course, I'm not stuck like they are. I can return to the Apaches or to Mexico and live fine."

Carrie Sue spoke softly, "T.J. Rogue was raised by the Chiricahua Apaches in Arizona." She told Kale about the experiences T.J. had while growing up in the Indian camp. She related her visit to Naiche's camp and her meeting on the trail with Geronimo. She revealed how T.J. had gone back to warn them of the Army's approach with Gatling guns, and how Naiche's tribe had fled into Mexico until it was safe to return. "You two are much alike, Kale; I think you'd make good friends."

"Now I see why Rogue is so powerful with his guns and wits—Apache training. You love this gunslinger, *chica?*"

Carrie Sue glanced at him and admitted, "Yes."

Kale probed, "You trust him?"

Carrie Sue hesitated before replying, "Because of my existence, Kale, it's hard for me to trust anybody fully except you and Darby. He had plenty of chances to betray me for money or glory, but he didn't. He took a lot of risks to help me. I think he loves me, too."

"Will he go to Montana with you?"

"I don't know. I did run out on him in El Paso. Several times he tried to persuade me to stop searching for Darby and get away. But I had to warn Darby about that other gang and let him see I was all right."

"Why did you leave Rogue behind?"

"Two reasons. I didn't want him joining us and getting into trouble, and I didn't want to endanger all of you if I'd misjudged him."

Kale liked the honesty of her answer, but wished she weren't so miserable over her decision. "If he crosses our trail and joins us, I will study him for you. Eyes and voices cannot lie to Apache wits."

"If he does lie, Kale, please don't kill him. He did save my life many times and he helped me get here. Just send him away."

"You love him too much, *chica,* if you do not wish his death even if he is an enemy. That is unlike the woman I helped raise and train. Love must be a powerful emotion, and a dangerous one." Kale eyed her closely. If Rogue made trouble for Darby, he would have to kill him. No threat to his friend could be allowed to live.

"When we reach San Angelo, let Kadry and Dillon go with Darby, and you stay in camp with me. After we finish with the reporter and I get some money, I'm gone, Kale. I have to. Understand?"

"Si, chica, I understand." He withdrew his knife and whetstone and began passing the blade back and forth along its surface.

"One day, *amigo,* you're going to cut off your fingers," she teased.

He chuckled. "A good knife can be your best friend if you take good care of it. I can peel off a man's hide in ten minutes or less."

She grimaced and asked, "Whyever would you want to do a gory thing like that, Kale?"

"A foe deserves no less than to lose his mask, *chica*."

She swallowed hard. "I wouldn't want you as a foe, Kale Rushton."

"Nor would I, *chica,* nor would I," he concurred honestly. "If anyone ever harmed you or Darby or one of the boys, you'd see what me and this shiny blade could do."

After a supper of venison stew and Johnnycakes, the camp quieted down. The boys began playing cards, making new plans, and sipping whiskey—especially Tyler Parnell. Kadry went to where Carrie Sue was standing near their brush corral with her new horse and asked her to take a walk with him.

When she refused as politely as possible, he asked, "Ye willna e'en gie me a chance tae fight fer ye?"

She focused her violet-blue eyes on him. "It won't do any good, Kadry. I don't love you. When are you going to accept that?"

He ran his spread fingers through his mixed blond hair. His sky blue eyes darkened. "Because o' this Rogue fellow?"

"Not really. I've known you for years, Kadry, and I haven't fallen in love with you. I tried it once to make you and Darby happy, but it didn't work, remember? Even if T.J. didn't exist, I still wouldn't love you and marry you. You're only making yourself miserable and me uncomfortable with this useless pursuit when you can't win."

"If that's a challenge, me darlin', I accept it."

She frowned to show her annoyance and to discourage him. "It wasn't a challenge, Kadry Sams, it's a fact."

He stroked her cheek and vowed, "One day, ye might find ye love me an' need me when this Rogue betrays ye or turns ye down."

"Whatever happens or doesn't happen between me and T.J. Rogue, it doesn't affect how I feel about you. I don't love you," she stressed. "You can't make somebody love you just because you want them to."

He argued, "I kin love enough fer both o' us, lass. Gie me a chance. Let me come ta Montana with ye. We kin start a new life. We kin buy a ranch, hae a home an' family. I kin make ye happy."

She shook her head. "No, Kadry, it wouldn't work. Please stop this. It isn't doing either of us any good to keep talking about it."

"I love ye an' want ye, Carrie Sue. I canna gie up on ye."

"I wish that weren't true. What can I say or do to make you stop pressing me? You're only punishing yourself. I don't want to hurt you, Kadry. Why do you force me to keep rejecting you?"

He captured her hand and carried it to his lips. "Tha only thin' I'ma forcing ye tae do, me luv, is face tha truth. Ye canna e'er hae a man like Rogue. He'd ne'er settle down. Men wad always be after him, challenging him. Ye'd ne'er be safe with him."

She pulled her hand away and placed it behind her. "The same can be said of you, my infamous friend."

"Nae in Montana, me luv, I promise ye, nae trouble."

Dillon Holmes joined them and halted Kadry's earnest pleas for love and marriage. The green-eyed southerner asked, "Why don't you let it go, Kadry? She's not going to choose you over me."

Carrie Sue groaned loudly. "I'm not going to choose either one of you, so please stop this bickering and pestering. You two are part of the reason I had to get away so many times. You drive me loco."

Dillon said, "I can give you anything you want or need, Carrie Sue."

She responded, "No, you can't, Dillon, nobody can. Please, both of you leave me alone. I'm tired. I'm going to

392

bed. We have a long ride ahead of us." She walked away, leaving the two outlaws bickering.

In her bedroll, Carrie Sue wondered if there was any way T.J. could track her here. If so, what would she do and say? She hoped he didn't. Much as she wanted to see his handsome face, she didn't want to cause trouble with any of the men or for her lover.

Carrie Sue pondered T.J.'s reaction to her escape. How had he felt? Where would he head to search for her, for surely he would? To Brownwood, she concluded, because that was where the gang was allegedly operating. She doubted that T.J. believed her note's claim that her brother wasn't to blame for those recent crimes. Even if he did believe her, he would still head for that area, either to take care of Quade Harding or hopefully to join up with her again. What would happen when Darby and T.J. met, if they did?

"Darby?" she whispered, her bedroll beside his.

"Yeah, Sis?" he responded, turning toward her in the dim light of a crescent moon. He was unable to make out much in the darkness.

She kept her voice low so the others couldn't overhear them. "Did you mean what you said earlier about going to Montana with me?"

Darby stayed silent.

Carrie Sue quivered in alarm and asked, "Did you hear me?"

"Yeah, I heard you. Once we get this mess cleared up about that false gang with that reporter, things should cool down for us. Me and the boys will probably head for Arizona after you leave. I hear there's lot of gold and silver to be had out there. You have a better chance of survival and making a new life if me and the boys aren't around to mess it up for you. If I leave them here, they'll only get into trouble and get themselves killed. I can't run out on them and I couldn't take them along to Montana 'cause we'd draw too much attention to you. I owe them, Sis; they've been with me from the start.

They're my friends, like family to me."

"You don't owe them your life, big brother."

"Yeah, maybe I do. They've risked theirs lots of times for me."

"You can't keep on with this, Darby. One day, one of those lawmen is going to outsmart you or one of those bounty hunters is going to catch up with you. They're going to kill you, Darby, all of you."

"I know, but we don't have any choice. It's too late for us."

"Yes, you do. You can pull out now. Let's forget about the reporter and money. Let's just leave from here and head north."

"I can't, Sis."

"You mean, you won't," she corrected, anger chewing at her.

After a pause, he replied, "Yeah, I guess you're right about that."

With teary eyes, she urged, "Darby, please."

Darby ignored her tone and words. "Why don't you leave from here, Sis? You can take some supplies and all the money we have left. The boys won't mind; we'll get more soon."

"No, I want to go to San Angelo with you and work with that reporter. I want the truth out before I take off." Carrie Sue didn't tell him she thought the reporter would trust her and believe her more than the men and she could make the newspaper man grasp the truth. She had to remove that threat to her brother before she deserted him for the last time. She owed Darby that much. Besides, she needed better supplies and more money if she was going to make it to Montana and have a real chance at a new beginning. If only she could get to Carolyn Starns's money in the Tucson bank, but that wasn't possible.

Carrie Sue also wanted to send T.J. a message through Hank Peterson to let her love know she was all right and was heading for safety far away. She realized there was no need to keep reasoning or arguing with her brother; she couldn't change his mind. She hated the fact he was choosing his friends over her, but Darby thought and felt like a man. Sometimes misguided loyalty was more important to men than family bonds. His male pride and his fealty to his gang would never let him desert them. He had pulled them together, led them, made all the decisions for them, and taken care of them. He felt responsible for the gang as a good father would for his family. They were six, and she was only one, so the odds were against her.

"Good-night, Darby," she murmured, her heart heavy with sadness.

" 'Night, Sis," he replied in a matching tone.

Carrie Sue spent a restless night with bad dreams about her brother's capture and death. Each time she awakened, she tried to return to sleep to dream about a bright future with T.J. Rogue, but her mind refused to cooperate. Whenever she saw her lover in her dreams, he was dogging her persistently and trying to destroy Darby and his gang.

Two hours before dawn, she finally fell into a deep slumber.

Saturday morning, June tenth, the Stover Gang left the cool and secluded canyon in the Guadalupe Mountains, heading for San Angelo. It was a journey which would require five days.

To the east in Brownwood, Ranger Dave Clemmens rode into a lethal trap by the gang impersonating Darby and his men. Pinned to the lawman's chest by his silver star was a note saying, "Stop chasing the Stover Gang or you'll all end up like this. You'll never catch us, so give it up and survive." It was signed "Darby Stover."

Tuesday night, a weary and moody T.J. Rogue arrived in San Angelo. He had tried to make town before the telegraph office closed for the day so he could pick up his messages. A storm had slowed him yesterday by forcing him to take cover for hours. He had no choice but to wait for morning to see what had taken place while he'd been out of touch. He also needed a newspaper to learn whatever he could.

He stabled Nighthawk, took his gear, and checked into a small hotel near the edge of town. Two buildings away was Miss Sally's Parlor House, a luxurious brothel famous for its food, music, drinks, gambling, and well-trained prostitutes. Tonight, he needed nothing more than a bath, hot meal, cool drink, and comfortable bed.

No, he corrected himself, what he needed and wanted most was Carrie Sue Stover in his arms. It had been seven days since he'd made love to her, then lost her to her recklessness. If, his mind scoffed, he could call her fleeing from his threat being rash. Lordy, he wished he knew where she was and how she was. Even if her posters were down, she was with the gang again, and in great peril. For all he knew, she could be captured or killed by now.

When morning came, after a long and troublesome night, T.J. arose early, had a quick breakfast, and headed for the telegraph office. There were two messages awaiting him. He read Hank Peterson's to discover his friend in Mesilla hadn't heard from Carrie Sue and didn't have any further news on the gang. Mitchell Sterling's message said that Ranger Dave Clemmens had been killed outside Brownwood last Saturday, allegedly by "Darby Stover."

T.J. knew from study that Carrie Sue's brother was not known to ambush and murder any man in cold blood, and Darby certainly never incriminated himself with reckless boasting! He wondered if Dave had stumbled onto something important about Quade Harding. The skilled Ranger had been working the Harding case for some time and had made a mistake somewhere along the trail. That meant T.J. needed to investigate Dave's death when he reached Brownwood. If Quade was in on more than a land grab and local crimes, his two cases would overlap. He hoped Harding was involved in the frame of the Stover Gang. If one existed, and he believed it did, that would give him another reason and way to entrap his foe.

Mitchell also said he had nothing new to report on the gang's movements and deeds since T.J. left El Paso. If Darby and his men had committed those recent crimes and Carrie Sue was back with them, they were laying low again and she would be safe, hopefully.

T.J. faced another reality. When he rode into Brownwood and confronted Quade Harding again, what would happen? The man knew he was Ranger Thad Jamison, and he would know his murder attempt had failed. Harding would be forced to try again to cover his guilt. T.J. asked himself if he should skip Brownwood for now, which could lead to him exposing his identity on this case. He couldn't arrest Quade without evidence and he couldn't get near the man to obtain it! If he revealed himself there, his undercover days were over. And, Carrie Sue would learn the wrong way who he was. Besides, Harding was probably on alert after that curious poster business.

The best thing to do was wait to learn if Dave Clemmens had reported anything before his death. T.J. sent a coded wire to the head of the Texas Ranger unit for which he worked. He told his superior about his suspicions of a frame and Quade Harding's possible involvement in that and Dave's murder. He asked the officer to reconsider a pardon for Carrie Sue, if she helped with the Stover and Harding cases. He vowed to marry her and keep her out of future trouble. He said he would take full responsibility for her, that he would do *anything* to get her pardoned.

T.J. sent a similar coded message to President Grant and prayed his old friend wouldn't let him down. If Grant didn't have a chance at a third term, then, this being an election year shouldn't control his decision on a pardon. If fact, the man whose life he had saved and whom he had served faithfully owed him this chance at happiness.

T.J. sent answers to Mitchell and Hank, then went to the newspaper office. He met William Ferguson, owner and reporter. He asked for the last seven day's papers to check out the news. While Ferguson gathered them, T.J. asked, "Hear much about the Stover Gang?"

"There was plenty of news for weeks, but nothing since that Wells Fargo office in Brady. Why are you so interested, son?"

T.J. used one of his genial and disarming smiles. "There's a ten thousand dollar reward out on Darby Stover and his sister and five each on his men. That's a lot of money. I travel around all the time, so if I run into them, I wouldn't mind collecting it. I hear she's a real beauty."

"Are you a bounty hunter?" William Ferguson asked.

T.J. sent him a scowl to reveal his feelings. "Nope. I'm what you might call a drifter or gunslinger. Name's T.J. Rogue."

William Ferguson looked the young man over and smiled. "In this business, I've heard of you many times, son. I must say it's a pleasure to meet such a famous man. I've printed stories about your . . . shall we say, colorful adventures? I also enjoy meeting the people I write about in my paper. I bet you could fill an entire edition with tall tales. You want to set the record straight? I always print the truth."

T.J. chuckled and shook his head, the man's words and mood telling him which approach to take to extract the most information. T.J. knew men like this had facts they often didn't or couldn't print. "Nope. If men learned I was tame as a kitten, they'd be stomping on my tail all the time. Some-times a bad reputation serves you well, sir, so I'd better keep mine a while. A fierce lone wolf gets challenged less than a pussycat, and I try to do as little killing as I can. It isn't like people think it is. It's a bad and hard way to survive."

Ferguson laughed heartily. He liked this direct young man and concluded he couldn't be evil. "You staying in town long?"

"I think I'll be leaving for Commanche in a few hours. That's one place the gang hasn't struck lately. Maybe I'll get lucky. I get tired of searching for odd jobs or taking offensive ones. It'll be nice to have enough money to maybe settle down some place peaceful. If you add up the Hardings' rewards and the law's, that comes to sixty-six thousand. A man can get out of the gunslinging business with that much."

"That's a wise and brave decision, son. I hope you succeed. But I wouldn't count on the Stover Gang being in central Texas. If they were, they'd be after whoever's impersonating them. I've studied and followed the Stover Gang for years and I can tell you, those last five crimes weren't committed by Darby's boys. Not his style, and a man doesn't change a perfect one and start acting crazy and reckless."

Tipping up the brim of his hat so the man could see his clear eyes better, T.J. chuckled and alleged, "That was my thinking too, sir. That's why I wanted your papers; I hear you're the best in Texas. From those I've been reading, something didn't sound right to me. I wonder if the law has noticed anything strange."

"I doubt it. They're too busy trying to capture and hang them to realize they're innocent of those charges. It's a real shame to see Darby's reputation sullied like this. He's been mighty careful over the years to shoot only when necessary. I think that's why people always yielded to him without a fight; they trusted him to ride off afterwards and leave them safe. These recent jobs all had vicious killings."

T.J. realized that Carrie Sue knew her brother well and she was right about suspecting impersonation. "You think somebody could be doing this on purpose, Mr. Ferguson? Say, framing Darby?"

"What makes you think that, son?" he asked, intrigued.

T.J. propped his elbows on the counter. He tucked his thumb under his chin and curled his index finger over it. "I'd say there has to be a traitor or spy somewhere, somebody who knows when his boss can play Darby. There hasn't been a robbery by both at the same time; that's why he looks guilty. Suppose one of his men is in cahoots with another gang and tipping them off on where and when to attack. Or," he began and paused dramatically, "what if some enemy is framing him to get him killed? Say, that Harding fellow in Brownwood who's so eager to get the Stovers. I hear he wants the sister alive or no payment. Isn't that a mite strange? I wonder what he's up to?" T.J. murmured, uncurling his fingers to stroke his jawline as if in deep study.

Ferguson was stimulated by the conversation. "I hadn't considered that angle, son. You could have something there. I thought it was strange that the Hardings took over the Stover ranch just before Darby became an outlaw. At first, he was Darby's only target, and the boy had done some shouting to the law about murder and theft. Could be a revenge motive in there some place. I'd give a box of gold pieces to question that boy and his sister about those early days."

"What would you say was their last strike, Mr. Ferguson?"

"That stage holdup near Sherman the end of April."

"That's over six weeks past. Isn't that a long time to lay low?"

The older man chuckled. "Not for Darby Stover. He doesn't need much money. Where can he go to spend it? He's wanted everywhere. He doesn't care about making a reputation for himself. I think he's stayed an outlaw because he had no choice in the matter. I think that boy would have gone straight long ago if the law had punished the Hardings. A real shame, but I believe he got himself into a trap trying to destroy the men who killed his parents and took his ranch."

"That's some theory, Mr. Ferguson. How could you prove it?"

"I can't, neither can he; that's why he's still on the run. I've worked on this story for years, son. It fascinates me how and why good men go bad. I've talked to folks who won't even talk to the law, scared to talk to them. I know things I can't even print because I can't back them up with proof or witnesses. Those Hardings have power and wealth, and they're real mean. It wouldn't surprise me any if there is a frame and they're behind it. I really hate seeing that boy and his sister get maligned and killed. You know something strange?" he said, then looked behind him to make certain no one was around.

"They put out a wanted poster on Carrie Sue Stover, then withdrew it, said it was a mistake, the wrong woman. Harding claims Carrie Sue Stover isn't the Texas Flame. He says he was with her when the Flame was seen with the Stover Gang. I can tell you, son, it wasn't the wrong woman. I don't know what's going on, but I'm trying to find out. The law isn't talking."

"How do you know it was her? And why would the law call it back?"

The older man moved closer and talked in a lowered tone. "I paid one of Quade Harding's ex-detectives for some information. He was fired from the agency for drinking too much, and he must have realized Quade wouldn't give him the chance to loosen his tongue while drunk. He identified the poster I showed him as Carrie Sue Stover. He swore she's the Flame, and he vowed that Quade Harding knows the truth. While he was considering my lucrative offer about coming forward with evidence, he was killed by a gambler for cheating. Blasted bad luck!" He glanced around again, then said, "Harding's son wants her badly, and it isn't for revenge. What I can't figure is why the law called in her posters and how they persuaded Harding to cooperate. They must have threatened him with legal action for withholding evidence all those years. I think the Rangers did it because they have one of their men with her and he's trying to get her to lead him to the gang. Sometimes she vanishes for months. It could be she's linked up with an undercover lawman and doesn't know it. They could be doing this to protect him and to give her time to lead him to her brother's gang."

"That means I don't stand a chance of locating them and bringing them in alive. I surely do hate to see bounty hunters get them."

"So do I, young man, so do I," the older man murmured sadly.

T.J. studied the gray-haired man for a time and made a quick decision. "Mr. Ferguson, I think you can be a big help to the law and possibly save their lives. What I'm about to tell you is in strictest confidence, but I need your help. You have a lot of knowledge we'll need if we're going to stop the Stover Gang and arrest the Hardings. I'm Thad Jamison, Texas Ranger, U.S. Marshal, and Special Agent to President Grant; I have official papers and badges to prove my claims if you need to see them. I've been on this case for weeks. Our man in Brownwood, Dave Clemmens, was killed recently, and I don't believe it was Darby's doing like that note on his chest claimed. Obviously he uncovered something about Quade Harding or this false gang and had to be silenced. I always work in secret, so I'll have to trust you not to tell anyone who or what I am." He divulged, "I was the one traveling with Carrie Sue Stover, but she gave me the slip in El Paso. From the message she left me, she was afraid she'd get T.J. Rogue into trouble for helping her. She said her brother was being framed, but how do we prove it? If we can, this will be the biggest story of your life." T.J. related most of the facts to the astonished man and entreated his help with this vital case.

After some thought, William Ferguson said, "If she's back with her brother by now, he knows about this frame job. If I know Darby Stover, he'll find a clever way to let people know the truth. Believe me, he'll make a strike this week and leave positive proof it was him."

"If Darby doesn't know her poster's down and he lets

Carrie Sue ride with him again, our ruse won't be worth a damn, and there's no way I can save her. Lordy, I can't even help her if she doesn't!" he stated angrily. "If she had only stuck with me a while longer."

Ferguson eyed him, then said, "You're in love with her, son."

"That's one story you can't ever print: Lawman Thad Jamison in love with the notorious Texas Flame. Can you help me save her?"

The newspaper owner and reporter smiled and said, "I'll try, son."

The two men discussed the case in length, comparing and sharing information. It was decided that T.J. would head on to Commanche while Ferguson tried to gather more facts through the sources. If anything was discovered, Ferguson was to wire T.J. in Commanche. If T.J. moved on, he was to let Ferguson know where to locate him. The two men shook hands and T.J. left the San Angelo newspaper.

He returned to the telegraph office and sent another coded message to McNelly, revealing these new facts and plans. By noon, T.J. was on his way to check the hideout which Carrie Sue had mentioned.

There was two hours of daylight left on Wednesday when the Stover Gang and Carrie Sue reached their old hideout west of San Angelo. It was little more than an old lean-to beside the Middle Concho River. Built in a heavily treed and bushy area, only a person riding in the water could see the cleverly concealed structure.

They had traveled for days across undulating fields of shortgrass with trees which often looked like balls of greenery. They had journeyed over lush, rolling hills and passed picturesque mesas and buttes. It had been easy riding, but everyone was tired.

Carrie Sue had not had a bath since the Pecos River, three

days ago. She was eager for the men to head into town to Miss Sally's so she could strip and dive into the river. Along the way, she had been lucky and careful to stay clear of Kadry and Dillon. She hoped she could continue avoiding them until she was gone.

Miss Sally's, Carrie Sue thought with a grin, was a delightful place for ranchers, soldiers from Fort Concho, cowboys, and other males to visit. The bawdyhouse had plenty to offer with its entertainment downstairs and upstairs. She had been there several times in the past and had gotten quite an eye, ear, and head full of enlightenment. Miss Sally more than liked Darby Stover and his boys. Often she had concealed them while they rested, and enjoyed her establishment.

Carrie Sue was not worried about her brother and his friends going there tonight. Miss Sally had a sly system of corded bells which warned men in certain rooms to flee out secret doors. Miss Sally's Parlor House was near the edge of town, and it would soon be dark. The men would be able to slip into and out of town without a problem, especially if Darby spent time with Miss Sally as usual.

After camp was set up, Carrie Sue encouraged all the men to go into town for diversion, but Kale Rushton refused. The half-Apache insisted on remaining with her for protection. She and Kale were relieved when Kadry and Dillon decided not to cause trouble tonight by trying to remain there to court her.

When the gang rode off, Carrie Sue glanced at Kale and said, "You stand guard, *amigo,* while I take a much needed bath. I want to look my best when they bring back that reporter. I hope the boys don't get too liquored up and make bad impressions on him. We need to clean up our image, not make it worse. I'm sure the man will start out prejudiced toward us, so we'll have to win him over with charm."

Kale told her, "Darby warned them to behave tonight because this task is important. The only one he'll need to watch is Tyler. He still drinks too much whiskey. I worry about him getting us caught. You know Darby and the boys wouldn't leave him behind if he got snared. Darby wouldn't leave any of us behind to face a rope."

"I know, Kale. He would die for any or all of you."

"You get cleaned up, *chica,* while I cook us some grub. I'm as hungry as a longhorn after a prairie fire burned all the grass."

It was long after midnight when Darby and his gang returned to camp. Kale Rushton and the redhead ceased their talk and set down their coffee cups. The half-Apache pocketed his whetstone and sheathed his knife before rising to go meet the boys. Two strangers were riding with them, and only one was blindfolded.

Darby dismounted and handed his reins to Kale. He grasped Carrie Sue's hand and said, "Come with me, Sis; we have to talk, now."

Carrie Sue realized something was wrong. She glanced at the man between Kadry and Dillon who was staring at her, then took a walk with her brother.

"What is it, Darby? Did anything happen in town tonight?"

"Plenty. Sis, there are a few things you and me need to discuss," he hinted, locking his eyes with hers.

Chapter Twenty-one

"What is it, Darby?" she asked when he continued to stare at her.

"We got that newspaper man and he was plenty willing to come along for the story. Sally said he's the best in Texas and a fair man. Name's William Ferguson. We'll give him our side tomorrow."

She smiled and hugged him. "That's wonderful, so why the sullen face? And who's the stranger with you?" she queried.

He replied to her last question, "Cliff Thomas. He was at Sally's tonight. I can use another man on the next few jobs. He rode with us when you were in Sante Fe all those months."

"That was years ago, Darby. You sure you can still trust him?"

"Yep, and it hasn't been years since our last job together. He rode with us after that ranch mess in Laredo and other times while you were holed up in camp."

"Why haven't I met him before?" she asked.

"He didn't come to camp between jobs. You know I never let many extras visit our hideout and see you; they met us other places. Now that your poster's out, it isn't necessary to protect your identity. That time we were on the trail for weeks, Cliff was with us. He's always been careful, so his face isn't known. He'll make a perfect scout for us like before. Don't worry about him; he's a good man."

"I'm confused," she murmured. "If everything went so

well in town, why are you acting so strangely? Was Sally mad at you?"

"Nope. Sally was better than ever tonight," he responded with a devilish grin. "She'd never betray me and the boys. What has me spooked is that friend of yours, T.J. Rogue, and your wanted posters."

Carrie Sue became alert. "Was he in town? Did you meet him?"

The auburn-haired man leaned against a tree. "He left yesterday morning, I'm sorry to say, 'cause I'd like a few words with your sweetheart about his feelings for you. If he loves you, maybe he'll help you escape when I get you some money. Least he can do is protect you in camp while me and the boys are raiding. He must be trying to locate you or he wouldn't be in this area. Too bad he's gone."

Carrie Sue wondered if T.J. was heading for Brownwood to battle Quade Harding like he said not long ago. If so, he was in danger. Quade had tried to kill him once and probably would try again. Or, he could be riding for Commanche just to see if she was there. Should she try to reach him, or was that a crazy idea?

"Cliff told me something real strange, Sis. Your posters were recalled by the Texas Rangers right after they were released. Most of them didn't even get put up anywhere. Cliff only saw two or three, 'cause they were yanked down quick as a wink. He said they weren't up any other place he's been lately. And that story about you in the papers was called a mistake. Now, the Rangers are claiming that new poster is Carrie Sue Stover, but you aren't the Texas Flame. They're saying that old poster is her and it ain't you."

"I don't understand," she murmured in total confusion.

"Quade told the law he was using your poster and reward to save your life until the real Texas Flame was captured. He said he was afraid you'd be killed by mistake before he could clear you. The law told Quade he couldn't put one out on someone who isn't a criminal, so they called them in. How do you make that out, Sis?"

She appeared baffled. "What could Quade be up to? It's crazy. T.J. showed me a poster, and Martin Ferris had one, and that sheriff who came to my room had one. For them to be called in so swiftly, a lot of them got loose! Are you sure Cliff's telling you the truth? I've never heard of wanted posters being withdrawn."

Her brother added, "I asked that newspaper man, and he said the same thing: no posters are out on Carrie Sue Stover with your picture, only one about a redhead called the Texas Flame. Mr. Ferguson said Quade Harding told the law they had the wrong woman. Said you'd worked for him for a long time and couldn't be involved. Quade vowed you two were together when the Flame was spotted riding with us. He's withdrawn his reward offer for Carrie Sue Stover."

She was shocked and alarmed. "Quade is crazy, but he's smart, too smart to pull this ridiculous stunt. How can he lie to the law? Doesn't he realize they'll discover the truth and arrest him?"

"Harding's never been worried about lying to the law. He's done it plenty of times. I think Curly wired him from Tucson and told him you weren't with us anymore, that you were starting a new life there. Harding was probably afraid you'd get killed before he could reach you, so he pulled that trick about the poster to get it called in. Don't you see, Sis? You aren't wanted now. Your name's been cleared. When I get you some money, you can get away clean." He tugged on a golden red curl and advised, "You need to cut this long hair and use some berries to darken it 'cause some folks have seen it. Thank goodness you were always masked. We'll make up a name for our famous sidekick and your past will be destroyed."

Carrie Sue paced in deep thought. Something wasn't right. Curly was killed right after seeing her, so he couldn't have wired Quade. Unless he wired Quade from El Paso after visiting Darby and told his boss she had quit the gang. It was like that sneaky Quade to disclaim her poster and guilt to give him time to locate her. Once she was cleared, he would assume he could force her to marry him! She related her conclusions to her brother, who agreed with them.

"You can always say you escaped Tucson because you were innocent but you knew no one would believe you. Good thing you didn't harm that sheriff and make yourself look guilty. This'll clear Rogue too."

She scoffed, "Until Quade admits he lied just to entrap me, or one of his hirelings does. It'll never work, Darby. There's something weird going on, and the law won't be fooled very long, if they're fooled at all. This could be a trick to ensnare Quade. They have to think it's odd that he's reversing his story. They'll figure out he lied and be on my trail again. I still have to vanish to be safe."

"You're right, Sis. I was too excited to think straight. Here in Texas, you'll always be Darby Stover's little sister. We'll let Harding help us clear you before I silence him forever. Once you're gone and Quade's dead, the law can't get to you or the truth. Let's get back to camp. We'll go over this again later."

He straightened up to leave. "I plan to hit the San Angelo bank tomorrow while you hold Ferguson captive here, talking his ears off. Then, we'll strike a gold coin shipment at Big Spring. Sally read a customer's telegram about it, a marshal who's to be there Monday to escort it to El Paso with his deputies. Me and the boys will take it on Sunday before they arrive. Gold coins can't be traced and they're worth plenty. Your freedom's in sight, Sis. You be sure to convince that newspaper man you've never ridden with us."

"That won't work, Darby. The minute Quade is dead, one of his men or hired detectives will come forward with the truth and I'll be on the wanted list again. He must be paying them plenty to keep them silent." Her violet-blue eyes enlarged and she frowned. "We know where he's getting the money for hush payments and our reward offers, from those frame jobs he's pulling. I have to tell Mr. Ferguson the truth so he can help us. Besides, people saw me in Tucson living as a woman killed during one of our robberies; that's too coincidental. It will make things worse for us, for me, if I mislead that reporter and the facts come out soon. People, especially the law, will assume that if we've lied about one thing, we've lied about others and we're no better off than before. He can get the truth out and lessen our perils."

Darby sighed heavily. "I guess I'm too tired to think straight. You're right, Sis. We need to unmask Harding and get you out of here."

William Ferguson spent hours questioning the men and taking notes. He couldn't believe his good fortune. He didn't mind that his legs and chest were secured to a chair when the gang got ready to leave camp to rob the bank in San Angelo. His hands were left free for writing and he promised not to pull any tricks with Carrie Sue, his guard.

Carrie Sue watched the eight men gallop away before taking a seat before the newspaper man with a pistol in her lap. She urged, "Please don't try anything, Mr. Ferguson, because I don't want you making me into a killer. Things have gotten desperate for us with that other gang on the loose, so I can't take any chances with my brother's life. It's time everyone learned the truth about us. I'm glad you came so willingly to hear it and report it."

They talked until two o'clock with the man taking down every word. Carrie Sue told him she was the Texas Flame and that Quade Harding had lied about knowing that fact. "Hopefully that will get him into deep trouble with the law. If they'll start investigating him, maybe they'll uncover other crimes. He's up to something, and I don't want to get entangled by his deceit."

William Ferguson knew Quade was not responsible for the poster ruse, but he could not tell her. "When I print this story, new posters will go out on you. This is a big risk, Carrie Sue."

"I know, but it'll unmask Quade Harding. I hate him."

"Why didn't you stick to Harding's lies and go free?"

She sighed wearily. "The law is too smart to be fooled very long, Bill. The truth would eventually come out and it would start over again. This is my one chance to tell our side. Your story can't clear us, but it can reveal the truth and help people understand."

Ferguson knew he couldn't print this story and endanger Thad Jamison's mission or risk having Quade expose the Ranger's demands. When it was over, he would print everything. He needed to get these facts to the lawman who might link up with her again soon.

In Commanche, T.J. was resentful over the two telegrams he picked up and read. His Ranger superior and the president still refused to consider a pardon for his love, and he was ordered to stay undercover as T.J. Rogue. That meant, no Brownwood and Harding yet. After he checked out the hiding place Carrie Sue had mentioned, he would decide what action to take next. It was frustrating. How, he worried, could he help her and protect her if he couldn't locate her? If anything happened to her, he'd never forgive himself. How could he live without his heart and soul, for she had stolen them. If he could just see her and reason with her, tell her the truth and convince her to comply with his plans.

In Stephenville, between Fort Worth and Brownwood, a train robbery was carried off by the alleged Stover Gang. One of the men was wounded while getting away. The masked Quade Harding reined in his horse, pulled his rifle, and shot his hireling to make certain he was dead and couldn't expose him. Before passing out, the outlaw saw Quade pull the trigger.

In San Angelo, the unmasked gang of Darby Stover was also having bad luck. After robbing the bank and handing the clerk a golden red lock from the Texas Flame, the frightened man pulled a small pistol from beneath the counter and shot the last man out the door: Cliff Thomas, who had turned to warn the people to stay quiet and motionless.

Walt Vinson checked Cliff quickly and said he was dead. Darby ordered the men to flee, and the gang got away with success.

In the Stover camp, Carrie Sue and William Ferguson were still talking, but she was calling him Bill now, as requested. She had given him their history and he had told her his impressions before and after meeting them, which pleased her. He believed the account of their frame and who was behind it. He told her about the witness he had found, the man who had been killed before speaking with the law.

"I can't print anything as fact without proof, Carrie Sue, but I can quote your statements. I think every newspaper in the country will print this. Everyone will be excited by it and wonder about your guilt. All you need to do is alert the authorities to Harding's mischief. They'll start an investigation which should help you. It won't clear any of you, but it will get many of those charges dropped. The shorter and weaker the list, the better your chances for a good defense when you're all captured. You have to face facts, Carrie Sue, criminals don't get away with their illegal deeds forever. What will happen to you?"

"As soon as the story's printed, I'm leaving. I may go to California, or Mexico, or Canada, or back East. I might even take a ship and get further away, maybe to England or one of those beautiful islands. I have to find a safe place to start over, Bill. You understand why I can't be clearer on that fact."

"Of course I do, young lady." He sent her an encouraging smile. "People want to know what makes honest folks go bad; this story will teach them something, maybe prevent other youngsters from taking the law into their own hands. It should also put a halt to the Hardings' crimes. After all these years, his treachery might get you justice in that matter. Is there anybody who can help you?"

Carrie Sue looked up from her evening meal preparations and gazed at him sadly for a moment as she thought about her lover. Where was T.J.? What was he doing and feeling? Would he trust her and want her back after her desertion and lies? Would any proud man? "No one. I told you what happened every time I tried to go straight or seek help."

"Those are some strong points in your favor that I believe the law will find of great interest, if you get a judge and jury who're fair. It's a shame you got in so deeply before this trouble could be cleared up with the Hardings. Those boys, too. They don't seem like bad fellows to me, not even that Kale Rushton. I could tell he didn't want to reveal anything about his experiences, but he did that just to help the rest of you. I don't often come across loyalty and love like that."

"The boys are real close, Bill. Any of them would die for the other."

"I'm sure of that, Carrie Sue. What else do you want me to print?"

The gang returned and halted their conversation. She was distressed to learn Cliff Thomas had been left behind. "Are you sure he was dead?"

"Yep, Walt checked him. Took a bullet in the heart. We left that lock of hair like you suggested, Sis. Make sure you put that in the story, Mr. Ferguson. That'll stop whoever's framing us."

"That was a clever idea, Carrie Sue, but a dangerous one. Those curls will tie you to the gang more tightly," Ferguson warned.

"It couldn't be helped. It was the only way to prove which

413

gang was attacking where. I'll be gone soon and out of danger."

The men eagerly devoured the beef stew and biscuits. Afterwards, they planned their departure in the morning for Big Spring. . . .

Darby asked Walt Vinson to show him his badge collection so he could find one or more to use during their next job, as Darby didn't want any trouble getting into the building where the gold was being held in secrecy. The men went to where Walt's possessions were outside near his bedroll, leaving Carrie Sue and William Ferguson in the shack.

When Darby saw the Texas Ranger badge with "Thad Jamison" on the back, he asked, "Where did you get this one, Walt?"

Walt looked at it and replied, "From that stage near Sherman. I took it offin that dead Ranger."

"What it is?" Kale questioned his friend's reaction.

"Read it, Kale. It says Thad Jamison. If we killed him, those Rangers will hunt us down forever. He's a legend."

"Legend," Dillon scoffed, "More like a mystery. You think he's for real?"

Kale Rushton responded, "He's for real, all right. He moves like a morning mist; you never see him, but you see where he's been. He hits an area, does his job secretly, then vanishes. Few people know him in person. You don't want to tangle with him; he's deadly, an expert in every area: guns, knives, bows, bare hands.

"We didn't kill Jamison, I met him at an Apache camp years ago. You remember that time I left you boys in camp and went to visit my mother's tribe. He was there, trying to work out some trouble between the whites and Indians. It wasn't him on the stage. Maybe that Ranger was carrying him a new badge."

Darby licked his lips nervously, then dropped the matter

414

from mind. "We have one U.S. Marshal badge and three deputy badges. I'll take this one. Kadry, Dillon, and Tyler will take the other three. With them, we'll get those guards to open the doors to that hotel room. After we get the drop on them, we'll let the rest of you inside. With these new beards and mustaches on me, Kadry, and Dillon, and with Tyler clean shaven, they won't recognize us 'til it's too late. I don't want any shooting, boys. We're trying to wash up our dirty reputations, not splatter 'em with fresh blood. If we make our next few hits without shedding blood, it'll go in our favor with that story."

At dawn on Friday, Darby Stover and his men rode off again, to return Monday night, leaving Carrie Sue to guard Ferguson once more.

Over coffee, she told him, "I'm sorry, Bill, but we can't release you until they return from Big Spring. I promise you will leave safely."

"Don't worry, Carrie Sue. We can talk easily for four more days. What was that talk about using badges last night?" he asked.

Carrie Sue explained how Darby intended to use badges which Walt Vinson collected to prevent any unnecessary killing during their holdup. "As I told you, my brother doesn't shoot unless his life's threatened, and he doesn't allow his men to do so either. Nearly every killing against us was committed by a man who was a temporary gangmember. Darby's always careful about who he lets join, but sometimes a bad seed gets past him. He gets rid of them the moment they disobey."

In San Angelo, the sheriff was questioning Cliff Thomas who had just aroused from his bullet wound. "You're damn lucky that slug was so small, Thomas. You can live through

415

this and get pardoned if you help us catch the Stover Gang. They can't have gotten too far. Which way were they heading? Speak up, man, or you'll hang tomorrow."

Cliff was in pain and was scared. "They didn't go nowhere, Sheriff. You put that promise in writing and I'll draw you a map to their camp."

The sheriff complied, but he knew he wouldn't keep his promise to this outlaw or to any criminal whom he tricked into capture. Cliff Thomas was propped up to draw a map to Darby's hideout on the Middle Concho River, west of town. "That ain't all, Sheriff," he hinted, but began to cough strenuously. He grabbed his chest as the bullet shifted in his heart and blocked a main artery, killing him before he could expose the Big Spring threat.

The doctor checked the outlaw and said, "Gone for sure this time."

"Don't matter; he would have hanged when he got well." He ordered his deputy to gather a posse, "a large one with plenty of guns."

Carrie Sue was glancing out the paneless window when she spotted movement around the trees and bushes. She hurried from side to side where wooden flaps were lifted for air flow and assessed the situation.

"What's wrong, Carrie Sue?" the gray-haired man asked.

"We've got a posse closing in on the shack. We're surrounded."

"Why don't you use me as a shield and hostage to bluff your way out?" he suggested, not wanting her captured.

"It's too dangerous, Bill. You could get shot by accident; posses are nervous men. I have to surrender peaceably to protect you." She went to William Ferguson and cut him free. Yanking off her bandanna, she ordered, "Tie my hands, Bill, quickly. Take my pistol and pretend you've overpowered me and captured me. There's no chance of escape for me, so it's rash to challenge them. I want you to get my reward, if there's one left. Just think what a wonderful story this will make: Newspaperman Captures Texas Flame!"

"Oh, my heavens," he murmured worriedly. He tied her wrists together, collected his valuable notes, and stuffed them inside his shirt. He led her outside at gunpoint with her bound hands lifted skyward. "Don't shoot!" he yelled when men showed their faces from behind trees. "It's me, William Ferguson, from the newspaper."

"Where are the others, Bill?" the sheriff shouted from cover.

"Gone. They left early this morning. I was kidnapped, but I got free and captured Darby's sister. She's harmless."

The sheriff and his posse came forward, eyeing the beautiful fugitive with great interest. "What in blazes are you doing here, Bill?"

The crafty newspaperman explained, "The Stovers say they're being framed. They vow they didn't commit any of those recent crimes. They abducted me to tell me their story so I could print it and inform the authorities. They claim Quade Harding, that fellow in Brownwood who offered those big rewards, is responsible. The gang's gone there to face him down and pull a job. She was guarding me, but I got the drop on her." He glanced at the silent beauty. "She's too nice and trusting," he added. "I believe their story."

The San Angelo sheriff studied Carrie Sue for a time. "It don't matter none. They're still outlaws. We'll catch 'em and they'll all hang."

No murmurs of approval were heard as the local men continued to stare at the ravishing creature beside William Ferguson, a woman whose expression was one of vulnerable innocence. They were awed by those large periwinkle eyes, her flowing tawny red mane, her soft rosy gold skin, and her gentle and delicate air.

"You say they left for Brownwood early this morning?" After Ferguson nodded, the sheriff said, "That should take them about three or four days round-trip. We'll have a posse waiting for them when they return. By Monday, we'll have them all in jail."

Carrie Sue recalled telling Ferguson that her brother always set out markers in all directions when leaving camp; that way Darby knew if it was safe to return there following a job. The gray-haired man also knew that the Stover Gang was heading northwest to Big Spring, not easterly. What she couldn't figure out was why this newspaper man lied to protect all of them because he knew Darby and his men, no matter which direction they had taken, would not ride back into a trap.

The offensive sheriff appeared to gloat when he said, "The Rangers called in your posters, but I guess this proves they were mistaken for a change. I'm sure the Flame's hair matches yours perfectly. I'll wire them we caught you dead-to-rights. You got anything to say, Miss Stover?" he asked tersely. "Where's the bank money?"

The redhead gazed at the belligerent lawman and, despite knowing it was a waste of breath, said, "I don't know. We're being framed, and the truth will come ot soon. That's all."

"I suppose you've been framed all these years?" he scoffed.

Carrie Sue glared at him. "Of course not, but I've nothing more to say. Mr. Peterson has all the facts. He'll print the truth."

"If the law lets him print such crap."

"Freedom of the press, Sheriff. I can print what they told me."

"Why would you want to do such a stupid thing, Bill?"

Calmly the man replied, "Two reasons, Sheriff. First, it's big news. No other paper has ever gotten an interview with the Stover Gang or any other gang. Second, I believe their account. I've studied this gang for years, and those recent crimes don't match their set style."

"Gangs don't have a style, Bill; they just rob and murder."

Ferguson smiled and shook his head. "I think the Rangers

will disagree with you there. I'm ready to get back to town and get moving on this news. For my story, how did you find this place?"

"That bastard they left behind recovered long enough to spill his guts about this place. Then, he keeled over before he could tell me about Brownwood. He's dead, not that it matters any."

Ferguson asked, "Can I come to the jail later and talk to her again?"

"Sure, but she'll be guarded heavily. I don't want that brother of hers busting her out. 'Course, he won't be back for a few days, and me and my men will be waiting right here to welcome him."

Ferguson didn't protest the grounds for her arrest. He figured jail was the safest place for her until he could reach Thad Jamison.

Carrie Sue's things were gathered and her horse was saddled. She was taken into town at the front of the posse and locked in the jail.

Time passed as the daring desperado contemplated her perilous predicament. She didn't think she needed to worry about her brother because he shouldn't fall for a trap. Yet, he might figure out what had happened to her and try to get her out of jail. Carrie Sue couldn't send word to Sally to warn him because that would expose the woman who loved and aided her brother. She couldn't get William Ferguson more involved than he already was. She dared not wire Hank Ferguson or Mitchell Sterling and call attention to them. If only T.J. were here, but she didn't know how or where to locate him. She was trapped, and all she could do was wait for the firm hand of justice to punish her.

William Ferguson sent a wire to Commanche, but T.J. Rogue didn't respond to it. He visited Carrie Sue briefly in her cell and was tempted to reveal news about Thad Jamison's help, but decided against exposing the lawman who had trusted him. He went back to his office and continued to work on the legendary story. He wished Jamison would answer his telegram and wondered why the man hadn't done so.

An hour later, the *San Angelo Tribune* owner and writer received news of a Stover Gang robbery in Stephenville which had occurred almost simultaneously with Darby's hit in San Angelo. A reporter there telegraphed that a wounded outlaw had been captured and jailed, and asked Ferguson to come interview the man and split the story. Ferguson chuckled — the Stephenville reporter said that Bill could get information out of a silence-vowed monk.

Ferguson went to see Carrie Sue again and told her about the other crime and his trip to Stephenville tomorrow. "I need to get there before he dies or decides not to talk, or gives somebody else his story. If he incriminates Quade Harding, this could be the break you need, Carrie Sue. But whatever happens with him, the law will realize Darby Stover couldn't be in two towns on the same day. They'll have to begin an investigation. I'm glad your brother hit the bank here yesterday to back up my story and your claims, but I surely did hate to lose my money in that holdup." He chuckled.

She promised in a serious tone, "Darby hid it, but I'll make certain he gets it back to you. And don't forget about collecting the reward for my capture. Good luck, Bill, and thanks . . . for everything."

Ferguson grasped the meaning of her last two words. He smiled and nodded. "I'll get you the best lawyer in the state, and I'll keep after the authorities until they listen to our side."

The sheriff unlocked the cell and ordered Bill to end his task.

Before leaving, Ferguson said, "I'm going to Stephenville for a story tomorrow. You take good care of Miss Stover. Make sure she isn't harmed or harassed, or you'll see yourself in bad print."

"Come on, Bill, don't threaten me," he said with a vexed laugh.

"No threat, Sheriff, a promise."

T.J. showed up at William Ferguson's home at nine o'clock. The newspaper owner was delighted and surprised to see the lawman. He told T.J. what had happened and of his impending plans.

The stunned T.J. said, "I heard about both robberies Thursday when I was in the telegraph office in Commanche, so I hightailed it back here when this one mentioned a fiery lock of hair as proof it was the Stover Gang's. Leaving such evidence against her was a stupid thing for her brother to do!" he stated with rising fury. He ordered himself to calm down and handle this matter with clear wits. "I didn't get your wire about her capture, but I wanted to see you before I met with three Rangers at the hotel. I wired them to meet me here tonight so we can make a plan to end this matter before she gets hurt. You head on to Stephenville and get that man to talk. Offer him anything, just open his mouth. I'll arrange a jailbreak for Carrie Sue tonight and get her to lead us to her brother's gang. I have to end this quickly."

Ferguson brushed over the highlights of his visit and interview with the gang. He cautioned, "Don't trust the sheriff here, Thad; he's set on taking them any way necessary. I said they were heading for Brownwood, but it's Big Spring like I told you. I knew it was better to give you that information rather than to tell him. You and those Rangers should head that way or they'll be gunned down if they return to his camp on the Concho River. You going to warn Big Spring?"

T.J. pondered his movements carefully. "Nope. If they plan an ambush for Darby and his boys on Sunday, it'll be a slaughter. Let them carry out the robbery and we'll capture them on their way back. With Rangers heading up the posse, everything should go smoothly."

"What will Carrie Sue say when she discovers the truth?"

"You didn't tell her anything about me, did you?"

"Certainly not, my friend, but I was sorely tempted."

"I'll have a talk with her before we reach her brother. I'll make her understand this is the only way to save his life. You get that evidence against Quade Harding because we'll need it at Darby's trial. I have another plan I'll need help with, Bill, so hurry back to town."

"What is it?" the newspaper owner inquired, intrigued.

When Lawman Thaddeus Jerome Jamison explained, William Ferguson's eyes widened in disbelief. Then, he smiled and nodded . . .

T.J. met with the three Texas Rangers who agreed with his bold plan to capture the Stover Gang in a location which wouldn't endanger town citizens. The San Angelo sheriff was summoned and persuaded to go along with her jailbreak. After the sheriff left to dismiss his deputies, T.J. told the Rangers how he would mark the trail for them to follow.

"Hang back at night, 'cause she's alert and wary. I'll need time to convince her I'm on her side. Monday morning, move in closer. That's when we should meet up with her brother on the trail back to San Angelo. We'll need a posse to prevent any gaps they can slip through. I want this case over with as quickly and cleanly as possible. Warn the men, no shooting unless fired upon and you give the signal. I want this gang taken alive. Understand?"

In Brownwood, Quade Harding left his ranch with his gang. The San Angelo sheriff had telegraphed him, in case the man was still interested in Carrie Sue Stover and her reward was still available. But Quade hadn't heard about the curious happening in Stephenville . . .

Carrie Sue realized she could not wait for Darby or T.J. to hear about her capture and risk freeing her. She had to escape, tonight! The sheriff seemed to cooperate unknowingly when he returned to the jail and dismissed his two deputies, telling them he was going to sleep there and to replace him at seven in the morning.

When the jail was quiet, she walked to the bars and called out, "Sheriff, can I see you a minute? I have something to say." As he got off the bunk, she pretended to trip and fall. She slammed her hand against the bars so it sounded as if her head had struck them. She groaned and lay still.

"Damn!" the man swore, worried about her being injured while in his care. How would he explain this to those Rangers? He hurriedly fetched the key and unlocked the door.

As he knelt beside the redhead and tried to help the dazed woman to her feet, Carrie Sue yanked the pistol from his holster. "Don't move or shout, Sheriff, or you're dead before help arrives. Just back away, real slow and careful."

While keeping her eyes on him, she left the cell and got his handcuffs. She returned to fasten them on his wrists. Afterwards, she gagged him, then secured him to the bars using his belt. The redhead locked the cell door and tossed the keys on the man's desk.

Ignoring her aching wrist, Carrie Sue strapped on her gunbelt and checked her revolvers. She gathered her belongings from a pile in the front corner. She would have to steal a horse, any one she could find close by. She stiffened in alarm when someone knocked on the door and called out in a muffled voice, "It's me, Sheriff, open up."

Carrie Sue knew she had to let the man inside or he would know something was wrong and sound a warning. She stood behind the door as she unlocked it and opened it, her pistol in her hand. She closed it quickly and said, "Don't move or you'll catch my bullets in your gut."

The masked man turned to face her, his twinkling eyes revealing his identity. He glanced toward the imprisoned sheriff, then back at her. He laughed and said, "I see you didn't need my help after all, Sis."

She smiled and said, "Darby! I knew you'd come, but this is reckless. Let's get moving before somebody sees us."

They gathered her things and sneaked out the door, locking it behind them. He had horses waiting around back. They mounted and left San Angelo quietly. Outside town, they changed to a swift gallop.

Chapter Twenty-two

They rode for over an hour before halting to speak briefly without dismounting. It was Saturday, June seventeenth, in the wee hours of the morning. They edged their mounts close together and caused their legs to make contact. Beneath the half-moon, they gazed at each other.

"You all right, love?" he asked, unable to pull his eyes from hers.

"Wonderful, partner. That was a good trick we pulled back there. I'm glad I told you Darby calls me Sis. That sheriff will be utterly confused and annoyed. At least I was quick-witted enough not to expose you. How did you find me, T.J., and why take such a big risk?"

He leaned forward and pulled her head toward him to kiss her before saying, "I should yank you off that horse, woman, and spank you good. Running out on me in El Paso was a dumb thing to do. See where it got you. From now on, you stick with me. Understand?"

Carrie Sue grinned as she caressed his stubbled jaw. "Yes sir, partner. Merciful Heavens, it's good to see your handsome face." She leaned toward him to kiss him again, savoring his lips and touch.

Both trembled and warmed. When they parted, he said, "We don't have time to fool around, you hotblooded vixen, so we'd better stop tempting each other before we lose our heads and lives. We need to put plenty of miles between us and San Angelo. We'll talk later, woman; you just behave for now."

"You didn't say how you found me," she pressed.

"I was in the Commanche telegraph office when word came in about the bank job here and your capture. I was sending Hank a message to see if he'd heard from you. I've been half-crazy with worry. Lordy, I'm glad you're safe and sound." He looked her over as if making certain she was unharmed. "You sent me on quite a wild chase, you sly woman. I checked out that place you mentioned near Commanche, but clearly you weren't heading there. I understand why you gave me the slip, Carrie Sue, but I don't agree with you being so impulsive just to protect me and Darby. I actually panicked when you were captured. I rushed here pronto to get you out of trouble. When that story comes out, the law won't know what to think or do."

"What story?" she inquired, new suspicions flooding her.

His eyes glowed. "Haven't you heard? That other band robbed a train in Stephenville and called themselves the Stover Gang. It happened on the same day Darby hit the bank here. The law has to realize somebody's framing them, just like your note said. Why did you think I wouldn't believe you? If anybody knows your brother, it's you."

"I was too scared and dull-witted. Quade Harding's to blame; I'm certain of it. You'll never guess what's been going on here," she hinted, then explained quickly what had taken place since they parted.

T.J. grinned as if her revelations were news to him. "That's a clever trick, woman, using the papers to clear yourselves. After those two holdups at the same time, the law will have to listen to your brother's side. I just wish all of his crimes were frame jobs." His tender gaze locked with hers. "You want to warn him before I take you far away? 'Cause that's exactly what I'm going to do, pronto."

She appeared surprised. "What about your revenge on Quade?"

"If the law doesn't get him this time, one day I'll come back

426

for him. Right now, you're my main concern. I love you, Carrie Sue Stover, and I want you to marry me when this mess is cleared up. I have to make certain you get out of this perilous existence."

Her mouth parted and her eyes enlarged with astonishment. "You what?" she asked, hoping she had heard him correctly.

He responded, "I love you and want to marry you. We'll go to Wyoming, or Montana, or some place and start a new life together. You did say you love me in that note. It wasn't a lie, was it?"

Happiness surged through her at his unexpected proposal, and at the engulfing look in his smokey gray eyes. "No, it wasn't a lie. I love you, T.J. Rogue, and I want to marry you. If we can just get far enough away from my past, it'll work."

He lifted her from her saddle and placed her on his thighs. He kissed her deeply and longingly. "I love you, woman, and I would do just about anything for you. I'll make certain you stay safe and happy from now on. I promise I won't ever let you change your mind about us."

"I could never stop loving you and wanting you," she murmured.

"I hope not, Carrie Sue, because you're mine forever."

They kissed and embraced again, then parted.

T.J. helped her back into her saddle. "We have to make tracks, love. There's only one question left: do we head for parts unknown this minute or do we locate your brother to warn him and say good-bye?"

Her heart bubbling with love and joy, she disclosed, "Darby's in Big Spring, waiting to pull off a robbery on Sunday. If we head that way, we'll meet him on the trail. I'd like to warn him and tell him good-bye, and I'd like him to meet my future husband. He heard you were in San Angelo before our arrival. He said he wished you'd hung around so he could question your intentions toward his little sister and entice you to take on my permanent protection."

A broad smile lifted the corners of T.J.'s mouth because she had told him the truth. At last, she trusted him completely. Lordy, how he hated to tell her his truth tomorrow night, at least part of it. Hopefully she wouldn't lose faith in him or change her feelings toward him before he could confide the rest of it. "That's the best job offer I've ever received, woman. Consider me hired."

Carrie Sue asked, "You think we should swing by the camp and make sure those warning markers are down in case we miss Darby and the boys on the road? Thoughts of a trap make me cringe."

"I think it's too dangerous. If that sheriff gets free before morning, he'll have a posse on our tail. He'll probably look in the last place he thinks we would think he wouldn't look." He chuckled.

Carrie Sue laughed too. "You're right, my love. Let's put some miles between us and talk later. Which way, partner?"

T.J. had taken off from town in an eastward direction to prevent suspicion. He took the lead and off they galloped northwesterly, to travel for many hours before taking a break, then journeying until dark.

William Ferguson left on the nine o'clock stage for Stephenville to question the bandit in jail there. He wanted to hurry this interview and return to San Angelo before the final story came to light. . . .

Quade Harding and his boys were heading toward San Angelo, but would arrive long after the posse — led by three Texas Rangers — left town to trail undercover Ranger Thad Jamison and his unsuspecting sweetheart Carrie Sue Stover . . .

Near Big Spring, Darby Stover and his gang camped outside town to await their action the next morning. The settlement had grown up around a natural spring on Sulphur Draw, a past and present watering hole for buffalo, antelope, wild mustangs, Indians, stage passengers, soldiers, and drifters. At ten o'clock in the morning, when most folks were in church, they would sneak into town, use their stolen badges, take the gold, and ride back for camp. It was a simple and crafty plan, and the boys were eager to get money for Carrie Sue's future.

As the last light of day was vanishing, T.J. and Carrie Sue halted to make camp. She asked, "You think it's safe to stop for the night?"

He gave a sly response, "You told me that sheriff thinks the gang was heading for Brownwood, and we did set a trail in that direction."

"But I called you Darby, so he'll think my brother rescued me. There's no telling which area he'll search, maybe all of them."

"You don't imagine he'll think Darby had a lookout posted who warned him about your capture so he could return and rescue you? Or maybe he'll think the guard rescued you," he hinted to mislead her.

Suddenly she laughed and said, "I bet he thinks I called the lookout Darby just to fool him into believing my brother wasn't heading for Brownwood. That sheriff was hateful. When he gets loose, after what that newspaper man told him, I'm sure he'll head straight for the Harding Ranch to look for the Stover Gang. Besides, we've ridden hard and fast for hours, so we have to be way ahead of any posse. They'll have to stop for rest, too, and they can't track in the dark."

T.J. noticed how she was flexing and rubbing her right wrist. "What's wrong, love. That wrist giving you trouble? Let me take a look."

He examined it and heard how she had injured it in the cell. "It's swollen and discolored, probably sprained." His fingers checked the area as gently as possible. "I don't feel any break. I'll wrap it tightly to take off the pressure. You should have told me sooner."

"We didn't have time to fiddle with a complaining wrist. It'll be fine in a day or two. Just sore and tingly. Ouch," she muttered when she flexed it too roughly to prove her point.

"You can't fool me, woman; I know it hurts. I've had sprains before. Holding that heavy pistol had to annoy it. You even burst a vein or two and it's bled under the skin." T.J. wrapped one of his bandannas securely around her wrist to remove the strain on it. "Try not to use it more than necessary. I'll do the chores. You rest."

He chuckled and teased, "I know how you love cold biscuits, beans from the can, and no coffee, so that's what I'll serve tonight. We shouldn't have a fire, just in case that sheriff is smarter than you think."

Carrie Sue observed her lover at work while she leaned against a tree and sipped water. She jested, "Maybe we should ride south to the Mexican border and ask King Fisher to hide us a while. From what Mitch was saying, the law's scared of him and can't snare him. I've met the King, twice."

"You have? When? How?"

"After that trouble in Laredo, we rode to Eagle Pass to cross the Rio Grande into Piedras Negras to lay low a while. He halted us and questioned us, then let us pass through his territory, after spending the night in his hidden camp, just like with Naiche. Then, he insisted we stop by again on our way back into Texas."

"You know where King Fisher's camp is located?"

"Sure, it's easy to find if you know where to look." She told the lawman how to reach the hideout of the bandit leader whom the Rangers were eager to apprehend, along with his band of around a hundred men.

T.J. sent her a pleased smile which she didn't grasp the

430

meaning of, which was one of relief. Surely this piece of valuable information would be worth something to the Texas authorities. If Carrie Sue could help him get the Stover Gang, Quade Harding, and King Fisher, surely that would earn her a pardon! What difference did it make to T.J. that she wasn't helping him willingly or knowingly? After the fact, he would claim she had assisted him in all three cases and make her agree! But if the authorities and his friends in high positions still didn't help him save his love, he would take that matter into his own hands!

Carrie Sue broke into his line of thought with, "We should link up with Darby by tomorrow afternoon, if nothing went wrong in Big Spring. He always travels one mile right of the road so me or the boys can catch up if any of us gets separated during a job. We'll ride in that area and eventually meet up with him. I can't wait to see his face when we turn up together. He'll be glad you're with me."

"I hope so; Darby sounds mighty protective to me. Where'd you get those clothes?" he asked, eyeing the Mexican garments which she had donned to look more feminine to William Ferguson.

"I stole them from Mitch's wife," she admitted. Carrie Sue related how she had disguised herself to get out of El Paso. "Was your friend upset with me for stealing his sorrel? How did you get him back?"

T.J. chuckled. "Seems our tastes run the same in horse-flesh, love. That's the horse I traded for Charlie. Mitch was going to take your pinto across the border to sell so he wouldn't get caught with it."

"You mean I stole my own horse?" she ventured merrily.

"Yep. But those clothes were definitely a theft. I'll send Mitch the money to pay for them. You do look good like that." He licked his lips and let his gaze roam her silky flesh before answering her other query. "I figured the sheriff had stabled Charo at the livery. I sneaked him and your saddle out before I came to rescue you."

"Charo, that's a good name. I'm glad you got him back for me."

After they ate and T.J. cleared the dishes, he asked, "Want to take a cool swim before we turn in? That was a hot and dusty ride."

Carrie Sue glanced at the inviting North Concho River nearby with moonlight dancing on its surface. "Yep, partner, sounds wonderful."

They walked to the bank and removed their clothes, after T.J. asked huskily if she needed any assistance with hers. He swam for a time, and the happy redhead was content to bathe and to watch her lover's sleek body.

T.J. knew they wouldn't be disturbed tonight because he had dropped a marker where he wanted the Rangers and posse to camp for the night, miles behind them. He had also warned them to hang back at night so as not to spook her. He needed to tell her part of the truth tonight, but he dreaded it because he couldn't decide how she would react.

The ebon-haired man joined her in the shallow water, resting on his knees before her. His smokey gray eyes studied her compelling beauty in the moonlight. "Lordy, you get me hotter than a horseshoe in the flames. I can't imagine what it's going to be like to have you as my wife forever, to be with you day and night, but I've surely dreamed about it countless times. How will I ever get any work done on our new ranch knowing you're in the house and I can go see you any time?"

Her wet hand drifted through his mussed hair. "The best way to solve that problem is to have me work at your side during the day and sleep there at night. I've worked a ranch twice, so I'll be helpful. We'll be good together, T.J., perfect."

T.J. captured her hand and pressed kisses to it. "I'm sure there's plenty I don't know about ranching, but you can teach me or we can learn together. Just like I'll help you in the house after we finish our chores outside. I've taken care of myself for years, so I know how to cook, sew on buttons and stitch up tears, wash dishes, and do other stuff. I've been in homes where an exhausted wife had to share the husband's chores during the day, then get no help with hers at night. I don't think that's fair, Carrie Sue, and it won't happen with us."

"You're one special man, T.J. Rogue. I love you." She pulled his mouth to hers and kissed him with a rising fever of desire.

Their lips fused into passionate kiss after tender kiss. Their hands caressed bare, wet flesh and caused each other to tingle and glow. Their bodies blazed with love's consuming flames. T.J. lifted her and placed her on the soft grass, and they embraced with eagerness.

T.J.'s lips seared over her face and his hands roved her body. He murmured hoarsely, "I love you, Carrie Sue. I've never told another woman that, and didn't know what love was until I met you. This has to be love because I feel all kinds of things for you. Not just physically," he confessed, "but everything. I want to be with you all the time. Just to talk or have fun. You make me feel good all over, taut as a bow and loose as a broken string at the same time. I get pleasure just from looking at you or hearing your voice. Sometimes I can't even control myself around you, and Lord knows that's never happened with a female before. I want to protect you and make you happy. Lordy, I'd die if I lost you."

"You won't ever lose me, my love. We're a perfect match in spirit, body, and lives. We'll be so happy together; I'm certain of it." Her fingers wandered over his firm shoulders and into the crevice of his spine. She loved the feel of his cool skin beneath her warm hands. She loved the possessive—but gentle—way he held her, touched her, responded to her, made love to her. Their relationship was nothing like the unions she had heard about at Sally's; her man didn't just take satisfaction from her. T.J. gave to her, shared with her, made sure she enjoyed their union as much as he did.

Carrie Sue sighed with contentment, knowing that soon she could have him any time she desired him and as many times as her body burned for his. Soon, they would have a home, a family, freedom. It was going to be sheer ecstasy to be his wife.

"The first time I saw you, T.J. Rogue, you scattered my wits and sent my mind to day-dreaming about you. That night at the burned station, I knew something was going to happen between us. I'd never been pulled toward a man like that before, and I didn't want to resist you. I was just too scared to chase you because of my past. After you visited my room that night, I was afraid not to tell you who and what I am, but I was more afraid you'd discover the truth one day and hate me. Merciful Heavens, I wanted and needed you so badly, but it was such a terrible risk to take. I love you so much."

Their loving words ceased as they kissed. Their bodies joined, fusing their spirits and souls. The blissful tensions mounted within them until they could no longer hold back the flood of desire which coursed through them. Their dams of restraint shattered and they were washed away by stormy passion.

Carrie Sue and T.J. were swept passed beautiful islands of sensation which tossed blossoms of delight into their paths. They were carried onward by powerful waves, caressed and stimulated by love's waters, and sent gasping for breath as they were pulled beneath the rapturous surface time and time again. The stormy tide seemed endless; yet, eventually they arrived on a peaceful shore. There, they lay exhausted from their stirring efforts, savoring their wondrous triumph.

They were tired, but it was a serene fatigue. They knew they needed sleep, so they didn't tarry long at their location. They rinsed in the river, dried off, and donned their riding clothes. They would sleep dressed, in case they had to make a fast getaway.

As T.J. put a dry wrap on Carrie Sue's sprained wrist, she laughed and said, "I don't even know your name. What does T.J. stand for?"

He completed his task and sat beside her on the bedroll.

"It's time for you to learn more about me since we're going to be married soon. Just hold your temper, Red, until I explain everything. I took the name Rogue because I was angry with my father for getting himself and my family killed. I was pretty bitter and was striking out at anything. When I was at the orphanage, the people in town called me a half-savage rogue, and the name stuck to me.,"

"You mean it isn't your name?" she inquired, all ears.

"Nope. My real name is Thaddeus Jerome Jamison, but I've gone by T.J. since I was born. Sometimes close friends call me Thad."

"Thad Jamison? *The* Thad Jamison, the mysterious legend?" she said, panic striking her when he nodded. "You're a . . . a *Texas Ranger,* aren't you?" When he kept his tender gaze locked to hers and nodded, her mouth went dry and her lips remained parted. Her heart pounded. Her chest rose and fell rapidly. She felt cold, weak, nauseous. She felt as if he had just stabbed her in the heart with a knife. She stared at him.

T.J. vowed in a serious tone, "I meant everything I said tonight, Carrie Sue. I love you and want to marry you. I want us to go to Montana where you'll be safe. If we stay here, I can't have you."

"But you're a lawman, a famous lawman. Why would you help me escape? Are you hoping I'll be tricked into leading you to Darby? That's what I suspected all along, but I let you get to me with your lies!"

He demanded, "Hear me out, Carrie Sue. Dammit, I love you and want to marry you. I swear I'm taking you to safety. I could never let you be captured, or jailed, or hanged. The only way to save you and have you is to leave Texas and the Rangers; that's what I'll do. Give me a chance to explain everything, please."

"What have I got to lose? I'm your prisoner already. Talk, Mr. Ranger, and I'll listen, but don't expect me to be duped again."

"Just keep an open mind until you hear what I have to say.

435

When I met you, I was on Curly James's trail, for the reason I told you. He did barbwire me to that tree and leave me to die, on Quade Harding's orders. Harding discovered who I was and that I was investigating him. The Rangers had received tips on his underhanded dealings and I was sent to check them out. He overheard me talking with another Ranger. That's why I've had to stay clear of him; he knows I'm Thad Jamison. We figured if he believed I was dead, he would relax and make a slip. We assigned another undercover Ranger to him, Dave Clemmens, but he was killed recently. When they found his body, there was a note pinned to his chest." He told her what the note said and how it was signed. When she gasped in shock and her eyes widened, he added, "You don't have to convince me your brother didn't do it. I know Darby Stover wasn't involved in any way."

Carrie Sue remained quiet and alert.

"If you're wondering if I was spying on you in Tucson, yes, I was. You can hardly blame me for being suspicious of a woman who acted so strangely and had such skills. But I had no idea who you were; I swear. I lied about Nighthawk's injury and collecting those rewards because I needed a logical reason to hang around town waiting for Curly."

"How did you know he was heading for Tucson?" she probed.

"The other two men told me before I killed them. They were to link up in El Paso, then head for Tucson to work for Ferris. I got them first, then beat Curly there. Mitch sent me a telegram about that Union Express job. That's the day you saw me coming out of the telegraph office when you were with Ferris. The Stover Gang was my next assignment, but I didn't connect you with the Texas Flame. I suppose because I was too involved with you to think clearly. You had my head clouded. But what could I do? I couldn't tell you who and what I am: I'm sworn to secrecy by the Rangers and the President. And I couldn't offer you anything without being honest with you. I figured, whatever would a proper schoolmarm see or want with a common gunslinger like T.J. Rogue? But Lordy you twisted up my guts with crazy feelings."

"Which is more important, T.J., your job or me?" she challenged.

He urged, "Let me finish first, then you'll know the answer. When Joe Collins came to my room the night before we escaped, he showed me the new poster for Carrie Sue Stover. I was stunned. I couldn't believe you were the Texas Flame, but it all made sense."

"Joe Collins? He's that lawman who came to my room?"

"Yep, but that was a ruse to force you to take me along when you fled. He wasn't hurt, and he was never on our trail. That's why I could come and go as usual; he wasn't after me. I'm sorry, love, but it was the only way I could get you out of town safely and quietly. I realized why you were in Tucson and I was sorry it wasn't going to work out for you, thanks to that damn Quade Harding!"

He mastered his anger so he could continue. "I wanted to save you and help you, Carrie Sue. I couldn't let you face posses and bounty hunters alone. And I wasn't about to put the woman I love in prison or at the end of a noose. At first, I was going to offer you a pardon if you'd help me capture your brother's gang. But I knew you'd never betray or endanger him for any reason. Yet, I hoped you'd want to stop his life of crime on innocent victims. If I could help you get a pardon, then you could lead a normal life somewhere, hopefully with me. I knew you must be tired of running and hiding and being an outlaw. I recalled little clues you dropped about your old life, about prison and such. I believed you wanted out, and I was determined to help you go straight. But first, I had to defeat your brother. Nobody's ever been able to get near Darby Stover, so I used you. I'm sorry and I feel guilty as hell, but I felt I had to get him any way necessary."

T.J. propped his elbows on his raised legs and rested his chin on interlocked hands. "But something happened along the way. I had rescued and was protecting a beautiful desperado with hopes of her assisting my case, but there was no one to protect me from you. I discovered I loved you and wanted you desperately. I had to find a way to clear you. The problem is, you're guilty; you're an outlaw. No frame or misunderstanding to clear up for exoneration. What could I do? Lordy, I was as ensnared by your past as you were. I didn't want to ask myself what you would do and say when you learned the truth about me. I didn't want to think about how my capturing your brother would affect our relationship. I kept telling myself I should be thinking only of my mission, but how could I with you nearby? Lordy, I've never been in such a predicament, such a scary trap."

"So what happens to me? To us?" she inquired sadly.

He didn't reply. "That day I vanished in the Chiricahuas, I went to tap into the telegraph line. I sent messages asking for the government to help the Apaches, as I promised Naiche when I saw him. I wired Collins about Martin Ferris. And I wired the Rangers and President about granting you a pardon. I told them you were aiding my case."

"But that was a lie!" she shrieked.

"I know, but I was desperate, Carrie Sue. I had to remove the threats to you. How could we have a life together if you were killed or imprisoned? I told you, I was going loco over our situation. When we reached Deming, I sent more telegrams and picked up some waiting for me. I learned about those jobs in Hillsboro, Eastland, and Big Spring which your brother supposedly committed. I know he's innocent of those charges, Carrie Sue, and I'm certain Harding's to blame. I also let Hank Peterson know we were on the way to his place."

She asked, "Who is Hank Peterson? And Mitchell Sterling?"

"Retired Rangers who still give help when we need it. They're deeply respected and the authorities listen to them. They're both good friends of mine. I've worked with them many times in the past and they agreed to help me in this matter. They know I love you and I'm trying to carry out this mission without damaging our relationship."

She murmured, "That can't be done, T.J. How can I marry you if you destroy my brother? How can you marry me if I'm captured?"

"That's why I found myself in such a tight bind, woman. To get the Stover Gang, I had to risk losing you. Unless I could get you pardoned. They've refused to cooperate on one, but I kept hoping they would reconsider because of all I've done for them," he revealed.

"And?" she hinted.

"No luck," he admitted. "One reason is the law thinks the gang's behind those recent crimes, and they're bad ones. When we were at Mitch's, I wired Dave Clemmens to speed up the Harding case, but he was killed a few days later. Maybe because I provoked him into doing something rash just to help us. After you ran out on me, I was afraid you'd messed up any chance I had of getting you exonerated. Then, I got word on the Brady holdup. I'd studied your brother's gang, so something didn't seem right. I came to the same conclusion you did, a frame job by Harding. I had to find you before you fell into his hands again, or got into more trouble with Darby."

Carrie Sue made no attempt to battle him or escape. "Quade is up to something more than framing us. He had my posters yanked until he could get to me. The law will know soon, because I told that newspaper man the truth to entrap Quade. I'm certain Curly was working for him, but you killed the snake before he could betray me."

T.J. gave her a stunning response. "It wasn't Quade, Carrie Sue. I convinced the Rangers to withdraw those posters so you would be safe on the trail. I told them I couldn't get near the gang with you if we were being chased. They were pulled down right after we left Tucson."

She stared at him. "I don't understand. William Ferguson

told me Quade did it. It was in all the papers."

"That's the story we put out to explain yanking them. We told Harding we had proof Carrie Sue Stover wasn't the Texas Flame, and we were pulling her posters. He was madder than a hornet with his nest shot down, but he was worried about how much we knew. He guessed we were up to something; either we were using you, or you were helping us to earn a pardon. He figured he'd better comply or risk exposure and charges for suppressing evidence for years. He agreed to tell the papers his poster and reward were put out to protect you until he could prove your innocence, which is what the lying bastard claims is true. In return, the Rangers said he didn't know what he did was illegal and no charges would be filed against him. Your posters were yanked and those old ones were put out again as the Flame."

"If I was cleared publicly, why was I arrested?"

"Because you were caught in Darby's camp, holding a prisoner. And that business with the Flame's lock proved you were guilty. The sheriff wired the Rangers and told them he had captured you red-handed." T.J. shifted his position. "I rode to Commanche with hopes you'd told the truth about going there, but you hadn't. While I was wiring Hank about news from you, I heard about the simultaneous San Angelo and Stephenville crimes. I knew Darby was on the move again and you'd be with him. Then, word came of your capture. Lordy, I was afraid Harding would bust you out of jail before I could."

Both were silent for a while. Then, the flaming haired fugitive asked, "Why do you hate my brother, T.J.? There had to be more than your job driving you after him. If you truly love me and want me, then you'd have given up this mission for our future. There has to be a personal motive in here somewhere. What is it?"

"As I always said, woman, you're too smart to be fooled very long. You're right; I did have revenge in mind. I insisted on having this assignment, before I met you and discovered who you are. Ever since March, all I could think about was killing the entire gang."

"Why?" she demanded when he fell silent again.

T.J. needed strength on his side to win her over to his until everything was resolved, and he hoped the truth would do that vital job for him. "There was a stage holdup near San Angelo on March twenty-second. A woman and child were murdered. Do you recall that incident, Carrie Sue? Were you along that day?"

At his tone and expression, a cold chill swept over her. "Yes I was there. I can't forget what happened."

"Do you also remember the robbery on April twenty-eighth when you became Carolyn Starns? A Ranger was killed when the stage was pursued and crashed. He was a good friend of mine. He saved my life when I was barbwired to that tree. I owed him justice, vengeance."

Her frantic mind was still lingering on his earlier hint, so she asked, "Who were the woman and child? Did you know them?"

"Arabella and Marie Jamison."

"Jamison?" she echoed in dread, wondering if his next words would be *my wife and child,* and she prayed they wouldn't be.

In a strained tone, he disclosed, "My brother's wife and daughter. Tim and I hadn't seen each other since our captures by the Apaches. We got news of each other's survival and location around Christmas time. We were planning to be reunited soon, but Tim was killed by Mexican bandits in February. When I received the news of his murder, I sent for his widow and child. I had intended to marry Arabella and raise Marie as my own daughter, but they didn't reach Fort Worth because of the Stover Gang."

Carrie Sue gaped at him as those staggering words sank in. Her heart was tormented by anguish and was filled with sympathy. "I'm sorry, T.J.; I didn't know. . . ." She lapsed into remorseful silence.

"Those three deaths in March came right atop my brother's in February. I was furious. Within two months, I'd gone from finding my family to not having one again. I wanted to kill every member of that gang, including Darby's sister. I was on Curly's trail, and the Stover Gang was laying low, so I decided to finish with him before taking off after your brother and his boys, which I figured would take a long time. Headquarters was keeping a file on Darby's movements, but I didn't know that the Sherman job was pulled by Darby until Joe Collins came to fill me in. You were acting strange, so I thought you were in trouble. I asked a Ranger friend to check you out so I could help you. Joe told me the Stover Gang pulled that holdup and he showed me your poster. That's the first time I knew about you; I swear it."

T.J. couldn't let her believe she was his second choice or that he fell in love with her because he was agonizing over a lost family. "There's something else I have to explain, Carrie Sue. I wasn't in love with Arabella — I didn't even know her — but I would have married her if she'd reached Fort Worth alive. You know from experience what happens to a woman alone, especially one with a child. I couldn't let anything happen to my brother's family. Maybe I was weakened by Tim's recent death, but I honestly was going to do my best to make a home for them. Then, a crazy thing happened to me: I met you while I was chasing Curly. I fell in love with you before I learned who you were. You're the only woman I've ever loved, and I could never have married Arabella after meeting you. When I discovered the truth about your identity, it was too late to back away from you and these feelings."

Tears were rolling down Carrie Sue's cheeks. T.J. turned to her and wiped them away, saying, "I don't hold you to blame, love."

"But we are to blame, T.J. That's why I was so desperate to get away; I couldn't stand the accidental deaths. If that driver hadn't tried to outrun us, that stage wouldn't have crashed and killed your friend and Carolyn. And if we hadn't attacked that other stage, that passenger wouldn't have panicked and shot your brother's wife and child. We didn't kill them, T.J., honestly. This man was babbling about them being captured and abused, so he shot them. Darby winged him, but it was too late. I swear we'd never kill women and children. If you can locate that coward, you can force the truth from him." As with T.J., she didn't know the irrational man had committed suicide following that grim incident.

"After all you've told me about Darby, I realized something didn't ring true. Your brother isn't what I imagined him to be. You said he ordered no killings, and I believe you. I understand that you two got shoved into this miserable life and were forced to stay there. But the accidents have to stop, Carrie Sue. I know you two don't deserve what happened to you, but neither do the innocent people the gang attacked. If Darby doesn't get out soon, he'll be dead, and we both know it, woman. You have to convince him to do the right thing, to turn himself in and face his punishment."

"He won't listen to me, T.J.; he thinks he's in too deep."

"When a man's in the right, sometimes he has to kill another man who wrongs him or challenges him. But when he's in the wrong, there's no justification for murder. That's why I never became an outlaw and why gunslinging never agreed with me, even as a cover for my job. I knew if I told you the truth about me, you'd offer me anything to give up this mission. But what kind of man shows such weakness and lack of character? I did change my mind about killing Darby and his boys, but I still felt I had to arrest the Stover Gang, for the law and for my friends and family. I was hoping after it was over, you'd love me enough to understand my predicament. I figured, if your love was strong and real, you'd keep on loving me even after I got justice."

"He's my brother, T.J.; I can't help you. I can't. Has it all been a lie? You've stayed with me and . . . just to get to Darby?"

"No, you frustrating vixen. I've pulled all kinds of tricks

with you and my superiors so I could stay with you for protection. I love you, Carrie Sue Stover, and want to marry you. You have to believe that much. I've done everything I could to secure you a pardon: bargained, begged, threatened, reasoned, misled. Nothing worked. I can't lose you, woman, so I have to quit the Rangers and leave Texas with you."

Carrie Sue looked deeply into his smokey gray eyes. "You really mean that don't you? You would give it all up to get me away safely."

"Yep. I can live without the Rangers and Texas, but I can't live without you, woman. If I led the law to your brother or told them where to locate his hideout, you'd be captured, too. I can't have that. To be honest, woman, if I could have gotten you a pardon, I'd have finished this mission to stop your brother's crimes. You love him, Carrie Sue, but what he's doing is wrong. Someone has to stop him."

Carrie Sue jumped up to pace. T.J. told her, "If you don't trust me near Darby, then we'll leave from here. Several times before I've given you the chance to test my word. I won't let anything happen to you. The only imprisonment you're facing is marriage to me."

"You'll forget your revenge?" she asked.

"You said Darby didn't kill Arabella and Marie; I believe you."

"What's in your saddlebags? You guard them like gold."

T.J. tossed them to her feet. "Look for yourself. You know the truth now. A telegraph key to tap into lines, a picture of Arabella and Marie, and a Ranger badge. That's what I couldn't let you see."

Carrie Sue unbuckled the straps and looked inside. Amidst clothing and ammunition were the items he stated. She didn't do more than glance at the picture because she would never forget those faces. She held his badge in the palm of her hand and wondered how much it meant to him. She was filled with mixed emotions: love, hope, joy, suspicion, and anger at his deceit. She studied the telegraph key and asked, "You won't use this to betray Darby after we see him and escape?"

"You can keep it or throw it away right now. I don't need it anymore. Maybe we can persuade Darby to turn himself in and serve his time. I can ask the Governor to intercede for him, and I can, too. Maybe he can get off with fifteen to twenty years with a chance of early parole for good behavior. After all, he didn't commit all the charges listed against him. He'll still be young when he gets out with a clean slate. That's better than being chased, hanged, or killed. He's welcome to join us in Montana."

Carrie Sue smiled at him, then flung the telegraph key into the river. She replaced the Ranger badge and picture of his brother's family in his saddlebag. "He'd never turn himself in," she said.

Her lover encouraged, "Still work on him because that may be the only way to save him. Surely you'd rather see him in jail for a few years than see him hanged or gunned down."

The redhead knelt before T.J. and cupped his knees with her palms. "Swear to me I'm not making a mistake to trust you."

T.J. gently captured her lovely face between his hands and pulled her closer to him. He worded his response carefully, trying to deceive her no more than necessary tonight. He had to stop the Stover Gang before he ran away with her, and he was being forced to flee afterwards. Once this matter was settled, he would expose everything to her and make her forgive him. "I love you and want to help you, woman. I swear to take you far away and marry you. I won't let you get harmed."

Carrie Sue knew those words were true, his clear gaze and calm voice told her they were. Besides, she mused, if they were being trailed by this lawman's order, T.J. wouldn't stop to make love! And if he was tricking her, he wouldn't tell her such things tonight. He had had her fooled into leading him to Darby, so he wouldn't take this risk. He wanted to prove he trusted her, and she must prove she trusted him. "We'll see Darby tomorrow, then head north, my love."

It was seven o'clock, not yet dusk, when Carrie Sue and T.J. found Darby Stover's camp on Sunday night. She hurriedly dismounted and raced toward her brother. She hugged and kissed him. Rapidly she related her capture, jailbreak, and flight with T.J. Rogue. "We're leaving at first light to head for Montana to get married, big brother. Are you sure you won't go with us?" she entreated.

Kale Rushton sneaked up behind the distracted lawman and put a gun to T.J.'s back and said, "This liar ain't going nowhere, *chica*. He may call himself Rogue to you and others, but he's Texas Ranger Thad Jamison, and your jailbreak was nothing but a sly trick."

Kadry and Walt grabbed T.J.'s arms and Dillon took his weapons.

Carrie Sue shouted, "Stop it! I know who he is. He's told me everything about him. He's giving up his badge and job to help me escape so we can start a new life together. Let him go!"

Darby faced T.J. and studied him. His brown eyes roved the lawman from head to foot, then settled on T.J.'s smokey gaze. Darby sensed power and peril, integrity and prowess. He perceived an undeniable strength of mind, body, and spirit. "You're wrong, Sis. He's used you to get to us. Tie him up, boys. We'll kill him later."

Carrie Sue yanked on her brother's arm. "You're mistaken, Darby! He loves me and is helping me escape. Don't you dare harm him!"

The auburn-haired man turned and glared at Carrie Sue to silence her. He was angry with his sister for being duped into a lethal trap by a crafty lawman, because he knew the treacherous Ranger had taken everything—everything—

from her. "There are things you don't know and understand, Sis. Jamison has to die. Tonight."

Chapter Twenty-three

"What don't I understand?" she shouted at her icy-eyed brother.

"Lawmen like Thad Jamison wouldn't give up a mission or toss away their job for a woman. He's charmed you into bringing him here. There's probably a posse tight on your tails. Tie him up snug, boys."

As T.J. was being bound, she refuted, "That isn't true, Darby. I watched him set a false trail out of town, and he's covered our tracks for miles. We weren't even heading in this direction. I was the one who insisted we find you and warn you before we headed north."

He scoffed in a sarcastic tone, "I bet. Don't you see, Sis? He let you think it was your idea. He knew you would be fooled after he busted you outta jail and filled your ears with pretty lies."

"From what I hear, Thaddeus Jamison can wipe out a whole gang by himself. Let's see how tough he is," Dillon suggested, then punched T.J. forcefully in the stomach.

Both rejected suitors vengefully attacked the helpless lawman who had stolen their love's heart and had betrayed her affections and trust. Kadry slammed his fist into T.J.'s gut. Dillon struck him across the jaw, making the lawman stagger backwards. When T.J. failed to go down, Kadry landed another, much harder, blow to his chin. That time, T.J. was sent to the dirt.

"Stop them, Darby, or I will," she threatened seriously,

448

fingering her gunbutts as she was tempted to draw against Darby and his men.

"Just because you're sweet on him, Sis, don't mean we have to get killed over it," her brother reasoned impatiently.

"My feelings for him have nothing to do with you allowing your men to murder him. If I loved him more than I love you, Darby, I wouldn't have come to warn you. I've proven myself to you plenty of times. You owe me this favor. Let us leave peacefully. He loves me."

"Sorry, Sis, but I have me and the boys to think about. Even if we let Jamison go or left you two behind, he'd be dogging us again the minute he's loose, or he'd alert his friends. It's him or us, Sis."

"No, it isn't. He's taking me to Montana; I swear it. He's even given up his revenge on us. That was his brother's wife and child that crazed man killed in March. T.J. thought we did it; that's why he was after us. I explained to him what happened that awful day. He knows the truth now, and he's giving up everything so I can go free and marry him. He even knows Quade Harding is framing us. He told me everything last night. If he was trying to trick me into leading him to you and the boys, he would have held silent. I trust him, Darby; that's why I brought him here to meet you."

Darby glared at her lover. "He's lying to you, Sis! He's been lying all along, and he'll keep on lying until we're all dead! I've met plenty of men like him, so I know his kind and feelings. He can't love you or want you. Don't be blind and stupid. We're riding out of here and you best come along. He probably has the law on to you."

T.J. was helpless, and decided against doing anything rash, but he couldn't let Darby's inflammatory words go unchallenged. "Don't listen to him, Carrie Sue. I love you, and I'll get you out of this mess if you'll trust me and convince them to let us go. That's no trick or lie."

"He lied tae ye, me darlin'. We hae tae kill him as punishment."

The redhead looked at the blond outlaw with her eyes chilled. "No, Kadry. There'll be no killing over me or I'll never forgive you."

"Whatcha gonna do, boss?" Walt asked.

"Give 'im time ta think, Cuz," Tyler suggested, his hazel eyes reddened by the whiskey everyone could smell on his breath.

"I say kill tha bastard now. Nae need tae wait until morn."

"Yeah," Dillon agreed with Kadry. "Kill him now. Let me do it." He lit a cigarillo as he eagerly awaited his leader's decision.

The black man pulled the ever-present chewing stick from between his snowy white teeth. "Missy Stover loves 'im, boss. Ya thinks ya ought to kill 'im a'fore 'er?"

Darby answered, "I have to, Griff. He's a threat to all of us."

"Yeah, he lied ta Miss Carrie Sue," Walt added, fingering his gun butts. As he looked at the lawman, fear permeated him.

Dillon tossed his cigarillo to the ground and crushed it forcefully. "I say get it over with, then pull out. If he's got a posse back there—"

Carrie Sue injected, "I told you he doesn't. Kale taught me plenty about tracking and covering trails. T.J. did a good job concealing it."

Kale Rushton reminded her, "He's Apache trained, *chica;* he could leave a trail you'd never notice. Maybe he is sweet on you, but I still think he was looking for our camp and planned to warn the others tomorrow before he left Texas with you. That's what I'd do in his place. A man like this doesn't give up once he has victory in sight. Now that he's found us, he can't just walk away and forget about us. That's not to his thinking and training."

She reasoned desperately, "How? He had a telegraph key, but he threw it into the river to prove he had no way to expose you."

The man with the red sash around his head asserted, "That was just another sly trick to keep you fooled."

"No, it wasn't," she protested. "I'm certain of it."

"Are you really certain, *chica,* certain enough to risk all our lives?"

She eyed Kale intently. "Don't put a burden like that on me. You're my friend. Make them listen. If anybody can read T.J., it's you."

"I know, *chica,* that's why I vote to kill him."

Panic flooded her. No one would take her side.

Darby said, "We're responsible for that Ranger's death on the stage. They'll never stop chasing us. They'll hound us into hell to capture us and kill us. Rangers don't forget or forgive."

Her voice was strained as she argued, "T.J. understands it was an accident. He holds the driver to blame for not yielding to us."

Darby tried to make her see his point of view. "I bet he recognized you from the start, Sis. He's been playing games with you. It's us he's after, not you."

"He didn't know who I was until he saw my poster the night before we escaped from Tucson. He's been protecting me and helping me."

T.J. spoke up and said, "That's true, Darby. I didn't know who she was until I was already in love with her. I'm telling you the truth; I'm going to take her far away to safety and marry her. If you kill me, she'll never forgive you."

"I wish I could believe you, Jamison, but I don't and can't. If she wasn't in love with you, she wouldn't trust you, either."

"She loves us both, man. She doesn't want to see us kill each other. The least you can do for her is leave us here and take off."

"Not after what you've done to my sister, you lying bastard."

Tyler said, "Let's kill 'im an' git outta 'ere before that posse comes."

Kale told them, "They can't track at night. They're probably camped by now. We should get some sleep and head out before daybreak."

Carrie Sue warned, "If you slay him, Darby, the Rangers will surely hunt you down and kill you. They don't know he's siding with me. They won't give up until you're dead, until you're all dead."

"Not if we head for Wyoming and lay low for months. We've got enough money. That'll be far enough away to fool them."

"He knew about the Big Spring job Friday night after he broke me out of jail. If he wasn't on my side, he would have wired them to set a trap for you. He could have captured me and had all of you ambushed."

"He just wanted tae catch us himself, lass, but we got him first."

"Capture seven men alone? Don't be ridiculous. No lawman is that good. He's had no chance to send for help, Darby; I swear it. You know I would never endanger you."

"There's a posse out there, *chica;* I can smell them miles away."

T.J. stated angrily, "Dammit, man, at least let her go. Stop dragging her into your crimes or you're going to get her killed."

"Dinna worry, Lawman. I'll take care o' her. I'll make her forget ye, ye cauld bastard. Ye took her frae me, but she'll be mine ag'in."

Carrie Sue eyed her brother and his men, then looked at the bound T.J. Rogue—no, she corrected herself, Thad Jamison, Ranger. T.J., R., the initials on his gun. Merciful Heavens, how she loved him and wanted to believe him. He had lied to her, but she knew he loved her and wanted to rescue him. Whatever was awaiting her out there, she couldn't let him die. It was useless to argue with the outlaws, so she made her decision. "Just wait until morning, Darby, and give yourself time to think this over. Don't kill him in haste. If you feel the same way at first light, then I'll leave and you can handle the matter. I'm going far away to where nobody has ever heard of the Stover Gang. I can't live this way. Whatever you do and wherever you go after tomorrow, just make certain you don't come near Montana and ruin things for me. The same goes for you two," she told Kadry and Dillon. "Don't ever try to find me."

"Ye canna mean that, me darlin' Carrie Sue."

"I've never meant anything more, Kadry Sams." She glanced from man to man. "If you kill him, I never want to see any of you again. You'll all be cold-blooded murderers, including you, big brother."

Darby said, "Let her be, boys; she's upset. Tie him to that tree and put a guard on him. We'll take care of him before we leave in the morning. Carrie Sue, you stay clear of him tonight, understand? I don't want to get tough with you, Sis, so let me handle this matter. When you've had time to cool down, you'll see I'm doing the right thing. Dammit, girl, he betrayed you in the worst way! How can you forgive him and take his side against me and the boys?"

"That isn't what I'm doing, Darby Stover! I just don't want you committing a rash murder. I know he lied to me and might have used me, but he had his reasons, just like we had good reasons for going on this outlaw trail years ago. No matter what he's done, murdering him is wrong. You never used to kill without good cause, Darby, and I'm sorry I've witnessed this wicked change in you."

Darby watched his sister walk away, and sighed deeply. He looked at T.J. and said, "This is your fault, Ranger. She doesn't understand I'm avenging her honor. You know you're guilty and deserve to die."

Thad Jamison said, "No matter what I've done to apprehend a notorious gang like yours or what you think about me, Darby, I do love her." He ordered through clenched teeth, "Leave her alone tomorrow. Give Carrie Sue the chance to be free and happy. If you really love her, you'll keep

453

your men away from her or they'll lead the law to her new location. Carrie Sue deserves better than what you've given her over the years."

To avoid suspicion, Carrie Sue ate her supper and didn't go near her lover, even to give him food and water. She had tended their horses, and prayed T.J. could ride bareback as skillfully as she could. The redhead knew she would be watched tonight, just like T.J. would. But the only man she had to worry about was Kale Rushton.

Carrie Sue lay on her bedroll until three o'clock. The longer she hesitated, the fewer doubts the men would feel about her. Darby had taken her weapons until morning, and she was furious with him for making her helpless. At least her brother hadn't ordered her bound!

She slipped from her bedroll and walked to the river which ran from San Angelo nearly to Big Spring. She sat on the bank, after placing a heavy rock beneath her full Mexican skirt. She knew the sharp-witted half-Apache would follow her and she would be forced to render him unconscious so she could do the same with Dillon and help her love escape. With luck, the boys wouldn't chase them. If they believed there was a posse nearby, they should take off swiftly in the other direction. *Please don't let anyone get hurt,* she prayed.

As expected and hoped, Kale Rushton joined her. "What's wrong, *chica,* can't sleep?"

Carrie Sue looked up at the man who was standing to her left. "You're my friend, Kale, so how can you do this to me?"

His dark eyes settled on her pale face. "To save our lives and to punish his tricks on you," came the easy answer.

"Have you never lied to someone you love to get what you wanted or to keep from hurting that person? Nearly all men deceive women for their own pleasures or reasons. T.J. is no different," she alleged.

"I've never told a woman I loved her just to use her."

"To let her believe you do is the same thing. Don't kill him."

"We have to, *chica,* or he'll dog us forever. Jamison is good, the best. If we get caught, he's the one who can do it."

"He'll leave with me today, honestly, Kale. He's not after you all anymore. He loves me and wants to get me away from this peril."

"Even if that's true, he'd expose us somewhere along the way or convince you to betray us."

She vowed heatedly, "I'd never do that; you know I wouldn't."

"He'll work on you until you weaken and see things his way. He's a lawman, *chica,* and he'll always be a lawman first. Jamison isn't the changing kind, or the relenting kind. He'll insist on finishing this last mission before running off with you, if that's the truth. He has a personal stake in this matter; have you forgotten about his brother's wife and child, and that Ranger friend of his? His honor will force him to destroy us. We're both Apache raised, so I know what he's like inside."

Carrie Sue stood up, holding the rock securely behind her in her left hand because her sprained right one was still weak. "You see that campfire in the distance," she remarked, pointing southward with her right hand. When he glanced that way, she lifted the rock and struck his head with it. He collapsed to the ground. She yanked the red sash from his bleeding head and bound his hands tightly behind his back. She knew his head would pain him but he wasn't badly injured. Taking Kale's bandanna, she gagged him for silence. She took his knife and gun and concealed them beneath her untucked blouse.

The redhead made her way to where Dillon was guarding the bound T.J. She whispered, "Can I see you privately for a minute, Dillon?"

Dillon knew the lawman couldn't escape as he was secured to a tree. He saw she was unarmed so he followed Carrie Sue into the bushes.

She turned to him and asked, "What do I have to do for you to let him escape before the others get up? I don't want him murdered."

Dillon studied her for a minute. "Anything for his freedom?"

"Yes," she replied guilefully. "What will it take to cut him loose?"

Dillon Holmes responded confidently, "Promise you'll marry me as soon as we reach Wyoming, 'cause you'll keep your word."

"What's that over there?" she asked, leaning forward and pretending to strain to see into the shadows. When Dillon turned, she rendered him unconscious with Kale's gun. She used his belt to bind his hands behind him and gagged him with his bandanna.

The desperate woman took Dillon's weapons and sneaked to her lover. Using Kale's sharp blade, she cut T.J. free and handed him Dillon's holster. "Let's get out of here," she whispered.

T.J. made no attempt to get the drop on the sleeping men because he knew Carrie Sue wouldn't stand for it, and wild shooting from the slumber-dazed outlaws could imperil her. He led her to their horses and they mounted bareback to prevent extra noise. They walked the horses from camp, then galloped southward.

At nearly four-thirty, they rode into the midst of the posse's camp before Carrie Sue realized what was taking place. Several men surrounded them and startled her.

One asked, "What's up, Thad? We trailing you too close?"

Carrie Sue stared at the Ranger badge on the man's chest and grasped his words. Kale had been right! It was a trap! She tried to bolt, but T.J. grabbed her from the sorrel's back. "Let me go, you lying bastard!" she shouted and struggled for freedom.

"Calm down, woman, this is for the best. I have to stop your brother's gang before he gets himself or more people

456

killed. I'll explain everything when I get back. Saddle up, men. We can take them while they're asleep. No shooting except in self-defense."

"No, T.J., he'll be gunned down. Please. You owe me!"

T.J. handed her to two men who held her captive between them. He pulled his silver star from his jeans pocket and pinned it on his shirt. "Sorry, Carrie Sue, but I have to do this. Darby's crimes have to stop and I'm the only one willing to take him alive. You'll be safe. Bob, you stay here and protect her," he commanded one of the men.

The posse mounted up and rode off with Rangers in the lead.

Carrie Sue paced frantically. Even if the posse sneaked up on Darby's camp, there would be shooting and killing. Darby would never surrender, nor would Kale or Kadry or Dillon, if Kale and Dillon weren't still disabled by her impulsive actions. This trap was her fault. She had trusted the wrong man, and he had used her vilely and betrayed her. He had sworn love, marriage, and freedom: all cruel lies! He had promised she would be safe, but she was a prisoner who would soon be facing either her Maker or a lengthy incarceration! He had alleged he couldn't pursue and capture the gang because she had no pardon and would be endangered, but he was doing it anyway! Her jailbreak had been a clever ruse to ensnare them, including her, because there was no way he could save her now that she was in custody. He had lied to her ever since their first meeting. Surely he had duped her in all areas, including lovemaking, which hurt the most. She had to escape. She had to ride like a blizzard wind and warn Darby to flee; she had to make up for her foolish mistakes.

She was standing near low hanging limbs. She pretended to toy with one while she asked, "Who planned this trap, Bob? How long has the posse been—" She yanked back the limb and released it, forcing the branch to slap the Ranger in the face and knock him backwards. She was on him in a flash, taking his weapon and getting the drop on him, a trick taught to her by Kale Rushton. Her friend had said that men could be duped easily by a female because they never expected or believed a mere woman could overpower and defeat them.

"Toss me your cuffs!" she demanded, then changed her mind. "No, snap one on your right wrist. Do it or I'll shoot you where a man doesn't want to be injured," she threatened, pointing the pistol at his groin. "I'm not a killer, Bob, but I can make you suffer badly if you don't do as I say. I'm not going to let them ambush my brother!"

After Bob obeyed, she gingerly stepped forward and locked the other cuff around his left wrist. She mounted Charo and, taking his horse along to prevent his pursuit, she galloped toward Darby's camp.

Before the posse reached their destination, T.J. halted them to give his final orders. "They're camped in those trees about a mile ahead on the river. I want the camp encircled. I don't want any of them to get away and risk a jailbreak later. I want them taken alive, all of them. They're outnumbered, so they should give up without a fight. Give 'em that chance." He told which men to take each position. "The Rangers will close in and order them to yield."

The groups quietly took their positions. T.J. sneaked to the spots where Kale and Dillon were still bound and only half-conscious. He led them back to the Rangers. "Hold these two, Harry. That leaves only five in camp. Let's go," he told the third Ranger.

They moved in closer and took cover behind two trees.

The lawman was distracted by worry over his love. Without thinking clearly, T.J. called out in a loud voice, "Darby Stover! This is Captain Thad Jamison and the Rangers. We have your camp surrounded. Give up peaceably and there

458

won't be any killing. We've captured Carrie Sue, Kale, and Dillon. There's only five of you and plenty of us."

Darby Stover was awakened by the commotion. He roused the other men fully. He warned, "Hold your fire until we see where the boys and Carrie Sue are. We don't want to hit them by mistake."

T.J. yelled out, "Give it up, Darby, and you'll get a fair trial. You don't stand a chance of escape. Don't force us to kill you."

Tyler Parnell panicked at the thought of being surrounded by Rangers and going to prison. He shouted, "Ya ain't gonna send me ta no jail." He ran for his horse, shooting wildly in all directions.

Several shots answered his challenge and he dropped to the ground.

Walt Vinson heard his first cousin moan and saw Tyler attempt to get up. He raced from cover, yelling, "I'll git ya, Cuz." He dodged back and forth, firing into the trees, as he ran to Tyler's aid.

More shots rang out and Walt went down near Tyler, both dead.

Seeing there were only three of them left, John Griffin threw down his pistols and stepped into the open with his hands raised. "Don't shoot. I'm comin' out," the black bandit shouted nervously.

"Hold your fire, men!" T.J. called out to the posse. To Griff he said, "Come this way and no tricks. You'll get a fair deal from us."

Griff followed the voice into the shadows and was taken prisoner by the Ranger with Thad Jamison.

Behind a tree, Kadry Sams turned to Darby. "I'm nae fool, man. I dinna want' tae die." He looked ruefully at his guns as he laid them down.

"I'm comin', tae, Rogue," he called out, then walked into the clearing with his hands above his head.

T.J. called to the gang leader, "It's just you left, Darby. Let me come in and talk to you. I don't want Carrie Sue seeing you gunned down, so don't be foolish. I'll get you a good lawyer. Harding will be captured soon and those fake charges against you will be dropped. Serve your time, man, and go free afterwards. You can't keep up this killing and robbing. Give it up, for your sister's sake."

There was no answer from the auburn-haired bandit. T.J. said, "I'm holstering my weapon and coming over there. Let's talk." T.J. told the Ranger, "I'll handle him." He left his cover and walked toward camp. "I'll help you, Darby, if you'll let me."

Darby allowed T.J. to get to within five feet of him. His revolvers were aimed at the lawman's chest. He yelled, "Any of you get itchy fingers out there and Jamison will be dead before I hit the ground!"

T.J. knew their words couldn't be overheard by the posse at that distance. He said, "I ordered them not to fire, Darby. Drop your guns and give yourself up. I promise you a fair trial. I'll do all I can to get you the shortest sentence possible, then you can join me and Carrie Sue in Montana. I'm serious about loving her and saving her."

"Where is my sister?" Darby demanded.

"She's safe with the Rangers, so are Kale and Dillon. This isn't for revenge, Darby, but I had to stop you. Can't you see this isn't any kind of life for you? You got into this mess by accident. I think the judge and jury will understand and be lenient. I have evidence to clear you of many false charges. One of Harding's men was wounded in that Stephenville train robbery. He talked plenty," T.J. alleged, hoping the witness had lived and chatted plenty to William Ferguson.

"You're a fool to walk into my gun sights," Darby told him.

"You aren't a cold-blooded killer, Darby Stover, and we both know that. When Harding's convicted, you'll probably get your ranch back. It's a prize piece of land, worth plenty. If you sell it and pay back those people you've robbed, the law will probably look on you with favor. You can serve your time and have a good life when you get out. Plenty of men go straight in prison and get paroled early. Hell, they'll probably hire a man like you as a lawman when you get out."

"You expect me to believe such crap?" Darby scoffed, but was intrigued by the man's words and expression.

T.J. saw the wavering in his love's brother. "I can help you, man, but only if you lay down those guns and come with me. I—"

T.J.'s words were cut off when Carrie Sue galloped into camp and dismounted near the two men. With a pistol in her hand, she ran toward them. "Darby!"

A shot rang out and Carrie Sue was thrown backwards by the force of the blast into her chest. T.J. and Darby raced toward her.

Thad Jamison shouted, "Hold your fire, damn you!"

Darby gathered the wounded Carrie Sue into his arms. "I didn't want it to go this way, Sis. Why did you do it? You can't help me."

"I know, Darby. I . . . love . . . you. Don't fight . . . them . . . or you'll . . . get killed," she murmured through a blackening haze. "It's over, Darby . . . finally over." Searing pain racked her shoulder and blood poured from the bullet wound.

T.J. knelt beside her and said, "You'll be all right, love. I'll get you to a doctor. Hold on, woman, or I'll beat you." Sheer terror flooded his body. Would he be the cause of her death? He couldn't lose her; he loved her and needed her.

With the last of her strength and awareness, Carrie Sue looked at her traitorous lover and murmured, "I . . . hate you. . . . Let me die . . . get . . . it over . . . with."

Before others reached them, T.J. told Darby, "I love her. I'll protect her. Don't worry or do anything foolish. They'll kill you."

Darby Stover met T.J.'s frantic gaze and knew the man was telling him the truth. He realized he should have let them go last night. "Get her away from this mess or I'll hunt you down

461

when I get out and kill you."

When the posse closed in on them, T.J. ordered, "Bring Kale Rushton over here. He's probably got some Indian medicine in his saddlebag. Get me something to use for bandages. I have to halt this bleeding. Harry, send one of the men to fetch the doctor in Big Spring."

Harry informed his panicked friend, "Doc Pritchard died last month. They don't have a doctor in Big Spring anymore. You'll have to get her back to San Angelo."

"That's too far and too rough a ride in her condition!"

"There's no choice, Thad," the Ranger reasoned.

T.J. thought swiftly. "There's a ranch a few miles away. Borrow a wagon from it while we tend her."

Harry sent two men to fetch the wagon. After cuffing Darby's hands, he searched the saddlebags for something to use as bandages. He handed them and a canteen of water to Thad Jamison.

The man who had done the impulsive shooting babbled anxiously, "She had a gun in 'er hand. I thought she was going to shoot Cap'ain Jamison. I didn't mean to kill 'er, just wound 'er."

Kale was unbound and brought forward to help Carrie Sue. T.J. ordered the posse to move away with the prisoners to give them working room and privacy. Harry urged the men backwards to the river.

After everyone cleared the area, Kale pushed the red splotched blouse to her waist and unlaced her camisole. He and T.J. studied the wound and glanced at each other.

"It's bad. Deep. Lots of bleeding," Kale remarked. He opened his Apache medicine pouch and withdrew a smaller pouch of powder. He shook some onto the wound, then bound it. "Bullet's in too far. If I dig around in there, I'll kill her. She needs a good doctor, fast."

T.J.'s voice was choked and his eyes were glittery with moisture as he asked, "You sure that's all you can do, Kale? She can't die on me. Dammit, I should have kept riding like I promised her."

Kale looked at the famous lawman. "She was right; you do love her."

"Yep, but I might have just killed her with my stubbornness. Not even the capture of the Stover Gang is worth her life. This was crazy."

"*Si, amigo,* but something a *verdadero hombre* had to do," Rushton remarked.

T.J. scoffed, "This is anything but honorable. No *real man* would do what I've done, but thanks, *-ch'uune'.*"

The outlaw was impressed when the Indian-raised lawman called him a friend and helper. "I wish I could do more. I can't."

"When that wagon arrives, I'll get her back to San Angelo and the doctor. I won't let her die on me," he vowed with determination.

While T.J. was busy with Carrie Sue, the other Rangers assigned men to return the gold to Big Spring. Harry took control of Walt Vinson's badge collection, pulling out Thad Jamison's to return it to him. The bodies of Walt and Tyler were secured to their horses for burial in San Angelo. The prisoners — Kadry Sams, Dillon Holmes, John Griffin, Kale Rushton, and Darby Stover — were ordered to mount up to be taken to the jail in San Angelo. From there, they would be escorted to Waco for trial and sentencing.

The wagon arrived. Darby entreated, "Please, let me ride with my sister. She could die along the way and I should be with her."

T.J. ordered, "Harry, you come along with me to guard Stover. I'm going to let him stay with his sister. I'll drive the wagon. The rest of you men take those prisoners back to town. Watch them closely, and no trouble. I promised them a fair trial, so get them to town alive and well or you'll answer to me personally."

T.J. and Darby loaded Carrie Sue with gentleness and worry. Her blouse had been replaced but the camisole was being used to help stop the continuing blood flow. Charo, Nighthawk, and Darby's mount were tied to the wagon gate. T.J. put their supplies in the wagon and told Darby to watch her carefully, to call out if he needed to halt and give her relief. Both men were scared because she hadn't regained consciousness. They pulled out with Harry riding beside them and guarding the notorious bandit leader whose lap cradled his sister's head.

It was a long and difficult trip back to San Angelo with T.J. and Darby trading places as the driver while the other man tended Carrie Sue. They halted only for the horses to rest and water. The men ate cold beans and chewed on dried strips of beef. They forced water into Carrie Sue, but she remained in her world of silent blackness.

They traveled all of Monday, most of Monday night, and part of Tuesday. The wagon had to move slowly to keep from jarring her too much and causing more bleeding. They reached town about five o'clock and took Carrie Sue to the doctor's office.

The physician checked the wound and shook his head. Carrie Sue moaned and moved slightly. The doctor said he had to use ether to make sure she held still while he removed the bullet. It was lodged near her lung and he didn't want to puncture it. He poured ether onto a clean rag and laid it over her nose and mouth. Soon, she quieted and lay motionless.

The skilled man took a long instrument with a slightly curved tip called a sound and probed the hole until he heard it make contact with metal. He eyed the spot and assessed the location. With slender gouging forceps, he wiggled them into the wound and grasped for the bullet. The bleeding was profuse now, but he couldn't stop groping. Finally he captured the lead between the forcep tips and carefully withdrew it. He tossed the bullet into a pan of water with his bloody instrument.

The doctor dabbed sweat from his brow and above his upper lip. He pressed a cloth to the fiery location to halt some of the bleeding so he could see to make stitches. He poured antiseptic—a wonder product by Robert Johnson—on the area, then sutured the wound with silk thread. After bandaging her, he said, "That's all I can do for her, Ranger Jamison. Keep her quiet and still. Try to force water and soup into her. If the bleeding stops soon and no infection sets in, she could survive. I would recommend holding her prisoner at the hotel. That jail isn't any place for her in this condition. As for me, I'd like to speak with that Indian fellow. Whatever he poured on the wound kept her alive until I could treat her. If he hadn't, she'd either have bled to death or been too enfevered to save. I've heard those Indians have magical cures we whites know nothing about. If he would work with me, we could advance medicine ten years."

"His name is Kale Rushton. He's half-Apache and half-Spanish. Talk to the Governor; maybe he'll work something out for you two."

The doctor smiled and said, "It's worth a try."

T.J. suggested, "You should check her right wrist; she sprained it badly a few days back."

After the doctor looked at it, then bandaged it snugly.

Carrie Sue was taken to the hotel and placed in bed. T.J. sat down to watch over her. To him, she looked so pale and weak lying there, and it ripped at his heart to know he was responsible.

"Don't leave me, love, and I promise you won't ever be harmed again," he murmured, placing kisses over her face and parted lips. He tasted and inhaled the bitter remains of the ether. He took a cloth and washed her face. "You're so beautiful, Carrie Sue Stover," he said as he gazed into her serene face. He wanted to see her lovely eyes open again. He stroked her tawny red hair and lifted her left hand to kiss each fingertip.

"I need you with me, woman. Hang on to life, love, please," he beseeched the unconscious redhead.

A knock summoned T.J. to the door. Two of the Rangers came inside and questioned her condition.

T.J. glanced toward the bed and informed them. "I don't think she's going to make it. Why don't you head on to Waco in the morning? If she gets well, I'll escort her there. If not, I'll join you soon."

"That's what we came to see you about, Thad. We need to keep the prisoners here a few days. Quade Harding and his boys left town late this morning. I've called the posse back together to ride after them at first light. You want to come along? I know you have a score to settle with him, and you are the superior officer here."

"I'm putting you in charge, Harry. Just get the bastard and his gang for me. I want to stay here with Carrie Sue. It's my fault she got shot helping me. With her brother in jail, she has no one to take care of her. We got close on the trail, so I'd prefer to tend her."

One of the Texas Rangers asked, "What will happen to her, Thad, if she survives?"

"I've requested a pardon for her from the President and Governor. I expect it to come through any day now. She did help us capture the Stover Gang and she's given evidence against Quade Harding. She also told me where and how to locate King Fisher's hideout." He drew a map and handed it to one man. "Wire this information to the Rangers near Eagle Pass. That should help Major Jones put a stop to his raids."

T.J. hated to lie to the Rangers — his friends — but if Carrie Sue was taken to Waco to stand trial with the Stover Gang, she would probably be convicted. He couldn't allow that to happen to his love. Since they had refused her a pardon, he had no choice but to get her away from there as soon as she was able to travel. He prayed that day would come. He had hoped the Rangers would depart for Waco in the morning with the prisoners and leave him here with Carrie Sue. Then, as soon as she was able to travel, instead of heading for Waco as he promised, he would sneak her to safety in Montana.

"She's a special woman, Thad, and I hope she makes it," Bob told him. "She's mighty clever, too. Got the drop on me in a flash."

The three men discussed their plans and case. Afterwards, the Rangers left him alone with his love.

William Ferguson arrived for a visit. "How is she, Thad?"

"Not doing good, Bill. I'm worried."

The newspaper man glanced in her direction and said, "I hope she pulls through; I really like her." Ferguson eyed Carrie Sue again before saying, "I told the other Rangers Harding just left town and, if they hurried, they could overtake him and capture him." He told T.J. about his interview with the wounded bandit in Stephenville and how he turned the evidence over to the Rangers today. "That outlaw talked his head off. It seems that Harding shot him and left him for dead so he couldn't expose him. The man was furious, but he was scared. He was afraid no one would believe his account against such a powerful and wealthy rancher. When I told him the law was investigating Harding and he would be arrested soon, he opened up and told me everything."

"That's good, Bill. Thanks for the help; I surely need it."

Ferguson took a seat and continued, "Curly James was feeding Quade Harding information, just like you suspected. From what that bandit said, Curly was suppose to join the Stover Gang after he left Tucson. Before he did, he was to wire Harding and warn him to cease those fake raids. That's how Harding messed up; he didn't know Curly was dead and Darby was on the move again, so he never got his warning against that Stephenville holdup. You'll be surprised how many raids they've pulled over the years and blamed the Stover Gang; that should help Darby's defense."

"I hope so. He's not a bad man by choice," T.J. murmured.

"I agree," the gray-haired man concurred. "I hired a good lawyer, one of the best available. He's to meet Darby in Waco. I'm going there myself to cover the end of this story. I've written up all the evidence I've gathered and I've recorded my conclusions for the lawyer and the authorities. I think those notes will aid Darby's defense."

"If we're lucky, but I haven't seen much luck lately."

"Don't get dispirited, Thad. I also sent a telegram to the President and Governor, asking them to pardon her."

T.J. muttered with resentment, "It won't do any good, Bill. I've begged them for a pardon, offered to do anything for one. They've refused. They've made up their minds the answer is no. I was going to sneak her away, but this shooting messes up things for us. When the posse gets back with Harding and his gang, if they don't leave with all the prisoners before she's well enough to travel, we're done for." He glanced at his injured love and murmured, "If she doesn't survive, it won't matter what I do."

The two men — new, but good, friends — talked and planned a while longer. . . .

T.J. watched and tended his love all night, forcing cool water between her dry lips. Not once did she arouse, and his fears increased. For a time, while the ether and her weakness held Carrie Sue entrapped in a dark world, he sneaked away to handle a pressing matter. . . .

Early the next morning, one of the Rangers stopped by to say they were pulling out to pursue the Harding gang. Harry remarked with concern, "You look terrible, Thad. Did you get any sleep?"

"Very little. There's no change. I doubt she'll survive to stand trial."

As he was flexing his stiff body, T.J. looked out the front window. He saw the doctor heading for the hotel. He went to Carrie Sue's bed and prepared her for this crucial examination.

When the doctor arrived, he checked the still unconscious woman. He tended her wound with antiseptic and placed new bandages on it. "No change, son. I'm sorry. It's real bad when they don't wake up soon. It could be that ether's fault; it can be unpredictable at times. I might have used too much," he said, detecting a faint odor of it on her.

"You think she'll pull through, Doc?" he queried, looking very worried.

"I'm afraid I don't, son," he revealed. "I have to go out of town to deliver a stubborn baby. I'll be back tonight. I'll check on her then."

The doctor reported to the local sheriff as ordered by the man. "She hasn't regained consciousness; that's a bad sign. I don't think she's going to make it, Sheriff, but that Ranger's trying his best to save her. If you asked me, I think he has strong feelings for her. He hasn't left her side for a minute, for the little good it's doing."

The sheriff said, "Maybe it'll be best if the Texas Flame doesn't recover to stand trial. Prison's a bad place for a woman like that." The lecherous man imagined the beauty as his helpless captive for years.

"Why didn't you ride out with the posse?" the doctor inquired.

"Those Rangers don't need any help," the offensive lawman scoffed.

Darby overheard those tormenting words about his sister's

condition and begged the lawman to let him go see her. The auburn-haired man was furious and distressed when the sheriff laughed and refused. "If she dies and I get loose, I'll kill you for this," he threatened.

T.J. forced water and soup into Carrie Sue again today as he had last night. He wanted her to have the strength to battle for her life.

William Ferguson came to visit again. He stayed with Carrie Sue while T.J. went to see Darby Stover. The Ranger and the outlaw talked privately for a time, then Thad Jamison returned to the hotel.

T.J. checked his love and said, "It's too late to change things, Bill. I'll handle the arrangements as we agreed. You sure about helping me with this?" When the man nodded, T.J. said, "You stay here until I return, then fetch your things. It'll be a long, hard day."

T.J. went to see the undertaker and ordered a coffin sent to his hotel room in an hour. As he was passing the dressmaker's store, he halted and went inside. He purchased the beautiful white gown in the window. With a heavy heart, he returned to the hotel room. Lordy, how he hated to do this, but he had no choice.

Ferguson left to fetch his camera. While he was gone, T.J. put the white dress on Carrie Sue and brushed her tawny gold mane. The coffin was delivered. When William returned, he and T.J. placed a lovely quilt in the bottom and a pillow. They put Carrie Sue inside. Ferguson placed flowers from his yard beneath her overlapping hands. T.J. straightened her white lace dress and flaming hair.

"All right, Bill, do what you must."

Ferguson set up his camera and took pictures of the grim sight. Tomorrow, his stories and pictures of the ill-fated Stover Gang would fill the *San Angelo Tribune*. "I have most of the articles written, Thad, and I'm going to re-run a few that I've already printed. I'll prepare the one on her death today. I'm also getting pictures of the gang in jail and taking their statements this afternoon. I'll go fetch the sheriff so he can bear witness to her demise. I'll see you at my house tonight. Make yourself at home there until the Rangers and posse return."

After the newspaper man departed, T.J. stood over the coffin and stared at the lovely face of the Texas Flame. "I'm sorry it had to be this way, love," he murmured, then bent forward to kiss her.

The sheriff arrived and looked into the coffin. "A real shame, she was a beauty. You burying her here?"

"Nope, in Waco where I live. I'm having her delivered to William Ferguson's home until we pull out of town. I don't want curious folks gaping at her on display. If they want to see her, they can buy one of Bill's papers tomorrow. He took pictures earlier to print. I want you to cuff Darby Stover and send him over with two deputies. Any man deserves to tell his sister good-bye, even an outlaw."

The sheriff argued, but had to obey the Ranger. Two deputies arrived shortly with a handcuffed Darby.

The bandit leader gazed at his sister a long time and kissed her cheek before murmuring, "Good-bye, Sis, I'll never forget you. This is all my fault and I'm sorry. I love you, Carrie Sue."

At the jail, one of the boys asked, "Is she really dead, boss?"

Darby leaned his head against the stone wall and said, "Yes."

The coldhearted sheriff remarked, "Don't worry, boys; you'll all be joining her soon when you swing from ropes in Waco."

Chapter Twenty-four

Thursday morning, the doctor came to Ferguson's home. "I got back to town too late last night to check on her. I saw the paper this morning. You sure she was dead, not just in deep unconsciousness?"

"I've seen plenty of people die, Doc. She had no heartbeat, no pulse in her throat. I put a mirror to her nose and mouth to check for breathing, and nothing happened."

"I didn't expect her to make it, not after staying unconscious so long." The doctor glanced at the sealed coffin, then at the disheveled lawman. "She was real special to you, so I'm mighty sorry she's gone."

Friday afternoon, the Rangers and posse returned to San Angelo with a few prisoners, but Quade Harding and others had been slain during a violent shoot-out on the trail. After filing their reports, the three Rangers went to William Ferguson's home to see Thad Jamison.

Harry related the news about Quade Harding and his gang. "We'll take the others back to Waco with us on Monday. We plan to rest here a couple of days." He shifted uneasily. "We heard about her passing on, Thad, and we're real sorry. What are your plans?"

T.J. took a hammer and loosened the coffin lid. He let the lawmen glance at Carrie Sue Stover before he nailed it shut again. He dropped into a chair as if soul-tired. His hair was mussed and he hadn't shaven for days. From the look of his wrinkled garments, he hadn't bothered to bathe or change them lately. "I'll head out with you on Monday morning. I'm taking her back to Waco to bury it so she'll be near me. That's the only place I spend much time." He sighed deeply before adding, "I'm thinking of quitting the Rangers. Playing T.J. Rogue gets as many innocent people killed as her brother's gang did. Besides, after she was shot, we blew my cover, so I won't be any more use to the Rangers or the President as T.J. Rogue."

"The Rangers still need Thad Jamison," Harry told him.

T.J. ran his fingers threw his ebony hair, then stroked his stubble. "I doubt they'll be too happy that I exposed myself on this case. I was ordered to remain undercover. After the trials, I think I'll find me a quiet town somewhere and settle down as a town marshal."

"Why don't you get cleaned up and join us for supper and a few drinks?" another of the Rangers asked. "You can use both, friend."

T.J. stood. He walked to the coffin and placed his hands on it. "Thanks, Bob, but I prefer to stay here and guard her until we leave town. I need to keep the curiosity seekers away. I won't let anyone gape at her or steal souvenirs. You know how folks behave when a famous person gets killed."

"Yep, I'm afraid I do. Will you be all right, Thad?"

He nodded. "I was going to marry this girl when her pardon came through. I just need some time alone to adjust."

"We understand," said Harry.

As they were leaving, William Ferguson returned home. Harry said, "You did a fine job on the Stovers' lives and on the Harding case. You want to report on King Fisher for your paper?"

"You have news on him already?" William inquired.

"Yep. The Rangers and Army joined forces and attacked that hideout she told us about. They didn't get King Fisher,

473

but they sent him on the run. Good thing is, his gang is scattered, what's left. Fisher won't be terrorizing that area any longer, thanks to Miss Stover."

"Why don't we have supper and you can give me all the facts on Harding and Fisher?" Ferguson suggested. "The restaurant at the hotel has a fine cook. When we're done, I'll bring Thad something to eat."

The four men left and T.J. bolted the door. Again, he checked all the windows and doors to make certain they were locked. He went to the coffin and unsealed it. He lifted Carrie Sue and carried her back to the bed. After removing the white dress, he checked her healing wound and put on her nightgown. He hoped the ether would wear off soon and he wouldn't have to use it again on her. Yet, he was glad it put her under deep enough to fool everyone into believing she was dead.

He murmured to the soundly sleeping woman, "I know you're getting tired of that foul ether, love, but I have to convince everyone you're dead. I just hope Doc won't miss what little I stole from his office the other night or figure out my ruse. 'Course, he's got no reason to mistrust a Texas Ranger." He stroked her hair and kissed the tip of her nose. "We'll be leaving Monday, love. Hank will have everything ready for us in Waco. Just as soon as the trials are over, we can sneak away without suspicion. But if I don't go there and retire, someone might realize what I've done and come after us. We'll be far away and safe soon, love. We'll get married and be happy forever."

As he tucked her in, he continued chatting to himself, "You don't have to worry about Darby suffering over your death; I told him my wild plan before I pulled it off. He played his part good and he's glad you'll be safe." He checked her wrist and saw it was doing fine now.

T.J. washed Carrie Sue's face and hands. He put the flowers in water and sat them near the bed. She had aroused only a few times since being shot—slipping in and out of consciousness — but not enough to comprehend what was happening. Her wound was looking better and no fever or infection had attacked her body, thanks to Kale's prompt treatment. She had swallowed the soup and water each time he had forced it into her mouth, and she was getting stronger.

T.J. felt bad about lying to his Ranger friends, but he had to think only of Carrie Sue now. His duty had been met, and he had done far more than should be expected of any man. He had used and betrayed his love and almost gotten her killed. They deserved freedom and happiness, and it was up to him to obtain them.

T.J. left her sleeping peacefully while he took a bath, shaved, and changed clothes. Until they left town, he would remain at her side. Once they were on the trail, the Rangers and prisoners would go on ahead while he drove slowly in a wagon with the coffin. When he and Carrie Sue were alone, he could unseal the wooden box. At the outskirts of Waco she would be compelled to hide again until he reached the house which Hank had rented for him. While he was filing his reports, attending the trials, and retiring from the Rangers, Hank Peterson would take care of her. Afterwards, it was off to Montana and a new life together.

As T.J. looked down at his love, he murmured, "From the moment I first laid eyes on you, I knew I couldn't rest until you were mine. I'll make you understand and forgive me, Carrie Sue. We're meant to be together."

T.J. stretched out beside her and closed his eyes. He was exhausted from nightly vigils and daily worry. He could relax and rest now because he knew she was going to get well and his ruse had worked perfectly.

Carrie Sue awakened off and on Saturday. T.J. was always at her side. While her head was clear, she was worried about her brother, but T.J. kept telling her that Darby was fine.

The last time she awakened that day, after feeding her

nourishing soup, T.J. told her of his impending plans.

In a weak voice, she asked, "You really are taking me away?"

"I never lied about that, Carrie Sue. I love you and want to marry you, but this is the only way. You have to trust me and cooperate."

Carrie Sue's eyes were heavy. She closed them and went to sleep, his last words running through her mind each time she stirred.

Sunday morning, Carrie Sue was more lucid and for a longer period of time. She asked for coffee, bringing a smile to T.J.'s lips.

"I hope this means you're feeling better," he hinted.

She was propped against pillows. "My shoulder hurts like heck. I feel as if I've honestly died and been dragged back to life."

T.J. stroked her silky hair — which he kept brushed — and said, "I was determined not to let you go, woman. You owe me."

Her violet-blue eyes gaped at him. "I owe you? How did you come to that crazy conclusion, you conniving lawman?"

"You're the one who tempted and teased me until I lost my head and heart over you. You're to blame for making me pull those stunts so I could have you. At least we got Harding, so you have your revenge and justice." He told her about Quade Harding's deeds and death.

"I feel too bad for that news to enliven me. What about Darby?"

T.J. explained what he had told Darby before and after her shooting. He related what he believed would happen to the bandit leader. "That's the best I can do for him, love." He sat beside her. "Aren't you relieved his outlaw days are over? Now, he can work on getting his head and life straight. I told him that when he gets out of prison, he can come live with us.

476

He knows where to look, and he's plenty welcome. None of the other boys know the truth. Darby and I figured it was too dangerous to tell them you aren't dead. This way, none of them will come looking for you after they get out of prison."

"You mean Kadry Sams and Dillon Holmes."

He grinned and chuckled. "That's right, my clever vixen. I'm a possessive and jealous man. I don't want either of those lovesick cowboys chasing my wife. I'd like a peaceful existence for a change."

She tried to move away from him, but she couldn't. She was too weak and it hurt her shoulder. Touching him caused a mixture of feelings: anger, irritation, confusion, love, and desire. "What if I refuse to marry you, Mr. Traitorous Rogue? Am I supposed to forget and forgive just because you had a mission to carry out? How do I know this isn't another one of your crafty tricks?"

He captured her hand and kissed it. "For what reason, woman? The Stover Gang is in jail. And you're in no condition to rescue them. Even if you were, I think you're smart enough to realize this is for the best. You don't want Darby killed or continuing as an outlaw. I saved his life, Carrie Sue, and he has a chance for a fresh start after he's served his time. There was no way you would help me stop him, so what did I do so wrong by tricking you for a while? I never lied about the important things like love and marriage."

She wanted to discuss this further, but she was drowsy. "The problem is . . . Rogue, I don't know . . . if I can ever trust you again."

"Let's get you tucked in and comfortable. You need sleep, love. You'll have lots of time to punish me with this sharp tongue later. Right now, you have to get plenty of rest. We leave in the morning. It'll be tough going for you until I get rid of them and unseal that coffin."

"I don't . . . want to . . . ride . . . in a coffin," she argued.

"Would you prefer to travel with the prisoners, stay in jail with them, stand trial with them, go to prison with them?

Are you that angry with me, Carrie Sue? Do you hate me that much?"

"Behave, Rogue, I'm . . . too tired to quarrel. Good-night." She closed her eyes and went to sleep.

T.J. settled her in bed and kissed her forehead. "You might be furious with me, woman, but you love me. It'll work out for us."

When she awakened again later, T.J. showed her the newspaper with her coffin picture and read the stories to her. He told her about the sheriff checking her at the hotel and what he told the doctor.

Carrie Sue was amazed, and impressed. "You're one clever and daring man, Rogue. Or should I call you Thad now?"

He grinned and shrugged. "Whichever name you prefer, love. I mostly go by T.J., but a few friends and Rangers call me Thad. You'll be Mrs. Thaddeus Jerome Jamison, Carrie Sue Jamison."

"If I marry you," she scoffed, jerking her hand from his.

He glued his gaze to hers. "You have no choice, woman. I saved your life and I'm keeping you out of prison. You belong to me."

"I see, swap one prison for another kind? Is that my choice?"

He sighed loudly in frustration. "Come on, Carrie Sue, give me another chance," he entreated.

"Another chance to use me and betray me?"

"Lordy, you stubborn vixen! You really want to punish me, don't you? What can I say or do to convince you I love you?"

She replied, "I don't doubt you love me, Ranger Jamison, but trust is a big part of love and marriage. You lied to me."

He countered, "And you didn't lie to me plenty of times?"

Carrie Sue felt a rush of guilt. "I suppose I did," she admitted. "But I had to," she claimed.

His voice tender, he responded, "Just like I had to deceive you, just for different reasons. Even so, I still trust you and love you."

Carrie Sue frowned in consternation. He was right, but . . .

"I know this is all hard on you, love, but I'll prove myself. Just give me time and patience and understanding. I promise you it's been just as hard on me. Imagine Thad Jamison, lawman, falling in love with an outlaw, the notorious fugitive he's sworn to arrest. Now, I'm turning my back on everything I know and have just to win you."

T.J. told her of his three badges and jobs. He went on to explain, "I was a Presidential agent and U.S. Marshal before I became a Texas Ranger in '74. That was when they were reorganized. Maybe you didn't know they were disbanded after the war by military authorities and corrupt politicians; I guess it was punishment for seceding from the Union in '61. The Texas Legislature passed a bill in '74 starting them up again with six companies. Major John Jones was assigned the Frontier Battalion to combat the Indian and border problems. I work under Captain L.H. McNelly of the Special Force. We're suppose to rid Texas of cattle thieves and outlaws, reestablish law and order. The President, Marshal's office, and Rangers sort of share me for various missions, but I've almost always used the gunslinger Rogue as a cover. My missions took me all over Texas and the surrounding territories. That's how I met Hank, Mitch, and Joe Collins." He related the full story of Arabella and Marie. Then, he filled in any gaps which she questioned.

With a sad tone, he said, "I tried to get you a pardon, Carrie Sue, but they won't grant one. And, if I hadn't brought your brother in alive, someone would have killed him. I've tried to do what's right for everyone. Can't you understand my side?"

Finally she said, "I need time, patience, and understanding, too. Maybe I'm just too weak and weary to think and feel right now."

"Just answer one question for me; do you love me and want me?"

She stared into his smokey gray eyes and said, "Yes, I do."

He smiled broadly. "That's plenty for now. Take a nap, love. Bill wants to visit later if that's all right with you."

"Why are we at his home? Why is he helping you? Don't tell me he's an ex-Ranger too," she jested, feeling as if an oppressing weight had been lifted from her body.

T.J. explained when and how he met the newspaper man. He told her what they had done together and separately. He explained why Bill hadn't betrayed the Stover Gang to the local sheriff. "By the way, the sheriff was killed last night trying to capture some rustlers. I doubt he'll be missed very much. He wasn't a good man."

"William Ferguson is," she remarked. "I'd like to see him later. I want to thank him for all he's done for me and Darby. See you next time, partner," she murmured and snuggled into bed.

Monday morning, June twenty-sixth, it had been a week since Carrie Sue was shot. She was recovering slowly and steadily. She asked, "What if they want to view my body again?"

"They won't, love. You've been dead too long. But just in case, I'll help you into that white dress again and you can hold these," he said, yanking the dead flowers from the vase. "We're damn lucky they didn't send for a prison wagon to haul those men to Waco. That would have caught us in a bind, made us travel at the same pace."

Carrie Sue was helped into the dress, and she admired it. "Where did you get this, Rogue? It's beautiful."

"At a local dress shop. I saw it in the window. Luckily it fit. You sure do look great in it. Why don't you wear it when we marry?"

She glanced at him, but didn't respond. She was trying to remain calm; she was trying to be understanding. She knew T.J. wouldn't allow her to recuperate here where he couldn't watch her. For now, the best thing was to cooperate. Also, she wanted to be near Darby's trial. T.J. had promised to find a way for them to visit one last time before he was sent to prison. Too, she wanted to see if T.J. truly meant what he had said about retiring and escaping with her.

Carrie Sue Stover loved Thad Jamison with all her heart and soul, but she was afraid to let down her guard this soon after his deceit. Time and his imminent actions would tell her what to do.

She was helped into the quilt-lined coffin. "I don't like this," she muttered as she lay down, wincing when her shoulder protested.

"You all right, love?" T.J. asked.

"Yep," she muttered unconvincingly.

He placed a canteen and some food in the wooden box within her reach. He laid a gun near her hand. "Just in case something happens to me and you need to protect yourself," he informed her when she glanced at him oddly. "Just stay quiet and still. I'll try to get rid of them as soon as possible. I love you, woman," he vowed, then bent forward to kiss her.

Carrie Sue looked at him when he straightened. She parted her lips to speak, but didn't. It was dark when he sealed the lid. She settled herself for the grueling experience ahead.

"It might get warm in here, love, but be patient." He cautioned, "They're here, so no more talking or moving."

T.J. and another man loaded the coffin onto a wagon. William tossed her saddlebags beside it. T.J. added his belongings and supplies. The lawman tied the reins of Nighthawk and Charo to the tail gate. He shook hands with William Ferguson and said, "I'll see you in Waco on Saturday. Thanks for everything, Bill."

"Take care of yourself, Thad. I'll be seeing you soon."

T.J. mounted the wagon seat, clicked the reins, and the team pulled out to join the group of men nearby. He glanced at Darby Stover, but their looks revealed nothing suspicious to the others. "Let's go."

Ten miles outside of San Angelo on the road which passed through Brownwood and Hamilton on the way to Waco, T.J. halted the men. "This is slow moving, Harry. Why don't you ride on and I'll catch up in Waco. If I go any faster, I'll bounce her coffin out of the wagon. I didn't think about it, but I could have headed out Saturday or Sunday. I guess my mind was elsewhere." He tried to look and sound sad, but it was hard with his love and happiness so close at hand.

Harry smiled sympathetically and said, "If you don't mind traveling alone, Thad, I would like to make better time."

T.J. despised lying to his friends and hated being compelled to take illegal actions, but he couldn't avoid this path and save his love too. "I wouldn't want to walk my horse that far. I'll be fine. I can use the peace and quiet, if you understand my meaning."

Harry thought he did, so he nodded. "All right, boys, let's pick up the pace and let the wind cool us."

Kadry Sams shouted, "I need tae see her an' sae good-bye. Just gie me one look at her."

Harry shook his head and replied, "She's been dead fornigh unto a week, boy; you don't want to look at her now. Remember her like she was."

When Bob offered to hang back with T.J., Harry said, "Let him be alone; he needs it before he puts her away for keeps."

The Rangers, appointed deputies, and prisoners galloped off and left the wagon there.

T.J. said, "Just a while longer, love. I want to make sure they're gone. You all right in there?"

When the wounded woman didn't respond, T.J. panicked. He knocked on the coffin and asked, "You all right, Carrie Sue?"

A muffled voice answered, "Just hot and sore, but fine."

They traveled for another half-hour, then halted. T.J.

482

removed the lid and lifted her out of the wooden confinement. Carrie Sue's cheeks were flushed and her skin glistened with moisture. T.J. poured water on a bandanna and washed the sweat from her face. He waved it before her, trying to cool her faster.

"How's the shoulder?" he inquired. "We'll get you out of this hot dress and into something cooler. I washed those Mexican garments; they should do the trick. I want to check for bleeding."

She noticed he had stopped near the eastern flow of the Concho River. She was glad. The grove he had selected was cool and shady. She let him remove the lovely white dress, check her wound, and rebind it with antiseptic bandages which he had stolen from the doctor. She helped him as much as possible as he pulled on her blouse and skirt.

"That better?" he asked.

"Much. Thanks." She sipped water slowly because she felt weak.

When he tossed the white lace dress into the wagon, she summoned the strength to scold, "Don't do that, T.J. Rogue! You fold that dress and put it away before you ruin it. Are your hands clean? I don't want you to stain it. It took all I had to keep from bleeding on it."

T.J. chuckled and said, "Yes, ma'am. Don't worry. I'm glad to see your spirit returning. You must feel better if that fiery temper is aglow today."

"I want to walk a minute. Can you help me? My legs feel like a mellow pear, so I can't do it alone. I need to get some blood flowing in this aching body. I'm not used to lying around for days. Makes me tense and moody."

T.J. smiled in pleasure. He put his right arm around her waist and held her left elbow with his free hand. He guided her around for a short time with her leaning against him for support. He felt her telltale tremors and the amount of pressure she was putting on his body. "I hope that ride wasn't too rough on you."

"I've had worse, and plenty better. Damn," she swore underbreath. "I hate feeling this way, helpless as a baby."

T.J. coaxed, "Just take it easy, love; you nearly died. You're strong and healthy; you'll be well soon. Until then, just lean on me. Whatever you want or need, I'll get it or do it for you."

For some inexplicable reason, Carrie Sue began to cry. "Damn," she swore again, feeling stupid, "First I'm feeling like a baby, now I'm bawling like one. I hate acting like this!"

T.J. knew what it was like to feel utterly helpless. He had experienced similar bouts of that offensive condition when he had been barbwired to that tree, when he hadn't been able to secure her a life-saving pardon, when she had been shot and nearly died, and when the Stover Gang had captured him. He knew how nerve-racking it was!

He swept her into his arms and walked to the riverbank with her. He sat her down and placed her feet in the refreshing water. "You're just hot and tired, love. You've been very sick. It's nothing but your body fussing at you and trying to heal. I was like this while recovering from Quade's little attack. I nearly died. I was weak and fussy and miserable, too. It'll pass, honest."

"I bet you didn't cry," she murmured, wiping at the tears.

He answered truthfully, "Nope, but I sure did want to lots of times. It was frustrating, maddening, irritating. My nerves stayed on edge. I was moody and bitter, downright foul-tempered all the time. I hurt like hell. I couldn't even take care of myself or defend myself. I had to be fed and tended for days. Really stung my pride." He didn't mention the Ranger who had saved his life and taken care of him; he didn't want to remind her of one of the Stover Gang's victims.

Carrie Sue looked at him. Maybe that was it: singed pride and damaged modesty. She hadn't even been able to tend to her private business alone! At least it was T.J. helping her and not a stranger. She dangled her feet in the soothing water and rested against his chest. "I feel nasty. What I need is a bath, a good bath, not just a light rinsing off. That would make me feel better; I know it would."

T.J. gently refused, "When we get to the house in Waco, I'll wash you from head to toe, woman, but it's too dangerous on the trail. I want you to take a nap and gather some energy before we pull out. Mind me, and I'll prop you up in the wagon for our afternoon ride."

She was exhausted, so she didn't battle him with foolish words. She stretched out on the bedroll he spread for her and closed her eyes.

T.J. saw the dust cloud down the road and knew someone was coming. He glanced at the sleeping Carrie Sue and didn't want to disturb her yet. He slipped to his horse, untied Nighthawk's reins, and headed in that direction to ward off any visitor to the wagon.

It was William Ferguson. "What is it, Bill? You were to catch the stage Thursday."

"How is Carrie Sue?" the newspaper man asked.

"She's doing fine, just tired and sleeping. What's up?" he pressed.

The excited man revealed, "Good news, Thad. Her pardons came through today. When the telegrams arrived for you, the man brought them to me because he knew you had been staying at my house and I was seeing you soon. It has to be a stroke of good fortune for them to arrive on the same morning, and before you're out of this area."

"From whom?" the shocked lawman asked.

"The President and Governor Hubbard. It seems our reports and pleas had a profound effect on them. What will you tell the Rangers about this death ruse?" Ferguson inquired.

T.J. shoved his hat to his shoulders and ran his fingers through his damp hair. "I don't have any idea, Bill. I didn't

485

give it any thought when I believed they weren't going to pardon her. To be honest, it didn't bother me as much when I thought they'd never learn I'd lied to them, but now they'll know the truth. Either I have to keep pretending she's dead, or I have to confess what I've done. You know what that means. I broke the law by faking the death of a fugitive so she could escape justice, so they could bring charges against me."

Ferguson reminded him, "But if you clear up this mess, then neither of you will have to go into hiding. Her name will be cleared. You won't have to run away."

"I still plan to head for Montana. We're both too well known here to have a real chance at a fresh start. Lordy, man, why couldn't this pardon have come through last week, or before she was shot?"

"Maybe you should read those telegrams," Ferguson hinted. "I hope you don't mind my opening them, but I figured if they were important, you needed to know immediately."

T.J. smiled and said, "You did the right thing, Bill." He read them and scowled. The wire from the Governor of Texas said reports on the evidence had been sent to him and he was requesting that the court go light on Darby Stover and his men, since all the charges against them weren't true, especially those violent killings and raids which the Harding gang had pulled off as a frame. Too, there were mitigating circumstances for Darby and his men becoming and remaining outlaws. With King Fisher, the Stover Gang, and Harding and his men halted, people would feel more comfortable about the law going lenient on the Stovers. Both telegrams said that official papers were enroute by mail, but wires had been sent to the Ranger Headquarters in Waco. Both men were particularly impressed with Carrie Sue Stover and affected by T.J.'s love for her.

Ferguson agreed, "People will be glad to have all of those villains taken off the roads. They'll be delighted to learn that

Darby Stover wasn't responsible for those terrible crimes. Folks have always liked him; he's a colorful legend in this area."

T.J. concurred, "Yeah, but that doesn't help me with my situation."

Ferguson suggested, "Why don't you get the President to say the death ruse was his idea until he could decide on her pardon? Who would say anything bad against him? Or hold you to blame? He's going out of office soon and has nothing more to lose, but you do."

T.J. argued, "But that means I'll have to tell him I lied. He'll lose all respect for me. One thing he knew was that he could trust me."

Ferguson reasoned, "Which is more important, Thad, his respect or you two going free?"

T.J. considered his words. He realized that was the only path to take. "It's best if I 'fess up and take any punishment coming my way."

Ferguson said, "Carrie Sue is going to be surprised and pleased when she hears this news."

T.J. informed him, "I can't tell her any time soon because she hasn't made up her mind about me yet. If she learns she's free to come and go as she chooses, there's no telling what that woman will do. She's still upset with me, so I don't want her taking off and doing something foolish or dangerous. I need for her to think she has to stay in hiding. Otherwise, she'll be at the court every day. I don't want her witnessing what happens to her brother, in case things don't go well with him."

Ferguson looked worried. "You've been honest with her lately, son. If I were you, I wouldn't risk deceiving her again."

"Lordy, man, do you know how headstrong that vixen is? I can't imagine what she'll do when she finds out she's been pardoned."

"I know, Thad. But you know what she'll do later when she discovers you've tricked her again."

Reluctantly T.J. admitted the older man was right. "Lordy, this thing called love is complicated. I guess I'm learning about it the wrong way because I keep making stupid mistakes with her. As soon as I find the best time, I'll tell her about the pardon."

Ferguson said he had to get back to San Angelo to complete his paper and business before packing and heading for Waco to cover the end of this fascinating story.

"You know where we'll be. Look us up when you arrive." T.J. gave the man a message to wire to President Grant, and T.J. prayed that the country's leader would understand his motive and forgive him.

Ferguson mounted and departed. T.J. returned to camp. While his love finished her nap, the lawman contemplated the requirements which Grant had placed on her pardon. . . .

When the redhead awakened, T.J. made her comfortable in the wagon and they continued their journey.

On Tuesday while they were camped, to distract her from her tension and discomfort, T.J. told Carrie Sue about Waco in the midst of the fertile and lovely Brazos River Valley. It was a town known for its cattle, cotton, corn, and culture: the four "C's." He explained how the town's cold springs had been popular with the Waco Indians and how the Ranger fort had been constructed there in '37. He spoke of the beautiful and prosperous plantations which had lined the river before the war, estates which had fallen greatly when the plantation economy had collapsed and the population had scattered. But, he said, renewed western movement following the war and the Chisholm Trail had brought new life into Waco, referred to as "Six-shooter Junction." He talked of Fort Fisher, Texas Ranger headquarters in this area, the place to where he reported after each mission. He mentioned the nation's largest suspension bridge across the Brazos River, built in '70 and rivaled by none in America.

When Carrie Sue's eyes glowed and she said she wanted to see all those wondrous sights, T.J. told her that maybe she could when this predicament was settled. He intended to wait until reaching Waco and getting the official papers and word before telling her about the pardon, which proved a wise decision.

On Wednesday night after they camped, they talked about their pasts, separately and together. Carrie Sue realized what good and gentle care he was taking of her. He had not pressed her romantically, nor had he argued with her or tried to browbeat her into thinking his way. He appeared to be giving her the time she had requested. Often along the way, he had halted at farms, ranches, or small towns to purchase hot meals for them, while she remained hidden in the coffin until they were out of sight and camped. He made certain she had nourishing food and plenty of rest, and that the journey wasn't too demanding on her condition. The longer she was with him, the harder it was to fault him for the necessary deceit.

She said, "You've been good to me, T.J., and I'm grateful. I'm feeling better every day, and it's because of your generous care."

He smiled at her relaxed air tonight. Her color and mood were improved. "I owed you, woman. I love you and you saved my life."

She placed her coffee cup aside and said, "Not really. Darby wouldn't have killed you or let his men murder you."

T.J. refuted in a tender tone, "Don't stay blinded by love and loyalty to him, Carrie Sue. We both know Darby would have killed me because he thought he had to. That's why I had to end this matter; I had to stop him from doing things he didn't want to do but felt he had to in order to survive. I think he's glad I stopped him."

Carrie Sue tried not to be miffed with him because his

answer was an honest one, even though it pained her deeply to admit the truth. "How was my brother when you last saw him?"

T.J. leaned against the wagon spokes. "Actually he was very calm, relieved, I must say. I think he's resigned himself to serving his time and starting over one day with a clean slate. At least he isn't furious with me anymore. He knows why I completed my mission before taking off with you to parts unknown. I believe your brother likes me and trusts me, even if you don't, my fickle vixen."

"I am not fickle," she retorted.

"What do you call it when a woman loves you in sunny weather but not during a storm?" he jested.

"This was more than a simple storm, T.J. Rogue. I mean, Thad."

"Exactly what was it, Carrie Sue?" he asked seriously.

She scoffed, "It was your damned deceit, Mr. Ranger!"

His gaze fused with hers. "Yep, one I was sworn to carry out long before I met a distracting spitfire who turned my life and guts inside out and seared them good. Tell me something, you feisty little wildcat, what would you think of me if I had turned my back on my duty and become an outlaw just for you?"

"I didn't want you to become an outlaw. I didn't want my brother to be an outlaw. I didn't want to be an outlaw. What's your point?"

"Then, what was an honest lawman supposed to do, woman? Let you go your merry way and get killed because you loved your brother too much to betray him? Let the Stover Gang continue their raids when I knew I could get to them and stop them? Was I suppose to look the other way to keep from hurting you? Was I suppose to forget I knew you, which was damned impossible? Should I have forgotten the law and my duty, the promises to my friends and superiors? Could I allow more innocent people to suffer or die like my brother's family, Miss Starns, and that Ranger when I had a

490

way to halt any future deaths? Surely you of all people can understand loyalty, desperation, and love. Look what you've done because of them."

T.J. seized her hand and compelled her gaze to his while he asked, "Tell me, Carrie Sue, if you had been in my place, what would you have done differently to solve this case without damaging our relationship? I did everything within my power to protect you and to save your life and Darby's. He's alive today because I used you to capture him. He has one of the best lawyers in Texas defending him. I gathered evidence to go in his favor and yours. I offered the President, the Governor, and the Rangers *anything* in exchange for your pardon. If you had been in my position, if you had met me and fallen in love with me after you were on this same trail to justice and revenge, what would you have done to end this matter while retaining your self-respect and mine? If you can honestly say you would have done anything differently, then I'll set you free as soon as you're fully recovered and I'll never trouble you again. Don't answer me now, just think about it."

Chapter Twenty-five

Carrie Sue had not answered T.J.'s question the night before, but she had given the matter serious consideration all morning as they traveled. She had to admit he was right. If he had done any less, she would not have respected him, nor would he have respected himself. He was a man of considerable honor and conscience, a good man, a strong and dependable one. She had spent more than a week nearly alone with him. They had talked many times on various subjects. No one could have done more for her than T.J. had.

It was evident to the redhead that Thad Jamison loved her and wanted her understanding. It was clear that he had done all in his power to help her and Darby. It was also undeniable that he could not have carried out his actions any differently for all concerned. He had taken big risks to protect her. She knew his mind must be in turmoil over betraying his friends, superiors, and his duty, all to save her. He was turning his back on all of them so she could be happy and free, and become his wife. Yes, she admitted, he had done his duty many times over to everyone, including her.

Both had been quiet all morning during their ride, and she knew why. Both were entrapped by deep thought and warring emotions. They had fallen in love, but were confronting serious problems. Both wanted a future together, a bright and happy fresh start. But if she couldn't forgive him, he—as vowed—would release her soon. She knew that that was not what she wanted and needed; Thad Jamison was.

At William's and along the way, they had been uneasy around each other, fearing to reach out, fearing to trust each other and themselves, but fearing not to do so. The strain had been tough on them, something they needed to end before they could make a new beginning. Each knew what a refusal of understanding and forgiveness would cost them. False pride and stubbornness had to be cast aside. They needed to relax, to reform their bond.

They reached the outskirts of Waco late that afternoon. Carrie Sue was concealed in the coffin one last time. T.J. drove the wagon to the house which Hank Peterson had rented for them. When they arrived, the ex-Ranger was waiting there and helped T.J. unload.

Inside the small house, T.J. removed the lid and assisted Carrie Sue out of the wooden box. He sat her in a chair and smiled, a loving and tender smile which warmed her from head to foot.

Hank said, "I think I have everything here you need, Thad. But if I overlooked something, I'm staying at the Merry Hotel." The man grinned as he thought of the happy news in his possession, but he would let his friend reveal it to Carrie Sue. When he had agreed to this daring ruse, somehow he had known the pardon would come through and dismiss them of guilt. He hadn't been able to allow this woman to go to prison or be hanged for mistakes in her past, mostly in her misguided and embittered youth. She hadn't wanted that vile existence and had tried to escape it many times. Carrie Sue Stover was worth saving and helping. Yet, if he had still been a Ranger, he couldn't have aided Thad with this illegal deception. Currently, he was only a private citizen, a good friend, and a romantic at heart.

Just as those last words traveled through Hank's mind, Carrie Sue asked, "Why are you doing this, Hank? It's against the law, I'm sure."

Hank sent her a genial smile. "Because I'm a darn fool, Carrie Sue, and Thad's my best friend. He wouldn't ask me to help him pull this off if it wasn't vital to his survival. I know you two love each other, and I know this is the right thing for me to do. I guess you could say the law sometimes needs a helping hand to make the right decision. For certain, I couldn't let you hang or go to prison, and I couldn't let Thad's life be ruined because of mistakes you were forced to commit long ago. You deserve another chance, Carrie Sue, and Thad deserves happiness. This was the only way to make both happen."

A radiant smile crossed her face and settled in her periwinkle eyes, eyes brightened by unshed tears of joy and gratitude. Those emotions were revealed in her voice when she replied, "Thank you; this is one of the nicest things anybody's ever done for me. I'll make certain you're never exposed because I wouldn't want you getting into trouble over me. I hope you don't mind if I consider you my friend, too."

The man responded with ease and verity, "I'd see it as an honor, Carrie Sue. I'm glad to see you survived your accident. Thad's telegram sounded a bit panicky when I got the news."

Carrie Sue glanced at T.J. and smiled. To show her lover she was relaxing and relenting, the redhead jested, "That's because my sneaky partner went to such trouble and pains to capture me."

T.J.'s heart fluttered wildly at her softened gaze and tone. He playfully retorted, "Only because my impulsive vixen went to such trouble and pains to thwart me. But I was determined not to give up hope. I needed a wife real bad to straighten me out and you're the only woman who's been able and willing to tolerate me and my craziness."

They all laughed. Then, Carrie Sue replied mirthfully, "Only because I had no choice, my sly and domineering partner."

"Right now, woman, I'm issuing another order. You need to hop into bed and take a nap. If you want to collect on that favor I promised you, you'll need lots of strength."

Carrie Sue blushed as she wondered how the word "favor"

struck Hank Peterson. "If you renege on my bath, I'll pitch a tantrum."

Hank laughed and said, "I need to get moving so you can rest. I'll see you tomorrow, Carrie Sue. You want me to stable that team and her horse at the livery?" he asked his friend.

"That would be a big help, Hank. I'll keep Nighthawk here. Just let me fetch the rest of our things from the wagon." He looked at Carrie Sue and said, "Stay in that chair, woman. I'll be right back and help you into bed. I don't want you falling and hurting yourself."

Outside, Hank passed the official pardon papers to Thad Jamison. "I'll sit with her tomorrow afternoon while you go to headquarters and straighten out this situation. I kept my mouth shut because I figured you'd want to tell her the good news. There's a telegram in there from President Grant; you might want to read it before you decide what to do. Oh, yes, there's food in the warming oven over the stove."

Hank tied his reins to the wagon with Carrie Sue's sorrel. He mounted the driver's seat and headed for the livery stable. T.J. secured Nighthawk's reins to the short hitching post out front, placed his saddle inside the door, and rejoined Carrie Sue.

"I want you to get a nap, love. Then, we'll have a long talk after supper." He lifted her and carried her to bed with her mildly protesting she could walk with his help. As he placed her on the bed, he chuckled and said, "But I love carrying you around, woman."

T.J. leaned over and kissed her, then gazed at her. "I love you, Carrie Sue, and everything's going to work out for us. You'll see."

"What if your friends come to visit? How will you explain me?"

"No one will find us here, love. They don't know we've reached town yet and they don't know about this house." He kissed her again and stroked her hair. "Sleep, woman," he ordered with a grin and left the lovely bedroom.

When she awakened nearly two hours later, T.J. washed her face and hands amidst shared laughter and playful jests. He helped her to the kitchen and into a chair. They devoured a hearty meal of fried chicken, brown gravy, biscuits, coffee, and green beans with small potatoes which he had warmed.

"Delicious," she murmured, licking her lips. "You're spoiling me."

"I wish I could say I cook this good, but Hank got it at the hotel. I only heated and served it, ma'am. And I'll clean it up while you rest."

"You've been doing all the work lately; let me help."

"No way, woman. Don't you realize how weak you are? That was a bad wound; you're still recovering."

"For once, partner, I won't be stubborn. You're right. My body still feels like flowing water, and this shoulder pains me to annoyance."

"How's the sprained wrist?" he queried.

"It's fine now. The pain and swelling are gone thanks to you, doc."

"Good. I'll take you in the parlor while I finish here."

"No, I'll drink coffee and watch you. I want to see how good you are in the kitchen, see if your skills here match those on the trail."

They exchanged smiles and laughter.

She observed and sipped coffee while he cleared the table and washed the dishes. "Who's home is this?" she inquired. "You said it was rented, but it's furnished. It's charming and lovely."

"It belonged to a widow who died recently. She had no family to claim her possessions. The bank has it for sale. The money's going to an orphanage like the woman requested. Hank lucked up on it."

"I'm glad he did; it's wonderful. When I worked at the Harding ranch, I had a small room in the back of the house. I had to stay there unless I was doing chores in the other rooms.

496

Then, while I was in Sante Fe working, I had a tiny room, which was all I could afford on that meager salary. Some businessmen really take advantage of women on their own by treating us like slaves and paying us hardly enough for survival, unless you're willing to do special chores after work," she hinted meaningfully. "The boarding house in Tucson was nice." She brightened, then looked sad.

"What's wrong?" he asked, noting her change in mood.

"I was thinking about Mrs. Thayer in Tucson. I wish I could write to her and explain things. She was so good and kind to me. But I'm suppose to be dead. I wonder if she's heard the news."

T.J. said, "You can still write her a letter. You can date it before June twenty-first. I'll mail it for you." After she learned of her pardon, she could write the woman with the whole truth.

"Thanks. I like this place," she murmured. "Except for that ranch in Laredo, this is the first home I've lived in since my parents—"

T.J. glanced up from his task when she fell silent. "I know how you feel, Carrie Sue; I haven't had a home since my parents died. It's either been strange hotel rooms or rowdy bunkhouses, crumbling shacks, or sleeping on the trail. I enjoyed our visits with Hank and Mitch, and I surely do like this place. Real homey and pretty."

"I liked visiting with them, too. We didn't have time in Laredo to fix up that place into a real home, but it was nice until Quade's detective made us flee. Being on the trail is a lousy existence, isn't it?"

"I didn't think much about it until I met you. Lordy, woman, you showed me how miserable my life was. Yep, this is real nice."

T.J. completed his chore and suggested, "Let's sit in the parlor, ma'am. We can behave like real folk here. No dessert or wine though."

Carrie Sue laughed and took his extended arm. With his

assistance, she walked into the cozy room and sat on the floral couch, leaving room for him. T.J. sat beside her. He leaned his head against the back and closed his eyes, sighing deeply in contentment.

"These next few days will be busy ones," he remarked without opening his smokey gray eyes. He dreaded what was ahead tonight.

She looked at him. "You're tired, aren't you?"

"Yep. Driving a slow wagon for days beats on your neck and back when you're used to a fast horse and a comfortable saddle."

"So does tending and hauling around a helpless invalid."

He turned his head and met her gaze. "You aren't heavy or any trouble, woman."

"I'm both, and you know it, Mr. Rogue." She laughed again. "It's going to be hard to get used to your real name. It's going to take a lot of attention and practice. Are your superiors mad at you for breaking your cover to help me?"

"I haven't given them the chance to fire me or scold me." He stood up and fetched an envelope. He returned to the couch and handed it to her. "Hank gave me this. You need to read it."

"What is it?" she questioned as she accepted the envelope.

"Good news for you. Maybe a bit of trouble for me."

She read the official notices of a full pardon for Carrie Sue Stover, then stared at the page with the President's seal and signature, and those of the Texas Governor on the other paper. Her astonished gaze shifted to T.J.'s face.

"Yep, those are for real, woman, just a little late."

"I'm free? I can come and go as I please?" she queried.

"Yep, but that would be dangerous until everyone learns the truth. Until it's written up in the newspapers and gets widely known, you'll still be in peril if anyone sees you. And, there's another problem. I have to figure out a way to explain your so-called death to everyone before they see you walking around, alive and well. I faked your death before this pardon was granted, so I have to clear up that deception before you come out. Else, Bill, Hank and me are in big trouble for breaking the law. You were a wanted criminal and we were helping you escape justice. I'll take those two pardons and go to Ranger headquarters tomorrow and try to straighten out this mess I've created."

As the reality of the joint pardons sank in, she said with excitement, "This means I can attend Darby's trial next week."

T.J. shook his head and dashed her joy and eagerness. "That's not a wise idea, Carrie Sue. Your presence would be much too distracting in the courtroom. People, including the judge and jury, will be gaping at you instead of paying attention to the evidence Bill and I gathered. They'll also realize I lied about your death, so they might assume I lied about the evidence to favor your brother. If I could fake your death, then I could fake evidence for him, which might cause Darby big trouble with his defense. That isn't all, woman. There'll be a large crowd observing and you're still weak and injured. I don't want you bumped around while people are trying to get a closer look at the Texas Flame. They'll be pushing and shoving just to touch you. They might even be yanking at your clothes to snatch souvenirs. You aren't well enough to face a mob scene like that. You need to stay here, resting and healing. I'll give you a full report every day."

Carrie Sue realized he hadn't given orders or threats. "But I could testify for him, T.J.; I know the truth. I might do him some good."

"I doubt it. Once everyone sees how beautiful you are and they discover the truth about our love and ruse, they won't believe a thing either of us says. Some of those envious women might convince their husbands you used your beauty to trick me into helping you and Darby. The President and Governor have requested the court to go lenient on Darby and the boys. If you show up and flaunt our deceit in their faces, it could be damaging for his case."

Carrie Sue realized he was right. She had to do what was best for Darby and everyone else involved — T.J., William, and

Hank. They had taken great risks to help her and she owed them her loyalty.

T.J. added, "There are some stipulations on your pardon, love. Grant's message was in code, but I've translated it for you. Read it."

Carrie Sue discovered that her freedom was based on Thad Jamison marrying her and keeping her out of trouble and on his resigning from the Rangers and as a Special Agent for the President who would be leaving office after this term. He was required to continue as a U.S. Marshal, but in Colorado. The decoded message also said that Grant was taking full responsibility for the death ruse, ordering T.J. to say it was his idea and command. The man claimed it was his hesitation which forced T.J. to become so desperate. Grant said he understood T.J.'s love for her and didn't fault his action. Clearly the President was giving her love a way out of his predicament. "If I don't marry you and go to Colorado as a marshal's wife, this pardon isn't effective?"

"Those are the conditions, what I promised in exchange. I told him I would do anything to get you pardoned, and he finally accepted my offer." When she became silent and thoughtful, T.J. walked to the window and gazed outside, worried about her reaction and response. He knew she loved him, but he had betrayed her. She was upset with him and was afraid to trust him again. He couldn't blame her.

Carrie Sue broke her silence by saying, "I'll do whatever you order here in Waco, T.J., because I'm certain you know what's best for everybody concerned. I would like to see Darby. Is that possible?"

T.J. didn't know how to take her oblique answer. "When his trial's over, I'll find some way to sneak Darby here or to slip you into the jail for a last visit. But right now, it's too dangerous. Too many curious people are hanging around the jail day and night. Once the trials ends, things will settle down and it'll be safe."

They both fell silent. T.J. felt dejected. Why was she so

quiet? What in blazes was going on inside her head?

"That's fine," she remarked. She said suddenly, "I'm going to marry you, T.J., not because of this pardon, but because I love you. I accept what you had to do in the line of duty."

T.J. turned and looked at her. He walked to the couch and sat down, pulling her into his embrace. He kissed her with a fiery passion which ignited his entire body, a passion which had been denied a long time. He cautioned himself not to let his hungers run wild; she was in no condition for urgent lovemaking tonight. When she cuddled against him, he vowed, "You won't be sorry, Carrie Sue. We'll be happy."

She hugged him and replied, "I know we will."

As her fingers absently teased over his chest and her body nestled to his, T.J. felt his control lessening by the instant. "You've been up long enough, woman. It's time for you to get back into bed. That journey here was hard on this healing body. I have to take care of you. I want you up and around soon so we can get married and head for our new home." When her head shifted and she gazed up at him, he added, "I know I promised you a bath, but it'll have to be in the morning after you're rested. I'll scrub this hair and body good; that'll give you some energy. I'm afraid it's too late to dry and you need to recover from that rough wagon ride. Is that all right with you?"

Carrie Sue felt her body aching for sweet release, but she knew he was exhausted and she hadn't had a bath in days. If she yielded to the temptation to cover his face with eager kisses, she would be unable to control her urgent desires. They hadn't been together as one since her jailbreak, nearly two weeks ago. She was starving for him. Yet, she wanted their reunion to be something special. Tomorrow night was the perfect occasion.

"You're the boss, my husband-to-be," she teased.

T.J. chuckled merrily as he carried her to the bed. Flames licked greedily at his body as she spread kisses on his neck. After she was tucked in, he only brushed her lips lightly with his, not daring to really kiss her. "See you in the morning, love."

She halted him at the door by saying, "Where are you sleeping?"

"I'll bed down in the parlor."

"A hard floor over a comfortable bed?" she hinted mirthfully.

"That's best, woman. You need a full night's sleep to get well. It would be much too dangerous for me to sleep in here tonight."

Carrie Sue gazed into his smokey gray eyes. She smiled knowingly. "It won't be hazardous tomorrow night," she hinted with a seductive smile.

His eyes glowed with happiness and desire. "The things you women will exchange for a bath," he teased.

Soft laughter left her throat. She mischievously retorted, "No more than a famous lawman would exchange to get himself a wife."

"Good-night, you lusty vixen," he murmured. "I love you."

"Good-night, my handsome Rogue. I love you, too."

After a delicious breakfast of bacon, scrambled eggs, biscuits, and coffee, T.J. heated plenty of water and filled the widow's tub in the kitchen. He helped Carrie Sue get undressed. Then, he scrubbed her hair and waited while she bathed.

Afterwards, he dried her quickly to prevent his kindled body from bursting into flames, and put on a fresh bandage on her shoulder. As he did so, he told her how he had stolen the ether and bandages from the doctor's office in San Angelo. Being careful with her wounded shoulder, he pulled on the cotton gown which she had brought along from Tucson. She sat in a kitchen chair while he brushed her hair, a task they both enjoyed.

"You're definitely spoiling me, my love. This is wonderful."

"Maybe you can repay my services when you get stronger."

"I'd love to, my virile Rogue." She tilted her head backwards and enticed her to kiss him.

"Behave, woman. I have work to do and it's back to bed with you."

"Sounds perfect to me," she could not help but say.

"I meant, I have to go to Ranger headquarters and settle our problem. Hank will be here soon to stay with you while I'm gone."

"You still don't trust me?" she jested.

"Of course I do. I just want him here for your protection. You're too weak to defend yourself if trouble struck. I'll stop by to see Darby and fill him in on the news. Up, vixen, it's nap time."

Since she didn't have a robe, Carrie Sue wrapped a lacy coverlet around her shoulders so she could visit with Hank Peterson in the parlor.

As they chatted, Hank told her how much T.J. loved her, how he had panicked after her escape in El Paso, and how frightened he had been after she was wounded. "You've made a big difference in his life, Carrie Sue, and he's done the same in yours. Thad and I have worked together and guarded each other's backs many times." To pass the time, Hank related some of their adventures.

Hank left when T.J. returned to the cozy house. Her love related his meeting with the Rangers, saying he had let the President take the blame since his authority outweighed the Texas law. "They don't like what I did, but they accepted it. I was a Special Agent before I was a Texas Ranger and that position carries more power. They realize I didn't have any choice but to obey President Grant's orders."

"Did you tell them about the President's requirements?"

T.J. shook his head. "That's a secret bargain between us, but I told them I was resigning to become a marshal in Colorado. Considering how well-known we both are, it sounded like a good idea to them." He grinned and quipped, "At least they were reluctant to lose me even after learning I had deceived them. I told them you agreed to stay in hiding until the trials were over, so they agreed to let you see Darby one night when it's safe. There's too much commotion in town for the next few days, so you'll have to wait a while. See where cooperation gets you, woman; right where you should be."

He chuckled, then revealed, "The story's being released today of your survival and pardon. It'll claim you've been sent back East to relatives. Nothing's going to be said about our love and marriage. That'll protect our privacy. The report will read that your death was faked until your pardon could arrive and you could be sent away secretly."

She sighed in relief. "I'm glad that worked out all right."

"Me too. Darby was in good spirits when I saw him. Even better after he heard you're doing fine and you've been pardoned. He's accepted his fate, Carrie Sue, and I'm glad. I told him you'd be seeing him before he left for prison. He's happy about that."

"How do you think the trial will go?" she queried with anxiety.

"His lawyer had just left. He thinks Darby has a strong defense. It helps that there wasn't a shoot-out when he was captured. And no one was hurt in either San Angelo or Big Spring, and all money was returned. That lawyer's as smart as Bill said he was; he's gotten those false charges of Quade's dropped. The newspapers have been filled with good reports on Darby and that frame's been exposed in colorful detail. The papers here picked up Bill's stories and interviews, so Darby's going to trial almost a hero, a real Western legend."

"Like I said, let the papers help you after they've hurt you."

T.J. went on, "I picked up some mighty interesting information today. Quinn Harding had a heart attack when he heard about his son; he's dead. The law has taken control of his ranch. They plan to return the stolen parcels to their rightful owners, including the Stover Ranch to Darby. His lawyer is handling a sale so the money can be used to pay back Darby's targets and get those charges reduced. The judge says it'll go in his favor. I hope you don't mind."

The redhead beamed with joy. "Certainly not. Besides, I have a new home to make in Colorado with my handsome husband. I don't have any money, so it's a good thing you'll have a job awaiting you."

T.J. smiled and informed her, "I have plenty of money saved, so we'll do just fine, Miss Stover. A man doesn't spend much money when he's on the trail alone most of the time."

Carrie Sue ventured, "Right now, partner, I'm not so fine. I have this ache all over that Dr. Jamison needs to tend."

"That's good, woman, because I'm suffering from that same condition. Let me lock up so we won't be disturbed for a long time."

After he did so, he carried the laughing Carrie Sue to bed. With gentle hands, quivering from anticipation, he undressed her. After she lay down, he removed his garments and boots and joined her.

He lay to her good side and gazed into her violet-blue eyes. His fingers carefully touched her bandaged shoulder as he murmured, "Lordy, I was afraid I had lost you forever when this happened. Then, I was afraid you'd never be able to forgive me and take me back. You don't know what it means to me for us to be together like this again. I love you, woman, and I need you. I'm glad you came to your senses," he teased, assailing her face and neck with kisses.

"I'm glad you came to your senses, too, Mr. Ranger Man," she murmured, embracing him. Overwhelming love and desire coursed through her body. She had never imagined she could be this content, this much in love. T.J. had entered her life and changed it, changed her.

A feeling of intermingled tranquility and tension consumed

her. At last, she felt totally safe and deliriously happy. It had been a long and hard road to this safe and loving location, but she was glad she had found it, discovered it with T.J.'s help and persistence. Her spirit was relaxed with T.J., and her body was highly susceptible to his actions. Her heart belonged to him.

It seemed as if this was the man she had awaited all her life, as if he was the only one who could unleash her passions, the only one who could tame her wild spirit, the only one who could fulfill her. Carrie Sue's fingers lightly skimmed his supple flesh — his powerful shoulders, his brawny arms, his hard chest — relishing the way it felt beneath them and responded to her touch. She hugged him tightly against her naked body and trembled at that stirring contact.

T.J.'s lips roamed her rosy gold face, placing kisses in each area. He loved the way her skin felt beneath his mouth and hands. He wanted to kiss and caress every inch of her. He wanted to give her enormous pleasure; yet, self-control to carry out that enticing task was difficult. He fingered her flaming hair and kissed the throbbing pulse at her throat. She seemed eager to join their bodies, and that thrilled him.

Carrie Sue realized how gentle and hesitant he was with her; she knew he was trying not to hurt her. She knew his body was aflame for hers, just as hers were burning wildly for his. No matter how many times they made love, each time was better, if that was possible.

T.J.'s skilled hands searched out those hidden places that made her squirm with rapture. His tongue worked in the hollows of her neck and between her breasts, then traveled to her snowy mounds and titillated the rosy brown peaks upon them. He loved the way she moaned in rising need, the way she reacted to his trek, the way she entreated him to continue his journey toward a mutual discovery of passion's haven. He explored her like a virginal area, slowly, thoroughly, excitedly. He yearned for their new life to begin, and knew it would soon.

Carrie Sue's tongue darted about T.J.'s sensual mouth, craving his taste. Her hands were bold and confident today, wandering over his virile frame at will and causing him to tremble with mounting intensity. She wanted to tantalize him beyond reality and endurance, and was doing a wonderful job of it. She wanted him to experience the most blissful union of his life, today, in her arms, within her.

They played their enticing games until both were breathless and consumed by a ravenous hunger. They joined their bodies to feed those fierce appetites which both had whet. They teased and tempted each other. They took and gave and shared. They were as one.

He looked down at her, enjoying the way her hair flamed a vivid golden red against the stark white pillow. He noted the flush on her face, but knew it was from a different kind of fever than he had feared last week. He listened to her moans, this time from passion, not physical pain. He watched her violet-blue eyes close, grateful it was from dreamy pleasure and not unconsciousness. He kissed the area around her bandage, and mutely thanked God for saving her life.

Carrie Sue was enraptured by his skilled lovemaking and gentleness. Her body felt aglow and her mind adrift. The sea of passion within her coursed back and forth between peaceful waves to stormy ones. She was swept along helplessly by the awesome force. She felt that blissful tension building higher and higher within her until she felt dizzy from its height and power.

T.J. trembled in restraint, fearing it was about to be lost uncontrollably. His body was searing from the heat of their union, burning from her touch, blazing from her brave actions. His manhood quivered in warning. It had been so long since they had made love, and he craved her urgently. His fingers roved her body, stimulating her. When he felt her clutch his shoulders and kiss him feverishly as she arched her back toward him, he knew the moment of victory had arrived. He cast aside his guard and raced swiftly to join her.

Surges of ecstasy shot through them like tiny bolts of lightning. Blood pounded in their ears like roaring thunder. They clung together to ride out passion's downpour of fiery sparks, their bodies glistening from its blissful rain. Their mouths meshed and their tongues danced wildly in their own mating ritual. The wondrous experience, the culmination of lovemaking, washed over them and carried them away to a serene shore where they lay panting for breath and savoring this special fusion of bodies, hearts, souls, and spirits.

They continued to kiss and caress, to lie enjoined in the paradise of contentment which they had built. As they cuddled, the strength of their love filled their minds and consumed them. Each knew their love had been predestined, their first encounter by fate guided.

T.J. looked into Carrie Sue's eyes and asked happily, "So you won't mind becoming a lawman's wife, my beautiful Texas Flame?"

Carrie Sue's hands lifted to caress his face. She stared into his smokey gray gaze and replied with a straight face. "Not at all, Marshal Thaddeus Jerome Jamison, but I still prefer being your vixen." Her face and eyes glowed as her naked body shook with merry laughter.

"You'll always hold that intoxicating position, my love," T.J. murmured, then closed his mouth over hers.

When their lips parted, she whispered mischievously, "I suppose you can teach this daring desperado to become a lawful citizen. After all, my handsome Rogue, you've taught me everything else."

"Not everything," he hinted with a devilish grin. "But give me time and I will." He knew that if anyone came to visit today, no one would answer the door, not with his tantalizing vixen beside him, not when love's urgent summons were being heard again. . . .

Epilogue

William Ferguson arrived Saturday afternoon to cover the upcoming trials of Darby Stover and his gang. He enjoyed a long visit with Carrie Sue and T.J. before he began his prize-winning work.

Carrie Sue and T.J. spent Sunday alone, making love and making plans for their bright future in Colorado.

Monday, July third, the trial of Darby Stover began. Excited crowds filled the courtroom and others packed around the building to listen through the open windows. Often they cheered the boyishly handsome man whom they considered a Wild West legend.

Tuesday was a big holiday, the country's centennial. Carrie Sue and T.J. celebrated in the cozy house with Hank Peterson and William Ferguson. A congratulatory telegram from Mitchell Sterling had arrived yesterday. He said he wished he could join them.

Wednesday, the trial resumed. It ended Thursday morning with an expected verdict of guilty and a sentence of fifteen years in prison. The crowd screamed for a pardon, but the judge finally quieted them down and told them it was impossible because Stover had broken the law. The crowds then shouted for an early parole for their hero, and the judge smiled.

Thursday night, Carrie Sue's and T.J.'s weapons were

taken by the Rangers who stood guard around the outside of the house while Darby Stover was allowed to have supper and a visit with his sister before leaving on Friday for a prison in eastern Texas. Following a delicious meal and a pleasant visit, Darby Stover and Thad Jamison shook hands and parted as friends.

T.J. had told her, "With good behavior, he'll be out sooner."

Darby had given T.J. a letter to Sally in San Angelo, thanking her for her help and love in the past, telling her not to wait for him. But Darby—and Sally—knew she would because she loved him. He had finally admitted to himself that he loved her.

On Friday, the trials of Kale Rushton, Kadry Sams, Dillon Holmes and John Griffin began, to end much the same way as Darby Stover's. The doctor from San Angelo attended Kale's trial and requested to be allowed to visit and work with the half-Apache while he was serving his prison term, hopefully to learn from the man and teach him as well. In fact, he hoped to persuade Kale to study in prison so he could become a doctor one day, combining the skills and knowledge of the Indian and white worlds. To everyone's surprise, Kale was open to the suggestion.

On that same day, Carrie Sue Stover wrote a letter to Mrs. Thayer in Tucson, explaining everything to the kind woman who had befriended her.

After church on Sunday, July nineth, Carrie Sue Stover, wearing the white lace dress, married Thad Jamison in a secret ceremony attended by their closest friends. A small party followed, and a passionate night.

On Monday, July twenty-fourth, Carrie Sue and Thad Jamison left the cozy house in Waco to head for their new life in Colorado. By then, they knew there would soon be three people riding in their wagon. . . .

Author's Note

I would like to thank the staffs of the Texas Ranger Museum in Waco (with its marvelous examples of barbwire and guns, and displays of Ranger exploits) and the Texas Tourist Bureaus for their extremely generous help. One Texan in particular, Richard Roberts, supplied me with loads of informative material, especially on early Texas.

I would also like to thank the people at the U.S. Department of Interior (National Park Service) for the many maps and brochures which provided information and guidance on the Guadalupe and Chiricahua Mountains.

One note to prevent confusion: In *The Great Chiefs* (Time/Life Books) it says "After both Cochise and his oldest son died, Naiche, the second son, succeeded to the position of chief of the Chiricahuas in 1876." But, *The Indian Wars* (Utley and Washburn) said, "In 1874 the legendary Cochise died. Neither of his sons, Taza or Nachez, proved equal to the test of chieftainship." You know which source I used.

Finally, I would like to thank each of you for your letters and encouragement over the years, and I look forward to writing many more enjoyable books for you. If you would like to receive a Janelle Taylor Newsletter, send a legal-sized Self-Addressed Stamped Envelope (or a stamp and a mailing label) to:

Janelle Taylor Newsletter
P.O. Box 11646
Martinez, Georgia 30917-1646

UNTIL NEXT TIME, GOOD READING . . .